"The Coldest Girl in Coldtown" by Holly Black

Fifty-seven days ago, Matilda had be~~~~~~~~~~~~~~~~~~~~~~named Julian, and they would dress up toge~~~~~~~~~~~~~~~~~~~wear skinny ties and glittery eye shadow. Sh~~~~~~~~~~~~~~~~~~s and boots that laced up so high that they wo~~~~~~~~~~~~~~~~ause they were busy tying them.

Matilda and Julian would dress up and prowl the streets and party at lockdown clubs that barred the doors from dusk to dawn. Matilda wasn't particularly careless; she was just careless enough.

She'd been at a friend's party. It had been stiflingly hot, and she was mad because Julian and Lydia were doing some dance thing from the musical they were in at school. Matilda just wanted to get some air. She opened a window and climbed out under the bobbing garland of garlic.

Another girl was already on the lawn. Matilda should have noticed that the girl's breath didn't crystallize in the air, but she didn't.

"Do you have a light?" the girl had asked.

Matilda did. She reached for Julian's lighter when the girl caught her arm and bent her backwards. Matilda's scream turned into a shocked cry when she felt the girl's cold mouth against her neck, the girl's cold fingers holding her off balance.

Then it was as though someone slid two shards of ice into her skin.

The spread of vampirism could be traced to one person—Caspar Morales. Films and books and television had started romanticizing vampires, and maybe it was only a matter of time before a vampire started romanticizing *himself*.

Crazy, romantic Caspar decided that he wouldn't kill his victims. He'd just drink a little blood and then move on, city to city. By the time other vampires caught up with him and ripped him to pieces, he'd infected hundreds of people. And those new vampires, with no idea how to prevent the spread, infected thousands.

When the first outbreak happened in Tokyo, it seemed like a journalist's prank. Then there was another outbreak in Hong Kong and another in San Francisco.

The military put up barricades around the area where the infection broke out. That was the way the first Coldtown was founded.

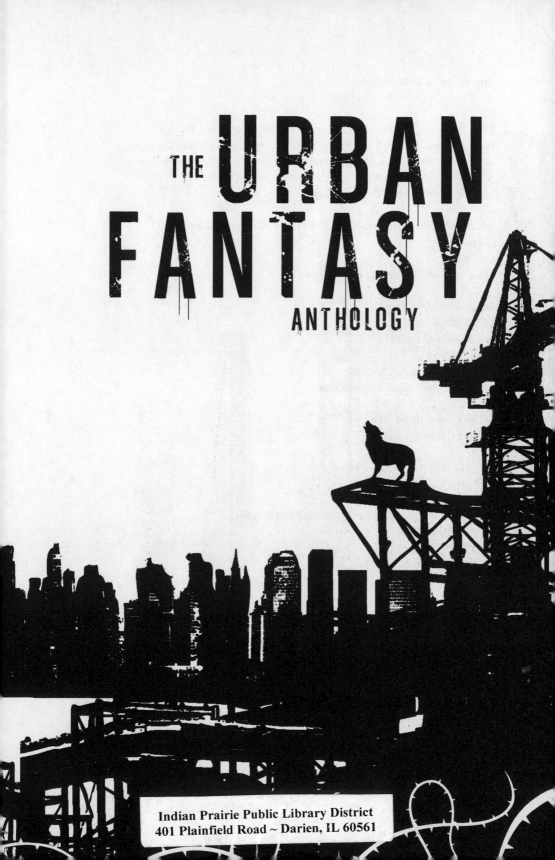

THE URBAN FANTASY

ANTHOLOGY

Cover and interior design by Elizabeth Story

Tachyon Publications
1459 18th Street #139
San Francisco, CA 94107
(415) 285-5615
www.tachyonpublications.com
tachyon@tachyonpublications.com

Series Editor: Jacob Weisman
Project Editor: Jill Roberts

ISBN 13: 978-1-61696-018-6
ISBN 10: 1-61696-018-3

Printed in the United States of America by Worzalla
First Edition: 2011
9 8 7 6 5 4 3 2 1

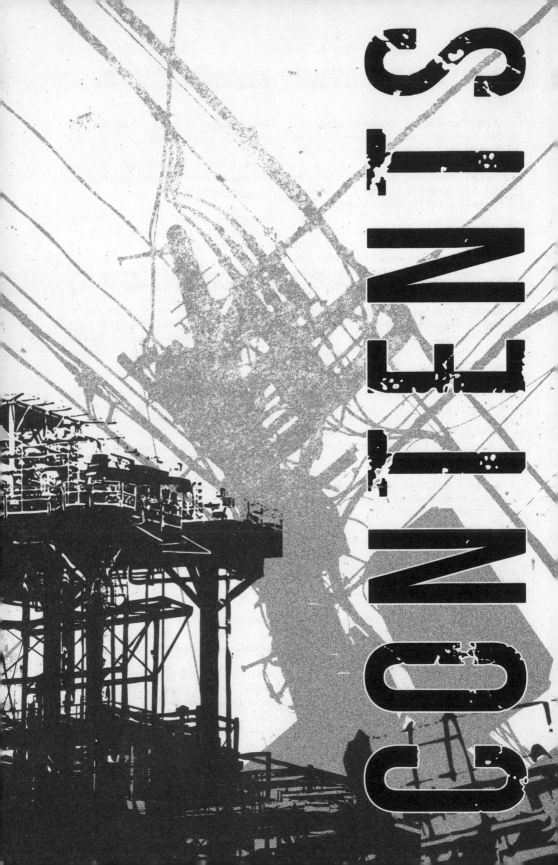

CONTENTS

THE
URBAN FANTASY
ANTHOLOGY

Introduction
Peter S. Beagle

I wish I could remember what writer or politician it was (we used to have remarkably literate politicians, even Republican ones) who said, "I am not an animal-lover. To me, an animal-lover is an animal who is in love with another animal."

In the same way, my main notion of urban fantasy is fantasy that takes place in an urban. Which to my mind—conditioned by years of *Pogo* and Dr. Seuss—is what's left when your favorite Sunday turban has gone one too many times through the wash.

But more seriously...

Jacob Weisman, Tachyon's publisher, has selected me to co-edit this book and to write this introduction because I have an affinity for *Buffy the Vampire Slayer* and because I once wrote a story called "Lila the Werewolf." That story, written long before the term "urban fantasy" would have meant anything to anybody, was about a New York werewolf, and the man who loved the werewolf, pursuing her late at night down mean, moonlit city streets. (I haven't included that story here because it wasn't written in the same spirit as the stories you'll find in this collection. Instead I have chosen to include a somewhat more recent story of my own involving another of that narrator's unusual girlfriends.) But as a subgenre, as a kind, as a trope, I still think that urban fantasy's most important distinction is that it isn't *The Lord of the Rings*: that is, it doesn't happen in a comfortable rural, pre-industrial setting where people still ride horses, swing swords, quaff ale in variously sinister pubs, and head off apocalypses and Armageddons that would make a *Buffy* episode look like a tussle in a schoolyard. Not that that's a bad thing...

What I *am* clear on is that, while I wasn't looking, urban fantasy has become so vibrant, and has evolved so rapidly, that it has emerged as a distinct marketing category, often with its own section in the bookstore. Because of that rapid growth the term means different things to different generations of readers. There have, in fact, been three distinct subgenres of urban fantasy: mythic fiction, paranormal romance, and noir fantasy. Elsewhere in these pages Charles de Lint, Paula Guran, and Joe R. Lansdale, all greater experts than I, will explain these to you in more depth then I will here.

The first popularization of the term urban fantasy (later rechristened by Charles de Lint and Terri Windling as mythic fiction), appearing in the mid to late 1980s, was used to apply to the work of writers such as de Lint, Emma Bull, Windling, and Will Shetterly, who wrote contemporary stories in which myths and fairy tales intruded into everyday life. Just about every generation of writers with a natural bent for the fantastic vision, from George MacDonald to Robert Nathan to Fritz Leiber, has been redefining fantasy as long as I've been reading the stuff, but there was a more concerted approach employed by the first generation of urban fantasists. Speaking for myself, I've never based whatever it is I do on any particular theoretical structure, other than "it seemed like a good idea at the time." These guys were *thinking* about it.

And then there was *Buffy*.

The much-deserved success of *Buffy the Vampire Slayer* meant that vampires, werewolves, and demons of all varieties—including the sort who were either as tormented about what they were as any teenager or as forlornly anxious to fit in—were suddenly fictional legal tender once again. A second wave of urban fantasy overtook the first: paranormal romance, in all of its dark, tawdry, and dysfunctional glory. These creatures of the night knew exactly what they'd become, and were at least half-aware that they were symbols and metaphors for the American experience. Our heroine, walking through the empty subway station, is no longer the meek shrinking-violet of previous generations. She is precocious, athletic, sexually aware, and regards kicking demonic ass, in Buffy's words, as "comfort food." (Okay, granted, *Twilight* and its sequels represent a decidedly reactionary backward step into the virgin-perpetually-at-physical-and-sexual-risk mode that began with in the eighteenth century with Samuel Richardson's *Clarissa*, but this too shall pass...) Around the time you have cheerful werewolf heroines running radio call-in shows—as in Laurel K. Hamilton's Anita Blake series—something has definitely changed.

The third generation of urban fantasy, noir fantasy, hearkens to a call for more realism, as exemplified by the novels of Charlie Huston, whose private-eye vampire detective is more profoundly worn down and plain weary than anyone Raymond Chandler ever envisioned. Think of one of Jim Thompson's or David Goodis's characters on a bad day, but with fangs. (Regrettably, Charlie Huston doesn't write that sort of material at shorter length, but I can strongly recommend his novels.) Noir fiction has been making inroads into fantasy and horror for many years. One need only look at Joe Lansdale's anthology *Crucified Dreams* (also published by Tachyon Publications) to see a map of the stories that lead from the works by masters of the craft like Harlan Ellison to the newer writers included here.

Urban fantasy counts on familiarity with mythology, fairy tales, and the earliest horror tropes like vampires, werewolves, and warlocks—in the same way that science fiction relies on faster-than-light drives and sentient robots—as shorthand to pull the reader through familiar territory quickly without wasting precious time. In old horror stories the tension built up slowly as the characters were drawn toward what the reader already knew would happen. A proper urban fantasy hero is always ready to grab a stake or a silver-bullet clip, and stalk down that dark alley, or into that dank sub-basement where red eyes glower from far corners, at a moment's notice. Or, when necessary, to be the thing behind those red eyes...to be, in the words of the bitter inversion of the 23rd Psalm that came out of the Vietnam War, "the meanest mother" in the Valley of Death.

This is not *The Secret History of Fantasy*. In that book, the previous anthology I edited for Tachyon, I gathered together a group of writers, all close to my heart, who were at once carving out new directions in fantasy while at the same time following in a tradition that owed little to the specter of J. R. R. Tolkien, or at least to those following slavishly in his footsteps. This was daring, auspicious work that took its joy in the telling, fiction that played with the very underpinnings of our genre, fiction that reveled in its own audacity and took itself seriously, without being ponderous or exclusionary about it.

The stories in this anthology represent the other side of that encampment—raw, consciously commercial fiction, feeding an unquenchable hunger for walks on the wild side, blending and shaking up familiar themes until they are transformed into something new and meaningful.

In this collection you will find a number of wonderful stories, some deeply provocative, others played for camp. You will be purely delighted by some of them and profoundly disturbed by others—I should be rather disappointed if it were otherwise. But you will not be bored.

Mythic
Fiction

A Personal Journey into Mythic Fiction
Charles de Lint

My journey into mythic fiction began early, with the books that I read as a child. Because my dad was a navigator for a surveying company, we moved around a lot. I didn't grow up or go to school with the same kids in the same neighbourhood, so I never felt the home roots that most children acquire.

While I often resented being the new kid on the block, in later years I came to appreciate what a mind-opening upbringing it was. It was also a time when I learned to amuse myself since books and my own imagination were the only entertainments I could take with me. Fairy tales and Enid Blyton's books and, later, *The Wind in the Willows* by Kenneth Grahame gave me my love of both story and illustrated books. As I got older, I devoured all the Tarzan and John Carter of Mars books in my father's library. When I reached my teens, I began to write.

I already appreciated mythology and folklore from my early years, but in my late teens I became totally enthralled by writers such as William Morris, Lord Dunsany, James Branch Cabell, Katharine Briggs and Colin Wilson. I spent my teen years reading everything esoteric that I could get my hands on. I was also intrigued by world religions, as well as by divination systems such as the I Ching, runes, etc.

There wasn't a great deal of fantasy fiction available but fortunately my appetite for fiction went beyond fantastic literature. Mainstream, westerns, mysteries, detective novels…anything with strong characters and a good story appealed to me.

I also developed a passion for music. This was the time of Beat poets and musicians like Bob Dylan, Donovan, The Incredible String Band. As a listener and as a musician, I developed an abiding love for Celtic music, which also happened to contain a great deal of myth and folklore.

During my teens and twenties I wrote reams of poetry and hundreds of songs, some of which contained fantasy elements. In the madness that comes with youth, one night I burned almost all of this in a magnificent bonfire. Ah, the drama and folly of it all.

By the late seventies I had evolved into writing stories and novels. When I first started out, I wrote high fantasy because that's what I thought fantasy had to be. My first few novels (not all of which were published, thankfully) were definitely influenced by Tolkien. My wife MaryAnn, while editing one of these early works, said, "You read all kinds of fiction. You should try this in a contemporary setting."

I replied, "Absolutely not. It wouldn't work." But the idea lodged in my head and it wouldn't go away. I wanted to write about the real world, but I also wanted to write fantasy. So I tried combining the two in one book and it didn't work. But the process showed me how it *could* work.

My next book was *Moonheart* (published in 1984), and I suppose the fusion of fantasy and realism in it was pretty successful since it remains in print to this day. I was blessed to have had that wealth of background reading from my youth. It allowed me to dip my proverbial ladle into that pool of myth, folklore and realism and play with various elements that intrigued me. And basically, I was doing the same thing that I do to this day: writing a story that I'd like to read but doesn't yet exist. Combining fantasy with the modern world let me push through self-imposed boundaries, and beyond what was being published in the fantasy genre at that time.

MaryAnn's suggestion got me going, but I had other help along the way. A few other fantasy writers had used contemporary settings in their work (Roger Zelazny, Peter S. Beagle and Roberta MacAvoy were among my favourites). But mostly, it was Terri Windling, my editor at Ace Books, who gave me sage advice that deeply influenced the trajectory of my work.

Terri had bought my high fantasy *The Riddle of the Wren* as well as *Moonheart*. After *Moonheart*, I turned in another high fantasy called *Eyes Like Leaves*. Although she'd accepted the book, Terri asked me if I was sure I wanted this to follow *Moonheart*. She cautioned me that with a couple of high fantasies already under my belt (*The Riddle of the Wren*, and *The Harp of the Grey Rose* from Starblaze/Donning), a third high fantasy might brand me forever as a high fantasy writer, no matter what else I subsequently produced.

THE URBAN FANTASY ANTHOLOGY

At the time I still liked high fantasy books. I liked them a lot. But I already knew I didn't want to keep writing them exclusively. So I swapped the manuscript of *Eyes Like Leaves* for *Yarrow*, a contemporary novel I'd just finished.

By the time I had a few more books under my belt (*Mulengro, Greenmantle*), I was calling what I wrote "contemporary fantasy." Then, when I turned in my modern retelling of the old fairy tale "Jack, The Giant-Killer," I made the mistake of calling it *The Jack of Kinrowan: A Novel of Urban Faerie* (the full title only showed up on the copyright page; everywhere else it was called *Jack, The Giant-Killer*).

Somehow the subtitle translated to "urban fantasy" in all subsequent references to my work.

I didn't fight it, but it never sat well. For one thing, while I enjoy setting magical stories on city streets, many of my tales have been set in more rural environs.

But I let it go.

Or at least I did until I was getting ready to go on tour for my novel *Someplace to Be Flying*. I'm not a naturally entertaining speaker the way some of my peers are. When it comes to writers like Joe Lansdale or Neil Gaiman, the *way* they do a reading is often as compelling as the story itself.

I felt I needed to do some prep work so I got together with Terri to talk about it. The first thing we realized was that I needed a way to describe what I did, because that's almost invariably the first thing that an interviewer asks. Somewhere in that conversation Terri said, "If we have to be in a genre, why don't we make up our own?"

I'm not sure which of us came up with the term "mythic fiction," but as soon as we had it, we knew it was perfect. Now, rather than paraphrase Terri, let me turn it over to her in some excerpts from correspondence to explain exactly why:

> We came up with the term because we wanted a way to describe
> novels and stories (including our own) that make conscious use of
> myth, medieval Romance, folklore, and/or fairy tales, but that are
> set in the real world, rather than in invented fantasy landscapes.
> "Fantasy" was inadequate for our purposes because it is a term

that is both too broad and too limiting. Broad, because it includes imaginary world novels, as well as works that aren't based on myth and folklore. Limiting, because "fantasy" has come to mean (to the average reader) fiction specifically published within the sf/fantasy genre, whereas the work we were trying to define was published in many other areas as well: mainstream fiction, historical fiction, horror fiction, postmodern fiction, surrealist fiction, young adult fiction, etc. We also found the terms "urban fantasy" and "contemporary fantasy" unsatisfactory—partly because of the connotations I've just described attached to "fantasy," and partly because not all the works we were looking at were urban, or set in the present day.

Some works of mythic fiction—such as John Barth's *Chimera* (in mainstream fiction), Delia Sherman's *The Porcelain Dove* (in historical fiction), or Robert Holdstock's *Mythago Wood* (in fantasy)—use mythic themes and tropes in obvious ways. Other works of mythic fiction are more subtle in their engagement with this material—such as the quiet bubbling of magic and folklore one finds within Alice Hoffman's tales, or Steven Millhauser's, or James P. Blaylock's. Like "magical realism," these stories use mythic and/or magical tropes to tell us something about the real world we live in, rather than (as in some other forms of fantasy) to remove us from that world altogether. Many magical realist tales also fall under the mythic fiction category—when they work with mythic or folkloric imagery rather than with surrealist imagery that is unrelated to these things. A story needn't have literal magic or fantastical elements to be considered mythic fiction, however; there are realist novels based on myth and folklore that also fall into this category—such as Brian Hall's *The Saskiad* (inspired by the *Iliad*).

To which I might add that I think that the best of these stories deal with character—people's relationships, trials and personal growth, using mythic and folkloric material either as a reflecting mirror, or to illuminate the tale by allowing inner landscapes and emotional states to appear physically "on stage" alongside real-world aspects.

The value in this kind of story is that it speaks to the obvious concerns that make up the physical world we all share with one another, but also addresses the individual worlds we carry inside ourselves—hopefully in a manner that allows us to understand ourselves, and each other, a little better and with more empathy.

By now you'll have noticed that Terri Windling's name has come up a lot in this piece. There's a reason she is almost synonymous with the term "mythic fiction" that goes beyond what I've written about so far.

The important thing to remember is that when she was an editor at Ace Books (from 1979 through the early '80s), and then later at Tor Books (late '80s through the '90s), she created a home for this sort of fiction. From time to time other publishers put out books of a similar ilk, but it was the lines Terri created and edited that set the standard in those early days when publishers and their publicity departments weren't quite sure what to do with such material.

Even if Terri hadn't been buying my books, I'm quite certain I would have continued to write this sort of story—once I realized it could be done, I wouldn't have been able to stop. And I'm sure the same is true for Emma Bull, Ellen Kushner, Stephen Brust, Will Shetterly, and all the rest of us. But we would have had to work really hard at selling these stories, taking precious time away from our writing. We wouldn't have had the safe haven that Terri provided, which allowed us to stretch and grow.

She became a spiritual center around which gathered not only fiction writers, but also visual artists, poets...in fact, anyone with a creative impulse who wanted to meld traditional folk, fairy tales and mythology with their art. Through her work as an editor, and as a talented painter and author in her own right, she was instrumental in creating a focus for this conversation on the mythic arts that exists between artists, and between their work in various mediums.

Putting aside her own wonderful paintings and stories, this community might well be her greatest legacy—a community that's still active today and continues to grow:

Her Endicott Studio website (www.endicott-studio.com) remains one of the best touchstones for the mythic arts, featuring art, essays, poetry, stories and links to other sites.

She also has a more personal blog at http://windling.typepad.com/blog/ in which she begins conversations in her posts that are often carried on in a lively discussion in the ensuing comments section.

Thirteen years after the last Bordertown book was published (a shared-world anthology series written by several of the writers Terri first nurtured at Ace and Tor), a new Bordertown book is coming out in 2011 featuring many of the old guard and some of the brightest new writers working today.

Folkroots, the column she initiated in *Realms of Fantasy* to explore the mythic arts, still appears in each issue with a new editor, Theodora Goss.

And while *The Year's Best Fantasy and Horror* series that she edited with Ellen Datlow is no longer being produced, the writers and poets she featured in her choices continue to create work for all of us to appreciate and enjoy.

These days a whole new group of writers have taken up the mantle of "urban fantasy." At first they came from the mystery and romance fields, combining elements of those genres with the tropes of more traditional fantasy—I'm speaking here of writers such as Charlaine Harris, Kim Harrison and Patricia Briggs. Soon after there was a whole new wave of writers inspired by *their* stories, in the same way writers are always inspired by what came before them, using what they like as a springboard to take the stories they want to tell in new directions.

As with any subgenre, some of the books are wonderful, some not so much. But the difference between what they do and what Terri and I call mythic fiction is that the magical/mythic/folkloric elements of these books is colour and shade, rather than the substance of the story. The new urban fantasy story remains rooted in the genres from which it sprang. Its magic is more often matter-of-fact—bricks and mortar—rather than something that leaves the reader with a sense of wonder.

There's nothing wrong with that, of course. Whether we call them urban fantasy, paranormal romance, or just "books we like to read," they provide full entertainment value. If they didn't, they wouldn't be as popular as they are, making inroads into television and film.

I'm sure their readership overlaps with that of mythic fiction, but the two styles remain very different for all that they use many of the same tropes. For me, the biggest difference is that mythic fiction has room for a story to be told at a slower pace. The preternatural elements are present, not only for their coolness factor (werewolves and witches and vampires, oh my!), but because fairy tales and mythology tap into a deeper part of the psyche than an adventure story can reach.

In the end it's apples and oranges. I'm just happy that we live in a literary world where there is room for both, as well as for whatever new things might be waiting for us on the other side of the days still to come.

As I've said before, I'm a writer and this is what I do no matter what name we put to it. Year by year, the world is turning into a darker and stranger place than any of us could want. Somewhere, there is always a war. Somewhere, there is always the threat of an act of terrorism. Somewhere, there is always a woman or a child in peril. Nature itself delivers devastating snowstorms, tsunamis, hurricanes and earthquakes. This is the only thing I do that has potential to shine a little further than my immediate surroundings. For me, each story is a little candle held up to the dark of night, trying to illuminate the hope for a better world where we all respect and care for each other.

A Bird That Whistles
Emma Bull

The dulcimer player sat on the back steps of Orpheus Coffeehouse, lit from behind by the bulb over the door. His head hung forward, and his silhouette was sharp against the diffused glow from State Street. The dulcimer was propped against his shoulder as if it were a child he was comforting. I'd always thought you balanced a dulcimer across your knees. But it worked; this sounded like the classical guitar of dulcimer playing. Then his chin lifted a little.

> 'Twas on one bright March morning, I bid New Orleans adieu,
> And I took the road to Jackson town, my fortunes to renew.
> I cursed all foreign money, no credit could I gain,
> Which filled my heart with longing for the lakes of Pontchartrain.

He got to the second verse before he stopped and looked up. Light fell on the side of his face.

"I like the bit about the alligators best," I said stupidly.

"So do I." I could hear his grin.

"'If it weren't for the alligators, I'd sleep out in the woods.' Sort of sums up life." He sounded so cheerful, it was hard to believe he'd sung those mournful words.

"You here for the open stage?" I asked. Then I remembered I was, and my terror came pounding back.

He lifted the shoulder that supported the dulcimer. "Maybe." He stood smoothly. I staggered up the steps with my banjo case, and he held the door for me.

In the full light of the back room his looks startled me as much as his music had. He was tall, slender and pale. His black hair was thick and long, pulled into a careless tail at the back, except for some around his face that was too short and fell forward into his eyes. Those were the ordinary things.

His clothes were odd. This was 1970 and we all dressed the way we thought Woody Guthrie used to: blue denim and workshirts. This guy wore a white T-shirt, black corduroys, and a black leather motorcycle jacket that looked old enough to be his father's. (I would have said he was about eighteen.) The white streak in his hair was odd. His face was odd; with its high cheekbones and pointed chin, it was somewhere out beyond handsome.

But his eyes—they were like green glass, or a green pool in the shadow of trees, or a green gemstone with something moving behind it, dimly visible. Looking at them made me uncomfortable; but when he turned away, I felt the loss, as if something I wanted but couldn't name had been taken from me.

Steve O'Connell, the manager, came out of the kitchen, and the green-eyed man handed him the dulcimer. "It's good," he said. "I'd like to meet whoever made it."

Steve's harried face lit up. "My brother. I'll tell him you said so."

Steve disappeared down the hall to the front room, and the green eyes came back to my face. "I haven't forgotten your name, have I?"

"No." I put my hand out, and he shook it. "John Deacon."

"Banjo player," he added. "I'm Willy Silver. Guitar and fiddle."

"Not dulcimer?"

"Not usually. But I dabble in strings."

That's when Lisa came out of the kitchen.

Lisa waited tables at Orpheus. She looked like a dancer, all slender and small and long-boned. Her hair was a cirrus cloud of red-gold curls; her eyes were big, cat-tilted, and grey; and her skin was so fair you should have been able to see through it. I'd seen Waterhouse's painting *The Lady of Shalott* somewhere (though I didn't remember the name of the painter or the painting then; be kind, I was barely seventeen), and every time I saw Lisa I thought of it. She greeted me by name whenever I came to Orpheus, and smiled, and teased me. Once, when I came in with the tail-end of the flu, she fussed over me so much I wondered if it was possible to get a chronic illness on purpose.

Lisa came out of the kitchen, my heart gave a great loud thump, she looked up with those big, inquiring eyes, and she saw Willy Silver. I recognised the disease that struck her down. Hadn't she already given it to me?

Willy Silver saw her, too. "Hullo," he said, and looked as if he was prepared to admire any response she gave.

"Hi." The word was a little breathless gulp. "Oh, hi, John. Are you a friend of John's?" she asked Willy.

"I just met him," I told her. "Willy Silver, Lisa Amundsen. Willy's here for open stage."

He gave me a long look, but said, "If you say so."

I must have been feeling masochistic. Lisa always gets crushes on good musicians, and I already knew Willy was one. Maybe I ought to forget the music and just commit seppuku on stage.

But you can't forget the music. Once you get the itch, it won't go away, no matter how much stage fright you have. And by the time my turn came—after a handful of guys-on-stools-with-guitars, two women who sang *a capella* for too long, a woman who did Leonard Cohen songs on the not-quite-tuned piano, and the Orpheus Tin-and-Wood Toejam Jug Band—I had plenty of stage fright.

Then Willy Silver leaned over from the chair next to me and whispered, "Take your time. Play the chord progression a couple of times for an intro— it'll settle you down."

I looked up, startled. The white streak in his hair caught the light, and his eyes gleamed green. He was smiling.

"And the worst that can happen isn't very bad."

I could embarrass myself in front of Lisa…and everyone else, and be ashamed to ever show my face in Orpheus again. But Willy didn't look like someone who'd understand that.

My hands shook as if they had engine knock. I wanted to go to the bathroom. Steve clumped up on stage, read my name from the slip of paper in his hand and peered out into the dark room for me. I hung the banjo over my shoulder and went up there to die for my art.

I scrapped the short opening I'd practised and played the whole chord progression instead. The first couple measures were shaky. But banjos give out a lively noise that makes you want to have a good time, and I could feel mine sending those messages. By the time I got around to the words, I could remember them, and sing them in almost my usual voice.

> I got a bird that whistles, honey, got a bird,
> Baby, got a bird that will sing.

Honey, got a bird, baby, got a bird that will sing.
But if I ain't got Corinna, it just don't mean,
It don't mean a natural thing.

At the back of the room, I could just see the halo of Lisa's hair. I couldn't see her face but at least she'd stopped to listen. And down front, Willy Silver sat, looking pleased.

I did "Lady Isabel and the Elf Knight" and "Newry Highwayman." I blew some chords and forgot some words, but I lived through it. And people applauded. I grinned and thanked them and stumbled off the stage.

"Do they clap because they like what you did," I asked Willy, "or because you stopped doing what they didn't?"

Willy made a muffled noise into his coffee cup.

"Pretty darn good," said Lisa, at my elbow. I felt immortal. Then I realised that she was stealing glances at Willy. "Want to order something, now that you're not too nervous to eat it?"

I blushed, but in the dark, who could tell? "PB and J," I told her.

"PB and J?" Willy repeated.

We both stared at him, but it was Lisa who said, "Peanut butter and jelly sandwich. Don't you call them that?"

The pause was so short I'm not sure I really heard it. Then he said, "I don't think I've ever been in a coffeehouse where you could order a peanut butter and jelly sandwich."

"This is it," Lisa told him. "Crunchy or smooth, whole wheat or white, grape jelly or peach preserves."

"Good grief. Crunchy, whole wheat, and peach."

"Non-conformist," she said admiringly.

He turned to me when she went towards the kitchen. "You *were* pretty good," he said. "I like the way you sing. For that last one, though, you might try mountain minor."

"What?"

He got an eager look on his face. "Come on," he said, sprang out of his chair, and led the way towards the back.

We sat on the back steps until the open stage was over, and he taught me about mountain minor tuning. His guitar was a deep-voiced old Gibson with the varnish worn off the strategic spots, and he flat-picked along with me, filling in the places that needed it. Eventually we went back inside, and he taught me about pull-offs. As Steve stacked chairs, we played "Newry Highwayman" as a duet. Then he taught me "Shady Grove," because it was mountain minor, too.

I'd worked hard at the banjo, and I enjoyed playing it. But I don't think I'd ever been aware of making something beautiful with it. That's what those two songs were. Beautiful.

And Lisa moved through the room as we played, clearing tables, watching us. Watching him. Every time I looked up, her eyes were following his face, or his long fingers on the guitar neck.

I got home at two in the morning. My parents almost grounded me; I convinced them I hadn't spent the night raising hell by showing them my new banjo tricks. Or maybe it was the urgency with which I explained what I'd learned and how, and that I had to have more.

When I came back to Orpheus two nights later, Willy was there. And Lisa, fair and graceful, was often near him, often smiled at him, that night and all the nights after it. Sometimes he'd smile back. But sometimes his face would be full of an intensity that couldn't be contained in a smile. Whenever Lisa saw that, her eyes would widen, her lips would part, and she'd look frightened and fascinated all at once. Which made me feel worse than if he'd smiled at her.

And sometimes he would ignore her completely, as if she were a cup of coffee he hadn't ordered. Then her face would close up tight with puzzlement and hurt, and I'd want to break something.

I could have hated him, but it was just as well I didn't. I wanted to learn music from Willy and to be near Lisa. Lisa wanted to be near Willy. The perfect arrangement. Hah.

And who could know what Willy wanted?

Fourth of July, Independence Day 1970, promised to be the emotional climax of the summer. Someone had organised a day of Vietnam War protests, starting with a rally in Riverside Park and ending with a torchlight march down State Street. Posters about it were everywhere—tacked to phone poles, stuck on walls, and all over the tables at Orpheus. The picture on the posters was the photo taken that spring, when the Ohio National Guard shot four students on the Kent State campus during another protest: a dark-haired woman kneeling over a dead student's body, her head lifted, her mouth open with weeping, or screaming. You'd think a photo like that would warn you away from protesting. But it gives you the feeling that someone has to do something. It gets you out on the street.

Steve was having a special marathon concert at the coffeehouse: Sherman and Henley, the Rose Hip String Band, Betsy Kaske, and—surprise—Willy Silver and John Deacon. True, we were scheduled to go on at seven, when the audience would be smallest, but I didn't care. I had been hired to play. For money.

The only cloud on my horizon was that Willy was again treating Lisa as one of life's non-essentials. As we set up for the show, I could almost see a dotted line trailing behind Willy that was her gaze, fixed on him.

Evening light was slanting through the door when we hit the stage, which made me feel funny. Orpheus was a place for after dark, when its shabby, struggling nature was cloaked with night-and-music magic. But Willy set his fiddle under his chin, leaned into the microphone, and drew out with his bow one sweet, sad, sustained note. All the awareness in the room—his, mine, and our dozen or so of audience's—hurtled to the sharp point of that one note and balanced there. I began to pick the banjo softly and his note changed, multiplied, until we were playing instrumental harmony. I sang, and if my voice broke a little, it was just what the song required:

> *The sun rises bright in France, and fair sets he,*
> *Ah, but he has lost the look he had in my ain country.*

We made enough magic to cloak *three* shabby coffeehouses with glamour. When I got up the nerve to look beyond the edge of the stage, sometime in our fourth song, we had another dozen listeners. They'd come to line State Street for the march and our music had called them in.

Lisa sat on the shag rug in front of the stage. Her eyes were bright, and for once, her attention didn't seem to be all for Willy.

Traditional music mostly tells stories. We told a lot of them that night. I felt them all as if they'd happened to friends of mine. Willy seemed more consumed by the music than the words, and songs he sang were sometimes almost too beautiful. But his strong voice never quavered or cracked like mine did. His guitar and fiddle were gorgeous, always, perfect and precise.

We finished at eight-thirty with a loose and lively rendition of "Blues in the Bottle," and the room was close to full. The march was due to pass by in half an hour.

We bounded off stage and into the back room. "Yo," said Willy, and stuck out his right hand. I shook it. He was touched with craziness, a little drunk with the music. He looked...not quite domesticated. Light seemed to catch more than usual in his green eyes. He radiated a contained energy that could have raised the roof.

"Let's go look at the street," I said.

We went out the back door and up the short flight of outside stairs to State Street. Or where State Street had been. The march, contrary to the laws of physics governing crowds, had arrived early.

Every leftist in Illinois might have been there. The pavement was gone beneath a winding, chanting snake of marchers blocks and blocks and *blocks* long. Several hundred people singing, "All we are saying/Is give peace a chance," makes your hair stand on end. Willy nudged me, beaming, and pointed to a banner that read, "Draft Beer, Not Boys." There really were torches, though the harsh yellow-tinted lights of State Street faded them. Some people on the edge of the crowd had lit sparklers; as the line of march passed over the bridge, first one, then dozens of sparklers, like shooting stars, arced over the railings and into the river, with one last bright burst of white reflection on the water before they hit.

I wanted to follow the march, but my banjo was in the coffeehouse, waiting for me to look after it. "I'm going to see what's up inside," I shouted at Willy. He nodded. Sparklers, fizzing, reflected in his eyes.

The crowd packed the sidewalk between me and Orpheus's front door, so I retraced our steps, down the stairs and along the river. I came into the parking lot, blind from the lights I'd just left, and heard behind me, "Hey, hippie."

There were two of them, about my age. They were probably both on their school's football and swimming teams; their hair was short, they weren't wearing blue jeans, they smelled of Southern Comfort, and they'd called me "hippie." A terrible combination. I started to walk away, across the parking lot, but the blond one stepped forward and grabbed my arm.

"Hey! I'm talking to you."

There's nothing helpful you can say at times like this, and if there had been, I was too scared to think of it. The other guy, brown-haired and shorter, came up and jabbed me in the stomach with two fingers. "You a draft dodger?" he said. "Scared to fight for your country?"

"Hippies make me puke," the blond one said thoughtfully.

They were drunk, for God's sake, and out on the town, and as excited in their way by the mass of people on the street above as I was. Which didn't make me feel any better when the brown-haired one punched me in the face.

I was lying on my back clutching my nose and waiting for the next bad thing to happen to me when I heard Willy say, "Don't do it." I'd heard him use his voice in more ways than I could count, but never before like that, never a ringing command that could turn you to stone.

I opened my eyes and found my two tormenters bracketing me, the blond one's foot still raised to kick me in the stomach. He lost his balance as I watched and got the foot on the ground just in time to keep from falling over. They were both looking toward the river railing, so I did, too.

The parking lot didn't have any lights to reflect in his eyes. The green sparks there came from inside him. Nor was there any wind to lift and stir his hair like that. He stood very straight and tall, six metres from us, his hands held a little out from his sides like a gunfighter in a cowboy movie. Around his right hand, like a living glove, was a churning outline of golden fire. Bits of it dripped away like liquid from the ends of his fingers, evaporating before they hit the gravel. Like sparks from a sparkler.

I'm sure that's what my two friends told each other the next day—that he'd had a sparkler in his hand, and the liquor had made them see something more. That they'd been stupid to run away. But it wasn't a sparkler. And they weren't stupid. I heard them running across the parking lot; I watched Willy clench the fingers of his right hand and close his eyes tight, and saw the fire dim slowly and disappear. And I wished like hell that I could run away, too.

He crouched down beside me and pulled me up to sitting. "Your nose is bleeding."

"What are you?" I croaked.

The fire was still there, in his eyes. "None of your business," he said. He put his arm around me and hauled me to my feet. I'm not very heavy, but it still should have been hard work, because I didn't help. He was too slender to be so strong.

"What do you mean, none of my business? Jesus!"

He yanked me around to face him. When I looked at him, I saw wildness and temper and a fragile control over both. "I'm one of the Daoine Sidhe, Johnny-lad," he said, and his voice was harsh and coloured by traces of some accent. "Does that help?"

"No," I said, but faintly. Because whatever that phrase meant, he was admitting that he was not what I was. That what I had seen had really been there.

"Try asking Steve. Or look it up, I don't care."

I shook my head. I'd forgotten my nose; a few drops of blood spattered from it and marked the front of his white shirt. I stood frozen with terror, waiting for his reaction.

It was laughter. "Earth and Air," he said when he caught his breath, "are we doing melodrama or farce out here? Come on, let's go lay you down and pack your face in ice."

There was considerable commotion when we came in the back door. Lisa got the ice and hovered over me while I told Steve about the two guys. I said Willy had chased them off; I didn't say how. Steve was outraged, and Lisa was solicitous, and it was all wasted on me. I lay on the floor with a cold nose and a brain full of rug fuzz, and let all of them do or say whatever they felt like.

Eventually I was alone in the back room, with the blank ceiling tiles to look at. Betsy Kaske was singing "Wild Women Don't Get the Blues." I roused from my self-indulgent stupor only once, when Steve passed on his way to the kitchen.

"Steve, what's a—" and I pronounced Daoine Sidhe, as best I could.

He repeated it, and it sounded more like what Willy had said. "Elves," he added.

"What?"

"Yeah. It's an Irish name for the elves."

"Oh, Christ," I said. When I didn't add to that, he went on into the kitchen.

I don't know what I believed. But after a while I realised that I hadn't seen Lisa go by in a long time. And she didn't know what I knew, or almost knew. So I crawled up off the floor and went looking for her.

Not in the front room, not in the kitchen, and if she was in the milling people who were still hanging out on State Street, I'd never find her anyway. I went out to the back steps, to see if she was in the parking lot.

Yes, sort of. They stood in the deep shadow where Orpheus's back wall joined the jutting flank of the next building. Her red-gold hair was a dim cascade of lighter colour in the dark. The white streak in his was like a white bird, flying nowhere. And the pale skin of her face and arms, his pale face and white shirt, sorted out the rest of it for me. Lisa was so small and light-boned, he'd lifted her off her feet entirely. No work at all for him. Her arms were around his neck. One of his hands was closed over her shoulder—I could see his long fingers against her dark blouse—and the gesture was so intense, so hungry, that it seemed as if that one hand alone could consume her. I turned and went back into Orpheus, cold, frightened, and helpless.

Lisa didn't come back until a little before closing, several hours later. I know; I was keeping watch. She darted in the back door and snatched her shoulder bag from the kitchen. Her eyes were the only colour in her face: grey, rimmed with red. "Lisa!" I called.

She stopped with her back to me. "What?"

I didn't know how to start. Or finish. "It's about Willy."

"Then I don't want to hear it."

"But—"

"John, it's none of your business. And it doesn't matter now, anyway."

She shot me one miserable, intolerable look before she darted out the back door and was gone. She could look like that and tell me it was none of my business?

I'd helped Steve clean up and lock up, and pretended that I was going home. But at three in the morning I was sitting on the back steps, watching a newborn breeze ruffle a little heap of debris caught against the doorsill: a crushed paper cup, a bit of old newspaper, and one of the flyers for the march. When I looked up from it Willy was standing at the bottom of the steps.

"I thought you'd be back tonight," I said.

"Maybe that's why I came back. Because you thought it so hard." He didn't smile, but he was relaxed and cheerful. After making music with him almost every day for a month, I could tell. He dropped loose-limbed onto the bottom step and stretched his legs out in front of him.

"So. Have you told her? What you are?"

He looked over his shoulder at me with a sort of stunned disbelief. "Do you mean Lisa? Of course not."

"Why not?" All my words sounded to me like little lead fishing weights hitting the water: plunk, plunk.

"Why should I? Either she'd believe me or she wouldn't. Either one is about equally tedious."

"Tedious."

He smiled, that wicked, charming, conspiratorial smile. "John, you can't think I care if Lisa believes in fairies."

"What *do* you care about?"

"John..." he began, wary and a little irritable.

"Do you care about her?"

And for the second time, I saw it: his temper on a leash. "What the hell does it matter to you?" He leaned back on his elbows and exhaled loudly. "Oh, right. You want her for yourself. But you're too scared to do anything about it."

That hurt. I said, a little too quickly, "It matters to me that she's happy. I just want to know if she's going to be happy with you."

"No," he snapped. "And whether she's going to be happy *without* me is entirely her lookout. Rowan and Thorn, John, I'm tired of her. And if you're not careful, I'll be tired of you, too."

I looked down at his scornful face, and remembered Lisa's: pale, red-eyed. I described Willy Silver, aloud, with words my father had forbidden in his house.

He unfolded from the step, his eyes narrowed. "Explain to me, before I paint the back of the building with you. I've always been nice to you. Isn't that enough?" He said "nice" through his teeth.

"Why are you nice to me?"

"You're the only one who wants something important from me."

"Music?"

"Of course, music."

The rug fuzz had been blown from my head by his anger and mine. "Is that why you sing that way?"

"What the devil is wrong with the way I sing?"

"Nothing. Except you don't sound as if any of the songs ever happened to you."

"Of course they haven't." He was turning stiff and cold, withdrawing. That seemed worse than when he was threatening me.

The poster for the protest march still fluttered in the doorway. I grabbed it and held it out. "See her?" I asked, jabbing a finger at the picture of the woman kneeling over the student's body. "Maybe she knew that guy. Maybe she didn't. But she cares that he's dead. And I look at this picture, and *I* care about *her*. And all those people who marched past you in the street tonight? They did it because they care about a lot of people that they're never even going to see."

He looked fascinated and horrified at once. "Don't you all suffer enough as it is?"

"Huh?"

"Why would you take someone else's suffering on yourself?"

I didn't know how to answer that. I said finally, "We take on each other's happiness, too."

He shook his head, slowly. He was gathering the pieces of himself together, putting all his emotional armour back on. "This is too strange even for me. And among my people, I'm notoriously fond of strange things." He turned and walked away, as if I'd ceased to exist.

"What about tonight?" I said. He'd taken about a half-dozen steps. "Why did you bother to scare off those guys who were beating me up?"

He stopped. After a long moment he half-turned and looked at me, wild-eyed and...frightened? Then he went on, stiffly, across the parking lot, and disappeared into the dark.

The next night, when I came in, Willy's guitar and fiddle were gone. But Steve said he hadn't seen him.

Lisa was clearing tables at closing, her hair falling across her face and hiding it. From behind that veil, she said, "I think you should give up. He's not coming."

I jumped. "Was I that obvious?"

"Yeah." She swept the hair back and showed a wry little smile. "You looked just like me."

"I feel lousy," I told her. "I helped drive him away, I think."

She sat down next to me. "I wanted to jump off the bridge last night. But the whole time I was saying, 'Then he'll be sorry, the rat.'"

"He wouldn't have been."

"Nope, not a bit," she said.

"But I would have."

She raised her grey cat-eyes to my face. "I'm not going to fall in love with you, John."

"I know. It's okay. I still would have been sorry if you jumped off the bridge."

"Me, too," Lisa said. "Hey, let's make a pact. We won't talk about The Rat to anybody but each other."

"Why?"

"Well..." She frowned at the empty lighted space of the stage. "I don't think anybody else would understand."

So we shared each other's suffering, as he put it. And maybe that's why we wouldn't have called it that.

I did see him again, though.

State Street had been gentrified, and Orpheus, the building, even the parking lot, had fallen to a downtown mall where there was no place for shabbiness or magic—any of the kinds of magic that were made that Fourth of July. These things happen in twice seven long years. But there are lots more places like that, if you care to look.

I was playing at the Greenbriar Bluegrass Festival in Pocahontas County, West Virginia. Or rather, my band was. A columnist in *Folk Roots* magazine described us so:

> Bird That Whistles drives traditional bluegrass fans crazy. They
> have the right instrumentation, the right licks—and they're likely
> to apply them to Glenn Miller's "In the Mood," or The Who's
> "Magic Bus." If you go to see them, leave your preconceptions
> at home.

I was sitting in the cookhouse tent that served as the musicians' green room, drinking coffee and watching the chaos that is thirty-some traditional musicians all tuning and talking and eating at once. Then I saw, over the heads, a raven's-wing black one with a white streak.

In a few minutes, he stood in front of me. He didn't look five minutes older than he had at Orpheus. He wasn't nervous, exactly, but he wasn't at ease, either.

"Hi," I said. "How'd you find me?"

"With this," he answered, smiling a little. He held out an article clipped from a Richmond, Virginia paper. It was about the festival, and the photo was of Bird That Whistles.

"I'm glad you did."

He glanced down suddenly. "I wanted you to know that I've been thinking over what you told me."

I knew what he was talking about. "All this time?"

Now it was the real thing, his appealing grin. "It's a damned big subject. But I thought you'd like to know...well, sometimes I understand it."

"Only sometimes?"

"Rowan and Thorn, John, have mercy! I'm a slow learner."

"The hell you are. Can you stick around? You could meet the band, do some tunes."

"I wish I could," he said, and I think he meant it.

"Hey, wait a minute." I pulled a paper napkin out of the holder on the table and rummaged in my banjo case for a pen.

"What's that?" he asked, as I wrote.

"My address. I'm living in Detroit now, God help me. If you ever need anything—or even if you just want to jam—let me know, will you?" And I slid the napkin across the table to him.

He reached out, hesitated, traced the edges of the paper with one long, thin finger. "Why are you giving me this?"

I studied that bent black-and-white head, the green eyes half-veiled with his lids and following the motion of his finger. "You decide," I told him.

"All right," he said softly, "I will." If there wasn't something suspiciously like a quaver in his voice, then I've never heard one. He picked up the napkin. "I won't lose this," he said, with an odd intensity. He put out his right hand, and I shook it. Then he turned and pushed through the crowd. I saw his head at the door of the tent; then he was gone.

I stared at the top of the table for a long time, where the napkin had been, where his finger had traced. Then I took the banjo out of its case and put it into mountain minor tuning.

Make a Joyful Noise
Charles de Lint

Every one thinks we're sisters, but it's not as simple as that. If I let my thoughts drift far enough back into the long ago—the *long* long ago, before Raven stirred that old pot of his and poured out the stew of the world—we were there. The two of us. Separate, but so much the same that I suppose we could have been sisters. But neither of us remember parents, and don't you need them to be siblings? So what exactly our relationship is, I don't know. We've never known. We just *are*. Two little mysteries that remain unchanged while the world changes all around us.

But that doesn't stop everyone from thinking they know us. In the Kickaha tradition we're the tricksters of their crow story cycles, but we're not really tricksters. We don't play tricks. Unless our trick is to look like we'd play tricks, and then we don't.

Before the Kickaha, the cousins had stories about us, too, though they were only gossip. Cousins don't buy into mythic archetypes because we all know how easy it is to have one attached to your name. Just ask Raven. Or Cody.

But gossip, stories, anecdotes...everybody seems to have something to pass on when it comes to us.

These days it's people like Christy Riddell that tell the stories. He puts us in his books—the way his mentor Professor Dapple used to do, except Christy's books are actually popular. I suppose we don't mind so much. It's kind of fun to be in a story that anyone can read. But if we have to have a Riddell brother in our lives, we'd much prefer it to be Geordie. There's nothing wrong with Christy. It's just that he's always been a bit stiff. Geordie's the one who knows how to have fun and that's why we get along with him so well, because we certainly like to have fun.

THE URBAN FANTASY ANTHOLOGY

But we're not only about mad gallivanting and cartwheels and sugar.

And we're not some single entity, either.

That's another thing that people get wrong. They see the two of us as halves of one thing. Most of the time they don't even recognize us when they meet us on our own. Apart, we're just like anybody else, except we live in trees and can change into birds. But when you put the two of us together, everything changes. We get all giddy and incoherence rules. It's like our being near each other causes a sudden chemical imbalance in our systems and it's almost impossible to be anything but silly.

We don't particularly mind being that way, but it does make people think they know just who and what and why we are, and they're wrong. Well, they're not wrong when the two of us are together. They're just wrong for who we are when we're on our own.

And then there are the people who only see us as who they want us to be, rather than who we really are—though that happens to everybody, I suppose. We all carry around other people's expectations of who we are, and sometimes we end up growing into those expectations.

It was a spring day, late in the season, so the oaks were filled with fresh green foliage, the gardens blooming with colour and scent, and most days the weather was balmy. Today was no exception. The sun shone in a gloriously blue sky and we were all out taking in the weather. Zia and I lounged on the roof of the coach house behind the Rookery, black-winged cousins perched in the trees all around us, and up on the roof of the Rookery, we could see Lucius's girlfriend Chlöe standing on the peak, staring off into the distance. That meant that Lucius was deep in his books again. Whenever he got lost in their pages, Chlöe came up on the roof and did her wind-vane impression. She was very good at it.

"What are you looking at?" we asked her one day.

It took her a moment to focus on us and our question.

"I'm watching a wren build a nest," she finally said.

"Where?" Zia asked, standing on her tip toes and trying to see.

"There," Chlöe said and pointed, "in that hedge on the edge of Dartmoor."

Neither of us were ever particularly good with geography, but even we knew that at least half a continent and an ocean lay between us and Dartmoor.

"Um, right," I said.

Other times she said she was watching ice melt in Greenland. Or bees swarming a new queen above a clover field somewhere in Florida. Or a tawny frogmouth sleeping in an Australian rainforest.

After a while we stopped asking. And we certainly didn't fly over and ask her what she was looking at today. We were too busy lounging—which is harder to do on a sloped roof than you might think—until Zia suddenly sat up.

"I," she announced, "have an astonishingly good idea."

I'd just gotten my lounging position down to an absolute perfection of casualness, so I only lifted a questioning eyebrow.

"We should open a store," she said.

"Selling what?"

"That's just it. It will be a store where people bring us things and we put them in the store."

"And when it gets all filled up?"

She grinned. "Then we open another. We just keep doing it until we have an empire of stores, all across the country."

"We don't have the money to buy anything," I said.

She nodded. "That's why they'd have to just give us the stuff. We'll be like a thrift shop, except we wouldn't sell anything we got."

"That seems greedy. What do we need with things?"

"We can give everything away once we've established our empire. It's just for fun."

"It seems more like a lot of work."

She sighed and shook her head. "You are so veryvery lazy."

"That's because today is a day especially made for being lazy."

"No, today's a day for building an empire of stores and if you won't help, I'll do it myself."

"I'll help later."

She nodded. "When all the hard work will probably be done."

"That's the risk I'll have to take."

She stuck her tongue out at me, then shifted to bird shape and a black crow went winging off above the oaks that line Stanton Street. I laid my head on the shingles again and went back to my very successful lounging.

I was so good at it that, eventually, I fell asleep.

When I woke, it was dark. Chlöe was still standing on the peak of the Rookery, and the trees around me were now filled with sleeping black birds. Above, the sky held a wealth of stars, only slightly dimmed by the city's pollution. I looked for Zia. She wasn't back yet so I slid to the bottom of the roof and then dropped the remaining distance to the dew-damp lawn. Cousins stirred in the trees at the soft thump of my descent on the grass, but went back to sleep when they saw it was only me.

I left the grounds of the Rookery and walked along Stanton Street, heading for downtown, where I supposed I'd find Zia. I wondered if she'd actually had any success getting her silly plan off the ground, or if she'd gotten distracted after leaving me and was now up to who knew what sort of mischief.

I could understand her getting distracted—it's such an easy thing to have happen. For instance, there were so many interesting houses and apartments on either side of the street as I continued to walk through Lower Crowsea. It was late enough that most of them were dark, but here and there I found lit windows. They were like paintings in an enormous art gallery, each offering small and incomplete views into their owner's lives.

Zia and I like to visit in people's houses when they're sleeping. We slip in and walk through the empty rooms, helping ourselves to sweets or fruit, if they're the sort of people to leave them out in small welcoming bowls or baskets. There might as well be a sign that says "Help yourself."

But we really don't take much else when we go inside. A bauble here, some unwanted trinket there. Mostly we just wander from room to room, looking, looking, looking. There are whole stories in the placement of vases and knickknacks, in what pictures and paintings have been hung, where and in what order. So we admire the stories on the walls and windowsills, the shelves and mantles. Or we sit at a desk, a dining room table, or on the sofa, leafing through a scrapbook, a school yearbook, a magazine that's important to whoever's home this is.

We're curious, yes, but not really all that snoopy, for all that it might seem the exact opposite. We're only chasing the ghosts and echoes of lives that we could never have.

So as I continued past Stanton Street, I forgot that I was looking for Zia. My gaze went up the side of the apartment building that rose tall above me and I chose a unit at random. Moments later I was inside, taking in the old lady smells: potpourri, dust and medicine. I stood quietly for a moment, then began to explore.

"Maddy?" an old woman's voice called from a room down the hall.

It was close enough to my name to make me sit up in surprise. I put down the scrapbook I'd been looking at and walked down the short hall, past the bathroom, until I was standing in the doorway of a bedroom.

"Is that you, Maddy?" the old woman in the bed asked.

She was sitting up, peering at me with eyes that obviously couldn't see much, if anything.

I didn't have to ask her who Maddy was. I'd seen the clippings from the newspaper, pasted into the scrapbook. She'd been the athletic daughter, winning prize after prize for swimming and gymnastics and music. The scrapbook was about half full. The early pages held articles clipped from community and city newspapers, illustrated with pictures of a happy child growing into a happy young woman over the years, always holding trophies, smiling at the camera.

She wasn't in the last picture. That photo was of a car, crumpled up against the side of an apartment building, under a headline that read "Drunk Driver Kills Redding High Student." The date on the clipping was over thirty years old.

"Come sit with Mama," the old lady said.

I crossed the room and sat cross-legged on the bed. When she reached out her hand, I let her take mine. I closed my fingers around hers, careful not to squeeze too hard.

"I've missed you so much," she said.

She went on, but I soon stopped listening. It was much more interesting to look at her because, even though she was sitting up and talking, her eyes open as though she was awake, I realized that she was actually still asleep.

Humans can do this.

They can talk in their sleep. They can go walking right out of their houses, sometimes. They can do all sorts of things and never remember it in the morning.

Zia and I once spent days watching a woman who was convinced she had fairies in her house, cleaning everything up after she'd gone to bed. Except she was the one who got up in her sleep and tidied and cleaned before slipping back under the covers. To show her appreciation to the fairies, she left a saucer of cream on the back steps—that the local cats certainly appreciated—along with biscuits or cookies or pieces of cake. We ate those on the nights we came by, but we didn't help her with her cleaning. That would make us bad fairies, I suppose, except for the fact that we weren't fairies at all.

After a while the old woman holding my hand stopped talking and lay back down again. I let go of her hand and tucked it under the covers.

It was a funny room that she slept in. It was full of memories, but none of them were new, or very happy. They made the room feel musty and empty, even though she used it every day. It made me wonder why people hung on to memories if they just made them sad.

I leaned over and kissed her brow, then got off the bed.

When I came back to the living room, there was the ghost of a boy around fifteen or sixteen sitting on the sofa where I'd been looking through the old lady's scrapbook earlier. He was still gawky, all arms and legs, with features that seemed too large at the moment, but would become handsome when he grew into them. Except, being a ghost, he never would.

Under his watchful gaze, I stepped up onto the coffee table and sat cross-legged in front of him.

"Who are you?" I asked.

He seemed surprised that I could see him, but made a quick recovery.

"Nobody important," he said. "I'm just the other child."

"The other..."

"Oh, don't worry. You didn't miss anything. I'm the one that's not in the scrapbooks."

There didn't seem much I could add to that, so I simply said, "I don't usually talk to ghosts."

"Why not?"

I shrugged. "You're not usually substantial enough, for one thing."

"That's true. Normally, people can't even see me, never mind talk to me."

"And for another," I went on, "you're usually way too focused on past wrongs and the like to be any fun."

He didn't argue the point.

"Well, I know why I'm here," he said, "haunting the place I died and all that. But what are you doing here?"

"I like visiting in other people's houses. I like looking at their lives and seeing how they might fit if they were mine."

I looked down at the scrapbook on the coffee table.

"So you were brother and sister?" I asked.

He nodded.

"Does she ever come back here?"

He laughed, but without any mirth. "Are you kidding? She hated this place. Why do you think she joined any school club and sports team that would have her? She'd do anything to get out of the house. Mother kept her on such a tight leash that she couldn't fart without first asking for permission."

"But you're here."

"Like I said, I died here. In my own room. I got bit by a bee that came in through the window. No one knew I was allergic. My throat swelled up and I asphyxiated before I could try to get any help."

"It sounds horrible."

"It was. They came back from one of Madeline's games and found me sprawled dead on the floor in my bedroom. It did warrant a small notice in the paper—I guess it was a slow news day—but that clipping never made it into a scrapbook."

"And now you're here..."

"Until she finally notices me," he finished for me.

"Why did she ignore you?" I asked. "When you were alive, I mean."

"I don't know. Madeline said it's because I looked too much like our dad. We were in grade school when he walked out on her, leaving her with a mess of debts and the two of us. I guess her way of getting over it was to ignore me and focus on Madeline, who took after her own side of the family."

"Humans are so complicated," I said.

"Which you're not."

"Oh, I'm very complicated."

"I meant human."

"What makes you say that?" I asked.

He kept count on his fingers. "One, you can see me, which most people can't. Two, you can talk to me, which most people really can't. Three, you're sitting there all calm and composed, when most people—most *human* people—would be flipping out."

I shrugged. "Does it matter what I am?"

"Not really."

He looked down the hall as though he could see through the walls to where his mother lay sleeping. The mother who'd ignored him when he was alive and now that he was dead, still ignored him. Her mind might be filled with old memories, but none of them were of him.

"Can you help me?" he asked.

"Help you with what?"

"With...you know. Getting her to remember me."

"Why is it so important?"

"How can I die and go on if no one remembers that I was ever alive?"

"Lots of people don't remember me," I said, "and it doesn't bother me."

He chuckled, but without any humour. "Yeah, like that's possible."

"No, it really doesn't."

"I meant that anybody would forget meeting you."

"You'd be surprised."

He held my gaze for a long moment, then shrugged.

"So will you help me?"

I nodded. "I can try. Maybe it's not so much that your mother should remember you more, but that she should remember your sister less. The way it is, there's no room inside her for anything else."

"But you'll try?"

Against my better judgment, I found myself nodding.

He did a slow fade and I was left alone in the living room. I sat for a while longer, looking at the place where he'd been sitting, then got down from the coffee table and walked back into the hall. There were two closed doors and two open ones. I knew one led into the old lady's bedroom, the other into a bathroom. I went to the first closed door. It opened into a room that was like stepping inside a cake, all frosty pinks and whites, full of dolls and pennants and trophies. Madeline's room. Closing its door, I continued down the hall and opened the other one.

Both rooms had the feel of empty places where no one lived. But while Madeline's room was bright and clean—the bed neatly made, the shelves dusted, the trophies shined—the boy's room looked as though the door had been closed on the day he died and no one had opened it until I had just this moment.

The bedding lay half-on, half-off the box spring, pooling on the floor. There were posters of baseball players and World War II planes on the wall. Decades of dust covered every surface, clustering around the model cars and plastic statues of movie monsters on the book shelves and windowsill. More planes hung from the ceiling, held in flight by fishing lines.

Unlike the daughter, he truly was forgotten.

I walked to the desk where a half-finished model lay covered in dust. Books were stacked on the far corner with a school notebook on top. I cleared the dust with a finger and read the handwritten name on the "Property of" line:

Donald Quinn.

I thought of bees and drunk drivers, of being remembered and forgotten. I knew enough about humans to know that you couldn't change their minds. You couldn't make them remember if they didn't want to.

Why had I said I'd help him?

Among the cousins, a promise was sacred. Now I was committed to an impossible task.

I closed the door to the boy's room and left the apartment.

The night air felt cool and fresh on my skin and the sporadic sound of traffic was welcome after the unhappy stillness of the apartment. I looked up at its dark windows, then changed my shape. Crow wings took me back to the Rookery on Stanton Street.

I think Raven likes us better when we visit him on our own. The way we explode with foolishness whenever Zia and I are together wears him down—you can see the exasperation in his eyes. He's so serious, that it's fun to get him going. But I also like meeting with him one-on-one. The best thing is he never asks where Zia is. He treats us as individuals.

"Lucius," I said the next morning. "Can a person die from a bee sting?"

I'd come into his library in the Rookery to find him crouched on his knees, peering at the titles of books on a lower shelf. He looked up at my voice, then stood, moving with a dancer's grace that always surprises people who've made assumptions based on his enormous bulk. His bald head gleamed in the sunlight streaming in through the window behind him.

"What sort of a person?" he asked. "Cousin or human?"

"What's the difference?"

He shrugged. "Humans can die of pretty much anything."

"What do you mean?"

"Well, take tobacco. The smoke builds up tar in their lungs and the next thing you know, they're dead."

"Cousins smoke. Just look at Joe, or Whiskey Jack."

"It's not the same for us."

"Well, what about the Kickaha? They smoke."

He nodded. "But so long as they keep to ceremonial use, it doesn't kill them. It only hurts them when they smoke for no reason at all, rather than to respect the sacred directions."

"And bee stings?"

"If you're allergic—and humans can be allergic to pretty much anything—then, yes. It can kill them. Why do you ask?"

I shrugged. "I met a boy who died of a bee sting."

"A dead boy," Lucius said slowly, as though waiting for a punchline.

"I meant to say a ghost."

"Ah. Of course."

"He's not very happy."

Lucius nodded. "Ghosts rarely are." He paused a moment, then added, "You didn't offer to help him, did you?"

He didn't wait for my reply. I suppose he could already see it in my face.

"Oh, Maida," he said. "Humans can be hard enough to satisfy, but ghosts are almost impossible."

"I thought they just needed closure," I said.

"Closure for the living and the dead can be two very different things. Does he want revenge on the bee? Because unless it was a cousin, it would be long dead."

"No, he just wants to be remembered."

Lucius gave a slow shake of his head. "You could be bound to this promise forever."

"I know," I said.

But it was too late now.

After leaving the Rookery, I flew up into a tree—not one of the old oaks on the property, but one further down the street where I could get a little privacy as I tried to figure out what to do next. Like most corbae, I think better on a roost or in the air. I knew just trying to talk to Donald's mother wouldn't be enough. At some point, I'd still have to, but first I thought I'd try to find out more about what exactly had happened to her children.

That made me cheer up a little because I realized it would be like having a case and looking into the background of it, the way a detective would. I'd be like a private eye in one of those old movies the Aunts liked to watch, late at night when everybody else was asleep except for Zia and me. And probably Lucius.

I decided to start with the deaths and work my way back from them.

There was no point in trying to find the bee. As Lucius had said, unless it was a cousin, it would be long dead by now, and it didn't make sense that it would be a cousin. I could look into it, I supposed, but first I'd try to find the driver of the car that had struck Madeline. A bee wouldn't even be alive after thirty years, anyway. But a human might.

Most people know there are two worlds, the one Raven made and the other-world, where dreams and spirits live. But there's another world that separates the two: the between. Thin as a veil in some places, as wide as the widest sea in others. When you know the way, it's easy to slip from one to another and that's what I do when I find myself standing in front of the locked door of Michael Clark's house. It's how Zia and I always get into places.

Slip into the between, take a step, then slip right back into Raven's world. It's as though you passed right through the door, except what you really did was take another, slightly more roundabout route.

I didn't like it in Clark's house when I got there that evening. There was an air of...unpleasantness about the place. I don't mean that it smelled bad, though there was a faint smell of mustiness and old body odour in the air. It was more that this was a place where not a lot of happiness had ever lived. Because places hold on to strong emotions just the way people do. The man who doesn't forgive? The house he lives in doesn't either. The house full of happy, laughing children? You can feel its smile envelop you when you step through the door.

Clark's name had been in that last clipping in the old lady's scrapbook.

When I looked it up in the telephone book, I found three listings for Michael Clark. The first two belonged to people much too young to be the man I was looking for, but this house...I knew as soon as I slipped inside that I was in the right place.

The front hall was messy with a few months' worth of flyers and old newspapers piled up against the walls, the kitchen garbage overflowing with take-out food containers and pizza boxes, the sink full of dirty mugs and other dishes. But there weren't any finished liquor bottles, or beer cases full of empties.

I found Clark sitting on the sofa in his living room, watching the TV with the sound off. Just as the rest of the place, this room was also a mess. Coming into it was like stepping onto a beach where the tide had left behind a busy debris of more food containers, newspapers, magazines, dirty clothes. A solitary, long-dead plant stood withered and dry in its pot on the windowsill.

Clark looked up when I came in and didn't even seem surprised to see me. That happens almost as often as it doesn't. Zia and I can walk into someone's kitchen while they're having breakfast and all they do is take down a couple of more bowls from the cupboard and push the cereal box over to us. Or they'll simply move over a little to give us room on the sofa they're sitting on.

In Clark's case, he might have thought that I was another one of those personal demons he was obviously wrestling with on a regular basis.

I didn't bother with any small talk.

"It's not like they made it out to be," the man said when I asked him about the night his car had struck Madeline. "I didn't try to kill her. And I wasn't drunk. I'd had a few beers, but I wasn't drunk. She just stepped out from behind a van, right in front of my car. She didn't even look. It was like she wanted to die."

"I've heard people do that," I said. "It seems so odd."

"I suppose. But there are times I can understand all too well. I lost everything because of that night. My business. My family. And that girl lost her life. *I* took her life."

There was more of that. A lot more.

When I realized I wasn't learning anything here except how to get depressed, I left him, still talking, only to himself. I looked up at the night sky, then took wing and headed for the scene of the accident that Michael Clark kept so fresh in his mind.

Between my ghost boy's mother and Michael Clark, I was beginning to see that the dead weren't the only ones haunted by the past.

The place where Madeline had died didn't look much different from any other part of the inner city. It had been so long since the accident, how could there be any sign that it had ever happened? But I thought, if her brother's ghost was still haunting the bedroom where he'd died, then perhaps she hadn't gone on yet either.

I walked along the sidewalk and down an alleyway, calling. "Hello, hello! Hello, hello!"

I did it, over and over again, until a man wrenched open one of the windows overlooking the alley. I looked up into his angry features, though with the light of the window behind him, he was more just a shadow face.

"It's three o'clock in the morning!" he yelled. "Are you going to shut up, or do I have to come down there and shut you up?"

"You'll have to come down," I called back, "because I can't stop."

"Why the hell not?"

"I need to find a dead girl. Have you seen her?"

"Oh, for Christ's sake."

His head disappeared back into the apartment and he slammed the window shut. I went back to calling for Madeline until I heard footsteps behind me. I turned, warm with success, but it was only the grumpy man from the window. He stood in the mouth of the alley, peering down its length to where I stood.

He was older than I'd thought when I'd seen him earlier—late fifties, early sixties—and though he carried more weight than he probably should, he seemed fit. If nothing else, he smelled good, which meant he at least ate well. I hate the smell of people who only eat fast food. All that grease from the deep-frying just seems to ooze out of their pores.

"What's this about a dead girl?" he asked.

I pointed to the street behind him. "She got hit by a drunk driver just out there."

"You're not answering my question."

"I just want to talk to her," I told him. "To see how she feels."

"You just said she was dead. I don't think she's feeling much of anything anymore."

"Okay. How her *ghost* feels."

He studied me for a long moment, then that thing happened that's always happening around Zia and me: he just took me at my word.

"I don't remember anybody dying around here," he said. "At least not recently."

"It was thirty years ago."

"Thirty years ago..."

I could see his mind turning inward, rolling back the years. He gave me a slow nod.

"I do remember now," he said. "I haven't thought about it in a long time." He turned from me and looked out at the street. "This was a good neighbourhood, and it still is, but it was different back then. We didn't know about things so much. People drank and drove because they didn't know any better. A policeman might pull you over, but then if it looked like you could drive, he'd give you a warning and tell you to be careful getting home."

He nodded and his gaze came back to me. "I remember seeing the guy that killed that poor girl. He didn't seem that drunk, but he was sure shook up bad."

"But you didn't see the accident itself?"

He shook his head. "We heard it—my Emily and me. She's gone now."

"Where did she go?"

"I mean she's dead. The cancer took her. Lung cancer. See, that's another of those things. Emily never smoked, but she worked for thirty years in a diner. It was all that secondhand smoke that killed her. But we didn't know about secondhand smoke back then."

I didn't know quite what to say, so I didn't say anything. I don't think he even noticed.

"Now they're putting hormones in our food," he said, "and putting God knows what kind of animal genes into our corn and tomatoes and all. Who knows what that'll mean for us, ten, twenty years down the road?"

"Something bad?" I tried.

"Well, it won't be good," he said. "It never is." He looked down the alley behind me. "Are you going to keep yelling for this ghost to come talk to you?"

"I guess not. I don't think she's here anymore."

"Good," he said. "I may not work anymore, but I still like to get my sleep."

He started to turn, then added, "Good luck with whatever it is you're trying to do."

And then he did leave and walked down the street.

I watched him step into the doorway of his apartment, listened to the door hiss shut behind him. A car went by on the street. I went back into the alley and looked around, but I didn't call out because I knew now that nobody was going to hear me. Nobody dead, anyway.

I felt useless as I started back to the mouth of the alley. This had been a stupid idea and I still had to help the dead boy, but I didn't know how, or where to begin. I felt like I didn't know anything.

"What are you doing?" someone asked.

I looked up to see Zia sitting on the metal fire escape above me.

"I'm investigating."

"Whatever for?"

I shrugged. "It's like I'm a detective."

"More like you're nosy."

I couldn't help but smile, because it was true. But it wasn't a big smile, and it didn't last long.

"That, too," I said.

"Can I help?"

I thought of how that could go, of how quickly we'd dissolve into silliness and then forget what it was we were supposed to be doing.

"I'll be veryvery useful," she said as though reading my mind. "You'll be in charge and I'll be your Girl Thursday."

"I think it's Girl Friday."

"I don't think so. Today's Thursday. *Tomorrow* I can be Girl Friday."

I gave her another shrug. "It doesn't matter. It turns out I'm a terrible detective."

She slid down the banister and plonked herself on the bottom step.

"Tell me about it," she said.

"It started out when I went looking for you and your store, but then I got distracted..."

"And now I feel like I'm forgetting what it's like to be happy," I said, finishing up. "It's like that stupid ghost boy stole all my happiness away, and now, ever since I talked to him, all I meet are unhappy people with very good reasons to be unhappy, and that makes me wonder, how could I ever have been happy? And what is being happy, anyway?"

Zia gave a glum nod. "I think it might be catching, because now I'm feeling the same way."

"You see? That's just what I mean. Why is it so easy to spread sadness and so hard to spread happiness?"

"I guess," Zia said, "because there's so much more sadness."

"Or maybe," I said, "it's that there's so much of it that nobody can do anything about."

"But we can do something about this, can't we?"

"What could we possibly do?

"Make the mother remember."

I shook my head. "Humans are very good at not remembering," I said. "It might be impossible for her to remember him now. She might not even remember him when she's dead herself and her whole life goes by in front of her eyes."

"Supposedly."

"Well, yes. If you're going to get precise, nobody knows if that's what really happens. But if it did, she probably wouldn't remember."

"And you can't just kill her to find out," Zia said.

"Of course not." I sighed. "So what am I going to do? I promised Donald I'd help him, but there's nothing I can do."

"I have an idea," Zia said, a mischievous gleam in her eye.

"This is serious—" I began, but she laid a finger across my lips.

"I know. So we're going to be serious. But we're also going to make her remember."

"How?"

Zia grinned. "That's easy."

She stood up and slapped a hand against her chest.

"I," she announced, "am going to be a ghost."

I had a bad feeling, but nevertheless, I let her lead me back to the apartment that Donald's mother was haunting as much as he was, and she wasn't even dead.

Zia practiced making spooky noises the whole way back to the ghost boy's apartment, which really didn't inspire any confidence in me, but once we were outside the building, she turned serious again.

"Is she alone in the apartment?" she asked me.

"There's the ghost boy."

"I know. But is there anybody in there to look after her? You made it sound like she'd need help to take care of herself."

"I don't know," I said. "There was no one else there last night. I suppose somebody could come by during the day."

"Well, let's go see."

We flew up to the fire escape outside her kitchen window, lost our wings and feathers, and then stepped into the between. A moment later we were standing inside the kitchen. I could only sense the old woman's presence—at least she was the only presence I could sense that was alive.

"Oh, Ghost Boy," Zia called in a loud whisper. "Come out, come out, wherever you are. If you come out, I have a nice little..." She gave me a poke in the shoulder. "What do ghosts like?"

"How should I know?"

She nodded, then called out again. "I have a nice little piece of ghost cake for you, if you'll just come out now."

Donald materialized in the kitchen by walking through a wall. He pointed a finger at Zia.

"Who's she?" he asked.

Zia looked at me.

"You didn't say he was so rude," she said before turning back to Donald. "I'm right here, you know. You could ask me."

"You look like sisters."

"And yet, we're not."

He ignored her, continuing to talk to me. "Is she here to help?"

"There, he's doing it again," Zia said.

"This is Zia," I said. "And Zia, this is Donald."

"I prefer Ghost Boy," she said.

"Well, it's not my name."

"She's here to help," I said.

"Really? So far, all she's been is rude and making promises she can't keep."

THE URBAN FANTASY ANTHOLOGY

Zia bristled at that. "What sort of promises can't I keep?"

He shrugged. "For starters, I'm here, but where's my cake?"

They held each other's gaze for a long moment, and it was hard to tell which one of them was more annoyed with the other. Then Zia's cheek twitched, and Donald's lips started to curve upward, and they were both laughing. Of course that set me off and soon all three of us were giggling and snickering, Zia and I with our hands over our mouths so that we wouldn't wake Ghost Boy's mother.

Donald was the first to recover, but his serious features only set us off again.

"Okay," he said. "It wasn't *that* funny. So why are you still laughing?"

"Because we can," Zia told him.

"Because we can-can!" I added.

Then Zia and I put our arms around each other's waist and began to prance about the kitchen like Moulin Rouge can-can dancers, kicking our legs up high in unison. It was funny until my toe caught the edge of the table, which jolted a mug full of spoons, knocking it over and sending silverware clattering all over the floor.

Zia and I stopped dead and we all three cocked our heads.

Sure enough, a querulous cry came from down the hall.

"Who's out there?" the old woman called. "Is there somebody out there?"

That was followed a moment later by the sound of her getting out of her bed and slowly shuffling down the hall towards us. Long moments later, she was in the doorway and the overhead light came on, a bright yellowy glare that sent the shadows scurrying.

Zia and I had stepped into the between, where we could see without being seen, but Donald stayed where he was, leaning against the kitchen counter, his arms folded across his chest. He was frowning when his mother came into the kitchen, the frown deepening when it became apparent that she wasn't able to see him.

We all watched as the old woman fussed about, trying to gather up the spoons that, with her poor eyesight, she couldn't really see. When she was done, there were still errant spoons—under the table, in front of the fridge—but she put the mug back on the table, gave the kitchen a last puzzled look, then switched off the overhead light and went back to her bedroom.

Zia and I stepped out of the between, back into the kitchen. Our sudden appearance startled Donald, which was kind of funny, seeing how he was the ghost and ghosts usually did the startling. But I didn't say anything because I didn't want to set us all off again—or at least it would be enough to set Zia and me off. I could feel that chemical imbalance spilling through me because she was so near—a sudden giddy need to turn sense into nonsense for the sheer fun of it—but I reminded myself why I was here. How if I didn't fulfill my promise, I'd be beholden to a ghost for the rest of my days, and if there's one thing that cousins can't abide, it's the unpaid debt, the unfulfilled promise. That's like flying with a long chain dangling from your foot.

"How did you do that?" Donald asked.

Zia gave him a puzzled look. "Do what?"

"Disappear, then just reappear out of nowhere."

"We didn't disappear," she told him. "We were just in the between."

I thought he was going to ask her to explain that, but he changed the subject to what was obviously more often on his mind than it wasn't.

"Did you see?" he asked us. "She was standing right in front of me and she didn't even notice me. Dead or alive, she's never paid any attention to me."

"Well, you *are* a ghost," Zia said.

I nodded. "And humans can't usually see ghosts."

"A mother should be able to see her own son," he said, "whether he's a ghost or not."

"The world is full of shoulds," Zia said, "but that doesn't make them happen."

It took him a moment to work through that. When he did, he gave a slow nod.

"Here's another should," he said. "I should never have gotten my hopes up that anyone would help me."

"We didn't say we wouldn't or that we couldn't," Zia said.

I nodded. "I made you a promise."

"And cousins don't break promises," Zia added. "It's all we have for coin and what would it be worth if our word had no value?"

"So you're cousins," he said.

He didn't mean it the way we did. He was thinking of familial ties, while for us it was just an easy way to differentiate humans from people like us whose

THE URBAN FANTASY ANTHOLOGY

genetic roots went back to the first days in the long ago, people who weren't bound to the one shape the way regular humans and animals are.

Instead of explaining, I just nodded.

"Show me your sister's room," Zia said.

Donald led us down the hall to Madeline's bedroom. He walked through the closed door, but I stopped to open it before Zia and I followed him inside.

"It's very girly," Zia said as she took in the all the lace and dolls and the bright frothy colours. Then she pointed to the pennants and trophies. "But sporty, too."

"Not to mention clean," Donald said. "You should see my room. Mother closed the door the day I died and it hasn't been opened since."

"*I've* been in there," I said.

"But Maddy's room," he went on as though I hadn't spoken. "Mother makes sure the cleaning lady sees to it every week—before she tackles any other room in the apartment."

"Why do you think that is?" Zia asked.

"Because so far as my mother was concerned, the sun and moon rose and set on my sister Maddy."

"But *why* did she think that?"

"I don't know."

"You told me something the last time I was here," I said. "Something about how maybe you reminded her too much of your father..."

"Who abandoned us," he finished. "That's just something Maddy thought."

Zia nodded. "Well, let's find out. Did your sister call you Donald?"

"What?"

"Your sister. What did she call you?"

"Donnie."

"Okay, good. That's all I needed."

"Hey, wait!" Donald said as she pulled back the covers and got into the bed.

Zia pretended he hadn't spoken.

"You two should hide," she said.

"But—"

"We don't want your mother to see anybody but me."

"Like she could see me."

That was true. But the mother *could* see me.

I didn't know what Zia was up to, but I went over to the closet and opened the door, pulling it almost closed again so that I was standing in the dark in a press of dresses and skirts and tops with just a crack to peer through. Donald let out a long theatrical sigh, but after a moment he joined me.

"Mama, mama!" Zia cried from the bed, her voice the high and frightened sound of a young girl waking from a bad dream.

Faster than she'd come into the kitchen earlier, the mother appeared in the doorway and crossed the room to the bed. She hesitated beside it, staring down at where Zia was sitting up with her arms held out for comfort. I could see the confusion in the old woman's half-blind gaze, but all it took was for Zia to call "Mama" one more time and a mother's instinct took over. She sat on the edge of the bed, taking Zia in her arms.

"I...I was so scared, Mama," Zia said. "I dreamed I was dead."

The old woman stiffened. I saw a shiver run from her shoulders, all the way down her arms and back. Then she pressed her face into Zia's hair.

"Oh, Maddy, Maddy," she said, her voice a bare whisper. "I wish it *was* a dream."

Zia pulled back from her, but took hold of her hands.

"I *am* dead, Mama," she said. "Aren't I?"

The old woman nodded.

"But then why am I here?" Zia asked. "What keeps me here?"

"M-maybe I...I just can't let you go..."

"But you don't keep Donnie here. Why did you let him go and not me?"

"Oh, Maddy, sweetheart. Don't talk about him."

"I don't understand. Why not? He's my brother. I loved him. Didn't you love him?"

The old woman looked down at her lap.

"Mama?" Zia asked.

The old woman finally lifted her head.

"I...I think I loved him too much," she said.

The ghost boy had no physical presence, standing beside me, here in the closet, but I could feel his sudden tension as though he was flesh and blood—a prickling flood of interest and shock and pure confusion.

"I still don't understand," Zia said.

THE URBAN FANTASY ANTHOLOGY

The old woman was quiet for so long I didn't think she was going to explain. But she finally looked away from Zia, across the room, her gaze seeing into the past rather than what lay in front of her.

"Donnie was a good boy," she said. "Too good for this world, I guess, because he was taken from it while he was still so young. I knew he'd grow up to make me proud—at least I thought I did. My eyesight's bad now, sweetheart, but I think I was blinder back then, because I never saw that he wouldn't get the chance to grow up at all."

Her gaze returned to Zia before Zia could speak.

"But you," the old woman said. "Oh, I could see trouble in you. You were too much like your father. Left to your own devices, I could see you turning into a little hellion. That you could be as bad as he was, if you were given half a chance. So I kept you busy—too busy to get into trouble, I thought—but I didn't do any better of a job raising you than I did him.

"You were both taken so young and I can't help but feel that the blame for that lay with me."

She fell silent, but I knew Zia wasn't going to let it go, even though we had what we needed.

The ghost boy's mother *did* remember him.

She *had* loved him.

I'd fulfilled my part of the bargain and I wanted to tell Zia to stop. I almost pushed open the closet door. I'd already lifted my hand and laid my palm against the wood paneling, but Donald stopped me before I could actually give it a push.

"I need to hear this," he said. "I...I just really do."

I let my hand fall back to my side.

"But why don't you ever talk about Donnie?" Zia asked. "Why is his room closed up and forgotten and mine's like I just stepped out for a soda?"

"When I let him die," the old woman said, after another long moment of silence, "all by himself, swelled up and choking from that bee sting..." She shook her head. "I was so ashamed. There's not a day goes by that I don't think about it...about him...but I keep it locked away inside. It's my terrible secret. Better to let the world not know that I ever had a son, than that I let him die the way he did."

"Except you didn't kill him."

"No. But I did neglect him. If I'd been here, instead of driving you to some piano class or gym meet or whatever it was that day, he'd still be alive."

"So it's my fault..."

"Oh no, honey. Don't even think such a thing. I was the one who made all the wrong choices. I was the one who thought he didn't need attention, but that you did. Except I was wrong about that, too. Look what happened to Donnie. And look how you turned out before...before..."

"I died."

She nodded. "You were a good girl. You were the best daughter a mother could have had. I was so proud of you, of all you'd achieved."

"And my room..."

"I keep it and your memory alive because it's the only thing left in this world that can give me any pride. It's the light that burns into the darkness and lets me forget my shame. Not always. Not for long. But even the few moments I can steal free of my shame are a blessed respite."

She fell silent again, head bowed, unable to look at what she thought was the ghost of her daughter.

Zia turned and glanced at where I was peering at her from the crack I'd made with the closet door. I knew her well enough to know what she was thinking. It was never hard. All I had to do was imagine I was in her shoes, and consider what I would say or do or think.

I turned to Donald.

"Is there anything you want to tell your mother?" I whispered.

He gave me a slow nod.

"Then just tell Zia and she'll pass it on to your mother."

He gave me another nod, but he still didn't speak.

"Donald?" I said.

"I don't know what to say. I mean, there's a million things I could say, but none of them seem to matter anymore. She's beating herself up way more than any hurt I could have wished upon her."

I reached out a comforting hand, but of course I couldn't touch him. Still, he understood the gesture. I think he even appreciated it.

"And I don't even wish it on her anymore," he added. "But then...while I feel bad about what she's going through, at the same time, I still feel hurt for the way she ignored me."

I opened the door a little more, enough to catch Zia's eye. She inclined her head to show that she understood.

"I've talked to Donnie," Zia said. "In the, you know. The hereafter. Before he went on."

The old woman lifted her head and looked Zia in the eye.

"You...you have?"

Zia nodded. "He understands, but he really wishes you'd celebrate his life the way you do mine. It...hurts him to think that you never think of him."

"Oh, god, there's not a day goes by that I don't think of him."

"He knows that now."

Zia's gaze went back to me and I made a continuing motion with my hand.

"And he wants," she went on, then caught herself. "He wanted you to know that he'll always love you. That he never held you to blame for what happened to him."

The old woman put her arms around Zia.

"Oh, my boy," she said. "My poor, poor boy."

"He wants you to be happy," Zia said. "We both do."

The woman shook her head against Zia's shoulder.

"I don't even know the meaning of the word anymore," she said.

"Will you at least try?"

The old woman sat up and dabbed at her eyes with the sleeve of her housecoat.

"How does one even begin?" she said.

"Well, sometimes, if you pretend you're happy, you can trick yourself into at least feeling better."

"I don't think I could do that."

"Try by celebrating our lives," Zia said. "Remember both your children with love and joy. There'll always be sadness, but try to remember that it wasn't always that way."

"No," the old woman said slowly. "You're right. It wasn't. I don't know if you can even remember, but we were once a happy family. But then Ted left and I had to go back to work, and you children...you were robbed of the life you should have had."

"It happens," Zia said—a touch too matter-of-factly for the ghost of a dead girl, I thought, but the old woman didn't appear to notice.

"It's time for me to go, Mama," Zia added. "Will you let me go?"

"Can't you stay just a little longer?"

"No," Zia said. "Let me walk you back to your bed."

She got up and the two of them left the room, the old woman leaning on Zia.

"I'm going to wake up in the morning," I heard the old woman say from the hall, "and this will all have just been a dream."

"Not if you don't want it to," Zia told her. "You've got a strong will. Look how long you kept me from moving on. You can remember this—everything we've talked about—for what it really was. And if you try hard, you can be happy again..."

Donald and I waited in the bedroom until Zia returned.

"Is she asleep?" I asked.

Zia nodded. "I think all of this exhausted her." She turned to Donald. "So how do you feel now?"

"I feel strange," he said. "Like there's something tugging at me...trying to pull me away."

"That's because it's time for you to move on," I told him.

"I guess."

"You're remembered now," Zia said. "That's what was holding you back before."

He gave a slow nod. "Listening to her...it didn't make me feel a whole lot better. I mean, I understand now, but..."

"Life's not very tidy," Zia said, "so I suppose there's no reason for death to be any different."

"I..."

He was harder to hear. I gave him a careful study and realized he'd grown much more insubstantial.

"It's hard to hold on," he said. "To stay here."

"Then don't," Zia told him.

I nodded. "Just let go."

"But I'm...scared."

Zia and I looked at each other.

"We were here at the beginning of things," she said, turning back to him, "before Raven pulled the world out of that old pot of his. We've been in the great beyond that lies on the other side of the long ago. It's..."

She looked at me.

"It's very peaceful there," I finished for her.

"I don't want to go to Hell," he said. "What if I go to Hell?"

His voice was very faint now and I could hardly make him out in the gloom of the room.

"You won't go to Hell," I said.

I didn't know if there was a Heaven or a Hell or *what* lay on the other side of living. Maybe nothing. Maybe everything. But there was no reason to tell him that. He wanted certainty.

"Hell's for bad people," I told him, "and you're just a poor kid who got stung by a bee."

I saw the fading remnants of his mouth moving, but I couldn't make out the words. And then he was gone.

I looked at Zia.

"I don't feel any better," I said. "Did we help him?"

"I don't know. We must have. We did what he wanted."

"I suppose."

"And he's gone on now."

She linked her arm in mine and walked me into the between.

"I had this idea for a store," she said.

"I know. Where you don't sell anything. Instead people just bring you stuff."

She nodded. "It was a pretty dumb idea."

"It wasn't that bad. I've had worse."

"I know you have."

We stepped out of the between onto the fire escape outside the apartment. I looked across the city. Dawn was still a long way off, but everywhere I could see the lights of the city, the headlights of cars moving between the tall canyons of the buildings.

"I think we need to go somewhere and make a big happy noise," Zia said. "We have to go mad and dance and sing and do cartwheels along the telephone wires like we're famous trapeze artists."

"Because...?"

"Because it's better than feeling sad."

So we did.

And later we returned to the Rookery and woke up all the cousins until every blackbird in every tree was part of our loud croaking and raspy chorus. I saw Lucius open the window of his library and look out. When he saw Zia and I, leading the cacophony from our high perch in one of the old oak trees in the backyard, he just shook his head and closed the window again.

But not before I saw him smile to himself.

I went back to the old woman's apartment a few weeks later to see if the ghost boy was really gone. I meant to go sooner, but something distracting always seemed to come up before I could actually get going.

Zia might tell me about a hoard of Mardi Gras beads she'd found in a dumpster and then off we'd have to go to collect them all, bringing them back to the Rookery where we festooned the trees with them until Lucius finally asked us to take them down, his voice polite, but firm, the way it always got when he felt we'd gone the step too far.

Or Chlöe might call us into the house because she'd made us each a sugar pie, big fat pies with much more filling than crust, because we liked the filling the best. We didn't even need the crust, except then it would just be pudding, which we also liked, but it wasn't pie, now was it?

Once we had to go into the far away to help our friend Jilly, because we promised we would if she ever called us. So when she did, we went to her. That promise had never been like a chain dangling from our feet when we flew, but it still felt good to be done with it.

But finally I remembered the ghost boy and managed to not get distracted before I could make my way to his mother's apartment. When I got there, they were both gone, the old woman and her dead son. Instead, there was a young man I didn't recognize sitting in the kitchen when I stepped out of the between. He was in the middle of spooning ice cream into a bowl.

"Do you want some?" he asked.

He was one of those people who didn't seem the least bit surprised to find me appearing out of thin air in the middle of his kitchen. Tomorrow morning, he probably wouldn't even remember I'd been here.

"What flavour is it?" I asked.

"Chocolate swirl with bits of Oreo cookies mixed in."

"I'd love some," I told him and got myself a bowl from the cupboard.

He filled my bowl with a generous helping and we both spent a few moments enjoying the ice cream. I looked down the hall as I ate and saw all the cardboard boxes. My gaze went back to the young man's face.

"What's your name?" I asked him.

"Nels."

He didn't ask me my name, but I didn't mind.

"This is a good invention," I said, holding up a spoonful of ice cream. "Chocolate and ice cream and cookies all mixed up in the same package."

"It's not new. They've had it for ages."

"But it's still good."

"Mmm."

"So what happened to the old woman who lived here?" I asked.

"I didn't know her," he told me. "The realtor brought me by a couple of days ago and I liked the place, so I rented it. I'm pretty sure he said she'd passed away."

So much for her being happy. But maybe there was something else on the other side of living. Maybe she and her ghost boy and her daughter were all together again and she *was* happy.

It was a better ending to the story than others I could imagine.

"So," I asked Nels, "are you happy?"

He paused with a spoonful of ice cream halfway to his mouth. "What?"

"Do you have any ghosts?"

"Everybody's got ghosts."

"Really?"

He nodded. "I suppose one of the measures of how you live your life is how well you make your peace with them."

My bowl was empty, but I didn't fill it up again. I stood up from the table.

"Do you want some help unpacking?" I asked.

"Nah. I'm good. Are you off?"

"You know me," I said, although of course he didn't. "Places to go, people to meet. Things to do."

He smiled. "Well, don't be a stranger. Or at least not any stranger than you already are."

I laughed.

"You're a funny man, Nels," I said.

And then I stepped away into the between. I stood there for a few moments, watching him.

He got up from the table, returned the ice cream to the freezer and washed out the bowls and utensils we'd used. When he was done, he walked into the hall and picked up a box which he took into the living room, out of my sight.

I could tell that he'd already forgotten me.

"Goodbye, Nels," I said, though he couldn't hear me. "Goodbye, Ghost Boy. Goodbye, old lady." I knew they couldn't hear me, either.

Then I stepped from the between, out onto the fire escape. I unfolded black wings and flew back to the Rookery, singing loudly all the way.

At least I thought of it as singing.

As I got near Stanton Street, a man waiting for his dog to relieve itself looked up to see me go by.

"Goddamned crows," he said.

He took a plastic bag out of his pocket and deftly bagged his dog's poop.

I sang louder, a laughing arpeggio of croaking notes.

Being happy was better than not, I decided. And it was certainly better than scooping up dog poop. If I was ever to write a story the way that Christy did, it would be very short. And I'd only have the one story because after it, I wouldn't need any more.

It would go like this:

Once upon a time, they all lived happily ever after. The end.

That's a much better sort of story than the messy ones that make up our lives. At least that's what I think.

But I wouldn't want to live in that story, because that would be too boring. I'd rather be caught up in the clutter of living, flying high above the streets and houses, making a joyful noise.

The Goldfish Pool and Other Stories
Neil Gaiman

It was raining when I arrived in L.A., and I felt myself surrounded by a hundred old movies.

There was a limo driver in a black uniform waiting for me at the airport, holding a white sheet of cardboard with my name misspelled neatly upon it.

"I'm taking you straight to your hotel, sir," said the driver. He seemed vaguely disappointed that I didn't have any real luggage for him to carry, just a battered overnight bag stuffed with T-shirts, underwear, and socks.

"Is it far?"

He shook his head. "Maybe twenty-five, thirty minutes. You ever been to L.A. before?"

"No."

"Well, what I always say, L.A. is a thirty-minute town. Wherever you want to go, it's thirty minutes away. No more."

He hauled my bag into the boot of the car, which he called the trunk, and opened the door for me to climb into the back.

"So where you from?" he asked, as we headed out of the airport into the slick wet neon-spattered streets.

"England."

"England, eh?"

"Yes. Have you ever been there?"

"Nosir. I've seen movies. You an actor?"

"I'm a writer."

He lost interest. Occasionally he would swear at other drivers, under his breath.

He swerved suddenly, changing lanes. We passed a four-car pileup in the lane we had been in.

"You get a little rain in this city, all of a sudden everybody forgets how to drive," he told me. I burrowed further into the cushions in the back. "You get rain in England, I hear." It was a statement, not a question.

"A little."

"More than a little. Rains every day in England." He laughed. "And thick fog. Real thick, thick fog."

"Not really."

"Whaddaya mean, no?" he asked, puzzled, defensive. "I've seen movies."

We sat in silence then, driving through the Hollywood rain; but after a while he said: "Ask them for the room Belushi died in."

"Pardon?"

"Belushi. John Belushi. It was your hotel he died in. Drugs. You heard about that?"

"Oh. Yes."

"They made a movie about his death. Some fat guy, didn't look nothing like him. But nobody tells the real truth about his death. Y'see, he wasn't alone. There were two other guys with him. Studios didn't want any shit. But you're a limo driver, you hear things."

"Really?"

"Robin Williams and Robert De Niro. They were there with him. All of them going doo-doo on the happy dust."

The hotel building was a white mock-gothic chateau. I said good-bye to the chauffeur and checked in; I did not ask about the room in which Belushi had died.

I walked out to my chalet through the rain, my overnight bag in my hand, clutching the set of keys that would, the desk clerk told me, get me through the various doors and gates. The air smelled of wet dust and, curiously enough, cough mixture. It was dusk, almost dark.

Water splashed everywhere. It ran in rills and rivulets across the courtyard. It ran into a small fishpond that jutted out from the side of a wall in the courtyard.

I walked up the stairs into a dank little room. It seemed a poor kind of a place for a star to die.

The bed seemed slightly damp, and the rain drummed a maddening beat on the air-conditioning system.

I watched a little television—the rerun wasteland: *Cheers* segued imperceptibly into *Taxi*, which flickered into black and white and became *I Love Lucy*—then stumbled into sleep.

I dreamed of drummers intermittently drumming, only thirty minutes away.

The phone woke me. "Hey-hey-hey-hey. You made it okay then?"

"Who is this?"

"It's Jacob at the studio. Are we still on for breakfast, hey-hey?"

"Breakfast...?"

"No problem. I'll pick you up at your hotel in thirty minutes. Reservations are already made. No problems. You got my messages?"

"I..."

"Faxed 'em through last night. See you."

The rain had stopped. The sunshine was warm and bright: proper Hollywood light. I walked up to the main building, walking on a carpet of crushed eucalyptus leaves—the cough medicine smell from the night before.

They handed me an envelope with a fax in it—my schedule for the next few days, with messages of encouragement and faxed handwritten doodles in the margin, saying things like *"This is Gonna be a Blockbuster!"* and *"Is this Going to be a Great Movie or What!"* The fax was signed by Jacob Klein, obviously the voice on the phone. I had never before had any dealings with a Jacob Klein.

A small red sports car drew up outside the hotel. The driver got out and waved at me. I walked over. He had a trim, pepper-and-salt beard, a smile that was almost bankable, and a gold chain around his neck. He showed me a copy of *Sons of Man*.

He was Jacob. We shook hands.

"Is David around? David Gambol?"

David Gambol was the man I'd spoken to earlier on the phone when arranging the trip. He wasn't the producer. I wasn't certain quite what he was. He described himself as "attached to the project."

"David's not with the studio anymore. I'm kind of running the project now, and I want you to know I'm really psyched. Hey-hey."

"That's good?"

We got in the car. "Where's the meeting?" I asked.

He shook his head. "It's not a meeting," he said. "It's a breakfast." I looked puzzled. He took pity on me. "A kind of pre-meeting meeting," he explained.

We drove from the hotel to a mall somewhere half an hour away while Jacob told me how much he enjoyed my book and how delighted he was that he'd become attached to the project. He said it was his idea to have me put up in the hotel—"Give you the kind of Hollywood experience you'd never get at the Four Seasons or Ma Maison, right?"—and asked me if I was staying in the chalet in which John Belushi had died. I told him I didn't know, but that I rather doubted it.

"You know who he was with, when he died? They covered it up, the studios."

"No. Who?"

"Meryl and Dustin."

"This is Meryl Streep and Dustin Hoffman we're talking about?"

"Sure."

"How do you know this?"

"People talk. It's Hollywood. You know?"

I nodded as if I did know, but I didn't.

People talk about books that write themselves, and it's a lie. Books don't write themselves. It takes thought and research and backache and notes and more time and more work than you'd believe.

Except for *Sons of Man*, and that one pretty much wrote itself.

The irritating question they ask us—us being writers—is: "Where do you get your ideas?"

And the answer is: Confluence. Things come together. The right ingredients and suddenly: *Abracadabra!*

It began with a documentary on Charles Manson I was watching more or less by accident (it was on a videotape a friend lent me after a couple of things I *did* want to watch): there was footage of Manson, back when he was first arrested, when people thought he was innocent and that it was the government picking on the hippies. And up on the screen was Manson—a charismatic, good-looking, messianic orator. Someone you'd crawl barefoot into Hell for. Someone you could kill for.

The trial started; and, a few weeks into it, the orator was gone, replaced by a shambling, apelike gibberer, with a cross carved into its forehead. Whatever

THE URBAN FANTASY ANTHOLOGY

the genius was was no longer there. It was gone. But it had been there.

The documentary continued: a hard-eyed ex-con who had been in prison with Manson, explaining, "Charlie Manson? Listen, Charlie was a joke. He was a nothing. We laughed at him. You know? He was a nothing!"

And I nodded. There was a time before Manson was the charisma king, then. I thought of a benediction, something given, that was taken away.

I watched the rest of the documentary obsessively. Then, over a black-and-white still, the narrator said something. I rewound, and he said it again.

I had an idea. I had a book that wrote itself.

The thing the narrator had said was this: that the infant children Manson had fathered on the women of The Family were sent to a variety of children's homes for adoption, with court-given surnames that were certainly not Manson.

And I thought of a dozen twenty-five-year-old Mansons. Thought of the charisma-thing descending on all of them at the same time. Twelve young Mansons, in their glory, gradually being pulled toward L.A. from all over the world. And a Manson daughter trying desperately to stop them from coming together and, as the back cover blurb told us, "realizing their terrifying destiny."

I wrote *Sons of Man* at white heat: it was finished in a month, and I sent it to my agent, who was surprised by it ("Well, it's not like your other stuff, dear," she said helpfully), and she sold it after an auction—my first—for more money than I had thought possible. (My other books, three collections of elegant, allusive and elusive ghost stories, had scarcely paid for the computer on which they were written.)

And then it was bought—prepublication—by Hollywood, again after an auction. There were three or four studios interested: I went with the studio who wanted me to write the script. I knew it would never happen, knew they'd never come through. But then the faxes began to spew out of my machine, late at night—most of them enthusiastically signed by one Dave Gambol; one morning I signed five copies of a contract thick as a brick; a few weeks later my agent reported the first check had cleared and tickets to Hollywood had arrived, for "preliminary talks." It seemed like a dream.

The tickets were business class. It was the moment I saw the tickets were business class that I knew the dream was real.

I went to Hollywood in the bubble bit at the top of the jumbo jet, nibbling smoked salmon and holding a hot-off-the-presses hardback of *Sons of Man*.

So. Breakfast.

They told me how much they loved the book. I didn't quite catch anybody's name. The men had beards or baseball caps or both; the women were astoundingly attractive, in a sanitary sort of way.

Jacob ordered our breakfast, and paid for it. He explained that the meeting coming up was a formality.

"It's your book we love," he said. "Why would we have bought your book if we didn't want to make it? Why would we have hired *you* to write it if we didn't want the specialness you'd bring to the project. The *you-ness*."

I nodded, very seriously, as if literary me-ness was something I had spent many hours pondering.

"An idea like this. A book like this. You're pretty unique."

"One of the uniquest," said a woman named Dina or Tina or possibly Deanna.

I raised an eyebrow. "So what am I meant to do at the meeting?"

"Be receptive," said Jacob. "Be positive."

The drive to the studio took about half an hour in Jacob's little red car. We drove up to the security gate, where Jacob had an argument with the guard. I gathered that he was new at the studio and had not yet been issued a permanent studio pass.

Nor, it appeared, once we got inside, did he have a permanent parking place. I still do not understand the ramifications of this: from what he said, parking places had as much to do with status at the studio as gifts from the emperor determined one's status in the court of ancient China.

We drove through the streets of an oddly flat New York and parked in front of a huge old bank.

Ten minutes' walk, and I was in a conference room, with Jacob and all the people from breakfast, waiting for someone to come in. In the flurry I'd rather missed who the someone was and what he or she did. I took out my copy of my book and put it in front of me, a talisman of sorts.

Someone came in. He was tall, with a pointy nose and a pointy chin, and his hair was too long—he looked like he'd kidnapped someone much younger and stolen their hair. He was an Australian, which surprised me.

He sat down.

He looked at me.

"Shoot," he said.

I looked at the people from the breakfast, but none of them were looking at me—I couldn't catch anyone's eye. So I began to talk: about the book, about the plot, about the end, the showdown in the L.A. nightclub, where the good Manson girl blows the rest of them up. Or thinks she does. About my idea for having one actor play all the Manson boys.

"Do you believe this stuff?" It was the first question from the Someone.

That one was easy. It was one I'd already answered for at least two dozen British journalists.

"Do I believe that a supernatural power possessed Charles Manson for a while and is even now possessing his many children? No. Do I believe that something strange was happening? I suppose I must. Perhaps it was simply that, for a brief while, his madness was in step with the madness of the world outside. I don't know."

"Mm. This Manson kid. He could be Keanu Reaves?"

God, no, I thought. Jacob caught my eye and nodded desperately. "I don't see why not," I said. It was all imagination anyway. None of it was real.

"We're cutting a deal with his people," said the Someone, nodding thoughtfully.

They sent me off to do a treatment for them to approve. And by *them*, I understood they meant the Australian Someone, although I was not entirely sure.

Before I left, someone gave me $700 and made me sign for it: two weeks *per diem*.

I spent two days doing the treatment. I kept trying to forget the book, and structure the story as a film. The work went well. I sat in the little room and typed on a notebook computer the studio had sent down for me, and printed out pages on the bubble-jet printer the studio sent down with it. I ate in my room.

Each afternoon I would go for a short walk down Sunset Boulevard. I would walk as far as the "almost all-nite" bookstore, where I would buy a newspaper. Then I would sit outside in the hotel courtyard for half an hour, reading a newspaper. And then, having had my ration of sun and air, I would go back into the dark, and turn my book back into something else.

There was a very old black man, a hotel employee, who would walk across the courtyard each day with almost painful slowness and water the plants and inspect the fish. He'd grin at me as he went past, and I'd nod at him.

On the third day I got up and walked over to him as he stood by the fish pool, picking out bits of rubbish by hand: a couple of coins and a cigarette packet.

"Hello," I said.

"Suh," said the old man.

I thought about asking him not to call me sir, but I couldn't think of a way to put it that might not cause offense. "Nice fish."

He nodded and grinned. "Ornamental carp. Brought here all the way from China."

We watched them swim around the little pool.

"I wonder if they get bored."

He shook his head. "My grandson, he's an ichthyologist, you know what that is?"

"Studies fishes."

"Uh-huh. He says they only got a memory that's like thirty seconds long. So they swim around the pool, it's always a surprise to them, going 'I never been here before.' They meet another fish they known for a hundred years, they say, 'Who are you, stranger?'"

"Will you ask your grandson something for me?" The old man nodded. "I read once that carp don't have set life spans. They don't age like we do. They die if they're killed by people or predators or disease, but they don't just get old and die. Theoretically they could live forever."

He nodded. "I'll ask him. It sure sounds good. These three—now, this one, I call him Ghost, he's only four, five years old. But the other two, they came here from China back when I was first here."

"And when was that?"

"That would have been, in the Year of Our Lord Nineteen Hundred and Twenty-four. How old do I look to you?"

THE URBAN FANTASY ANTHOLOGY

I couldn't tell. He might have been carved from old wood. Over fifty and younger than Methuselah. I told him so.

"I was born in 1906. God's truth."

"Were you born here, in L.A.?"

He shook his head. "When I was born, Los Angeles wasn't nothin' but an orange grove, a long way from New York." He sprinkled fish food on the surface of the water. The three fish bobbed up, pale-white silvered ghost carp, staring at us, or seeming to, the O's of their mouths continually opening and closing, as if they were talking to us in some silent, secret language of their own.

I pointed to the one he had indicated. "So he's Ghost, yes?"

"He's Ghost. That's right. That one under the lily—you can see his tail, there, see?—he's called Buster, after Buster Keaton. Keaton was staying here when we got the older two. And this one's our Princess."

Princess was the most recognizable of the white carp. She was a pale cream color, with a blotch of vivid crimson along her back, setting her apart from the other two.

"She's lovely."

"She surely is. She surely is all of that."

He took a deep breath then and began to cough, a wheezing cough that shook his thin frame. I was able then, for the first time, to see him as a man of ninety.

"Are you all right?"

He nodded. "Fine, fine, fine. Old bones," he said. "Old bones."

We shook hands, and I returned to my treatment and the gloom.

I printed out the completed treatment, faxed it off to Jacob at the studio.

The next day he came over to the chalet. He looked upset.

"Everything okay? Is there a problem with the treatment?"

"Just shit going down. We made this movie with..." and he named a well-known actress who had been in a few successful films a couple of years before. "Can't lose, huh? Only she is not as young as she was, and she insists on doing her own nude scenes, and that's not a body anybody wants to see, believe me.

"So the plot is, there's this photographer who is persuading women to take their clothes off for him. Then he *shtups* them. Only no one believes he's doing it. So the chief of police—played by Ms. Lemme Show the World My Naked

Butt—realizes that the only way she can arrest him is if she pretends to be one of the women. So she sleeps with him. Now, there's a twist..."

"She falls in love with him?"

"Oh. Yeah. And then she realizes that women will always be imprisoned by male images of women, and to prove her love for him, when the police come to arrest the two of them she sets fire to all the photographs and dies in the fire. Her clothes burn off first. How does that sound to you?"

"Dumb."

"That was what we thought when we saw it. So we fired the director and recut it and did an extra day's shoot. Now she's wearing a wire when they make out. And when she starts to fall in love with him, she finds out that he killed her brother. She has a dream in which her clothes burn off, then she goes out with the SWAT team to try to bring him in. But he gets shot by her little sister, who he's also been *shtupping*."

"Is it any better?"

He shakes his head. "It's junk. If she'd let us use a stand-in for the nude sequences, maybe we'd be in better shape."

"What did you think of the treatment?"

"What?"

"My treatment? The one I sent you?"

"Sure. That treatment. We loved it. We all loved it. It was great. Really terrific. We're all really excited."

"So what's next?"

"Well, as soon as everyone's had a chance to look it over, we'll get together and talk about it."

He patted me on the back and went away, leaving me with nothing to do in Hollywood.

I decided to write a short story. There was an idea I'd had in England before I'd left. Something about a small theatre at the end of a pier. Stage magic as the rain came down. An audience who couldn't tell the difference between magic and illusion, and to whom it would make no difference if every illusion was real.

That afternoon, on my walk, I bought a couple of books on Stage Magic and Victorian Illusions in the "almost all-nite" bookshop. A story, or the seed of it anyway, was there in my head, and I wanted to explore it. I sat on the bench in the courtyard and browsed through the books. There was, I decided, a specific atmosphere that I was after.

I was reading about the Pockets Men, who had pockets filled with every small object you could imagine and would produce whatever you asked on request. No illusion—just remarkable feats of organization and memory. A shadow fell across the page. I looked up.

"Hullo again," I said to the old black man.

"Suh," he said.

"Please don't call me that. It makes me feel like I ought to be wearing a suit or something." I told him my name.

He told me his: "Pious Dundas."

"Pious?" I wasn't sure that I'd heard him correctly. He nodded proudly.

"Sometimes I am, and sometimes I ain't. It's what my mamma called me, and it's a good name."

"Yes."

"So what are you doing here, suh?"

"I'm not sure. I'm meant to be writing a film, I think. Or at least, I'm waiting for them to tell me to start writing a film."

He scratched his nose. "All the film people stayed here, if I started to tell you them all now, I could talk till a week next Wednesday and I wouldn't have told you the half of them."

"Who were your favorites?"

"Harry Langdon. He was a gentleman. George Sanders. He was English, like you. He'd say, 'Ah, Pious. You must pray for my soul.' And I'd say, 'Your soul's your own affair, Mister Sanders,' but I prayed for him just the same. And June Lincoln."

"June Lincoln?"

His eyes sparkled, and he smiled. "She was the queen of the silver screen. She was finer than any of them: Mary Pickford or Lillian Gish or Theda Bara or Louise Brooks…. She was the finest. She had 'it.' You know what 'it' was?"

"Sex appeal."

"More than that. She was everything you ever dreamed of. You'd see a June Lincoln picture, you wanted to…" he broke off, waved one hand in small circles, as if he were trying to catch the missing words. "I don't know. Go down on one knee, maybe, like a knight in shinin' armor to the queen. June Lincoln, she was the best of them. I told my grandson about her, he tried to find something for the VCR, but no go. Nothing out there anymore. She only lives in the heads of old men like me." He tapped his forehead.

"She must have been quite something."

He nodded.

"What happened to her?"

"She hung herself. Some folks said it was because she wouldn't have been able to cut the mustard in the talkies, but that ain't true: she had a voice you'd remember if you heard it just once. Smooth and dark, her voice was, like an Irish coffee. Some say she got her heart broken by a man, or by a woman, or that it was gambling, or gangsters, or booze. Who knows? They were wild days."

"I take it that you must have heard her talk."

He grinned. "She said, 'Boy, can you find what they did with my wrap?' and when I come back with it, then she said, 'You're a fine one, boy.' And the man who was with her, he said, 'June, don't tease the help' and she smiled at me and gave me five dollars and said 'He don't mind, do you, boy?' and I just shook my head. Then she made the thing with her lips, you know?"

"A *moue?*"

"Something like that. I felt it here." He tapped his chest. "Those lips. They could take a man apart."

He bit his lower lip for a moment, and focused on forever. I wondered where he was, and when. Then he looked at me once more.

"You want to see her lips?"

"How do you mean?"

"You come over here. Follow me."

"What are we...?" I had visions of a lip print in cement, like the handprints outside Grauman's Chinese Theatre.

He shook his head, and raised an old finger to his mouth. *Silence.*

I closed the books. We walked across the courtyard. When he reached the little fish-pool, he stopped.

"Look at the Princess," he told me.

"The one with the red splotch, yes?"

He nodded. The fish reminded me of a Chinese dragon: wise and pale. A ghost fish, white as old bone, save for the blotch of scarlet on its back—an inch-long double-bow shape. It hung in the pool, drifting, thinking.

"That's it," he said. "On her back. See?"

"I don't quite follow you."

He paused and stared at the fish.

"Would you like to sit down?" I found myself very conscious of Mr. Dundas's age.

"They don't pay me to sit down," he said, very seriously. Then he said, as if he were explaining something to a small child, "It was like there were gods in those days. Today, it's all television: small heroes. Little people in the boxes. I see some of them here. Little people.

"The stars of the old times: They was giants, painted in silver light, big as houses...and when you met them, they were *still* huge. People believed in them.

"They'd have parties here. You worked here, you saw what went on. There was liquor, and weed, and goings-on you'd hardly credit. There was this one party...the film was called *Hearts of the Desert*. You ever heard of it?"

I shook my head.

"One of the biggest movies of 1926, up there with *What Price Glory* with Victor McLaglen and Dolores del Rio and *Ella Cinders* starring Colleen Moore. You heard of them?"

I shook my head again.

"You ever heard of Warner Baxter? Belle Bennett?"

"Who were they?"

"Big, big stars in 1926." He paused for a moment. "*Hearts of the Desert*. They had the party for it here, in the hotel, when it wrapped. There was wine and beer and whiskey and gin—this was Prohibition days, but the studios kind of owned the police force, so they looked the other way; and there was food, and a deal of foolishness; Ronald Colman was there and Douglas Fairbanks—the father, not the son—and all the cast and the crew; and a jazz band played over there where those chalets are now.

"And June Lincoln was the toast of Hollywood that night. She was the Arab princess in the film. Those days, Arabs meant passion and lust. These days... well, things change.

"I don't know what started it all. I heard it was a dare or a bet; maybe she was just drunk. I thought she was drunk. Anyhow, she got up, and the band was playing soft and slow. And she walked over here, where I'm standing right now, and she plunged her hands right into this pool. She was laughing, and laughing, and laughing...

"Miss Lincoln picked up the fish—reached in and took it, both hands she took it in—and she picked it up from the water, and then she held it in front of her face.

"Now, I was worried, because they'd just brought these fish in from China and they cost two hundred dollars apiece. That was before I was looking after the fish, of course. Wasn't me that'd lose it from my wages. But still, two hundred dollars was a whole lot of money in those days.

"Then she smiled at all of us, and she leaned down and she kissed it, slow like, on its back. It didn't wriggle or nothin', it just lay in her hand, and she kissed it with her lips like red coral, and the people at the party laughed and cheered.

"She put the fish back in the pool, and for a moment it was as if it didn't want to leave her—it stayed by her, nuzzling her fingers. And then the first of the fireworks went off, and it swum away.

"Her lipstick was red as red as red, and she left the shape of her lips on the fish's back.—There. Do you see?"

Princess, the white carp with the coral red mark on her back, flicked a fin and continued on her eternal series of thirty-second journeys around the pool. The red mark did look like a lip print.

He sprinkled a handful of fish food on the water, and the three fish bobbed and gulped to the surface.

I walked back in to my chalet, carrying my books on old illusions. The phone was ringing: it was someone from the studio. They wanted to talk about the treatment. A car would be there for me in thirty minutes.

"Will Jacob be there?"

But the line was already dead.

The meeting was with the Australian Someone and his assistant, a bespectacled man in a suit. His was the first suit I'd seen so far, and his spectacles were a vivid blue. He seemed nervous.

"Where are you staying?" asked the Someone.

I told him.

"Isn't that where Belushi...?"

"So I've been told."

He nodded. "He wasn't alone, when he died."

"No?"

He rubbed one finger along the side of his pointy nose. "There were a couple of other people at the party. They were both directors, both as big as you could get at that point. You don't need names. I found out about it when I was making the last Indiana Jones film."

An uneasy silence. We were at a huge round table, just the three of us, and we each had a copy of the treatment I had written in front of us. Finally I said:

"What did you think of it?"

They both nodded, more or less in unison.

And then they tried, as hard as they could, to tell me they hated it while never saying anything that might conceivably upset me. It was a very odd conversation.

"We have a problem with the third act," they'd say, implying vaguely that the fault lay neither with me nor with the treatment, nor even with the third act, but with them.

They wanted the people to be more sympathetic. They wanted sharp lights and shadows, not shades of gray. They wanted the heroine to be a hero. And I nodded and took notes.

At the end of the meeting I shook hands with the Someone, and the assistant in the blue-rimmed spectacles took me off through the corridor maze to find the outside world and my car and my driver.

As we walked, I asked if the studio had a picture anywhere of June Lincoln.

"Who?" His name, it turned out, was Greg. He pulled out a small notebook and wrote something down in it with a pencil.

"She was a silent screen star. Famous in 1926."

"Was she with the studio?"

"I have no idea," I admitted. "But she was famous. Even more famous than Marie Prevost."

"Who?"

"'A winner who became a doggie's dinner.' One of the biggest stars of the silent screen. Died in poverty when the talkies came in and was eaten by her dachshund. Nick Lowe wrote a song about her."

"Who?"

"'I knew the bride when she used to rock and roll.' Anyway, June Lincoln. Can someone find me a photo?"

He wrote something more down on his pad. Stared at it for a moment. Then wrote down something else. Then he nodded.

We had reached the daylight, and my car was waiting.

"By the way," he said, "you should know that he's full of shit."

"I'm sorry?"

"Full of shit. It wasn't Spielberg and Lucas who were with Belushi. It was Bette Midler and Linda Ronstadt. It was a coke orgy. Everybody knows that. He's full of shit. And he was just a junior studio accountant for chrissakes on the Indiana Jones movie. Like it was his movie. Asshole."

We shook hands. I got in the car and went back to the hotel.

The time difference caught up with me that night, and I woke, utterly and irrevocably, at 4 A.M.

I got up, peed, then I pulled on a pair of jeans (I sleep in a T-shirt) and walked outside.

I wanted to see the stars, but the lights of the city were too bright, the air too dirty. The sky was a dirty, starless yellow, and I thought of all the constellations I could see from the English countryside, and I felt, for the first time, deeply, stupidly homesick.

I missed the stars.

I wanted to work on the short story or to get on with the film script. Instead, I worked on a second draft of the treatment.

I took the number of Junior Mansons down to five from twelve and made it clearer from the start that one of them, who was now male, wasn't a bad guy and the other four most definitely were.

They sent over a copy of a film magazine. It had the smell of old pulp paper about it, and was stamped in purple with the studio name and with the word ARCHIVES underneath. The cover showed John Barrymore, on a boat.

The article inside was about June Lincoln's death. I found it hard to read and harder still to understand: it hinted at the forbidden vices that led to her death, that much I could tell, but it was as if it were hinting in a cipher to which modern readers lacked any key. Or perhaps, on reflection, the writer of her obituary knew nothing and was hinting into the void.

More interesting—at any rate, more comprehensible—were the photos. A full-page, black-edged photo of a woman with huge eyes and a gentle smile, smoking a cigarette (the smoke was airbrushed in, to my way of thinking very clumsily: had people ever been taken in by such clumsy fakes?); another photo of her in a staged clinch with Douglas Fairbanks; a small photograph of her standing on the running board of a car, holding a couple of tiny dogs.

She was, from the photographs, not a contemporary beauty. She lacked the transcendence of a Louise Brooks, the sex appeal of a Marilyn Monroe, the sluttish elegance of a Rita Hayworth. She was a twenties starlet as dull as any other twenties starlet. I saw no mystery in her huge eyes, her bobbed hair. She had perfectly made-up cupid's-bow lips. I had no idea what she would have looked like if she had been alive and around today.

Still, she was real; she had lived. She had been worshipped and adored by the people in the movie palaces. She had kissed the fish, and walked in the grounds of my hotel seventy years before: no time in England, but an eternity in Hollywood.

I went in to talk about the treatment. None of the people I had spoken to before were there. Instead, I was shown in to see a very young man in a small office, who never smiled and who told me how much he loved the treatment and how pleased he was that the studio owned the property.

He said he thought the character of Charles Manson was particularly cool, and that maybe—"once he was fully dimensionalized"—Manson could be the next Hannibal Lecter.

"But. Um. Manson. He's real. He's in prison now. His people killed Sharon Tate."

"Sharon Tate?"

"She was an actress. A film star. She was pregnant and they killed her. She was married to Polanski."

"*Roman* Polanski?"

"The director. Yes."

He frowned. "But we're putting together a deal with Polanski."

"That's good. He's a good director."

"Does he know about this?"

"About what? The book? Our film? Sharon Tate's death?"

He shook his head: none of the above. "It's a three-picture deal. Julia Roberts is semiattached to it. You say Polanski doesn't know about this treatment?"

"No, what I said was—"

He checked his watch.

"Where are you staying?" he asked. "Are we putting you up somewhere good?"

"Yes, thank you," I said. "I'm a couple of chalets away from the room in which Belushi died."

I expected another confidential couple of stars: to be told that John Belushi had kicked the bucket in company with Julie Andrews and Miss Piggy the Muppet. I was wrong.

"Belushi's dead?" he said, his young brow furrowing. "Belushi's not dead. We're doing a picture with Belushi."

"This was the brother," I told him. "The brother died, years ago."

He shrugged. "Sounds like a shithole," he said. "Next time you come out, tell them you want to stay in the Bel Air. You want us to move you out there now?"

"No, thank you," I said. "I'm used to it where I am."

"What about the treatment?" I asked.

"Leave it with us."

I found myself becoming fascinated by two old theatrical illusions I found in my books: "The Artist's Dream" and "The Enchanted Casement." They were metaphors for something, of that I was certain; but the story that ought to have accompanied them was not yet there. I'd write first sentences that did not make it to first paragraphs, first paragraphs that never made it to first pages. I'd write them on the computer, then exit without saving anything.

I sat outside in the courtyard and stared at the two white carp and the one scarlet and white carp. They looked, I decided, like Escher drawings of fish, which surprised me, as it had never occurred to me there was anything even slightly realistic in Escher's drawings.

Pious Dundas was polishing the leaves of the plants. He had a bottle of polisher and a cloth.

"Hi, Pious."

"Suh."

"Lovely day."

He nodded, and coughed, and banged his chest with his fist, and nodded some more.

I left the fish, sat down on the bench.

"Why haven't they made you retire?" I asked. "Shouldn't you have retired fifteen years ago?"

He continued polishing. "Hell no, I'm a landmark. They can *say* that all the stars in the sky stayed here, but *I* tell folks what Cary Grant had for breakfast."

"Do you remember?"

"Heck no. But *they* don't know that." He coughed again. "What you writing?"

"Well, last week I wrote a treatment for this film. And then I wrote another treatment. And now I'm waiting for...something."

"So what *are* you writing?"

"A story that won't come right. It's about a Victorian magic trick called 'The Artist's Dream.' An artist comes on to the stage, carrying a big canvas, which he puts on an easel. It's got a painting of a woman on it. And he looks at the painting and despairs of ever being a real painter. Then he sits down and goes to sleep, and the painting comes to life, steps down from the frame and tells him not to give up. To keep fighting. He'll be a great painter one day. She climbs back into the frame. The lights dim. Then he wakes up, and it's a painting again..."

"...and the other illusion," I told the woman from the studio, who had made the mistake of feigning interest at the beginning of the meeting, "was called 'The Enchanted Casement.' A window hangs in the air and faces appear in it, but there's no one around. I think I can get a strange sort of parallel between the enchanted casement and probably television: seems like a natural candidate, after all."

"I like *Seinfeld*," she said. "You watch that show? It's about nothing. I mean, they have whole episodes about nothing. And I liked Garry Shandling before he did the new show and got mean."

"The illusions," I continued, "like all great illusions, make us question the nature of reality. But they also frame—pun, I suppose, intentionalish—the issue of what entertainment would turn into. Films before they had films, telly before there was ever TV."

She frowned. "Is this a movie?"

"I hope not. It's a short story, if I can get it to work."

"So let's talk about the movie." She flicked through a pile of notes. She was in her mid-twenties and looked both attractive and sterile. I wondered if she was one of the women who had been at the breakfast on my first day, a Deanna or a Tina.

She looked puzzled at something and read: "*I Knew the Bride When She Used to Rock and Roll?*"

"He wrote that down? That's not this film."

She nodded. "Now, I have to say that some of your treatment is kind of... *contentious*. The Manson thing...well, we're not sure it's going to fly. Could we take him out?"

"But that's the whole point of the thing. I mean, the book is called *Sons of Man*; it's about Manson's children. If you take him out, you don't have very much, do you? I mean, this is the book you bought." I held it up for her to see: my talisman. "Throwing out Manson is like, I don't know, it's like ordering a pizza and then complaining when it arrives because it's flat, round, and covered in tomato sauce and cheese."

She gave no indication of having heard anything I had said. She asked, "What do you think about *When We Were Badd* as a title? Two *d*'s in Badd."

"I don't know. For this?"

"We don't want people to think that it's religious. *Sons of Man*. It sounds like it might be kind of anti-Christian."

"Well, I do kind of imply that the power that possesses the Manson children is in some way a kind of demonic power."

"You do?"

"In the book."

She managed a pitying look, of the kind that only people who know that books are, at best, properties on which films can be loosely based, can bestow on the rest of us.

"Well, I don't think the studio would see that as appropriate," she said.

"Do you know who June Lincoln was?" I asked her.

She shook her head.

"David Gambol? Jacob Klein?"

She shook her head once more, a little impatiently. Then she gave me a typed list of things she felt needed fixing, which amounted to pretty much everything. The list was TO: me and a number of other people, whose names I didn't recognize, and it was FROM: Donna Leary.

I said, Thank you, Donna, and went back to the hotel.

I was gloomy for a day. And then I thought of a way to redo the treatment that would, I thought, deal with all of Donna's list of complaints.

Another day's thinking, a few days' writing, and I faxed the third treatment off to the studio.

Pious Dundas brought his scrapbook over for me to look at, once he felt certain that I was genuinely interested in June Lincoln—named, I discovered, after the month and the president, born Ruth Baumgarten in 1903. It was a leatherbound old scrapbook, the size and weight of a family Bible.

She was twenty-four when she died.

"I wish you could've seen her," said Pious Dundas. "I wish some of her films had survived. She was so big. She was the greatest star of all of them."

"Was she a good actress?"

He shook his head decisively. "Nope."

"Was she a great beauty? If she was, I just don't see it."

He shook his head again. "The camera liked her, that's for sure. But that wasn't it. Back row of the chorus had a dozen girls prettier'n her."

"Then what was it?"

"She was a star." He shrugged. "That's what it means to be a star."

I turned the pages: cuttings, reviewing films I'd never heard of—films for which the only negatives and prints had long ago been lost, mislaid, or destroyed by the fire department, nitrate negatives being a notorious fire hazard; other cuttings from film magazines: June Lincoln at play, June Lincoln at rest, June Lincoln on the set of *The Pawnbroker's Shirt*, June Lincoln wearing a huge fur coat—which somehow dated the photograph more than the strange bobbed hair or the ubiquitous cigarettes.

"Did you love her?"

He shook his head. "Not like you would love a woman..." he said.

There was a pause. He reached down and turned the pages.

"And my wife would have killed me if she'd heard me say this..."

Another pause.

"But yeah. Skinny dead white woman. I suppose I loved her." He closed the book.

"But she's not dead to you, is she?"

He shook his head. Then he went away. But he left me the book to look at.

The secret of the illusion of "The Artist's Dream" was this: It was done by carrying the girl in, holding tight on to the back of the canvas. The canvas was supported by hidden wires, so, while the artist casually, easily, carried in the canvas and placed it on the easel, he was also carrying in the girl. The painting of the girl on the easel was arranged like a roller blind, and it rolled up or down.

"The Enchanted Casement," on the other hand, was, literally, done with mirrors: an angled mirror which reflected the faces of people standing out of sight in the wings.

Even today many magicians use mirrors in their acts to make you think you are seeing something you are not.

It was easy, when you knew how it was done.

"Before we start," he said, "I should tell you I don't read treatments. I tend to feel it inhibits my creativity. Don't worry, I had a secretary do a précis, so I'm up to speed."

He had a beard and long hair and looked a little like Jesus, although I doubted that Jesus had such perfect teeth. He was, it appeared, the most important person I'd spoken to so far. His name was John Ray, and even I had heard of him, although I was not entirely sure what he did: his name tended to appear at the beginning of films, next to words like EXECUTIVE PRODUCER. The voice from the studio that had set up the meeting told me that they, the studio, were most excited about the fact that he had "attached himself to the project."

"Doesn't the précis inhibit your creativity, too?"

He grinned. "Now, we all think you've done an amazing job. Quite stunning. There are just a few things that we have a problem with."

"Such as?"

"Well, the Manson thing. And the idea about these kids growing up. So we've been tossing around a few scenarios in the office: try this for size. There's a guy called, say, Jack Badd—two *d*'s, that was Donna's idea—"

Donna bowed her head modestly.

"They put him away for satanic abuse, fried him in the chair, and as he dies he swears he'll come back and destroy them all.

"Now, it's today, and we see these young boys getting hooked on a video arcade game called *Be Badd*. His face on it. And as they play the game he like, starts to possess them. Maybe there could be something strange about his face, a Jason or Freddy thing." He stopped, as if he were seeking approval.

So I said, "So who's making these video games?"

He pointed a finger at me and said, "You're the writer, sweetheart. You want us to do all your work for you?"

I didn't say anything. I didn't know what to say.

Think movies, I thought. *They understand movies.* I said, "But surely, what you're proposing is like doing *The Boys from Brazil* without Hitler."

He looked puzzled.

"It was a film by Ira Levin," I said. No flicker of recognition in his eyes. "*Rosemary's Baby.*" He continued to look blank. "*Sliver.*"

He nodded; somewhere a penny had dropped. "Point taken," he said. "You write the Sharon Stone part, we'll move heaven and earth to get her for you. I have an in to her people."

So I went out.

That night it was cold, and it shouldn't have been cold in L.A., and the air smelled more of cough drops than ever.

An old girlfriend lived in the L.A. area and I resolved to get hold of her. I phoned the number I had for her and began a quest that took most of the rest of the evening. People gave me numbers, and I rang them, and other people gave me numbers, and I rang them, too.

Eventually I phoned a number, and I recognized her voice.

"Do you know where I am?" she said.

"No," I said. "I was given this number."

"This is a hospital room," she said. "My mother's. She had a brain hemorrhage."

"I'm sorry. Is she all right?"

"No."

"I'm sorry."

There was an awkward silence.

"How are you?" she asked.

"Pretty bad," I said.

I told her everything that had happened to me so far. I told her how I felt.

"Why is it like this?" I asked her.

"Because they're scared."

"Why are they scared? What are they scared of?"

"Because you're only as good as the last hits you can attach your name to."

"Huh?"

"If you say yes to something, the studio may make a film, and it will cost twenty or thirty million dollars, and if it's a failure, you will have your name attached to it and will lose status. If you say no, you don't risk losing status."

"Really?"

"Kind of."

"How do you know so much about all this? You're a musician, you're not in films."

She laughed wearily: "I live out here. Everybody who lives out here knows this stuff. Have you tried asking people about their screenplays?"

"No."

"Try it sometime. Ask anyone. The guy in the gas station. Anyone. They've all got them." Then someone said something to her, and she said something back, and she said, "Look, I've got to go," and she put down the phone.

I couldn't find the heater, if the room had a heater, and I was freezing in my little chalet room, like the one Belushi died in, same uninspired framed print on the wall, I had no doubt, same chilly dampness in the air.

I ran a hot bath to warm myself up, but I was even chillier when I got out.

White goldfish sliding to and fro in the water, dodging and darting through the lily pads. One of the goldfish had a crimson mark on its back that might, conceivably, have been perfectly lip-shaped: the miraculous stigmata of an almost-forgotten goddess. The gray early-morning sky was reflected in the pool.

I stared at it gloomily.

"You okay?"

I turned. Pious Dundas was standing next to me.

"You're up early."

"I slept badly. Too cold."

"You should have called the front desk. They'd've sent you down a heater and extra blankets."

"It never occurred to me."

His breathing sounded awkward, labored.

"You okay?"

"Heck no. I'm old. You get to my age, boy, you won't be okay either. But I'll be here when you've gone. How's work going?"

"I don't know. I've stopped working on the treatment, and I'm stuck on 'The Artist's Dream'—this story I'm doing about Victorian stage magic. It's set in an English seaside resort in the rain. With the magician performing magic on the stage, which somehow changes the audience. It touches their hearts."

He nodded, slowly. "'The Artist's Dream'..." he said. "So. You see yourself as the artist or the magician?"

"I don't know," I said. "I don't think I'm either of them."

I turned to go and then something occurred to me.

"Mister Dundas," I said. "Have you got a screenplay? One you wrote?"

He shook his head.

"You *never* wrote a screenplay?"

"Not me," he said.

"Promise?"

He grinned. "I promise," he said.

I went back to my room. I thumbed through my U.K. hardback of *Sons of Man* and wondered that anything so clumsily written had even been published, wondered why Hollywood had bought it in the first place, why they didn't want it, now that they had bought it.

I tried to write "The Artist's Dream" some more, and failed miserably. The characters were frozen. They seemed unable to breathe, or move, or talk.

I went into the toilet, pissed a vivid yellow stream against the porcelain. A cockroach ran across the silver of the mirror.

I went back into the sitting room, opened a new document, and wrote:

> I'm thinking about England in the rain,
> a strange theatre on the pier: a trail
> of fear and magic, memory and pain.
>
> The fear should be of going bleak insane,
> the magic should be like a fairytale.
> I'm thinking about England in the rain.
>
> The loneliness is harder to explain—
> an empty place inside me where I fail,
> of fear and magic, memory and pain.
>
> I think of a magician and a skein
> of truth disguised as lies. You wear a veil.
> I'm thinking about England in the rain...
>
> The shapes repeat like some bizarre refrain
> and here's a sword, a hand, and there's a grail
> of fear and magic, memory and pain.
>
> The wizard waves his wand and we turn pale,
> tells us sad truths, but all to no avail.
> I'm thinking about England, in the rain
> of fear and magic, memory and pain.

I didn't know if it was any good or not, but that didn't matter. I had written something new and fresh I hadn't written before, and it felt wonderful.

I ordered breakfast from room service and requested a heater and a couple of extra blankets.

The next day I wrote a six-page treatment for a film called *When We Were Badd*, in which Jack Badd, a serial killer with a huge cross carved into his forehead, was killed in the electric chair and came back in a video game and took over four young men. The fifth young man defeated Badd by burning the original electric chair, which was now on display, I decided, in the wax museum where the fifth young man's girlfriend worked during the day. By night she was an exotic dancer.

The hotel desk faxed it off to the studio, and I went to bed.

I went to sleep, hoping that the studio would formally reject it and that I could go home.

In the theater of my dreams, a man with a beard and a baseball cap carried on a movie screen, and then he walked off-stage. The silver screen hung in the air, unsupported.

A flickery silent film began to play upon it: a woman who came out and stared down at me. It was June Lincoln who flickered on the screen, and it was June Lincoln who walked down from the screen and sat on the edge of my bed.

"Are you going to tell me not to give up?" I asked her.

On some level I knew it was a dream. I remember, dimly, understanding why this woman was a star, remember regretting that none of her films had survived.

She was indeed beautiful in my dream, despite the livid mark which went all the way around her neck.

"Why on earth would I do that?" she asked. In my dream she smelled of gin and old celluloid, although I do not remember the last dream I had where anyone smelled of anything. She smiled, a perfect black-and-white smile. "I got out, didn't I?"

Then she stood up and walked around the room.

"I can't believe this hotel is still standing," she said. "I used to fuck here." Her voice was filled with crackles and hisses. She came back to the bed and stared at me, as a cat stares at a hole.

"Do you worship me?" she asked.

I shook my head. She walked over to me and took my flesh hand in her silver one.

"Nobody remembers anything anymore," she said. "It's a thirty-minute town."

There was something I had to ask her. "Where are the stars?" I asked. "I keep looking up in the sky, but they aren't there."

She pointed at the floor of the chalet. "You've been looking in the wrong places," she said. I had never before noticed that the floor of the chalet was a sidewalk and each paving stone contained a star and a name—names I didn't know: Clara Kimball Young, Linda Arvidson, Vivian Martin, Norma Talmadge, Olive Thomas, Mary Miles Minter, Seena Owen...

June Lincoln pointed at the chalet window. "And out there." The window was open, and through it I could see the whole of Hollywood spread out below me—the view from the hills: an infinite spread of twinkling multicolored lights.

"Now, aren't those better than stars?" she asked.

And they were. I realized I could see constellations in the street lamps and the cars.

I nodded.

Her lips brushed mine.

"Don't forget me," she whispered, but she whispered it sadly, as if she knew that I would.

I woke up with the telephone shrilling. I answered it, growled a mumble into the handpiece.

"This is Gerry Quoint, from the studio. We need you for a lunch meeting."

Mumble something mumble.

"We'll send a car," he said. "The restaurant's about half an hour away."

The restaurant was airy and spacious and green, and they were waiting for me there.

By this point I would have been surprised if I *had* recognized anyone. John Ray, I was told over hors d'oeuvres, had "split over contract disagreements," and Donna had gone with him, "obviously."

Both of the men had beards; one had bad skin. The woman was thin and seemed pleasant.

They asked where I was staying, and, when I told them, one of the beards told us (first making us all agree that this would go no further) that a politician

THE URBAN FANTASY ANTHOLOGY

named Gary Hart and one of the Eagles were both doing drugs with Belushi when he died.

After that they told me that they were looking forward to the story.

I asked the question. "Is this for *Sons of Man* or *When We Were Badd?* Because," I told them, "I have a problem with the latter."

They looked puzzled.

It was, they told me, for *I Knew the Bride When She Used to Rock and Roll.* Which was, they told me, both High Concept and Feel Good. It was also, they added, Very Now, which was important in a town in which an hour ago was Ancient History.

They told me that they thought it would be a good thing if our hero could rescue the young lady from her loveless marriage, and if they could rock and roll together at the end.

I pointed out that they needed to buy the film rights from Nick Lowe, who wrote the song, and then that, no, I didn't know who his agent was.

They grinned and assured me that that wouldn't be a problem.

They suggested I turn over the project in my mind before I started on the treatment, and each of them mentioned a couple of young stars to bear in mind when I was putting together the story.

And I shook hands with all of them and told them that I certainly would.

I mentioned that I thought that I could work on it best back in England.

And they said that that would be fine.

Some days before, I'd asked Pious Dundas whether anyone was with Belushi in the chalet, on the night that he died.

If anyone would know, I figured, he would.

"He died alone," said Pious Dundas, old as Methuselah, unblinking. "It don't matter a rat's ass whether there was anyone with him or not. He died alone."

It felt strange to be leaving the hotel.

I went up to the front desk.

"I'll be checking out later this afternoon."

"Very good, sir."

"Would it be possible for you to...the, uh, the groundkeeper. Mister Dundas. An elderly gentleman. I don't know. I haven't seen him around for a couple of days. I wanted to say good-bye."

"'To one of the groundsmen?"

"Yes."

She stared at me, puzzled. She was very beautiful, and her lipstick was the color of a blackberry bruise. I wondered whether she was waiting to be discovered.

She picked up the phone and spoke into it, quietly.

Then, "I'm sorry, sir. Mister Dundas hasn't been in for the last few days."

"Could you give me his phone number?"

"I'm sorry, sir. That's not our policy." She stared at me as she said it, letting me know that she *really* was *so* sorry...

"How's your screenplay?" I asked her.

"How did you know?" she asked.

"Well—"

"It's on Joel Silver's desk," she said. "My friend Arnie, he's my writing partner, and he's a courier. He dropped it off with Joel Silver's office, like it came from a regular agent or somewhere."

"Best of luck," I told her.

"Thanks," she said, and smiled with her blackberry lips.

Information had two Dundas, P's listed, which I thought was both unlikely and said something about America, or at least Los Angeles.

The first turned out to be a Ms. Persephone Dundas.

At the second number, when I asked for Pious Dundas, a man's voice said, "Who is this?"

I told him my name, that I was staying in the hotel, and that I had something belonging to Mr. Dundas.

"Mister. My grandfa's dead. He died last night."

Shock makes clichés happen for real: I felt the blood drain from my face; I caught my breath.

"I'm sorry. I liked him."

"Yeah."

"It must have been pretty sudden."

"He was old. He got a cough." Someone asked him who he was talking to, and he said nobody, then he said, "Thanks for calling."

I felt stunned.

"Look, I have his scrapbook. He left it with me."

"That old film stuff?"

"Yes."

A pause.

"Keep it. That stuff's no good to anybody. Listen, mister, I gotta run."

A click, and the line went silent.

I went to pack the scrapbook in my bag and was startled, when a tear splashed on the faded leather cover, to discover that I was crying.

I stopped by the pool for the last time, to say good-bye to Pious Dundas, and to Hollywood.

Three ghost white carp drifted, fins flicking minutely, through the eternal present of the pool.

I remembered their names: Buster, Ghost, and Princess; but there was no longer any way that anyone could have told them apart.

The car was waiting for me, by the hotel lobby. It was a thirty-minute drive to the airport, and already I was starting to forget.

On the Road to New Egypt
Jeffrey Ford

One day when I was driving home from work, I saw him there on the side of the road. He startled me at first, but I managed to control myself and apply the brakes. His face was fixed with a look somewhere between agony and elation. That thumb he thrust out at an odd angle was gnarled and had a long nail. The sun was setting and red beams danced around him. I stopped and leaned over to open the door.

"You're Jesus, right?" I said.

"Yeah," he said and held up his palms to show the stigmata.

"Hop in," I told him.

"Thanks, man," he said as he gathered up his robe and slipped into the front seat.

As I pulled back out onto the road, he took out a pack of Camel Wides and a dark blue Bic lighter. "You don't mind, do you?" he asked, but he already had a cigarette in his mouth and was bringing a flame to it.

"Go for it," I said.

"Where you headed?" he asked.

"Home, unless you're here to tell me different," I said, forcing a laugh.

"Easy, easy," he said.

After a short silence, Christ took a couple of deep drags and blew the smoke out the partially opened window.

"Where are *you* going?" I asked.

"You know, just up the road a piece."

We stopped at a red light and I looked over at him. That crown of thorns must have itched like hell. I shook my head and said, "Wait till I tell my wife about this."

"She religious?" he asked.

"Not particularly, but still, she'll get the impact."

He smiled and flicked some ashes into his palm.

We drove on for a while through the vanishing light, past fields of pumpkins and dried corn stalks. A few minutes later, night fell, and I turned on the headlights. I didn't see it at first, but a possum darted out into the road right in front of the car. *Bump, bump,* we were over it in a microsecond. I looked at Christ.

He shrugged as if to say, "What can you do?"

"...and Heaven?" I asked as the car traveled into a valley where the trees from either side of the road had, above, grown together into a canopy.

"Angels, blue skies, your relatives are all there. The greats are there. Basically everybody is there. It gets a little tense sometimes, a little close."

"You said that 'basically' everybody is in Heaven," I said. "Who isn't?"

"You know," he said, "those other people."

We kept going past the fences of the horse farms, the edges of barren fields, until Christ had me stop at McDonald's and order him a quarter pounder with cheese, and a chocolate shake. I paid for it with my last couple of dollars.

He said, "I'll pay you back in indulgences."

"Hey, it's on me," I said.

He wolfed down that burger like the Son of man that he was.

"So what have you seen in your travels?" I asked.

"You name it," he said, sucking at his shake. "The human drama."

"Do you ever stop anywhere?"

"Sometimes. I'm always on the look-out for an old Howard Johnson." There was a short pause and then he said, "Could you step on it a little, I have to be in New Egypt by eight."

"Sure thing," I said and put down the pedal. "You meeting someone?"

"I've been seeing this woman there on and off for the past couple of years. Every once in a while I'll appear, give her a little push and then split by sunup."

"She must be pretty special."

"Yeah," he said, and took out a flattened wallet. "Here she is."

He showed me an old photo of this forty-five-year-old ex-blonde-bombshell in a leopard bikini.

"Nice," I said.

"Nice isn't the word for it," he said, with a wink.

"What's she do?" I asked.

"A little of this and a little of that," he said.

"No, I mean where does she work?"

"At the funeral parlor. She sews mouths and lids shut. She lives in a small house in the center of town. When I get there, she's usually in bed. I step out of the armoire, minus the robe, and slip between the sheets with her. We eat of the fruit of the knowledge of good and evil for a few hours and then lay back, have a smoke."

"Does she know who you are?"

"I hope by this time she's figured it out," he said.

"She'll end up going to the tabloids with the story," I warned.

"Screw it, she already has. We were in that one recently with Bigfoot on the cover and the story about the woman who turned to stone on page three."

"I missed that one, but I remember the cover."

All of a sudden Christ sat straight up and pointed out the windshield. "Whoa, whoa," he said, "pull over like you're going to pick this guy up."

Only when he spoke did I see the shadowy figure up ahead on the side of the road. I could see it was a guy and that he was hitchhiking. I passed by him a few feet and then pulled over to the shoulder. We could hear him running toward the car.

"Okay, peel out," Christ said.

I did and we left that stranger in the dust.

"I love that one," said the savior.

A few minutes passed and then I heard a hatchet of a voice from the back seat. "You fuckers," it said. I looked in the rearview mirror and there was the Devil—horns, red skin, cheesy whiskers in a goatee. As I looked at him his grin turned into a wide smile.

Jesus reached back and offered a hand.

"Who's the stiff at the wheel?" asked the Devil.

"You mean fat boy here?" Christ said and they both burst out laughing. "He's cool."

"Nice to meet you," said the Devil.

I reached back and shook a hand that was a tree branch with the power to grip. "Name's Jeff," I said.

"I am legion," he hissed.

Then he stuck his head in the space between us and shot a little burp of flame into the air. Christ doubled over with silent laughter. "I got a bag of Carthage Red on me, you got any papers?" the Devil asked, putting his hand on Christ's shoulder.

"Does the Pope shit in the woods?" asked the Son of God.

The Devil got the papers and started rolling one in the back seat. "Jeff, you ever try this shit?"

"I never heard of it."

"It's old, man, it'll make you see God."

"By the way," Christ said, interrupting, "what ever happened with that guy in Detroit?"

"I took him," said the Devil. "Mass murderer, just reeking evil. He hung himself in the jail cell. They conveniently forgot to remove his belt."

"I thought I told you I wanted him," said Christ.

"I thought I cared," said the Devil. "Anyway, you get that old woman from Tampa. She's going to make canonization. I guarantee it."

"I guess that's cool," he said.

"Eat me if it isn't," said the Devil. They both started laughing and each patted me on the back. The Devil lit up the enormous joint he had created and the odd pink smoke began to permeate the car.

It tasted like cinnamon and fire and even with only the first toke, I was stunned. Paranoia set in instantly, and I slowed the car down to about thirty. I drove blindly while in my head I saw the autumn afternoon woods of my childhood, where it was so still and the leaves silently fell. I thought of home and it was far away.

When my mind returned to me at a red light, I realized that the radio was on. New Age music, a piano, and some low moaning formed a backdrop to the conversation of my passengers.

"What do you think?" Christ had just asked.

"I think this music has to go," said the Devil. His fingers grew like snakes from the back seat, and he kept pressing the scan button on the radio until he came to the oldies station. "Back seat memories," he said.

Somehow it was decided that we would go to Florida and check out the lady who was going to become a saint. "Maybe she'll pop a miracle," said the Devil.

"No sweat," said Christ.

"My wife's expecting me home around nine," I said.

The Devil laughed really loud. "I'll tell you what I'll do," he said. "I'll split myself in two, and half of me will go to your house and boff your wife till we get back."

Christ leaned over and put his hand on my knee. "Don't be an idiot," he said to me with a smile. "I have to be in New Egypt by eight."

"You can do things?" I asked.

"Look," said Christ, nodding toward the windshield, "we're there. Just make a right at this corner. It's the third house on the left."

I looked up and saw that we were in a suburban neighborhood with palm trees lining the side of the road. The houses were all one-story ranch styles and painted in pastel colors. When I pulled the car over in front of the house, I could hear crickets singing quickly in the night heat.

Before we got out, the Devil leaned toward the front seat and said to Christ, "I'll make you a bet she doesn't do a miracle while we're here."

"Bullshit," said Christ.

"What do you want to bet?" asked the Devil.

"How about *him*," said the savior and pointed that weird thumb at me.

"Quite the high roller," said the Devil.

As we were walking up the driveway to the front door, the Devil lagged a little behind us. I leaned over and, in a whisper, asked Christ if he thought she would perform.

He shrugged and rolled his eyes. "Have faith, man," he said. "Sometimes you win, sometimes you lose."

"I heard that," said the Devil. "I don't like whispering."

We walked right through the front door and into the living room where a woman was sitting in front of the television. At first, I thought she was deaf, but it soon became clear that we were completely invisible to her.

The Devil walked up behind me and handed me a sixteen-ounce Rolling Rock. "There she is in all her splendor," he said, as he handed a beer to Christ. "Doesn't look like much of an opportunity here unless she's gonna get better looking."

We stood and stared at her. She was about sixty-five with short hair dyed brown and wearing a flowered bathrobe. On the coffee table in front of her set an ashtray with a lit cigarette in one of the holders. In her left hand she held a glass of dark wine. As the daily reports of mayhem and greed came through the box, she shook her head from time to time and sipped her drink.

"What's she done?" I asked.

"She brought a kid back from the dead a few months ago," said the Devil. "A girl was hit by a car outside a local grocery store. Mrs. Lumley, here, was present and just touched the girl's hand. The kid got right up off the stretcher and walked away."

"Strange shit," said Christ. "We don't really know how it works."

"You mean," I said, "that you can't make her do a miracle?"

"Not exactly," said Christ.

"That's a bitch, isn't it?" said the Devil. "Now drink your beer and calm down."

The Devil walked around behind Mrs. Lumley's chair and used two fingers to make horns behind her head. Christ went to pieces over that one. I even had to laugh while we watched her pick her nose. She was at it for a good five minutes. Christ applauded her every strategy, and the Devil said, "The one that got away."

"We better sit down. This may take a few minutes," said Christ.

The Devil and I sat down on the couch and Christ took an old rocker across from us. The evil one rolled another huge joint and listened intently to the report on the television of a murder/suicide in California. Mrs. Lumley began singing "The Whispering Wind" to herself in between sips of wine while Christ hummed a duet with her.

"I've had more fun in church," said the Devil, as he passed me the joint. Again, I tasted the cinnamon and fire, and I took big gulps of beer to soothe my throat.

Christ begged off and just rocked contentedly in his chair.

The news eventually ended and *Jeopardy* came on the television. "Wait till I get my hooks into *this* asshole," the Devil said, nodding toward the host of the show.

"He's yours," said Christ. "It's on me." Then he pointed his finger at Mrs. Lumley and made her change the channel to a *Star Trek* rerun.

While we waited for something to happen, the Devil showed me a trick. He took a big draw of Carthage Red and then exhaled it in a perfect globe of smoke. The globe hovered in the air before my eyes and turned crystal clear. Then it was filled with an image of my wife and kids reading bedtime stories. When I reached for it, the globe popped like a soap bubble.

"Parlor tricks," said Christ.

Eventually, Mrs. Lumley got up, turned off the set and went into her bedroom. We followed her as far as the door, where we looked in at her. She was kneeling next to the bed, saying her prayers.

"I hope you like the heat," the Devil said to me.

Then Christ said, "Look."

Mrs. Lumley lay on the floor, her body twitching. A steady groan escaped through her clenched teeth. In seconds, her skin had become a metallic blue and her head had doubled in size. Fangs, claws, gills, audibly popped from her features. She turned her head to face us, and I could feel she was actually seeing us with her expanding eyes.

"Shit," said the Devil, and turned and ran toward the door.

"Let's get out of here," said Christ, and he too turned and ran. I followed close behind.

By the time we got outside, the Devil was sticking his head out the back-seat window of the car. "Move your asses!" he yelled.

I ran around the front of the car and climbed in the driver's seat as fast as I could. Mrs. Lumley, now some kind of rapidly changing blue creature, growled from the front lawn. I turned on the ignition and hit the gas.

"What the fuck was that supposed to be?" said Christ, catching his breath as he passed us each a cigarette.

"Your old man is out of his mind," said the Devil. "It's all getting just a little too strange."

"Tell me about it," said Christ. "Remember, I warned you back when they first walked on the moon."

"This is some really evil shit, though," said the Devil.

"The whole ball of wax is falling apart," said Christ.

"I actually had a break-out in the ninth bole of Hell last week," said the Devil. "A big bastard—he smashed right through the ice. Killed one demon with his bare hands and broke another one's back."

"Did you get him?" I asked.

"One of my people said she saw him in Chicago."

"Purgatory is spreading like the plague," said Christ.

The Devil leaned up close behind me and put his claw hand on my shoulder. I could feel his hot breath on the back of my neck. "His old man is reading Nietzsche," he whispered, his tongue grazing my earlobe.

"What's he saying?" Christ asked me.

"Which way am I supposed to turn to get out of this development?" I asked.

Just then there was an abrupt bump on the top of the car. It startled me and I swerved, almost hitting a garbage can.

"You gotta check this out," said the Devil. "Saint Lumley of the Bad Trips is flying over us."

"Punch the gas," yelled Christ, and I floored it. I drove like a maniac, screeching around corners as the pastel ranches flew by.

"We're starting to lose her," the Devil called out.

"What are you carrying?" Christ asked.

"I've got a full minute of fire," said the Devil. "What have you got?"

"I've got the Machine of Eden," said Christ.

"Uhh, not *The* fucking Machine of Eden," said the Devil, and slammed the back of my seat.

"What do you mean?" said Christ.

"When was the last time that thing worked?"

"It works," said Christ.

"Pull off and go through the gate up on your right," said the Devil. "We've got to take her out or she'll dog us for eternity."

"I don't like this at all," said Christ.

After passing the gate, I drove on a winding gravel road that led to the local landfill. There were endless moonlit hills of junk and garbage. I parked the car and we got out.

"We've got to get to the top of that hill before she gets here," said Christ, pointing to a huge mound of garbage.

I scrabbled up the hill, clutching at old car seats and stepping on dead appliances. Startled rats scurried through the debris. When I reached the top I was sweating and panting. Christ beat me, but I had to reach back down and help the Devil up the last few steps.

"It's the hooves," he said, "they're worse than high heels."

"There's some cool old stuff here," said Christ.

"I saw a whole carton of *National Geographics* I want to snag on the way out," said the Devil.

Off in the distance, I saw the shadow of something passing in front of the stars. It was too big to be a bird. "Here she comes," I yelled and pointed. They both spun around to look. "What do I do?" I asked.

"Stay behind us," said Christ. "If she gets you, it's going to hurt."

The next thing I knew, Mrs. Lumley had landed and we three were backed against the edge of the hill with a steep drop behind us. Her blue skin shone in the moonlight like armor, but there were tufts of hair growing from it. She had this amazing aqua body and an eight-foot wingspan, but with the exception of the gills and fangs, she still had the face of a sixty-five-year-old woman. She moved slowly toward us, burping out words that made no sense.

When she came within a few feet of us, Christ said, "Smoke 'em if you got 'em," and the Devil stepped forward. Tentacles began to grow from her body toward him. One managed to wrap itself around his left horn when he opened his mouth to assault her with a minute of fire. The flames discharged like a blowtorch and stopped her cold. When she was completely engulfed in the blaze, the tentacles retracted, but she would not melt.

As soon as the evil one finished, coughing out great clouds of gray smoke, Mrs. Lumley opened her eyes and the tentacles began again to grow from her sides. I looked over and saw that Christ was holding something in his right hand. It appeared to be a remote control, and he was furiously pushing its buttons.

The Devil had jumped back beside me, his hand clutching my arm. He had real fear in his serpent eyes, yet he could not help but laugh at Christ messing around with the Machine of Eden.

"What's with the cosmic garage door opener?" he shouted.

"It works," said Christ, as he continued to nervously press buttons. Then I felt one of the tentacles wrap itself around my ankle. Mrs. Lumley opened her mouth and crowed like a rooster. Another of the blue snake appendages entwined itself around the Devil's midsection. We both screamed as she pulled us toward her.

"Three," Christ yelled, and a beam of light shot out of the end of the Machine. I then heard the sound of celestial voices singing in unison. Mrs.

Lumley took the blast full in the chest and began instantly to shrivel. Before my eyes, like the special effects in a crappy science fiction movie, she turned into a tree. Leaves sprouted, pink blossoms grew, and as the singing faded, pure white fruit appeared on the lower branches.

"Not fun," said the Devil.

"I thought she was going to suck your face off," said Christ.

"What exactly was she," I asked, "an alien?"

Christ shook his head. "Nah," he said, "just a fucked-up old woman."

"Is she still a saint?" I asked.

"No, she's a tree," he said.

"You and your saints," said the Devil and plucked a piece of fruit. "Take one of these," he said to me. "It's called the *Still Point of the Turning World*. Only eat it when you need it."

I picked one of the white pears off the tree and put it in my pocket before we started down the junk hill. The Devil found the box of magazines and Christ came up with a lamp made out of seashells. We piled into the car and I started it up.

I heard Christ say, "Holy shit, it's 8:00!"

The next thing I knew I was on my usual road back in Jersey. The car was empty but for me, and I was just leaving New Egypt.

Julie's Unicorn
Peter S Beagle

The note came with the entree, tucked neatly under the zucchini slices but carefully out of range of the seafood crepes. It said, in the unmistakable handwriting that any graphologist would have ascribed to a serial killer, "Tanikawa, ditch the dork and get in here." Julie took her time over the crepes and the spinach salad, finished her wine, sampled a second glass, and then excused herself to her dinner partner, who smiled and propped his chin on his fingertips, prepared to wait graciously, as assistant professors know how to do. She turned right at the telephones, instead of left, looked back once, and walked through a pair of swinging half-doors into the restaurant kitchen.

The heat thumped like a fist between her shoulder blades, and her glasses fogged up immediately. She took them off, put them in her purse and focused on a slender, graying man standing with his back to her as he instructed an earnest young woman about shiitake mushroom stew. Julie said loudly, "Make it quick, Farrell. The dork thinks I'm in the can."

The slender man said to the young woman, "Gracie, tell Luis the basil's losing its marbles, he can put in more oregano if he wants. Tell him to use his own judgment about the lemongrass—I like it myself." Then he turned, held out his arms and said, "Jewel. Think you strung it out long enough?"

"My dessert's melting," Julie said into his apron. The arms around her felt as comfortably usual as an old sofa, and she lifted her head quickly to demand, "God damn it, where have you been? I have had very strange phone conversations with some very strange people in the last five years, trying to track you down. What the hell happened to you, Farrell?"

"What happened to me? Two addresses and a fax number I gave you, and nothing. Not a letter, not so much as a postcard from East Tarpit-on-the-Orinoco, hi, marrying tribal chieftain tomorrow, wish you were here. But just

THE URBAN FANTASY ANTHOLOGY

as glad you're not. The story of this relationship."

Julie stepped back, her round, long-eyed face gone as pale as it ever got. Almost in a whisper, she asked, "How did you know? Farrell, how did you know?" The young cook was staring at them both in fascination bordering on religious rapture.

"What?" Farrell said, and now he was gaping like the cook, his own voice snagging in his throat. "You did? You got married?"

"It didn't last. Eight months. He's in Boston."

"That explains it." Farrell's sudden bark of laughter made Gracie the cook jump slightly. "By God, that explains it."

"Boston? Boston explains what?"

"You didn't want me to know," Farrell said. "You really didn't want me to know. Tanikawa, I'm ashamed of you. I am."

Julie started to answer him, then nodded toward the entranced young cook. Farrell said, "Gracie, about the curried peas. Tell Suzanne absolutely not to add the mango pickle until just before the peas are done, she always puts it in too early. If she's busy, you do it—go, go." Gracie, enchanted even more by the notion of getting her hands into actual food, fled, and Farrell turned back to face Julie. "Eight months. I've known you to take longer over a lithograph."

"He's a very nice man," she answered him. "No, damn it, that sounds terrible, insulting. But he is."

Farrell nodded. "I believe it. You always did have this deadly weakness for nice men. I was an aberration."

"No, you're my friend," Julie said. "You're my friend, and I'm sorry, I should have told you I was getting married." A waiter's loaded tray caught her between the shoulderblades just as a busboy stepped on her foot, and she was properly furious this time. "I didn't tell you because I knew you'd do exactly what you're doing now, which is look at me like that and imply that you know me better than anyone else ever possibly could, which is not true, Farrell. There are all kinds of people you don't even know who know things about me you'll never know, so just knock it off." She ran out of breath and anger more or less simultaneously. She said, "But somehow you've gotten to be my oldest friend, just by goddamn attrition. I missed you, Joe."

Farrell put his arms around her again. "I missed you. I worried about you. A whole lot. The rest can wait." There came a crash and a mad bellow from the steamy depths of the kitchen, and Farrell said, "Your dork's probably missing you too. That was the Table Fourteen dessert, sure as hell. Where can I call you? Are you actually back in Avicenna?"

"For now. It's always for now in this town." She wrote the address and telephone number on the back of the Tonight's Specials menu, kissed him hurriedly and left the kitchen. Behind her she heard another bellow, and then Farrell's grimly placid voice saying, "Stay cool, stay cool, big Luis, it's not the end of the world. Change your apron, we'll just add some more brandy. All is well."

It took more time than they were used to, even after more than twenty years of picking up, letting go and picking up again. The period of edginess and uncertainty about what questions to ask, what to leave alone, what might or might not be safe to assume, lasted until the autumn afternoon they went to the museum. It was Farrell's day off, and he drove Madame Schumann-Heink, his prehistoric Volkswagen van, over the hill from the bald suburb where he was condo-sitting for a friend and parked under a sycamore across from Julie's studio apartment. The building was a converted Victorian, miraculously spared from becoming a nest of suites for accountants and attorneys and allowed to decay in a decently tropical fashion, held together by jasmine and wisteria. He said to Julie, "You find trees, every time, shady places with big old trees. I've never figured how you manage it."

"Old houses," she said. "I always need work space and a lot of light, and only the old houses have it. It's a trade-off—plumbing for elbow room. Wait till I feed NMC." NMC was an undistinguished black and white cat who slept with six new kittens in a box underneath the tiny sink set into a curtained alcove. ("She likes to keep an eye on the refrigerator," Julie explained. "Just in case it tries to make a break for freedom.") She had shown up pregnant, climbing the stairs to scratch only at Julie's door, and sauntering in with an air of being specifically expected. The initials of her name stood for Not My Cat. Julie opened a can, set it down beside the box, checked to make sure that each kitten was securely attached to a nipple, briefly fondled a softly thrumming throat and told her, "The litter tray is two feet to your left. As if you care."

At the curb, gazing for a long time at Madame Schumann-Heink, she said, "This thing has become absolutely transparent, Joe, you know that. I can see the Bay right through it."

"Wait till you see her by moonlight," Farrell said. "Gossamer and cobwebs.

The Taj Mahal of rust. Tell me again where the Bigby Museum is."

"North. East. In the hills. It's hard to explain. Take the freeway, I'll tell you where to turn off."

The Bigby City Museum had been, until fairly recently, Avicenna's nearest approach to a Roman villa. Together with its long, narrow reflecting pool and its ornamental gardens, it occupied an entire truncated hilltop from which, morning and evening, its masters—copper-mining kinglets—had seen the Golden Gate Bridge rising through the Bay mist like a Chinese dragon's writhing back. With the death of the last primordial Bigby, the lone heir had quietly sold the mansion to the city, set up its contents (primarily lesser works of the lesser Impressionists, a scattering of the Spanish masters, and the entire oeuvre of a Bigby who painted train stations) as a joint trust, and sailed away to a tax haven in the Lesser Antilles. Julie said there were a few early Brueghel oils and drawings worth the visit. "He was doing Bosch then—maybe forgeries, maybe not—and mostly you can't tell them apart. But with these you start seeing the real Brueghel, sort of in spite of himself. There's a good little Raphael too, but you'll hate it. An Annunciation, with *putti*."

"I'll hate it," Farrell said. He eased Madame Schumann-Heink over into the right-hand lane, greatly irritating a BMW, who honked at him all the way to the freeway. "Practically as much as I hate old whoever, the guy you married."

"Brian." Julie punched his shoulder hard. "His name is Brian, and he's a lovely, wonderful man, and I really do love him. We just shouldn't have gotten married. We both agreed on that."

"A damn Brian," Farrell said. He put his head out of the window and yelled back at the BMW, "She went and married a Brian, I ask you!" The BMW driver gave him the finger. Farrell said, "The worst thing is, I'd probably like him, I've got a bad feeling about that. Let's talk about something else. Why'd you marry him?"

Julie sighed. "Maybe because he was as far away from you as I could get. He's sane, he's stable, he's—okay, he's ambitious, nothing wrong with that—"

Farrell's immediate indignation surprised him as much as it did Julie. "Hey, I'm sane. All things considered. Weird is not wacko, there's a fine but definite line. And I'm stable as a damn lighthouse, or we'd never have stayed friends this long. Ambitious—okay, no, never, not really. Still cooking here and there, still playing a bit of obsolete music on obsolete instruments after hours. Same way you're still drawing cross sections of lungs and livers for medical students. What does old ambitious Brian do?"

"He's a lawyer." Julie heard herself mumbling, saw the corner of Farrell's mouth twitch, and promptly flared up again. "And I don't want to hear one bloody word out of you, Farrell! He's not a hired gun for corporations, he doesn't defend celebrity gangsters. He works for non-profits, environmental groups, refugees, gay rights—he takes on so many pro bono cases, half the time he can't pay his office rent. He's a better person than you'll ever be, Farrell. Or me either. That's the damn, damn trouble." Her eyes were aching heavily, and she looked away from him.

Farrell put his hand gently on the back of her neck. He said, "I'm sorry, Jewel." Neither of them spoke after that until they were grinding slowly up a narrow street lined with old sycamore and walnut trees and high, furry old houses drowsing in the late-summer sun. Julie said, "I do a little word-processing, temp stuff," and then, in the same flat voice, "You never married anybody."

"Too old," Farrell said. "I used to be too young, or somebody was, I remember that. Now it's plain too late—I'm me, finally, all the way down, and easy enough with it, but I damn sure wouldn't marry me." He braked to keep from running over two cackling adolescents on skateboards, then resumed the lumbering climb, dropping Madame Schumann-Heink into second gear, which was one of her good ones. Looking sideways, he said, "One thing anyway, you're still the prettiest Eskimo anybody ever saw."

"Get out of here," she answered him scornfully. "You never saw an Eskimo that wasn't in some National Geographic special." Now she looked back at him, fighting a smile, and he touched her neck again, very lightly. "Well, I'm getting like that myself," she said. "Too old and too cranky to suit anybody but me. Turn right at the light, Joe."

The Bigby City Museum came upon them suddenly, filling the windshield just after the last sharp curve, as they rolled slightly downward into a graveled parking lot which had once been an herb garden. Farrell parked facing the Bay, and the two of them got out and stood silently on either side of Madame Schumann-Heink, staring away at the water glittering in the western sun. Then they turned, each with an odd, unspoken near-reluctance, to face the Museum. It would have been a beautiful building, Julie thought, in another town. It was three stories high, cream white, with a flat tile roof the color of red wine. Shadowed on three sides by cypress trees, camellia bushes softening the rectitude of the corners, a dancing-dolphin fountain chuckling in the sunny courtyard, and the white and peach rose gardens sloping away from the reflecting pool, it was a beautiful house, but one that belonged in Santa Barbara, Santa Monica or Malibu, worlds and wars, generations and elections removed from silly, vain, vainly perverse Avicenna. Farrell finally sighed and said, "Power to the people, hey," and Julie said, "*A bas les aristos*," and they went inside. The ticketseller and the guest book were on the first floor, the Brueghels on the second. Julie and Farrell walked up a flowing mahogany stairway hung with watercolors from the Southwestern period of the train-station Bigby. On the landing Farrell looked around judiciously and announced, "Fine command of plastic values, I'll say that," to which Julie responded, "Oh, no question, but those spatio-temporal vortices, I don't know." They laughed together, joined hands and climbed the rest of the way.

There were ten or twelve other people upstairs in the huge main gallery. Most were younger than Farrell and Julie, with the distinct air of art students on assignment, their eyes flicking nervously from the Brueghels to their fellows to see whether anyone else had caught the trick, fathomed the koan, winkled out the grade points that must surely be hiding somewhere within those depictions of demon priests and creatures out of anchorite nightmares. When Julie took a small pad out of her purse, sat down on a couch and began copying certain corners and aspects of the paintings, the students were eddying silently toward her within minutes, just in case she knew. Farrell winked at her and wandered off toward a wall of train stations. Julie never looked up.

More quickly than she expected, he was back, leaning over her shoulder, his low voice in her hair. "Jewel. Something you ought to see. Right around the corner."

The corner was actually a temporary wall, just wide and high enough to hold three tapestries whose placard described them as "...mid-fifteenth century, artist unknown, probably from Bruges." The highest tapestry, done in the terrifyingly detailed millefleurs style, showed several women in a rich garden being serenaded by a lute-player, and Julie at first thought that Farrell—a lutanist himself—must have meant her to look at this one. Then she saw the one below.

It was in worse shape than the upper tapestry, badly frayed all around the edges and darkly stained in a kind of rosette close to the center, which showed a knight presenting a unicorn to his simpering lady. The unicorn was small and bluish-white, with the cloven hooves, long neck and slender quarters of a deer The knight was leading it on a silvery cord, and his squire behind him was prodding the unicorn forward with a short stabbing lance. There was a soapbubble castle in the background, floating up out of a stylized broccoli forest. Julie heard herself say in a child's voice, "I don't like this."

"I've seen better," Farrell agreed. "Wouldn't have picked it as Bruges work myself." The lance was pricking the unicorn hard enough that the flesh dimpled around the point, and the unicorn's one visible eye, purple-black, was rolled back toward the squire in fear or anger. The knight's lady held a wreath of scarlet flowers in her extended right hand. Whether it was meant for the knight or the unicorn Julie could not tell.

"I wish you hadn't shown me this," she said. She turned and returned to the Brueghels, trying to recapture her focus on the sliver of canvas, the precise brushstroke, where the young painter could be seen to step away from his master. But time after time she was drawn back, moving blindly through the growing crowd to stare one more time at the shabby old imagining of beauty and theft before she took up her sketchpad again. At last she gave up any notion of work, and simply stood still before the tapestry, waiting patiently to grow numb to the unicorn's endless woven pain. The lady looked directly out at her, the faded smirk saying clearly, "Five hundred years. Five hundred years, and it is still going on, this very minute, all to the greater glory of God and courtly love."

"That's what you think," Julie said aloud. She lifted her right hand and moved it slowly across the tapestry, barely brushing the protective glass. As she did so, she spoke several words in a language that might have been Japanese, and was not. With the last syllable came a curious muffled jolt, like an underwater explosion, that thudded distantly through her body, making her step back and stagger against Farrell. He gripped her shoulders, saying, "Jewel, what the hell are you up to? What did you just do right then?"

"I don't know what you're talking about," she said, and for that moment it was true. She was oddly dizzy, and she could feel a headache coiling in her temples. "I didn't do anything, what could I do? What do you think I was doing, Joe?"

Farrell turned her to face him, his hands light on her shoulders now, but his dark-blue eyes holding her with an intensity she had rarely seen in all the years they had known each other. He said, "I remember you telling me about your grandmother's Japanese magic. I remember a night really long ago, and a goddess who came when you called her. It all makes me the tiniest bit uneasy."

The strange soft shock did not come again; the art students and the tourists went on drifting as drowsily as aquarium fish among the Brueghels; the figures in the tapestry remained exactly where they had posed for five centuries. Julie said, "I haven't done a damn thing." Farrell's eyes did not leave her face. "Not anything that made any difference, anyway," she said. She turned away and walked quickly across the gallery to examine a very minor Zurbaran too closely.

In time the notepad came back out of her purse, and she again began to copy those scraps and splinters of the Brueghels that held lessons or uses for her. She did not return to the unicorn tapestry. More time passed than she had meant to spend in the museum, and when Farrell appeared beside her she was startled at the stained pallor of the sky outside the high windows. He said, "You better come take a look. That was one hell of a grandmother you had."

She asked no questions when he took hold of her arm and led her—she could feel the effort it cost him not to drag her—back to the wall of tapestries. She stared at the upper one for a long moment before she permitted herself to understand.

The unicorn was gone. The knight and his squire remained in their places, silver cord hauling nothing forward, lance jabbing cruelly into helpless nothing. The lady went on smiling milkily, offering her flowers to nothingness. There was no change in any of their faces, no indication that the absence of the reason for their existence had been noticed at all. Julie stared and stared and said nothing.

"Let you out of my sight for five minutes," Farrell said. He was not looking at her, but scanning the floor in every direction. "All right, main thing's to keep him from getting stepped on. Check the corners—you do that side, I'll do all this side." But he was shaking his head even before he finished. "No, the stairs, you hit the stairs. If he gets down those stairs, that's it, we've lost him. Jewel, go!" He had not raised his voice at all, but the last words cracked like pine sap in fire.

Julie gave one last glance at the tapestry, hoping that the unicorn would prove not to be lost after all, but only somehow absurdly overlooked. But not so much as a dangling thread suggested that there had ever been any other figure in the frame. She said vaguely, "I didn't think it would work, it was just to be doing something," and sprang for the stairway.

By now the art students had been mostly replaced by nuzzling couples and edgy family groups. Some of them grumbled as Julie pushed down past them without a word of apology; a few others turned to gape when she took up a position on the landing, midway between a lost-contact-lens stoop and a catcher's crouch, looking from side to side for some miniature scurry, something like a flittering dust-kitten with a tiny blink at its brow...*But will it be flesh, or only dyed yarn? And will it grow to full size, now it's out of the frame? Does it know, does it know it's free, or is it hiding in my shadow, in a thousand times more danger than when there was a rope around its neck and a virgin grinning at it? Grandma, what have we done?*

Closing time, nearly, and full dark outside, and still no trace of the unicorn. Julie's heart sank lower with each person who clattered past her down the stairs, and each time the lone guard glanced at her, then at Farrell, and then pointedly wiped his snuffly nose. Farrell commandeered her notepad and prowled the floor, ostentatiously scrutinizing the Brueghels when he felt himself being scrutinized, but studying nothing but dim corners and alcoves the rest of the time. The museum lights were flicking on and off, and the guard had actually begun to say, "Five minutes to closing," when Farrell stopped moving, so suddenly that one foot was actually in the air. Sideways-on to Julie, so that she could not see what he saw, he slowly lowered his foot to the floor; very slowly he turned toward the stair; with the delicacy of a parent maneuvering among Legos, he navigated silently back to her. He was smiling as carefully as though he feared the noise it might make.

"Found it," he muttered. "Way in behind the coat rack, there's a water cooler on an open frame. It's down under there."

"So what are you doing down here?" Julie demanded. Farrell shushed her frantically with his face and hands. He muttered, "It's not going anywhere, it's too scared to move. I need you to distract the guard for a minute. Like in the movies."

"Like in the movies." She sized up the guard: an over-age rent-a-cop, soft and bored, interested only in getting them out of the museum, locking up and heading for dinner. "Right. I could start taking my clothes off, there's that. Or I could tell him I've lost my little boy, or maybe ask him what he thinks about fifteenth-century Flemish woodcuts. What are you up to now, Joe?"

"Two minutes," Farrell said. "At the outside. I just don't want the guy to see me grabbing the thing up. Two minutes and gone."

"Hey," Julie said loudly. "Hey, it is not a thing, and you will not grab it." She did lower her voice then, because the guard was glancing at his watch, whistling fretfully. "Joe, I don't know if this has sunk in yet, but a unicorn, a real unicorn, has been trapped in that miserable medieval scene for five centuries, and it is now hiding under a damn water cooler in the Bigby Museum in Avicenna, California. Does that begin to register at all?"

"Trouble," Farrell said. "All that registers is me being in trouble again. Go talk to that man."

Julie settled on asking with breathy shyness about the museum's legendary third floor, always closed off to the public and rumored variously to house the secret Masonic works of Rembrandt, Goya's blasphemous sketches of Black Masses, certain Beardsley illustrations of de Sade, or merely faded pornographic snapshots of assorted Bigby mistresses. The guard's money was on forgeries: counterfeits donated to the city in exchange for handsome tax exemptions. "Town like this, a town full of art experts, specialists—well, you wouldn't want anybody looking at that stuff too close. Stands to reason."

She did not dare look to see what Farrell was doing. The guard was checking his watch again when he appeared beside her, his ancient bomber jacket already on, her coat over his arm. "On our way," he announced cheerfully; and, to the guard, "Sorry for the delay, we're out of here." His free right hand rested, casually but unmoving, on the buttonless flap of his side pocket.

They did not speak on the stairs, nor immediately outside in the autumn twilight. Farrell walked fast, almost pulling her along, until they reached the van. He turned there, his face without expression for a very long moment before he took her hand and brought it to his right coat pocket. Through the cracked leather under her fingers she felt a stillness more vibrant than any struggle could have been: a waiting quiet, making her shiver with a kind of fear and a kind of wonder that she had never known and could not tell apart. She whispered, "Joe, can it—are you sure it can breathe in there?"

"Could it breathe in that damn tapestry?" Farrell's voice was rough and tense, but he touched Julie's hand gently. "It's all right, Jewel. It stood there and looked at me, and sort of watched me picking it up. Let's get on back to your place and figure out what we do now."

Julie sat close to him on the way home, her hand firmly on his coat-pocket flap. She could feel the startlingly intense heat of the unicorn against her palm as completely as though there were nothing between them; she could feel the equally astonishing sharpness of the minute horn, and the steady twitch of the five-century-old heart. As intensely as she could, she sent the thought down her arm and through her fingers: we're going to help you, we're your friends, we know you, don't be afraid. Whenever the van hit a bump or a pothole, she quickly pressed her hand under Farrell's pocket to cushion the legend inside.

Sitting on her bed, their coats still on and kittens meowling under the sink for their absent mother, she said, "All right, we have to think this through. We can't keep it, and we can't just turn it loose in millennial California. What other options do we have?"

"I love it when you talk like a CEO," Farrell said. Julie glared at him. Farrell said, "Well, I'll throw this out to the board meeting. Could you and your grandmother possibly put the poor creature back where you got it? That's what my mother always told me to do."

"Joe, we can't!" she cried out. "We can't put it back into that world, with people capturing it, sticking spears into it for the glory of Christian virginity. I'm not going to do that, I don't care if I have to take care of it for the rest of my life, I'm not going to do that."

"You know you can't take care of it." Farrell took her hands, turned them over, and placed his own hands lightly on them, palm to palm. "As somebody quite properly reminded me a bit back, it's a unicorn."

"Well, we can just set it free." Her throat felt dry, and she realized that her hands were trembling under his. "We'll take it to the wildest national park we can get to—national wilderness, better, no roads, people don't go there—and we'll turn it loose where it belongs. Unicorns live in the wilderness, it would get on fine. It would be happy."

"So would the mountain lions," Farrell said. "And the coyotes and the foxes, and God knows what else. A unicorn the size of a pork chop may be immortal, but that doesn't mean it's indigestible. We do have a problem here, Jewel."

They were silent for a long time, looking at each other. Julie said at last, very quietly, "I had to, Joe. I just never thought it would work, but I had to try."

Farrell nodded. Julie was looking, not at him now, but at his coat pocket. She said, "If you put it on the table. Maybe it'll know we don't mean it any harm. Maybe it won't run away."

She leaned forward as Farrell reached slowly into his pocket, unconsciously spreading her arms to left and right, along the table's edge. But the moment Farrell's expression changed she was up and whirling to look in every direction, as she had done on the museum stair. The unicorn was nowhere to be seen. Neither was the cat NMC. The six kittens squirmed and squeaked blindly in their box, trying to suck each other's paws and ears.

Farrell stammered, "I never felt it—I don't know how..." and Julie said, "Bathroom, bathroom," and fled there, leaving him forlornly prowling the studio, with its deep, murky fireplace and antique shadows. He was still at it when she returned, empty-handed as he, and her wide eyes fighting wildness.

Very quietly, she said, "I can't find the cat. Joe, I'm scared, I can't find her."

NMC—theatrical as all cats—chose that moment to saunter grandly between them, purring in throaty hiccups, with the unicorn limp between her jaws. Julie's gasp of horror, about to become a scream, was choked off by her realization that the creature was completely unharmed. NMC had it by the back of the neck, exactly as she would have carried one of her kittens, and the purple eyes were open and curiously tranquil. The unicorn's dangling legs—disproportionately long, in the tapestry, for its deerlike body—now seemed to Julie as right as a peach, or the nautilus coil inside each human ear. There was a soft, curling tuft under its chin, less like hair than like feathers, matched by a larger one at the end of its tail. Its hooves and horn had a faint pearl shine, even in the dim light.

Magnificently indifferent to Farrell and Julie's gaping, NMC promenaded to her box, flowed over the side, and sprawled out facing the kittens, releasing her grip on the unicorn's scruff as she did so. It lay passively, legs folded under it, as the squalling mites scrimmaged across their mother's belly. But when Farrell reached cautiously to pick it up, the unicorn's head whipped around faster than any cat ever dreamed of striking, and the horn scored the side of his right hand. Farrell yelped, and Julie said wonderingly, "It wants to be there. It feels comforted with them."

"The sweet thing," Farrell muttered, licking the blood from his hand. The unicorn was shoving its way in among NMC's kittens now: as Julie and Farrell watched, it gently nudged a foster brother over to a nipple next down from the one it had chosen, took the furry tap daintily into its mouth, and let its eyes drift shut. Farrell said it was purring. Julie heard no sound at all from the thin blue-white throat, but she sat by the box long after Farrell had gone home, watching the unicorn's flanks rise and fall in the same rhythm as the kittens' breathing.

Surprisingly, the unicorn appeared perfectly content to remain indefinitely in Julie's studio apartment, living in an increasingly crowded cardboard box among six growing kittens, who chewed on it and slept on it by turns, as they chewed and slept on one another. NMC, for her part, washed it at least twice as much as she bathed any of the others ("To get rid of that nasty old medieval smell," Farrell said), and made a distinct point of sleeping herself with one forepaw plopped heavily across its body. The kittens were not yet capable of climbing out of the box—though they spent most of their waking hours in trying—but NMC plainly sensed that her foster child could come and go as easily as she. Yet, unlike its littermates, the unicorn showed no interest in going anywhere at all.

"Something's wrong," Farrell said after nearly a week. "It's not acting properly—it ought to be wild to get out, wild to be off about its unicorn business. Christ, what if I hurt it when I picked it up in the museum?" His face was suddenly cold and pale. "Jewel, I was so careful, I don't know how I could have hurt it. But I bet that's it. I bet that's what's wrong."

"No," she said firmly. "Not you. That rope around its neck, that man with the spear, the look on that idiot woman's face—there, there's the hurt, five hundred years of it, five hundred frozen years of capture. Christ, Joe, let it sleep as long as it wants, let it heal." They were standing together, sometime in the night, looking down at the cat box, and she gripped Farrell's wrist hard.

"I knew right away," she said. "As soon as I saw it, I knew it wasn't just a religious allegory, a piece of a composition. I mean, yes, it was that too, but it was real, I could tell. Grandma could tell." NMC, awakened by their voices, looked up at them, yawning blissfully, round orange eyes glowing with secrets and self-satisfaction. Julie said, "There's nothing wrong with it that being out of that damn tapestry won't cure. Trust me, I was an art major."

"Shouldn't it be having something beside cat milk?" Farrell wondered. "I always figured unicorns lived on honey and—I don't know. Lilies, morning dew. Tule fog."

Julie shook her head against his shoulder. "Serenity," she said. Her voice was very low. "I think they live on serenity, and you can't get much more serene than that cat. Let's go to bed."

"Us? Us old guys?" Farrell was playing absently with her black hair, fanning his fingers out through it, tugging very gently. "You think we'll remember how it's done?"

"Don't get cute," she said, harshly enough to surprise them both. "Don't get cute, Farrell, don't get all charming. Just come to bed and hold me, and keep me company, and keep your mouth shut for a little while. You think you can manage that?"

"Yes, Jewel," Farrell said. "It doesn't use the litter box, did you notice?"

Julie dreamed of the unicorn that night. It had grown to full size and was trying to come into her bedroom, but couldn't quite fit through the door. She was frightened at first, when the great creature began to heave its prisoned shoulders, making the old house shudder around her until the roof rained shingles, and the stars came through. But in time it grew quiet, and other dreams tumbled between her and it as she slept with Farrell's arm over her, just as the unicorn slept with NMC.

In the morning, both of them late for work, unscrambling tangled clothing and exhuming a fossilized toothbrush of Farrell's ("All right, so I forgot to throw it out, so big deal!"), they nearly overlooked the unicorn altogether. It was standing—tapestry-size once again—at the foot of Julie's bed, regarding her out of eyes more violet than purple in the early light. She noticed for the first time that the pupils were horizontal, like those of a goat. NMC crouched in the doorway, switching her tail and calling plaintively for her strange foundling, but the unicorn had no heed for anyone but Julie. It lowered its head and stamped a mini-forefoot, and for all that the foot came down in a bright puddle of underwear it still made a sound like a bell ringing under the sea. Farrell and Julie, flurried as they were, stood very still.

The unicorn stamped a second time. Its eyes were growing brighter, passing from deep lavender through lilac, to blazing amethyst. Julie could not meet them. She whispered, "What is it? What do you want?"

Her only answer was a barely audible silver cry and the glint of the fierce little horn as the unicorn's ears slanted back against its head. Behind her Farrell, socks in hand, undershirt on backwards, murmured, "Critter wants to tell you something. Like Lassie."

"Shut up, Farrell," she snapped at him; then, to the unicorn, "Please, I don't understand. Please."

The unicorn raised its forefoot, as though about to stamp again. Instead, it trotted past the bed to the rickety little dressing table that Farrell had helped Julie put together very long ago, in another country. Barely the height of the lowest drawer, it looked imperiously back at them over its white shoulder before it turned, reared and stretched up as far as it could, like NMC setting herself for a luxurious, scarifying scratch. Farrell said, "The mirror."

"Shut up!" Julie said again; and then, "What?"

"The Cluny tapestries. *La Dame à la Licorne*. Unicorns like to look at themselves. Your hand mirror's up there."

Julie stared at him for only a moment. She moved quickly to the dressing table, grabbed the mirror and crouched down close beside the unicorn. It shied briefly, but immediately after fell to gazing intently into the cracked, speckled glass with a curious air almost of puzzlement, as though it could not quite recognize itself. Julie wedged the mirror upright against the drawer-pull; then she rose and nudged Farrell, and the two of them hurriedly finished dressing, gulping boiled coffee while the unicorn remained where it was, seemingly oblivious of everything but its own image. When they left for work, Julie looked back anxiously, but Farrell said, "Let it be, don't worry, it'll stay where it is. I took Comparative Mythology, I know these things."

True to his prediction, the unicorn had not moved from the mirror when Julie came home late in the afternoon; and it was still in the same spot when Farrell arrived after the restaurant's closing. NMC was beside it, now pushing her head insistently against its side, now backing away to try one more forlorn mother-call, while the first kitten to make it into the wide world beyond the cat box was blissfully batting the tufted white tail back and forth. The tail's owner paid no slightest heed to either of them; but when Julie, out of curiosity, knelt and began to move the mirror away, the unicorn made a sound very like a kitten's hiss and struck at her fingers, barely missing. She stood up calmly, saying, "Well, I'm for banana cake, *Bringing Up Baby*, and having my feet rubbed. Later for Joseph Campbell." The motion was carried by acclamation.

The unicorn stayed by the mirror that night and all the next day, and the day after that. On the second day Julie came home to hear the sweet rubber-band sound of a lute in her apartment, and found Farrell sitting on the bed playing Dowland's "The Earl of Essex's Galliard." He looked up as she entered and told her cheerfully, "Nice acoustics you've got here. I've played halls that didn't sound half as good."

"That thing of yours about locks is going to get you busted one day," Julie said. The unicorn's eyes met hers in the hand mirror, but the creature did not stir. She asked, "Can you tell if it's listening at all?"

"Ears," Farrell said. "If the ears twitch even a bit, I try some more stuff by the same composer, or anyway the same century. Might not mean a thing, but it's all I've got to go by."

"Try Bach. Everything twitches to Bach."

Farrell snorted. "Forget it. Bourrees and sarabandes out the yingyang, and not a wiggle." Oddly, he sounded almost triumphant. "See, it's a conservative little soul, some ways—it won't respond to anything it wouldn't have heard in its own time. Which means, as far as I can make out, absolutely nothing past the fifteenth century. Binchois gets you one ear. Dufay—okay, both ears, I'm pretty sure it was both ears. Machaut—ears and a little tail action, we're really onto something now. Des Pres, jackpot—it actually turned and looked at me. Not for more than a moment, but that was some look. That was a look."

He sighed and scratched his head. "Not that any of this is any help to anybody. It's just that I'll never have another chance to play this old stuff for an informed critic, as you might say. Somebody who knows my music in a way I never will. Never mind. Just a thought."

Julie sat down beside him and put her arm around his shoulders. "Well, the hell with unicorns," she said. "What do unicorns know? Play Bach for me."

Whether Farrell's music had anything to do with it or not, they never knew; but morning found the unicorn across the room, balancing quite like a cat atop a seagoing uncle's old steamer trunk, peering down into the quiet street below. Farrell, already up and making breakfast, said, "It's looking for someone."

Julie was trying to move close to the unicorn without alarming it. Without looking at Farrell, she murmured, "By Gad, Holmes, you've done it again. Five hundred years out of its time, stranded in a cat box in California, what else would it be doing but meeting a friend for lunch? You make it look so easy, and I always feel so silly once you explain—"

"Cheap sarcasm doesn't become you, Tanikawa. Here, grab your tofu scramble while it's hot." He put the plate into the hand she extended backwards toward him. "Maybe it's trolling for virgins, what can I tell you? All I'm sure of, it looked in your mirror until it remembered itself, and now it knows what it wants to do. And too bad for us if we can't figure it out. I'm making the coffee with a little cinnamon, all right?"

The unicorn turned its head at their voices; then resumed its patient scrutiny of the dawn joggers, the commuters and the shabby, ambling pilgrims to nowhere. Julie said, slowly and precisely, "It was woven into that tapestry. It began in the tapestry—it can't know anyone who's not in the tapestry. Who could it be waiting for on East Redondo Street?"

Farrell had coffee for her, but no answer. They ate their breakfast in silence, looking at nothing but the unicorn, which looked at nothing but the street; until, as Farrell prepared to leave the apartment, it bounded lightly down from the old trunk and was at the door before him, purposeful and impatient. Julie came quickly, attempting for the first time to pick it up, but the unicorn backed against a bookcase and made the hissing-kitten sound again. Farrell said, "I wouldn't."

"Oh, I definitely would," she answered him between her teeth. "Because if it gets out that door, you're going to be the one chasing after it through Friday-morning traffic." The unicorn offered no resistance when she picked it up, though its neck was arched back like a coiled snake's and for a moment Julie felt the brilliant eyes burning her skin. She held it up so that it could see her own eyes, and spoke to it directly.

"I don't know what you want," she said. "I don't know what we could do to help you if we did know, as lost as you are. But it's my doing that you're here at all, so if you'll just be patient until Joe gets back, we'll take you outside, and maybe you can sort of show us..." Her voice trailed away, and she simply stared back into the unicorn's eyes.

When Farrell cautiously opened the door, the unicorn paid no attention; nevertheless, he closed it to a crack behind him before he turned to say, "I have to handle lunch, but I can get off dinner. Just don't get careless. It's got something on its mind, that one."

With Farrell gone, she felt curiously excited and apprehensive at once, as though she were meeting another lover. She brought a chair to the window, placing it close to the steamer trunk. As soon as she sat down, NMC plumped into her lap, kittens abandoned, and settled down for some serious purring and shedding. Julie petted her absently, carefully avoiding glancing at the unicorn, or even thinking about it; instead she bent all her regard on what the unicorn must have seen from her window. She recognized the UPS driver, half a dozen local joggers—each sporting a flat-lipped grin of agony suggesting that their Walkman headphones were too tight—a policewoman whom she had met on birdwatching expeditions, and the Frozen-Yogurt Man. The Frozen-Yogurt Man wore a grimy naval officer's cap the year around, along with a flapping tweed sport-jacket, sweat pants and calf-length rubber boots. He had a thin yellow-brown beard, like the stubble of a burned-over wheatfield, and had never been seen, as far as Julie knew, without a frozen-yogurt cone in at least one hand. Farrell said he favored plain vanilla in a sugar cone. "With M&Ms on top. Very California."

NMC raised an ear and opened an eye, and Julie turned her head to see the unicorn once again poised atop the steamer trunk, staring down at the Frozen-Yogurt Man with the soft hairs of its mane standing erect from nape to withers. (Did it pick that up from the cats? Julie wondered in some alarm.) "He's harmless," she said, feeling silly but needing to speak. "There must have been lots of people like him in your time. Only then there was a place for them, they had names, they fit the world somewhere. Mendicant friars, I guess. Hermits."

The unicorn leaped at the window. Julie had no more than a second's warning: the dainty head lowered only a trifle, the sleek miniature hindquarters seemed hardly to flex at all; but suddenly—so fast that she had no time even to register the explosion of the glass, the unicorn was nearly through. Blood raced down the white neck, tracing the curve of the straining belly.

Julie never remembered whether she cried out or not, never remembered moving. She was simply at the window with her hands surrounding the unicorn, pulling it back as gently as she possibly could, praying in silent desperation not to catch its throat on a fang of glass. Her hands were covered with blood— some of it hers—by the time the unicorn came free, but she saw quickly that its wounds were superficial, already coagulating and closing as she looked on. The unicorn's blood was as red as her own, but there was a strange golden shadow about it: a dark sparkling just under or beyond her eyes' understanding. She dabbed at it ineffectually with a paper towel, while the unicorn struggled in her grasp. Strangely, she could feel that it was not putting forth its entire strength; though whether from fear of hurting her or for some other reason, she could not say.

"All right," she said harshly. "All right. He's only the Frozen-Yogurt Man, for God's sake, but all right, I'll take you to him. I'll take you wherever you want—we won't wait for Joe, we'll just go out. Only you have to stay in my pocket. In my pocket, okay?"

The unicorn quieted slowly between her hands. She could not read the expression in the great, bruise-colored eyes, but it made no further attempt to escape when she set it down and began to patch the broken window with cardboard and packing tape. That done, she donned the St. Vincent de Paul duffel coat she wore all winter, and carefully deposited the unicorn in the wrist-deep right pocket Then she pinned a note on the door for Farrell, pushed two kittens away from it with her foot, shut it, said aloud, "Okay, you got it," and went down into the street.

The sun was high and warm, but a chill breeze lurked in the shade of the old trees. Julie felt the unicorn move in her pocket, and looked down to see the narrow, delicate head poke out from under the flap. "Back in there," she said, amazed at her own firmness. "Five hundred, a thousand years—don't you know what happens by now? When people see you?" The unicorn retreated without protest.

She could see the Frozen-Yogurt Man's naval cap a block ahead, bobbing with his shuffling gait. There were a lot of bodies between them, and she increased her own pace, keeping a hand over her pocket as she slipped between strollers and dodged coffeehouse tables. Once, sidestepping a skateboarder, she tripped hard over a broken slab of sidewalk and stumbled to hands and knees, instinctively twisting her body to fall to the left. She was up in a moment, unhurt, hurrying on.

When she did catch up with the Frozen-Yogurt Man, and he turned his blindly benign gaze on her, she hesitated, completely uncertain of how to approach him. She had never spoken to him, nor even seen him close enough to notice that he was almost an albino, with coral eyes and pebbly skin literally the color of yogurt. She cupped her hand around the unicorn in her pocket, smiled and said, "Hi."

The Frozen-Yogurt Man said thoughtfully, as though they were picking up an interrupted conversation, "You think they know what they're doing?" His voice was loud and metallic, not quite connecting one word with another. It sounded to Julie like the synthesized voices that told her which buttons on her telephone to push.

"No," she answered without hesitation. "No, whatever you're talking about. I don't think anybody knows what they're doing anymore."

The Frozen-Yogurt Man interrupted her. "I think they do. I think they do. I think they do." Julie thought he might go on repeating the words forever; but she felt the stir against her side again, and the Frozen-Yogurt Man's flat pink eyes shifted and widened. "What's that?" he demanded shrilly. "What's that watching me?"

The unicorn was halfway out of her coat pocket, front legs flailing as it yearned toward the Frozen-Yogurt Man. Only the reluctance of passersby to make eye contact with either him or Julie spared the creature from notice. She grabbed it with both hands, forcing it back, telling it in a frantic hiss, "Stay there, you stay, he isn't the one! I don't know whom you're looking for, but it's not him." But the unicorn thrashed in the folds of cloth as though it were drowning.

The Frozen-Yogurt Man was backing away, his hands out, his face melting. Ever afterward, glimpsing him across the street, Julie felt chillingly guilty for having seen him so. In a phlegmy whisper he said, "Oh, no—oh, no, no, you don't put that thing on me. No, I been watching you all the time, you get away, you get away from me with that thing. You people, you put that chip behind my ear, you put them radio mice in my stomach—you get away, you don't put nothing more on me, you done me enough." He was screaming now, and the officer's cap was tipping forward, revealing a scarred scalp the color of the sidewalk. "You done me enough! You done me enough!"

Julie fled. She managed at first to keep herself under control, easing away sedately enough through the scattering of mildly curious spectators; it was only when she was well down the block and could still hear the Frozen-Yogurt Man's terrified wailing that she began to run. Under the hand that she still kept in her pocket, the unicorn seemed to have grown calm again, but its heart was beating in tumultuous rhythm with her own. She ran on until she came to a bus stop and collapsed on the bench there, gasping for breath, rocking back and forth, weeping dryly for the Frozen-Yogurt Man.

She came back to herself only when she felt the touch of a cool, soft nose just under her right ear. Keeping her head turned away, she said hoarsely, "Just let me sit here a minute, all right? I did what you wanted. I'm sorry it didn't work out. You get back down before somebody sees you."

A warm breath stirred the hairs on Julie's arms, and she raised her head to meet the hopeful brown eyes and all-purpose grin of a young golden retriever. The dog was looking brightly back and forth between her and the unicorn, wagging its entire body from the ears on down, back feet dancing eagerly. The unicorn leaned precariously from Julie's pocket to touch noses with it.

"No one's ever going to believe you," Julie said to the dog. The golden retriever listened attentively, waited a moment to make certain she had no more to confide, and then gravely licked the unicorn's head, the great red tongue almost wrapping it round. NMC's incessant grooming had plainly not prepared the unicorn for anything like this; it sneezed and took refuge in the depths of the pocket. Julie said, "Not a living soul."

The dog's owner appeared then, apologizing and grabbing its dangling leash to lead it away. It looked back, whining, and its master had to drag it all the way to the corner. Julie still huddled and rocked on the bus stop bench, but when the unicorn put its head out again she was laughing thinly. She ran a forefinger down its mane, and then laid two fingers gently against the wary, pulsing neck. She said, "Burnouts. Is that it? You're looking for one of our famous Avicenna loonies, none with less than a master's, each with a direct line to Mars, Atlantis, Lemuria, Graceland or Mount Shasta? Is that it?" For the first time, the unicorn pushed its head hard into her hand, as NMC would do. The horn pricked her palm lightly.

For the next three hours, she made her way from the downtown streets to the university's red-tiled enclave, and back again, with small side excursions into doorways, subway stations, even parking lots. She developed a peculiar cramp in her neck from snapping frequent glances at her pocket to be sure that the unicorn was staying out of sight. Whenever it indicated interest in a wild red gaze, storks'-nest hair, a shopping cart crammed with green plastic bags, or a droning monologue concerning Jesus, AIDS, and the Kennedys, she trudged doggedly after one more street apostle to open one more conversation with the moon. Once the unicorn showed itself, the result was always the same.

"It likes beards," she told Farrell late that night, as he patiently massaged her feet. "Bushy beards—the wilder and filthier, the better. Hair, too, especially that pattern baldness tonsure look. Sandals, yes, definitely—it doesn't like boots or sneakers at all, and it can't make up its mind about Birkenstocks. Prefers blankets and serapes to coats, dark hair to light, older to younger, the silent ones to the walking sound trucks—men to women, absolutely. Won't even stick its head out for a woman."

"It's hard to blame the poor thing," Farrell mused. "For a unicorn, men would be a bunch of big, stupid guys with swords and whatnot. Women are betrayal, every time, simple as that. It wasn't Gloria Steinem who wove that tapestry." He squeezed toes gently with one hand, a bruised heel with the other. "What did they do when they actually saw it?"

The unicorn glanced at them over the edge of the cat box, where its visit had been cause for an orgy of squeaking, purring and teething. Julie said, "What do you think? It was bad. It got pretty damn awful. Some of them fell down on their knees and started laughing and crying and praying their heads off. There were a couple who just sort of crooned and moaned to it—and I told you about the poor Frozen-Yogurt Man—and then there was one guy who tried to grab it away and run off with it. But it wasn't having that, and it jabbed him really hard. Nobody noticed, thank God." She laughed wearily, presenting her other foot for treatment. "The rest—oh, I'd say they should be halfway to Portland by now. Screaming all the way."

Farrell grunted thoughtfully, but asked no more questions until Julie was in bed and he was sitting across the room playing her favorite Campion lute song. She was nearly asleep when his voice bumbled slowly against her half-dream like a fly at a window. "It can't know anyone who's not in the tapestry. There's the answer. There it is."

"There it is," she echoed him, barely hearing her own words. Farrell put down the lute and came to her, sitting on the bed to grip her shoulder.

"Jewel, listen, wake up and listen to me! It's trying to find someone who was in that tapestry with it—we even know what he looks like, more or less. An old guy, ragged and dirty, big beard, sandals—some kind of monk, most likely. Though what a unicorn would be doing anywhere near your average monk is more than I can figure. Are you awake, Jewel?"

"Yes," she mumbled. "No. Wasn't anybody else. Sleep."

Somewhere very far away Farrell said, "We didn't see anybody else." Julie felt the bed sway as he stood up. "Tomorrow night," he said. "Tomorrow's Saturday, they stay open later on Saturdays. You sleep, I'll call you." She drifted off in confidence that he would lock the door carefully behind him, even without a key.

A temporary word-processing job, in company with a deadline for a set of views of diseased kidneys, filled up most of the next day for her. She was still weary, vaguely depressed, and grateful when she returned home to find the unicorn thoroughly occupied in playing on the studio floor with three of NMC's kittens. The game appeared to involve a good deal of stiff-legged pouncing, an equal amount of spinning and side-slipping on the part of the unicorn, all leading to a grand climax in which the kittens tumbled furiously over one another while the unicorn looked on, forgotten until the next round. They never came close to laying a paw on their swift littermate, and the unicorn in turn treated them with effortless care. Julie watched for a long time, until the kittens abruptly fell asleep.

"I guess that's what being immortal is like," she said aloud. The unicorn looked back at her, its eyes gone almost black. Julie said, "One minute they're romping around with you—the next, they're sleeping. Right in the middle of the game. We're all kittens to you."

The unicorn did a strange thing then. It came to her and indicated with an imperious motion of its head that it wanted to be picked up. Julie bent down to lift it, and it stepped off her joined palms into her lap, where—after pawing gently for a moment, like a dog settling in for the night—it folded its long legs and put its head down. Julie's heart hiccuped absurdly in her breast.

"I'm not a virgin," she said. "But you know that." The unicorn closed its eyes.

Neither of them had moved when Farrell arrived, looking distinctly irritated and harassed. "I left Gracie to finish up," he said. "Gracie. If I still have my job tomorrow, it'll be more of a miracle than any mythical beast. Let's go."

In the van, with the unicorn once again curled deep in Julie's pocket, Farrell said, "What we have to do is, we have to take a look at the tapestry again. A good long look this time."

"It's not going back there. I told you that." She closed her hand lightly around the unicorn, barely touching it, more for her own heartening than its reassurance. "Joe, if that's what you're planning—"

Farrell grinned at her through the timeless fast-food twilight of Madame Schumann-Heink. "No wonder you're in such good shape, all that jumping to conclusions. Listen, there has to be some other figure in that smudgy thing, someone we didn't see before. Our little friend has a friend."

Julie considered briefly, then shook her head. "No. No way. There was the knight, the squire, and that woman. That's all, I'm sure of it."

"Um," Farrell said. "Now, me, I'm never entirely sure of anything. You've probably noticed, over the years. Come on, Madame, you can do it." He dropped the van into first gear and gunned it savagely up a steep, narrow street. "We didn't see the fourth figure because we weren't looking for it. But it's there, it has to be. This isn't Comparative Mythology, Jewel, this is me."

Madame Schumann-Heink actually gained the top of the hill without stalling, and Farrell rewarded such valor by letting the old van free-wheel down the other side. Julie said slowly, "And if it is there? What happens then?"

"No idea. The usual. Play it by ear and trust we'll know the right thing to do. You will, anyway. You always know the right thing to do, Tanikawa."

The casual words startled her so deeply that she actually covered her mouth for a moment: a classic Japanese mannerism she had left behind in her Seattle childhood.

"You never told me that before. Twenty years, and you never said anything like that to me." Farrell was crooning placatingly to Madame Schumann-Heink's brake shoes, and did not answer. Julie said, "Even if I did always know, which I don't, I don't always do it. Not even usually. Hardly ever, the way I feel right now."

Farrell let the van coast to a stop under a traffic light before he turned to her. His voice was low enough that she had to bend close to hear him. "All I know," he said, "there are two of us girls in this heap, and one of us had a unicorn sleeping in her lap a little while back. You work it out." He cozened Madame Schumann-Heink back into gear, and they lurched on toward the Bigby Museum.

A different guard this time: trimmer, younger, far less inclined to speculative conversation, and even less likely to overlook dubious goings-on around the exhibits. Fortunately, there was also a university-sponsored lecture going on: it appeared to be the official word on the Brueghels, and had drawn a decent house for a Saturday night. Under his breath, Farrell said, "We split up. You go that way, I'll ease around by the Spanish stuff. Take your time."

Julie took him at his word, moving slowly through the crowd and pausing occasionally for brief murmured conversations with academic acquaintances. Once she plainly took exception to the speaker's comments regarding Brueghel's artistic debt to his father-in-law, and Farrell, watching from across the room, fully expected her to interrupt the lecture with a discourse of her own. But she resisted temptation; they met, as planned, by the three tapestries, out of the guard's line of sight, and with only a single bored-looking browser anywhere near them. Julie held Farrell's hand tightly as they turned to study the middle tapestry.

Nothing had changed. The knight and squire still prodded a void toward their pale lady, who went on leaning forward to drape her wreath around captive space. Julie imagined a bleak recognition in their eyes of knotted thread that had not been there before, but she felt foolish about that and said nothing to Farrell. Silently the two of them divided the tapestry into fields of survey, as they had done with the gallery itself when the unicorn first escaped. Julie took the foreground, scanning the ornamental garden framing the three human figures for one more face, likely dirty and bearded, perhaps by now so faded as to merge completely with the faded leaves and shadows. She was on her third futile sweep over the scene when she heard Farrell's soft hiss beside her.

"Yes!" he whispered. "Got you, you godly little recluse, you. I knew you had to be in there!" He grabbed Julie's hand and drew it straight up to the vegetable-looking forest surrounding the distant castle. "Right there, peeping coyly out like Julia's feet, you can't miss him."

But she could, and she did, for a maddening while; until Farrell made her focus on a tiny shape, a gray-white bulge at the base of one of the trees. Nose hard against the glass, she began at last to see it clearly: all robe and beard, mostly, but stitched with enough maniacal medieval detail to suggest a bald head, intense black eyes and a wondering expression. Farrell said proudly, "Your basic resident hermit. Absolutely required, no self-respecting feudal estate complete without one. There's our boy."

It seemed to Julie that the lady and the two men were straining their

THE URBAN FANTASY ANTHOLOGY

embroidered necks to turn toward the castle and the solitary form they had forgotten for five centuries. "Him?" she said. "He's the one?"

"Hold our friend up to see him. Watch what happens."

For a while, afterward, she tried to forget how grudgingly she had reached into her coat pocket and slowly brought her cupped hand up again, into the light. Farrell shifted position, moving close on her right to block any possible glimpse of the unicorn. It posed on Julie's palm, head high, three legs splayed slightly for balance, and one forefoot proudly curled, (*exactly like every unicorn I ever drew when I was young.*) She looked around quickly—half afraid of being observed, half wishing it—and raised her hand to bring the unicorn level with the dim little figure of the hermit.

Three things happened then. The unicorn uttered a harsh, achingly plain cry of recognition and longing, momentarily silencing the Brueghel lecturer around the corner. At the same time, a different sound, low and disquieting, like a sleeper's teeth grinding together, seemed to come either from the frame enclosing the tapestry or the glass over it. The third occurrence was that something she could not see, nor ever after describe to Farrell, gripped Julie's right wrist so strongly that she cried out herself and almost dropped the unicorn to the gallery floor. She braced it with her free hand as it scrambled for purchase, the carpet-tack horn glowing like abalone shell.

"What is it, what's the matter?" Farrell demanded. He made clumsily to hold her, but she shook him away. Whatever had her wrist tightened its clamp, feeling nothing at all like a human hand, but rather as though the air itself were turning to stone—as though one part of her were being buried while the rest stood helplessly by. Her fingers could yet move, enough to hold the unicorn safe; but there was no resisting the force that was pushing her arm back down toward the tapestry foreground, back to the knight and the squire, the mincing damsel and the strangling garden. *They want it. It is theirs. Give it to them. They want it.*

"Fat fucking chance, buster," she said loudly. Her right hand was almost numb, but she felt the unicorn rearing in her palm, felt its rage shock through her stone arm, and watched from very far away as the bright horn touched the tapestry frame.

Almost silently, the glass shattered. There was only one small hole at first, popping into view just above the squire's lumpy face; then the cracks went spidering across the entire surface, making a tiny scratching sound, like mice in the walls. One by one, quite deliberately, the pieces of glass began to fall out of the frame, to splinter again on the hardwood floor.

With the first fragment, Julie's arm was her own once more, freezing cold and barely controllable, but free. She lurched forward, off-balance, and might easily have shoved the unicorn back into the garden after all. But Farrell caught her, steadying her hand as she raised it to the shelter of the forest and the face under the trees.

The unicorn turned its head. Julie caught the brilliant purple glance out of the air and tucked it away in herself, to keep for later. She could hear voices approaching now, and quick, officious footsteps that didn't sound like those of an art historian. As briskly as she might have shooed one of NMC's kittens from underfoot, she said, in the language that sounded like Japanese, "Go on, then, go. Go home."

She never actually saw the unicorn flow from her hand into the tapestry. Whenever she tried to make herself recall the moment, memory dutifully producing a rainbow flash or a melting movie-dissolve passage between worlds, irritable honesty told memory to put a sock in it. There was never anything more than herself standing in a lot of broken glass for the second time in two days, with a faint chill in her right arm, hearing Farrell's eloquently indignant voice denying to guards, docents and lecturers alike that either of them had laid a hand on this third-rate Belgian throw rug. He was still expounding a theory involving cool recycled air on the outside of the glass and warm condensation within as they were escorted all the way to the parking lot. When Julie praised his passionate inventiveness, he only growled, "Maybe that's the way it really was. How do I know?"

But she knew without asking that he had seen what she had seen: the pale shadow peering back at them from its sanctuary in the wood, and the opaline glimmer of a horn under the hermit's hand. Knight, lady and squire—one another's prisoners now, eternally—remained exactly where they were.

That night neither Farrell nor Julie slept at all. They lay silently close, peacefully wide-awake, companionably solitary, listening to her beloved Black-Forest-tourist-trash cuckoo clock strike the hours. In the morning Farrell said it was because NMC had carried on so, roaming the apartment endlessly in search of her lost nursling. But Julie answered, "We didn't need to sleep. We needed to be quiet and tell ourselves what happened to us. To hear the story."

Farrell was staring blankly into the open refrigerator, as he had been for some time. "I'm still not sure what happened. I get right up to the place where you lifted it up so it could see its little hermit buddy, and then your arm...I can't ever figure that part. What the hell was it that had hold of you?"

"I don't see how we'll ever know," she said. "It could have been them, those three—some force they were able to put out together that almost made me put the unicorn back with them, in the garden." She shivered briefly, then slipped past him to take out the eggs, milk and smoked salmon he had vaguely been seeking, and close the refrigerator door.

Farrell shook his head slowly. "They weren't real. Not like the unicorn. Even your grandmother couldn't have brought one of them to life on this side. Colored thread, that's all they were. The hermit, the monk, whatever—I don't know, Jewel."

"I don't know either," she said. "Listen. Listen, I'll tell you what I think I think. Maybe whoever wove that tapestry meant to trap a unicorn, meant to keep it penned up there forever. Not a wicked wizard, nothing like that, just the weaver, the artist. It's the way we are, we all want to paint or write or play something so for once it'll stay painted, stay played, stay put, so it'll still be alive for us tomorrow, next week, always. Mostly it dies in the night—but now and then, now and then, somebody gets it right. And when you get it right, then it's real. Even if it doesn't exist, like a unicorn, if you get it really right..."

She let the last words trail away. Farrell said, "Garlic. I bet you don't have any garlic, you never do." He opened the refrigerator again and rummaged, saying over his shoulder, "So you think it was the weaver himself, herself, grabbing you, from back there in the fifteenth century? Wanting you to put things back the way you found them, the way he had it—the right way?"

"Maybe." Julie rubbed her arm unconsciously, though the coldness was long since gone. "Maybe. Too bad for him. Right isn't absolutely everything."

"Garlic is," Farrell said from the depths of the vegetable bin. Emerging in triumph, brandishing a handful of withered-looking cloves, he added, "That's my Jewel. Priorities on straight, and a strong but highly negotiable sense of morality. The thing I've always loved about you, all these years."

Neither of them spoke for some while. Farrell peeled garlic and broke eggs into a bowl, and Julie fed NMC. The omelets were almost done before she said,

"We might manage to put up with each other a bit longer than usual this time. Us old guys. I mean, I've signed a lease on this place, I can't go anywhere."

"Hand me the cayenne," Farrell said. "Madame Schumann-Heink can still manage the Bay Bridge these days, but I don't think I'd try her over the Golden Gate. Your house and the restaurant, that's about her limit."

"You'd probably have to go a bit light on the garlic. Only a bit, that's all. And I still don't like people around when I'm working. And I still read in the bathroom."

Farrell smiled at her then, brushing gray hair out of his eyes. "That's all right, there's always the litter box. Just don't you go marrying any Brians. Definitely no Brians."

"Fair enough," she said. "Think of it—you could have a real key, and not have to pick the lock every time. Hold still, there's egg on your forehead." The omelets got burned.

Paranormal
Romance

A Funny Thing Happened
On the Way to Urban Fantasy

Paula Guran

No publishing mastermind creates genres, subgenres, or categories. They arise due to public demand. No writer sets out to invent them. An imaginative author—who is influenced by what she or he has experienced, heard, seen, knows—writes her or his unique work. Often, around the same time, there is another writer or two who—through sheer serendipity or cultural zeitgeist—may be writing stories that have a similar appeal. For various reasons that one can theorize about, but no one really understands, the fiction gains popularity. If a type of fiction is seen as marketable, the places that sell books want more of "that sort of book," and the publishers provide them. An example, as Joe R. Lansdale has pointed out elsewhere in this volume, is horror. It did not become a commercial category until the 1980s after the phenomenon named Stephen King came along.

More recently, readers wanted a type of fantasy novel that was set in an alternate version of our contemporary/near-contemporary (but not always urban) world with a female (sometimes male) protagonist who usually (but not always) has (or develops) a certain amount of "kickassitude." She possesses supernatural powers or a connection to those with such powers (or gains them for herself). The books often had a detective-style plot—or at least something that had to be revealed/discovered—with (usually but not always) a romantic relationship as at least one subplot. Action-oriented, they often included horrific elements balanced with humor. The comedy might be snarky, twinged with morbidity, or downright funny, but the universe was still, overall, dark. When romance (and/or sex) was involved it was written either from the female perspective or a balance of female and male. The protagonist was also usually involved in a journey of self-discovery. This evolving character development, complex universe, and complicated storylines usually required more than one book to resolve.

A type of fiction that didn't really have a name, this nameless genre/subgenre/genre blend became the most popular and bestselling fantasy of the last ten years.

How did it come to be known as urban fantasy?

In the 1990s and first years of the twenty-first century, the term *paranormal romance* was often used by the media and reviewers in publications such as the *New York Times, Publishers Weekly, USA Today,* etc. to describe fantasy books like those written by Laurell K. Hamilton and Charlaine Harris as well as those by Christine Feehan, Maggie Shayne, and others. Previously, Anne Rice's work—her *Interview with the Vampire* was published in 1976—had often been referred to as paranormal romance.

The romance genre has identified one of its many subgenres as paranormal romance for at least two decades. (The Romance Writers of America introduced a Futuristic/Fantasy/Paranormal category for the organization's RITA awards in 1991. It is currently called, more succinctly, Best Paranormal Novel.) As with any long-established subgenre, its definition has changed over the years, but it has never been confined only to a contemporary setting; it included time-travel, historical fantasy, and science fictional romance too.

But of the examples mentioned above, only Maggie Shayne's (her Wings in the Night series, started in 1993 with *Twilight Phantasies*) and Feehan's books (*Dark Prince,* first of her Dark series, was published in 1999) were published as romance and conformed to that genre's expectations of a love relationship central to the plot with a positive, satisfying ending in which the reader is assured the couple will remain together.

Rice, although her fame has come from writing about vampires and witches, has always shunned labels and her books are commonly shelved in bookstores simply as "fiction." It certainly isn't genre romance.

Hamilton's first Anita Blake Vampire Hunter novel, *Guilty Pleasures,* was published in 1993. Set in an alternate world where the supernatural is known to exist and the preternatural have been granted equal rights in the U.S., Hamilton's earliest books did have a romantic aspect, but Anita Blake was closer to a horrific version of mystery novelist Sue Grafton's character Kinsey Millhone than a romance heroine.

Charlaine Harris's first Southern Vampire Mysteries novel, *Dead Until*

Dark, won an Anthony Award as Best Paperback *Mystery* of 2001. Her heroine, Sookie Stackhouse, lives in a world where supernatural creatures have recently "come out" and co-exist with humans. As a secret telepath, Sookie has problems dating fellow humans until she meets a vampire whose mind she can't read.

Nobody called these books "urban fantasy," at the time. Nor, at first, were Kelley Armstrong's Women of the Otherworld series (first book: *Bitten*, 2001) or Kim Harrison's *Dead Witch Walking* (2004), the first of her Rachel Morgan novels, or any of the other novels of this increasingly popular fantasy. It wasn't romance and even though it was dark and vampires, werewolves, and other supernatural creatures were involved, you couldn't call it horror. For the most part it was just "fantasy"—even if reviewers, journalists, and others sometimes misnamed it as paranormal romance.

Meanwhile true paranormal romance set in an alternate world similar to our own—some with the romance occurring in a well-built fantasy universe, some with only a nod to meaningful fantastic elements—was selling well too. Heroines and heroes found each other and a happy-ever-after ending (even if one's true love happened to be a vampire or demon or werewolf) while saving the world from supernatural nastiness (often in the form of vampires, demons, werewolves, etc.)

[I edited *The Year's Best Paranormal Fiction* anthology in 2006, with a lengthy introduction about the romance tradition and definition. It pointed out the difference between "fantasy with some romance" and fiction from the marketing category called romance, but suggested we just call it all paranormal romance. It was a lame attempt and I now disavow it. The next volume was called *The Year's Best Romantic Fantasy* and then (against the publisher's wishes at the time) I killed the series. But that is another story. Let's just say I saw the light.]

Around 2005, the term *urban fantasy* started to be used to differentiate novels that were not "paranormal romance-according-to-romance-genre." Outside of the simple fact there were starting to be a lot of books of this type being published and they were being published as fantasy—printed on the spine and categorized by BISAC Subject Code (a list used to categorize books based on topical content that theoretically determines where the work is shelved or the genre under which it can be searched for in a database)—I suspect, but have no proof, that the term popped up for two reasons.

First, although some fans could not care less about labels, readers who wanted romance resented books not fitting their expectations being called romance. There seemed to be a suspicion, too, among some more vociferous fans that "someone" was trying to sneak non-romance into the romance sections of bookstores. That being said, many romance readers seemed to be receptive to fantasy and flexible about "crossing the aisle" without prejudice.

Perhaps more importantly, writers of fantasy of this type, primarily women, weren't getting respect from their peers or the fantasy "experts." (Books by male authors—most notably Jim Butcher—whose books appealed to the same readership weren't being called paranormal romance.) They wrote fantasy and wanted it to be recognized as such. These books were the hottest thing in the fantasy field and bringing in throngs of new readers—many of whom had previously read mostly romance or mystery or were discovering fantasy for the first time or realizing fantasy wasn't what they had thought it was—yet the authors and the fiction as a whole were being ignored (even derided) by the field itself and most of its established mavens.

Somehow or another—sometimes appropriately, sometimes not—this type of fantasy came to be called urban fantasy. It gave readers and authors something new to debate, but I'm not sure it made much of a corrective dent in the perspectives of many in the sf/f community or the media.

Of course there are authors of "this stuff" who can't neatly be labeled as either paranormal romance or urban fantasy. There are writers like MaryJanice Davidson, Shanna Swendson, and Julie Kenner who write lighter fare that has been placed into one category or another almost arbitrarily. Books can be unintentionally or even intentionally mislabeled by publishers, or series can evolve out of or into one genre or the other.

But, trust me, the terms are not interchangeable.

Calling these books urban fantasy, however, confused longtime fantasy lovers and ruffled some definitional feathers. The term (and the fiction it then described) first gained popularity in the 1980s. To quote John Clute on "Urban Fantasy" in *The Encyclopedia of Fantasy* (ed. by J. Clute & J. Grant, 1997):

THE URBAN FANTASY ANTHOLOGY

Urban fantasy.... A city may be seen from afar, and is generally seen clear; the UF is told from within and from the perspective of characters acting out their roles, it may be difficult to determine the extent and nature of the surrounding reality. UFs are normally texts where fantasy and the mundane world interact, intersect and interweave throughout a tale which is significantly about a real city.

Authors (and landmark works) most commonly cited as early examples of urban fantasy include Jonathan Carroll (*The Land of Laughs*, 1980), John Crowley (*Little, Big*; 1981), Charles de Lint (*Moonheart*, 1984), and Emma Bull (*War for the Oaks*, 1987). Additionally, Terri Windling's shared-world anthology for teens (co-edited with Mark Alan Arnold), *Borderland*, (1986) and its subsequent series of anthologies and novels are important early works. When discussing this type of urban fantasy in a larger context, authors like Neil Gaiman, China Miéville, and Caitlín R. Kiernan are often mentioned.

As for the ruffling of feathers, well, most of those feathers belonged to folks unacquainted with a broad enough range of this "new" urban fantasy to make any judgment calls to start with. But, hey, not really knowing much about playing a sport doesn't keep anyone from second-guessing a team or its coaches, either.

Charles de Lint wrote that he feels the subtitle of his novel *Jack of Kinrowan: A Novel of Urban Faerie* led to his work becoming termed urban fantasy. He and Terri Windling came up with "mythic fiction" to better describe their strain of the fantastic. It is an admirable and workable definition and now used by knowledgeable readers, critics, and academics.

I don't like less-than-well-thought-out labels any more than Joe Lansdale does, and agree the more a type of fiction is "directed" like cows through a chute the more likely it is "all going to end in the slaughterhouse."

I am in awe of these two gentlemen (and gentlemen both truly are). Their intelligence, imaginations, talents, and works are breathtaking. They are masters of the art and craft of storytelling. They (and others of their kind) create wonderful tales that I wish could magically attract folks simply by being what it is: superlative reading.

In a perfect world, great fiction—or even entertainingly adequate fiction—would not be a commodity that has to be packaged and sold.

But publishing is not only an imperfect world, it's a world with an absurd business model where no one has any real idea why a particular book sells or how to reliably get proper attention for its products. In the last few years, it's gotten to be an even stranger and more dangerous a place for writers to survive. What little guidance the best publishers and editors might once have provided doesn't matter as much. More than ever, whatever simplistic label can be stuck to a book—or, better yet, what already highly successful, previously published book/author that a new title can be compared to—matters a great deal. It matters because without such tagging, books don't get into brick-and-mortar stores at all and don't get favorably grouped for online sales.

The chutes are used because they help at least some of the cattle get fat so they can retire to nice green meadows rather than winding up as part of a Big Mac. Some others can at least chew their cud and moo a little longer than they might have otherwise.

Readers and writers of books that became known as urban fantasy—let's call it urban fantasy/paranormal from here on out—were ready for it because, well, its time had come. Outside of literary influences—including comic book heroines—strong women heroes like Ellen Ripley in the *Alien* series (1979, 1986, 1992, and 1997) and Sarah Connor in the first two *Terminator* movies (1984 and 1991) made an impression in film. And although the protagonist is male, *The Crow* (1994) was, at its core, a supernatural love story inextricably tied to the modern city. Like *The Crow*, the 1998 vampire-action film *Blade* (1998) was based on a comic. Its macho human-vampire hybrid protected humans against vampires—but why couldn't a woman do the same?

Television series were another influence. *Beauty and the Beast* (original run: 1987–1990 on CBS) updated the old tale of the noble man-beast. His love was a smart assistant district attorney in New York. He lived among other social outcasts under the city. *Nick Knight*, a TV movie released in 1989, was about a vampire working as a police detective in modern day Los Angeles. In 1992, CBS reshaped it as a series, *Forever Knight*. It ran three seasons, ending in 1996. *The X-Files* (originally aired from 1993 to 2002 on Fox) is considered by many as the defining series of the nineties. Despite its science fictional trappings and conspiracy theories, true believer Fox Mulder and skeptic Dana Scully were paranormal investigators. The protagonist of the *Xena: Warrior Princess*, a supernatural fantasy adventure series that aired in syndication 1995–2001, may not have been modern or urban, but she was a formidable fighter seeking her redemption by helping others.

Since the first books that became known as urban fantasy/paranormal were written before its existence, the authors can't be said to have been directly inspired by Joss Whedon's *Buffy the Vampire Slayer* television series (1997–2003) [and its spin-off series *Angel* (1999–2004)]. But many of those who later became its readers and writers probably were.

The *Buffy* series was darker than Whedon's action-comedy/horror parody film of the same name (1992) and better conveyed his concept of an empowered woman fighting monsters (metaphors for problems that humans, especially teenagers, face).

Buffy Summers had "kickassitude"—and by kickassitude I don't necessarily mean violence. In slang, the word originally meant awesome, cool, something that "kicks ass" in a positive manner. As far as female examples, the easiest comparisons are women in rock who displayed kickassitude: Joan Jett, Chrissie Hynde, Patti Smith, Janis Joplin, Lita Ford, Deborah Harry, etc.

And, like rock-and-roll, *Buffy* had meaning but was also a lot of fun.

Books have been written on the pop cultural meaning and impact of *Buffy*. Let's just sum it up by saying *Buffy* borrowed from folklore, myth, literature, film, and television for serialized episodes that were part of a larger story arc. Although a drama, there was plenty of comedy and genre-blending from romance, science fiction, martial arts, action, and more. Buffy and her friends were saving the world from supernatural threat with a combination of investigation, physical combat, and magic. She was also struggling with her role as a "chosen" heroine and learning about herself as a person.

But even if not recognized as such, the urban fantasy/paranormal heroine was definitely around pre-Buffy (and even pre-Hamilton) in fantasy literature.

Mercedes Lackey's Diana Tregarde first appeared in a couple of short stories and then in three novels: *Burning Water* (1989), *Children of the Night* (1990), and *Jinx High* (1991). An American witch whose day job is writing romance novels, Diana is a Guardian. This gives her more magical power, but also the responsibility of providing aid to those who ask her for help. In the three books (published by Tor as horror) she provides protection from angry deities, vampires, and a sorceress.

Tanya Huff's Blood books (five novels and a collection of short stories) mixed a strong heroine with vampires, mystery, suspense, and romance. *Blood Price* (1991) introduced Vicki Nelson, a homicide detective forced to retire when her eyesight fails due to Retinitis pigmentosa. Vicki teams up with Henry Fitzroy—a 450-year-old vampire and bastard son of Henry VIII—and becomes a private investigator. The other man in her life is Detective-Sergeant Mike Celluci. The series is set in Toronto. The books became the basis of a short-lived TV series, *Blood Ties*, which premiered on Lifetime in 2007.

The urban fantasy/paranormal heroine owes a lot to the tradition of the hard-boiled tough-guy American detective genre—there were tough gals, too, like Gale Gallagher, Honey West, V. I. Warshawski, and Kinsey Millhone—and to stories of "occult detectives" and various "vampire detectives." She is also derived from sword and sorcery and is a female incarnation of the action-adventure hero. Most of all, she's relevant to the here and now. It may be fantasy, but urban fantasy/paranormal says a lot about our fears and hopes, our cynicism and angst, our personal journeys and cultural climate.

In the last five years—a period that saw the phenomenal success of Stephenie Meyer's young adult vampire-romance fantasy series and its consequent film versions; movies like *Underworld*; *Blood Ties* on TV; Charlaine Harris's Sookie Stackhouse novels become the HBO series *True Blood*; and young adult urban fantasy/paranormal romance series were introduced—urban fantasy/paranormal boomed. So many titles were published—some good, some bad, some in-between; some derivative, some highly original—it became impossible for even the most devoted fan to keep up with it all, especially since it takes multiple volumes for the whole story to be told.

That's one disadvantage of uf/p: It tends to be written best in novel form—in multiple sequential volumes at that! You simply don't find many high-caliber short stories that completely fit the model. I'm not even sure all the fine stories selected for the pertinent section of this anthology can be assigned to this subgenre.

What I think you will find, however, is that all of the fiction collected here has something in common: An intersection of "the other"—the magical, the strange, the weird, the wondrous, the dark that illumines, the revelation of the hidden—with the mundane, the world we know.

Our world is in perpetual need of this otherness. It entertains and, at its best, enlightens. We need both.

Companions to the Moon
Charles de Lint

"I think Edric's cheating on me."

Gwen's eyes widen, then fill with sympathy.

We're sitting across from each other at a small table in the Half Kaffe Café. It's a regular haunt of ours—as Bohemian as Gwen can tolerate, and about as uptown as I'll go. They make an excellent cup of regular coffee, but they also serve the fancy chi-chi drinks that she likes. Decaf soy lattes. Chai teas.

"Oh, Mary," she says. "That's awful."

I've known Gwen forever. We were best friends from kindergarten all the way through to our final year of high school when I made a sharp turn into garage rock-slash-punkdom, while Gwen suddenly became this responsible young woman aiming for university whom I couldn't recognize anymore. It felt like it happened overnight. One moment we were doing everything together— Girl Guides, piano lessons, messing about in the woods behind her house— the next we were strangers.

But while we drifted apart—I couldn't care less about a house in the suburbs, or worry about finding a good job, and the last thing Gwen would do is listen to the Clash or come to a Stooges concert with me—we made an effort to stay friends. Once or twice a month we had lunch, or the occasional dinner, and caught up. Sometimes we even brought our husbands.

Okay, Edric and I aren't married. But seven years together is almost as good as, don't you think?

"How did you find out?" she asks.

"Well, I haven't, exactly. It's just this feeling I get."

Gwen nods wisely. She starts to tick off points on her fingers. "Doesn't seem as interested in you anymore. Hang-ups when you pick up the phone. Has to work late a lot more often than he used to."

"None of the above. You forget, he's always out late."

"Duh," she says and slaps her brow with the palm of her hand. "Working musician."

"Anyway, I can't quite put my finger on it. We just don't seem to do as much together. I mean, we used to do the shopping as a couple. Yard work, household chores. Now, he's says that if I'm getting groceries, it's more efficient if he puts in a laundry, or does some weeding in the garden. I *liked* that we did that kind of thing together, but now we hardly do."

"So tell him."

"I have. It doesn't help."

"And is he taking more out-of-town gigs than he used to?"

I shake my head. "No, but that's a funny thing. I was looking at the calendar the other day and noticed that most of his out-of-town gigs are during a full moon. Then I checked the website his booking agent put up for him, and he's *always* out of town during the full moon."

Gwen smiles. "Maybe he's a werewolf."

"That's not helping."

"I'm sorry," she says. "But there's always been something different about him."

Different? I suppose. There's certainly always been a part of him that I can't reach—that I feel I'll never know—but that touch of mysteriousness is half of what attracted me to him in the first place. And I've never been the kind of person who believes in changing the person I'm with. You fall in love with them because of who they are. Unless they acquire some new, destructive habit, why would you want to change them?

"Just remember," Gwen says. "*You're* not defined by your relationship to him."

"I *know* that."

"And besides, you're not even married."

That's so Gwen. For her, a piece of paper always has more weight than the knowledge we acquire beyond school or university, or the depth of the feelings people carry around in their hearts.

For me, the feeling is everything.

We fall silent for a few moments. I drink some of my coffee and consider getting one of the café's fancy scones. Gwen has a sip of latte and I know she's not even tempted by the treats behind glass at the counter. She's looking out the window. It's a beautiful autumn day out there, but that's not what has her attention.

I'm not sure if she's fascinated or repulsed by the parade of people with their tats and piercings and individual fashion sense. Probably a little of both. She so doesn't fit into the scene down here in Crowsea, but I feel right at home.

"You know," she says, "whenever I hear about something like this, a big change that comes out of nowhere, I..."

She gets this look that I'm beginning to recognize. This has come up before. Her gaze turns to meet mine.

"What happened that last year of high school?" she asks. "I thought we'd be friends forever."

"We're still friends," I say, my voice mild.

She nods. "But you know what I mean. You just changed overnight."

"I didn't change. I evolved. If anyone changed, it was you."

"I didn't..."

"Besides," I say before she can go on. "Change doesn't automatically mean bad. Sometimes we need to change, to become who we really are."

"And who are you, really, Mary?"

This is new. I'm about to brush off her question with a joke, but I think about what's happened to me, my suspicions about Edric, and the way it has me feeling stupid, spying on him, grasping for some, *any* kind of understanding.

"I don't know," I tell her.

I manage a CD shop over on Williamson, but I don't believe that people are defined by their jobs any more than they are by their relationships. Both can tell you something about a person, but they're only pieces of the big puzzle. And that's what I am to myself right now. A big puzzle.

"This is going to sound awful," she says, "and I'm totally sympathetic to your situation, but I have to admit that there's a little piece of me that feels relieved that you can be going through all of this."

"What is *that* supposed to mean?"

"It's just...well, I found out that Bill's been going to this website called SuicideGirls. You know, it's one of those pay porn sites where girls pose naked. Girls who, you know..."

"Are all tattooed and pierced like me."

She nods. "Everywhere you turn, *that's* the cool thing. Actors, musicians, *porn* stars for god's sake. *They're* all cool. It's like you're a Neanderthal if you don't have a half-dozen tattoos and something stuck in your tongue, or dangling from a place that was never meant to dangle anything."

"In your opinion."

"In my opinion, yes. All of you are the people who are sexy and cool while the rest of us are just, I don't know, drones or something."

"I don't think you're a drone," I tell her. "And I don't think that there's anything innately cool about tats or piercings. They're either something you use to express yourself, or they're not."

"That's not what the media seems to be telling us these days."

I smile. "Except mostly what I see in the media are skinny women with big boobs and blonde hair. They're not exactly Goths, or punks."

"No, but they make it out like there's this whole exotic underground that ordinary people can't be a part of."

"Do you *want* to be a part of it?"

"That's not the point. They're selling it as the new cool. I mean, Angelina Jolie's already way more beautiful than any of us could ever hope to be. Do they really need to add in tattoos when they hype her?"

"So don't listen to them."

We fall silent for a moment.

"I'm sorry," she says. "I shouldn't have said anything like that."

I can't help but smile. I know I should be a little pissed off, but this is Gwen. She's so square that they check rulers against her to make sure they're straight.

"But you can't help but feel relieved to find out that 'cool' people—" I mark quotations in the air between us. "—have their problems, too."

"I know. I'm an awful friend, aren't I?"

I shake my head. "No, you're just being honest. We've earned the right to that between us." I wait a beat, then add, "So you think Bill's cheating on you, too. Maybe with some little tattooed Goth girl?"

"Oh, God, no. I just find it weird that that kind of thing could turn him on."

"Did you ask him about it?"

She shook her head. "In a vague sort of way. But he thought I was accusing him of lusting after you."

"And you didn't correct him?"

"No. Because then he'd know I was poking through his browser history. Oh, come on," she adds at the look on my face. "Everybody does that. Don't tell me you never have."

"I never have," I say. "And even if Edric wasn't a complete Luddite and actually used our computer, I still wouldn't."

"He doesn't use a computer?"

"He doesn't like any kind of modern technology. I got him a cell phone, but while he carries it around, he doesn't even have it turned on. When I asked him why he kept it, he said he thought of it as a talisman to remind him of me."

"That's...different."

"No, that's just Edric."

"So what are you going to do about him?"

I shrug. "What else can I do? The next full moon, I should follow him to whatever gig he's supposed to have."

"Or you could just ask him," Gwen says.

"Right."

"You seem to think I should have done that with Bill."

"This is different."

"How's it different?"

I nod slowly. "I guess, it's not really, is it? It's just women being insecure and doesn't it suck that with all these strides we're supposed to have made, we still come around to this: letting our confidence be undermined by our relationships. God, it's like high school all over again."

"Except you've already got the tattoos and piercings this time," she says.

"Ha ha."

But she's right.

"Have you been cheating on me?" I ask Edric.

Here's the thing when people have something to hide. Usually, they don't answer you right away. Instead, they come back with a question, like "Why would you think that?" Or maybe they just say, "I can't believe you think that." They beat around the bush until you make them answer you, yes or no, simple as that.

Edric looks at me with what appears to be genuine surprise.

"No," he says.

We've just finished dinner. He doesn't have a gig tonight. We have the whole evening, so what better way to spend this time together than accusing my partner of being unfaithful?

"It's just...things feel different between us," I say when he doesn't fill the silence.

But that awkward bit of conversation never happens.

I agree with Gwen. It's what I should do, but while Edric and I do have the evening free, he spends it practicing his guitar, while I stay busy scanning pictures of musicians from British music magazines, and then making buttons out of the print-outs that I can sell in the store.

It's Tuesday night. This Wednesday's a full moon. And of course Edric's got an out-of-town gig. So I'm going to do the stupid, senseless thing. I'm going to follow him to the gig and see what, if anything, is going on. I've already got one of my part-timers coming in so that I can have the two days off.

I know, I know. He could be doing the dirty deed while I'm at the store during the day, but I don't think so. I'd know if he was having somebody in the apartment besides his music buddies, and there are none of the usual signs when he comes back from being out. It's only these nights of the full moon. Now that I'm paying attention, I can sense some tension in him as the time approaches, and he's...I don't know. Relieved when he comes back.

You could put it down to gig nerves, but the one place he's entirely at home is on stage with his guitar in his hand.

Wednesday morning I leave the apartment the same time I always do, but instead of walking to the store, I take El Sub to my friend Karen's place in Upper Foxville. She's lending me her car. And a blonde wig to hide my black hair.

"You're sure you don't want me to come with?" she asks. "Because these things never turn out well."

"No, I'm good. And really, how bad can it be?"

"If you find out he *is* cheating on you? Really bad." She pauses to give me a considering look. "Unless you don't care anymore."

"Oh, I care."

"Then maybe you should have some company."

"No," I repeat. "This is going to turn out to be all in my own head."

Karen sighs, but she lets it go.

Thirty minutes later I'm parking behind the store. I'm working the morning since I know Edric won't be leaving until around three or so. His gig's in Sweetwater tonight, which isn't that far out of town. He'll want to miss the rush hour traffic, but it's not like he has a whole day of driving ahead of him.

"I sure hope your uncle's going to be okay," Cassidy says when I come in the back door.

See, that's what this has done to me. Not only am I going all weird about Edric, I'm lying to people about it. Cassidy thinks I'm going to take care of a sick uncle for a couple of days.

I nod. "It's only until my cousin gets back. I'm just going to make sure everything's okay at the house—get him some groceries, that kind of thing."

I leave the lie hanging between us in the back room and go out into the front to make sure everything's okay. I check that there's plenty of stock on this week's sale items, ask Laura if we need change and if she'll put up the buttons I made last night, then I go into my office to get yesterday's deposit ready for the bank.

The day drags the way it only can when you're waiting on something, but finally it's time for me to get going. I don't put on the wig until I'm in the car, adjusting it in the rearview mirror, then I ease out into the traffic and head for home.

Or rather, a half block away from home where I can see our car parked in front of the apartment building. My timing's pretty good, because by the time I get parked myself, I see Edric coming out of the building. He loads his guitar and gear, then pulls out.

And right away my fears seem to be confirmed. Instead of taking any of the eastbound streets, which is what he'll need to do to get to Sweetwater, he works his way over to Williamson Street and then heads north. I stay a few cars back as I follow him out of town and onto the highway.

This so sucks.

I want to turn around and return Karen's car to her, go back to the store and just forget about all of this. But it's way too late for that. Now I *have* to know where he's going, what he's up to. *Who* he's doing it with.

It's so pathetic. I should have just confronted him last night instead of going through all of this crap. Right now I should just pull him over to the side of the road and demand he level with me. But no, I feel trapped in this stupid plan I've put into motion and all I do is follow him.

We go up as far as an old deserted motel that sits on the inside of a curve of the highway. He signals and turns into its parking lot, steering around the clumps of weeds and broken asphalt. I drive by, stopping on the side of the road when the curve takes me out of sight. I yank off the wig, jump out of my own vehicle and run back through the woods and brush. By the time I can see the motel, the car's no longer there.

Hidden around back, I'm guessing.

This is gross. Couldn't he and his girlfriend at least get a room in a working motel?

I cut across the parking lot, then follow the wall of the building to the rear. There I see the car, its engine still pinging. I lift my gaze and spot Edric heading into the woods on the far side of a wide field behind the motel.

Now I don't know what to think. He can't have some girl stashed away in the forest, can he? So what's he *doing*? What could possibly bring him out here every full moon?

Gwen's stupid comment about werewolves comes to mind, but I dismiss it before it can even start to take hold. This isn't a story about boogiemen. Whatever sordid secret Edric's got hidden in these woods, it relates to this world, not the make-believe world of horror movies or fairy tales.

When Edric disappears in between the trees, I jog across the field, aiming for the big oak tree that marks the place where he vanished from my view. I slow down when I get near, trying to walk carefully, but I'm a city girl, not some Indian tracker. I know I'm making noise. I just hope it's not enough to give me away.

It's cooler under the trees, but surprisingly clear of brush. I button up my coat, and step under the oak's boughs. They're heavy with dead leaves, brown and golden. Beyond the oak, it's all tall pine trees and next to no underbrush. The forest floor is littered with their needles. I can see a fair distance through the trees, but it still takes me a few moments to find Edric. When I do, I duck behind the fat trunk of a big pine tree and mouth a silent curse when I lean against it and my hand comes away sticky with sap.

I peer around the trunk to see that Edric's stopped. He's about a hundred yards away, reaching into what I assume is a hollow of a tree trunk until I realize his hands are going right into the wood. That barely has time to register before he starts pulling something...no. Some*one* out of the trunk.

And then I realize that it's not just someone. It's himself. He's pulling a mirror image of himself out of the tree.

I try to make sense out of what I'm seeing, but it's no use. It can't make sense because it's impossible.

I can feel myself starting to shut down.

This isn't real. This can't be real.

I sink to my haunches and lean against the pine, not caring if I get sap on my clothes or hair. With bark rough against my face, I watch as Edric talks to his double.

There has to be a rational explanation for this, I think, as Edric's double takes the car keys from Edric's hand, then turns away to retrace Edric's path through the trees. I move around the tree so that I won't be in his line of sight as he comes by.

Okay. Figure this out.

Edric has a twin he hasn't told me about. That's possible—and the only probable explanation. And since people can't exist inside trees, Edric's twin must have been standing on the other side of the tree and it just *looked* as if he'd stepped out of it.

It doesn't explain why they're meeting here in the woods, but at least I no longer have to feel like I've gone off the deep end.

I peek around my tree and see that Edric's walking off, deeper into the woods. I look around the other side. His twin goes by, heading for the field. The resemblance is eerie. They're even wearing the exact same clothes. I start when a twig snaps under his feet.

I wait and watch until he steps into the field, then I force myself to my feet. I still feel a little shaky, but I can deal with all of this now. I give the twin a last glance, just to make sure he's really leaving, then set off in the direction Edric took.

When I think about what I've seen, I realize that the twins are switching places and I wonder what that means for this relationship I've had with Edric for the past seven years. Was it with him, with his twin brother, or some weird combination of the two?

It's not him cheating on me with another woman—at least not so far as I've seen yet—but the more I think about it, the angrier I get.

I should just leave. I should go home and pack up his crap and leave it waiting for him or his twin out on the curb. Because there's something particularly twisted about how all of this is playing out.

I slow down when I see that Edric has stopped up ahead. He's standing in a small clearing. To get to that clearing myself, I have to leave the quiet carpet of pine needles for the underbrush that's growing up on the edges of the meadow. I look left and right, then spy a ridge of granite that rises steadily on the north side. It could give me a view of the meadow. It just depends how much foliage there is in the way.

It's starting to get dark now, so I hurry over to the ridge and clamber up the rock. It's steeper than I thought, but I find plenty of hand- and toe-holds and soon I'm jogging along the top of the ridge, my running shoes quiet on the granite.

I keep an eye on the meadow as I go. Edric's still just standing there. Waiting for something, I guess. Probably for some bush girl who lives out here where sensible people don't even visit, never mind live.

Finally, I reach the part of the ridge that's closest to the meadow. There are pine boughs in the way, but I find places where I can peer through them and get a good line of view. Behind Edric is another of the massive oaks that seem to be scattered through this mostly evergreen wood. I'm close enough that I could call out to him and he'd hear me.

The dusk is steadily falling. I can still make Edric out. He's wearing a pale tan fleece and the light from the moon picks it out. Around me, the forest falls deeper and deeper into shadows.

I'm not sure when I start to hear the music—fiddles and drums and bells playing a soft marching rhythm. I just know I've been hearing it for a few moments before I see lights approaching on the far side of the meadow. And then...

I have to shake my head.

It figures. Who else would Edric be meeting out here but some back-to-the-earth Renaissance Fayre types. These ones are riding horses and they're all decked out in fancy gowns and robes. Edric's played the Fayres for years—he took me there on one of our first dates and didn't I fit in, all in black with my tats and my hair cut short and spiked. I'd laughed when Edric put on the hose, doublet and all to play the wandering minstrel, but had to admit he had the build that could pull it off.

They all took it so seriously. Apparently, a lot of them were part of something called the Society for Creative Anachronism and they had this whole role-playing thing set up where they dressed like medieval lords and ladies and had feasts and jousts and, of course, the Fayres.

I ended up liking a lot of them—once we got over our mutual culture shock. But today? Not so much. Between finding out Edric's got a twin who's apparently been sharing his conjugal rights, traipsing around in the autumn woods, which is not my idea of fun, and now this, I'm not feeling particularly charitable toward them.

I figure the looker on the front horse is the woman he's here to see. She's wearing the usual SCA low-cut bodice, a blue-green cape flowing over her mount's withers. She has a crown—naturally—and her hair is a dark waterfall that goes all the way to the small of her back in a curtain of ringlets. The rest of them are acting like they are her court—like she's the queen her crown says she is. I start to look for a safe way down to confront them when it occurs to me that none of the riders are carrying the lights. The lanterns are bobbing in the air, floating above the little entourage. And then I see...then I see...

Children, I tell myself. They're just children.

Except some of them have wings and they're no bigger than cats. They're flying—*flying!*—above the riders, carrying their lanterns and...and...

My knees feel weak. I sit down on the stone under my feet before my legs give way.

I try to convince myself that I'm not seeing what my eyes are telling me I am. They're doing it all with wires. Mirrors. It's just a trick. That's all.

Just.

A.

Trick.

The music falls silent when the lead rider stops her horse directly in front of Edric. She says something to him. I can hear her voice—high and musical—but I can't make out what she's saying. It's in some language I've never heard before.

Then they both look in my direction.

Oh crap.

They don't know I'm here. They *can't* know I'm here.

But then a pair of those flying cat-sized people come zipping from the meadow and my pulse goes into overdrive. I want to bolt, but I can't even get to my feet. The pair dart between the boughs of the spruce, holding their lanterns, until they're circling above me. I'm blinded by the light and hold my arm up to cover my eyes. They make a last circle above me—so close the hummingbird motion of their wings has my hair lifting and fluttering and I can smell the sweet oil from their lanterns—then they're gone again. I see stars until my eyes adjust to the darkness.

My heartbeat is still drumming in my chest when I hear the woman speak once more—this time in English.

"You know what happens now," she says.

I see Edric nod. His shoulders are drooped.

He knows, and I can guess. They're going to do something to me—I don't know what. Wipe my mind of the memory of seeing them, maybe. Banish me into some weird Fairyland prison.

Or they could just kill me.

I sit straighter and stare at them, waiting for I don't know what. My sentence to be pronounced, I suppose. But I won't go without a fight.

I look around and reach for a branch that's lying on the stone nearby. I make myself get up—*will* the shaking in my legs to stop. When I'm sure I have my balance, I break the branch against my knee. That gives me two small clubs with which to defend myself.

The snap is loud in the night. Edric and the fairy court turn in my direction. I can see the queen frowning from where I stand, but then she lifts her arm. I stiffen and try to psyche myself for the attack I'm sure she's about to command. But when she brings her hand down, the whole fairy court simply vanishes and the woods are plunged into night.

It takes my eyes a long moment to adjust to the darkness again. When they do, I can't see Edric anymore. I have the sudden thought that I've just dreamed the whole thing. Any moment I'll wake up—back home, in my own bed—and everything will be back to normal. But then I hear a scuffling on the rock below. I step closer to the edge and see Edric working his way up a switchback to the top of the ridge.

There are only three turns—the ridge is no more than twenty-or-so feet high. I step back from the edge when he comes into view, my clubs held out in front of me. The light's poor, even with the bright moonshine coming down through the trees, but I know he sees me. Sees what I'm holding.

"Mary," he says.

I glare at him.

"So, what did she tell you to do?" I demand. "Are you supposed to try to kill me?"

He shakes his head. I can't read his features.

"Nothing like that," he says.

"Yeah, right."

Neither of us say anything for a long moment.

"Why couldn't you just leave well enough alone?" he finally asks.

"Why did you have to have secrets?"

"I was under a geas," he says. "Do you know what that means?"

I nod. "Some kind of old promise or something."

"I wasn't allowed to tell you. I wasn't allowed to tell anyone. It was like...like a fairy tale, you know? Like Bluebeard's room."

"Oh, that's a great example," I say, "considering he turned out to be some kind of serial killer freak. And if we're going to use folklore as an ethical barometer, what about all those sailor boys who are gone seven years, but then come back and try to trick their loyal girlfriends with some sleazy pick-up shtick?"

"Okay, you're right. What I mean is—"

"Who *are* you?"

"We're of the sidhe."

"She who? What's that supposed to mean? Are you talking about that woman on the horse?"

He shakes his head. "Sidhe," he repeats and spells it out for me. "They're one of the elfin races."

"Elfin."

"As in pixies, fairies..."

"And you're one of them?"

He nods.

"I guess this is a whole new twist on having your boyfriend come out of the closet to tell you he's a fairy." I think about it for a moment, then add, "Is this why you never wanted to have kids?"

He nods again.

"*Could* we even have had kids?"

"Yes, but our children would be half-breeds."

"Jesus, would you listen to yourself."

He winces. "I'm sorry. I'm not saying I agree. But that's what my people would call him. The Court—for the most part—is against mixed-marriages, and *especially* the children that result."

"Why would they even have to know?" I say. "And we wouldn't have had to tell anyone—not even our little girl. No one would have to know except for us."

"Because our child...she would be different. She would be able to do things that we would have to teach her to control."

I'd noticed that we both had our own ideas about the gender of this child we'll never have. Apparently Edric did, too. But his attempt to soothe me by coming over to my side just pisses me off. Everything about this pisses me off. I know I should be trying to see some way past this, some way we can work things out. We've been together for so long. We were happy for so long. But there's this huge lie rearing up between us now. And that twin of his, taking his place who knows how many times when I thought it was him?

I can't stop the fury, burning up all the love and good memories. Knowing what I now know, I'm not sure I even want to.

"And I suppose this fairy queen's your little bit on the side?" I ask.

"God, no. She's my sister."

"Your sister. And I guess that was your brother you pulled out of the tree earlier?"

He shakes his head. "That was a kind of changeling—made to take my place in the world while I conducted my business here."

"And did that business include him banging me when you were too busy to do it yourself?"

"No, no."

"So what *kind* of business?"

"Court business. I'm a prince of the Court. No matter how much I'm not interested in it, I have responsibilities I can't shirk. So we made an agreement— my parents and I. I could live in the world of men so long as I came back once a lunar cycle to fulfill my obligations to the Court." He pauses for a moment, then adds, "And so long as no one discovered the truth."

"Do you know how stupid that sounds?"

"Why? Because it doesn't fit in with your concept of living life as a free spirit, the establishment be damned?"

I don't have an answer for that.

"I have to go now," he says.

"Of course you do."

"I didn't want it to work out this way."

"Of course you didn't—but here we are, all the same."

"I..." He stops. When he goes on, I know this isn't what he started to say. "The changeling...he gets to have my life now. I'm not going to tell you what to do or not to do, but I don't recommend you see him. He's not human and he can be dangerous."

"Except, apparently, you're not human either."

"No, but—"

"Oh, don't worry. I don't want anything more to do with either you or your doppelganger."

"Changeling."

"Whatever."

He sighs. "*Why* did you have to follow me?" he asks.

I have to laugh. "I thought you were having an affair."

"If you'd trusted me—"

"What? We could have happily lived a lie for a while longer?"

"It wasn't like that for me."

I shake my head. "You knew everything about me, but it turns out I didn't know the first thing about you. Was everything you told me a lie?"

"No, I just didn't give you all the specific details."

"Like what?"

He shrugs. "We don't have a cottage—we have a lakeside palace. I didn't go to a one-room country school, but we did have a small class with a private tutor."

"Kind of a big difference."

"I truly do love you."

"Yeah, well, I saw *The Little Mermaid*. You could have given up all the magic and stuff to be with me."

"I would have—but that isn't an option for royalty."

"Right. Prince Edric."

"Don't make this harder than it needs to be," he says.

I shake my head. "No, I have the right to make this as hard on you as I want."

He nods. "I suppose you do."

I don't want it to be like this. Moments ago I was so angry—I'm *still* angry—but we had so much love between us. We gave each other seven years of our lives. You don't just walk away from something like that without trying to fix it.

I take a breath to steady myself.

"There's got to be a way around this," I say.

"There isn't. If there was *any* way I could fix it, I would."

"So you're just going to walk away from me—from what we have. Had."

"If I don't, they'll hurt you. I won't let that happen."

"We'll go to the police..." I start to say, then realize how stupid that has to sound.

"And tell them what?" he asks. "They could hide us away, but the Court would find us. There's no place we could go that they wouldn't find us."

"And they would really hurt us—like kill us or something?"

He studies me for a long moment, then nods.

"I should go," he says.

I feel empty. And the only thing I can find to fill that emptiness is anger.

"Yeah," I tell him, my voice sharp. "They'll all be waiting on you."

"Mary, I—"

I put up my hand to stop him. It's still holding my makeshift club, so I throw it and its partner away.

"Don't," I tell him. "Don't say anything else."

He nods. He gives me another long look, then he steps to one side, and just like the fairy Court, he vanishes.

I've managed to hold back my tears, but now that he's gone, I go down on my knees on the top of that granite ridge and let them come.

It takes me a while to get back to where I left Karen's car. I get turned around a few times, but I finally find the big field and from there on it's pretty easy. I half-expected to find a ticket on the car, or that it had been towed away by the highway patrol, but it's right where it's supposed to be.

I have another crying jag, once I'm behind the wheel. It's a long time before I can wipe my face on my sleeve and start up the engine.

I feel wrung out. Empty. Sadder than anyone has a right to feel.

And then the anger comes back.

I know Edric was right. I shouldn't have anything to do with his changeling twin. But when I turn the car around, I don't head south, back into the city. Instead, I cut east, aiming the car for The Custom House in the little town of Sweetwater. That's the bar where Edric was supposed to be playing tonight. Where his changeling twin is playing.

I have a moment of disassociation when I step through the front door of the bar and see him on stage. Because I can't tell it's not him—Edric, I mean. He looks exactly the same. He plays exactly the same. It's not until the end of the set when I go up to the side of the stage as he's retuning his guitar that I see the difference.

Actually, there is no difference—at least nothing you can measure. It's in the way he looks at me. In the tone of his voice.

"You," he says.

I have to clear my throat, but when I do manage to speak, my voice is steady.

"Yeah, me," I say.

"What are you doing here?"

"I just had to see for myself."

He scowls at me.

"I'm the one who's real now," he says. "This is my life now."

I shrug.

"I'm grateful for the part you played in my getting it, but—"

"I'm not here for your thanks."

"—this ends here. We're not taking up together or anything."

I pull a face. "Like I'd want to."

"I'll just come get my stuff tomorrow, and that'll be it."

"You don't have any stuff," I tell him, "so don't bother."

His eyes narrow. "Well, then you don't have a car anymore."

"Fine. If you want the cops to pull you in for car theft, don't bring it back."

"Then I'll get a warrant to get my stuff back."

"I told you. You don't have any stuff. But Edric's crap is going to be sitting on the curb just as soon as I get home from here."

"*I'm* Edric now."

I shake my head. "No, you're not. You're just some pathetic little changeling that he grew out of a tree."

He takes an angry step towards me.

"Temper temper," I say. "You don't want the good people who came here buying into your peaceful guitar groove to find out you're really just a nasty little creep, do you?"

He glares, but he stays where he was and I leave the bar.

Well, that went well, I think as I get into the car. Venting like that was just so mature, wasn't it?

But it felt good.

I have another long cry before I start up the car and head home to put Edric's belongings on the curb.

"You know," Gwen says when we're sitting in the Half Kaffe Café the next day, "I didn't really mean that I was happy you were having problems."

"Yeah, I know."

I had Karen commiserating with me when I brought her car back earlier this morning. Mine was parked where it was supposed to be, on the street, with my resident's parking pass displayed on the dashboard. Edric's stuff was all gone—but whether the changeling got it, or street people, I don't know. Or care.

Now I've got Gwen figuratively holding my hand.

"So he really was having an affair," she says.

I didn't say anything to either her or Karen about changelings and fairy courts and the fairy tale geas that pushed Edric and I apart. I simply told them there'd been another woman—which wasn't entirely a lie. He just wasn't sleeping with her.

"He has this whole other life," I tell her. "It's been going on from before we even met and he won't—he says can't—give it up. So what am I supposed to do?"

"That sucks," she says, then she cocks her head. "And there you were, wanting me to ask Bill about his fixation with the SuicideGirls."

"I wouldn't bother," I say. "Not unless he starts listening to Goth music and starts talking about getting a tattoo or a piercing."

"As if." Then Gwen sighed and added, "You really just put all Edric's stuff out on the curb?"

"I wasn't going to keep it—and I didn't want to see him again."

Only it would be the changeling coming by, not Edric, and there's no way I can explain that without sounding completely mental.

"I'm still surprised you didn't want to try to work things out," Gwen says. "I mean, you of all people..."

"I agree there are relationships you can work on, but for ours to stay good, either he or I would have had to have a complete makeover—and you know how I feel about that kind of thing."

Gwen shakes her head. "I still don't get it. When we started going our separate ways back in high school, you didn't give up on us."

"That's because, for all our differences, we were actually willing to work on our friendship. You *and* me. It takes two."

"I guess. But you and Edric were together for *seven* years."

"During which time, he had a secret life that he kept hidden from me. And he won't give it up, so what can I do?"

"I hate this," Gwen says.

She reaches across the table and gives my hand a squeeze. The rest of our conversation goes on much the way the one with Karen did, me saying I was okay, really, her being supportive and telling me if there was anything I needed, all I had to do was ask.

There's something I need, but she can't give it to me.

I need to turn back the clock, maybe.

Or I need to be a fairy girl myself—or at least someone who trusts her partner, without questions.

But I'm just not built that way.

I realize just how true that is when Gwen asks me, "If you could take it all back, would you?"

"Before or after the suspicions?"

"After, I guess. Before you had them, there wasn't a decision to be made, was there?"

"I guess not."

The problem is, she doesn't know the whole truth, the fairy tale puzzle lying underneath the mess that has become my life. I can't tell her or anybody without someone suggesting that I should check myself into the Zeb for a psychological evaluation. Maybe I should anyway, but I'm not going to.

"So would you?" she asks.

I shake my head. "You know me. I can never let something just lie. I have to worry at it until I understand."

The look in her eyes tells me she gets it.

"But that doesn't mean it hurts any less now," she says.

I think of the big ache that fills my whole chest and give her a slow nod.

"No," I agree. "It doesn't make it hurt any less."

A Haunted House of Her Own
Kelley Armstrong

Tanya couldn't understand why realtors failed to recognize the commercial potential of haunted houses. This one, it seemed, was no different.

"Now, these railings need work," the woman said as she led Tanya and Nathan out onto one of the balconies. "But the floor is structurally sound, and that's the main thing. I'm sure these would be an attractive selling point to your bed-and-breakfast guests."

Not as attractive as ghosts.

"You're sure the house doesn't have a history?" Tanya prodded again. "I thought I heard something in town...."

She hadn't, but the way the realtor stiffened told Tanya that she was onto something. After pointed reminders about disclosing the house's full history, the woman admitted there was, indeed, something. Apparently a kid had murdered his family here, back in the seventies.

"A tragedy, but it's long past," the realtor assured her. "Never a spot of trouble since."

"Damn," Tanya murmured under her breath, and followed the realtor back inside.

Nathan wanted to check out the coach house, to see if there was any chance of converting it into a separate "honeymoon hideaway."

Tanya was thrilled to see him taking an interest. Opening the inn had been her idea. An unexpected windfall from a great-aunt had come right after she'd lost her teaching job and Nathan's office-manager position teetered under end-of-year budget cuts. It seemed like the perfect time to try something new.

"You two go on ahead," she said. "I'll poke around in here, maybe check out the gardens."

"Did I see a greenhouse out back?" Nathan asked the realtor.

She beamed. "You most certainly did."

"Why don't you go take a look, hon? You were talking about growing organic vegetables."

"Oh, what a wonderful idea," the realtor said. "That is so popular right now. Organic local produce is all the rage. There's a shop in town that supplies all the..."

As the woman gushed, Tanya backed away slowly, then escaped.

The house was perfect—a six-bedroom, rambling Victorian perched on a hill three miles from a suitably quaint village. What more could she want in a bed-and-breakfast? Well, ghosts. Not that Tanya believed in such things, but haunted inns in Vermont were all the rage, and she was determined to own one.

When she saw the octagonal Victorian greenhouse, though, she decided that if it turned out there'd never been so much as a ghostly candle spotted on the property, she'd light one herself. She had to have this place.

She stepped inside and pictured it with lounge chairs, a bookshelf, maybe a little woodstove for winter. Not a greenhouse, but a sunroom. First, though, they'd need to do some serious weeding. The greenhouse *conservatory*, she amended—sat in a nest of thorny vines dotted with red. Raspberries? She cleaned a peephole in the grime and peered out.

A head popped up from the thicket. Tanya fell back with a yelp. Sunken brown eyes widened, and wizened lips parted in a matching shriek of surprise.

Tanya hurried out as the old woman made her way from the thicket, a basket of red berries in one hand.

"I'm sorry, dear," she said. "We gave each other quite a fright."

Tanya motioned at the basket. "Late for raspberries, isn't it?"

The old woman smiled. "They're double-blooming. At least there's one good thing to come out of this place." She looked over at the house. "You aren't... looking to buy, are you?"

"I might be."

The woman's free hand gripped Tanya's arm. "No, dear. You don't want to do that."

"I hear there's some history."

"History?" The old woman shivered. "Horrors. Blasphemies. Murders. Foul murders. No, dear, you don't want this house, not at all."

Foul murders? Tanya tried not to laugh. If they ever did a promotional video, she was hiring this woman.

"Whatever happened was a tragedy," Tanya said. "But it's long past, and it's time—"

"Long past? Never. At night, I still hear the moans. The screams. The chanting. The chanting is the worst, as if they're trying to call up the devil himself."

"I see." Tanya squinted out at the late-day sun, dropping beneath the horizon. "Do you live around here, then?"

"Just over there."

The woman pointed, then shuffled around the conservatory; still pointing. When she didn't come back, Tanya followed, wanting to make note of her name. But the yard was empty.

Tanya poked around a bit after that, but the sun dropped fast over the mountain ridge. As she picked her way through the brambles, she looked up at the house looming in the twilight—a hulking shadow against the night, the lights inside seeming to flicker like candles behind the old glass.

The wind sighed past and she swore she heard voices in it, sibilant whispers snaking around her. A shadow moved across an upper window. She'd blame a drape caught in a draft...only she couldn't see any window coverings.

She smiled as she shivered. For someone who didn't believe in ghosts, she was quite caught up in the fantasy. Imagine how guests who did believe would react.

She found Nathan still in the coach house, measuring tape extended. When she walked up, he grinned, his boyish face lighting up.

"It's perfect," he said. "Ten grand and we'd have ourselves a honeymoon suite."

Tanya turned to the realtor. "How soon can we close?"

The owners were as anxious to sell as Tanya was to buy, and three weeks later, they were in the house, with the hired contractors hard at work. Tanya and Nathan were working, too, researching the house's background, both history and legend.

The first part was giving them trouble. The only online mention Nathan found was a secondary reference. But it proved that a family had died in their house, so that morning he'd gone to the library in nearby Beamsville, hoping a search there would produce details.

Meanwhile, Tanya would try to dig up the less-tangible ghosts of the past.

She started in the gardening shop, and made the mistake of mentioning the house's history. The girl at the counter shut right down, murmuring, "We don't talk about that," then bustled off to help the next customer. That was fine. If the town didn't like to talk about the tragedy, she was free to tweak the facts and her guests would never hear anything different.

Next, she headed for the general store, complete with rocking chairs on the front porch and a tub of salty pickles beside the counter. She bought supplies, then struck up a conversation with the owner. She mentioned that she'd bought the Sullivan place, and worked the conversation around to, "Someone over in Beamsville told me the house is supposed to be haunted."

"Can't say I ever heard that," he said, filling her bag. "This is a nice, quiet town."

"Oh, that's too bad." She laughed. "Not the quiet part but..." She lowered her voice. "You wouldn't believe the advertising value of ghosts."

His wife poked her head in from the back room. "She's right, Tom. Folks pay extra to stay in those places. I saw it on TV."

"A full house for me means more customers for you," Tanya said.

"Well, now that you mention it, when my boys were young, they said they saw lights..."

And so it went. People might not want to talk about the true horrors of what had happened at the Sullivan place, but with a little prodding they spun tales of imagined ones. Most were secondhand accounts, but Tanya didn't even care if they were true. Someone in town said it, and that was all that mattered. By the time she headed home, her notebook was filled with stories.

She was at the bottom of the road when she saw the postwoman putting along in her little car, driving from the passenger seat so she could stuff the mailboxes. Tanya got out to introduce herself. As they chatted, Tanya mentioned the raspberry-picking neighbor, hoping to get a name.

"No old ladies around here," the postwoman said. "You've got Mr. McNally to the north. The Lee gang to the south. And to the back, it's a couple of new women. Don't recall the names—it isn't my route—but they're young."

"Maybe a little farther? She didn't exactly say she was a neighbor. Just pointed over there."

The woman followed her finger. "That's the Lee place."

"Past that, then."

"Past that?" The woman eyed her. "Only thing past that is the cemetery."

Tanya made mental notes as she pulled into the darkening drive. She'd have to send Nathan to the clerk's office, see if he could find a dead resident who resembled a description of the woman she'd seen.

Not that she thought she'd seen a ghost, of course. The woman probably lived farther down the hill. But if she found a similar deceased neighbor, she could add her own spooky tale to the collection.

She stepped out of the car. When a whisper snaked around her, she jumped. Then she stood there, holding the car door, peering into the night and listening. It definitely sounded like whispering. She could even pick up a word or two, like come and join. Well, at least the ghosts weren't telling her to get lost, she thought, her laugh strained and harsh against the quiet night.

The whispers stopped. She glanced up at the trees. The dead leaves were still. No wind. Which explained why the sound had stopped. As she headed for the house, she glanced over her shoulder, checking for Nathan's SUV. It was there, but the house was pitch black.

She opened the door. It creaked. Naturally. No oil for that baby, she thought with a smile. No fixing the loose boards on the steps, either. Someone was bound to hear another guest sneaking down for a midnight snack and blame ghosts. More stories to add to the guest book.

She tossed her keys onto the table. They hit with a jangle, the sound echoing through the silent hall. When she turned on the light switch, the hall stayed dark. She tried not to shiver as she peered around. *That's quite enough ghost stories for you*, she told herself as she marched into the next room, heading for the lamp. She tripped over a throw rug and stopped.

"Nathan?"

No answer. She hoped he wasn't poking around in the basement. He'd been curious about some boxes down there, but she didn't want to get into that. There was too much else to be done.

She eased forward, feeling the way with her foot until she reached the lamp. When she hit the switch, light flooded the room. Not a power outage, then. Good; though it reminded her they had to pick up a generator. Blackouts would be a little more atmospheric than guests would appreciate.

"Nathan?"

She heard something in the back rooms. She walked through, hitting lights as she went—for safety, she told herself.

"Umm-hmm." Nathan's voice echoed down the hall. "Umm-hmm."

On the phone, she thought, too caught up in the call to realize how dark it had gotten and turn on a light. She hoped it wasn't the licensing board. The inspector had been out to assess the ongoing work yesterday. He'd seemed happy with it, but you never knew.

She let her shoes click a little harder as she walked over the hardwood floor, so she wouldn't startle Nathan. She followed his voice to the office. From the doorway, she could see his back in the desk chair.

"Umm-hmm."

Her gaze went to the phone on the desk. Still in the cradle. Nathan's hands were at his sides. He was sitting in the dark, looking straight ahead, at the wall.

Tanya rubbed down the hairs on her neck. He was using his cell phone earpiece, that was all. Guys and their gadgets. She stepped into the room and looked at his ear. No headset.

"Nathan?"

He jumped, wheeling so fast that the chair skidded across the floor. He caught it and gave a laugh, shaking his head sharply as he reached for the desk lamp.

"Must have dozed off. Not used to staring at a computer screen all day anymore."

He rubbed his eyes, and blinked up at her.

"Everything okay, hon?" he asked.

She said it was and gave him a rundown of what she'd found, and they had a good laugh at that, all the shopkeepers rushing in with their stories once they realized the tourism potential.

"Did you find anything?"

"I did indeed." He flourished a file folder stuffed with printouts. "The Rowe family. Nineteen seventy-eight. Parents, two children, and the housekeeper, all killed by the seventeen-year-old son."

"Under the influence of Satan?"

"Rock music. Close enough." Nathan grinned. "It was the seventies. Kid had long hair, played in a garage band, partial to Iron Maiden and Black Sabbath. Clearly a Satanist."

"Works for me."

Tanya took the folder just as the phone started to ring. The caller ID showed the inspector's name. She set the pages aside and answered as Nathan whispered that he'd start dinner.

There was a problem with the inspection—the guy had forgotten to check a few things, and he had to come back on the weekend, when they were supposed to be away scouring estate auctions and flea markets to furnish the house. The workmen would be there, but apparently that wasn't good enough. And on Monday, the inspector would leave for two weeks in California with the wife and kids.

Not surprisingly, Nathan offered to stay. Jumped at the chance, actually. His enthusiasm for the project didn't extend to bargain hunting for Victorian beds. He joked that he'd have enough work to do when she wanted her treasures refinished. So he'd stay home and supervise the workers, which was probably wise anyway.

It was an exhausting but fruitful weekend. Tanya crossed off all the necessities and even a few wish-list items, like a couple of old-fashioned washbasins.

When she called Nathan an hour before arriving home, he sounded exhausted and strained, and she hoped the workers hadn't given him too much trouble. Sometimes they were like her grade-five pupils, needing a watchful eye and firm, clear commands. Nathan wasn't good at either. When she pulled into the drive and found him waiting on the porch, she knew there was trouble.

She wasn't even out of the car before the workmen filed out, toolboxes in hand.

"We quit," the foreman said.

"What's wrong?" she asked.

"The house. Everything about it is wrong."

"Haunted," an older man behind him muttered.

The younger two shifted behind their elders, clearly uncomfortable with this old-man talk, but not denying it, either.

"All right," she said slowly. "What happened?"

They rhymed off a litany of haunted-house tropes—knocking inside the walls, footsteps in the attic, whispering voices, flickering lights, strains of music.

"Music?"

"Seventies rock music," Nathan said, rolling his eyes behind their backs. "Andy found those papers in my office, about the Rowe family.

"You should have warned us," the foreman said, scowling. "Working where something like that happened? It isn't right. The place should be burned to the ground."

"It's evil," the older man said. "Evil soaked right into the walls. You can feel it."

The only thing Tanya felt was the recurring sensation of being trapped in a B movie. Did people actually talk like this? First the old woman. Then the townspeople. Now the contractors.

They argued, of course, but the workmen were leaving. When Tanya started to threaten, Nathan pulled her aside. The work was almost done, he said. They could finish up themselves, save some money, and guilt these guys into cutting their bill even more.

Tanya hated to back down, but he had a point. She negotiated 20 percent off for the unfinished work and another 15 for the inconvenience—unless they wanted her spreading the word that grown men were afraid of ghosts. They grumbled, but agreed.

The human mind can be as impressionable as a child. Tanya might not believe in ghosts, but the more stories she heard, the more her mind began to believe, with or without her permission. Drafts became cold spots. Thumping pipes became the knocks of unseen hands. The hisses and sighs of the old furnace became the whispers and moans of those who could not rest. She knew better: that was the worst of it. She'd hear a pipe thump and she'd jump, heart pounding, even as she knew there was a logical explanation.

Nathan wasn't helping. Every time she jumped, he'd laugh. He'd goof off and play ghost, sneaking into the bathroom while she was in the shower and writing dirty messages in the condensation on the mirror. She was spooked; he thought it was adorable.

The joking and teasing she could take. It was the other times, the ones when she'd walk into a room and he'd be standing or sitting, staring into nothing, confused, when he'd start out of his reverie, laughing about daydreaming, but nervously, like he didn't exactly know what he'd been doing.

They were three weeks from opening when she returned from picking up the brochures and, once again, found the house in darkness. This time, the hall light worked—it'd been nothing more sinister than a burned-out bulb before. And this time she didn't call Nathan's name, but crept through the halls looking for him, feeling silly, and yet...

When she approached the kitchen, she heard a strange rasping sound. She followed it and found Nathan standing in the twilight, staring out the window, hands moving, a *skritch-skritch* filling the silence.

The fading light caught something in his hands—a flash of silver that became a knife, a huge butcher's knife moving back and forth across a whetting stone.

"N-Nathan?"

He jumped, nearly dropping the knife, then stared down at it, frowning. A sharp shake of his head and he laid the knife and stone on the counter, then flipped on the kitchen light.

"Really not something I should be doing in the dark, huh?" He laughed and moved a carrot from the counter to the cutting board, picked up the knife, then stopped. "Little big for the job, isn't it?"

She moved closer. "Where did it come from?"

"Hmm?" He followed her gaze to the unfamiliar knife. "Ours, isn't it? Part of the set your sister gave us for our anniversary? It was in the drawer." He grabbed a smaller knife from the wooden block. "So, how did the brochures turn out?"

Two nights later, Tanya was startled awake and bolted up, blinking hard, hearing music. She rubbed her ears, telling herself it was a dream, but she could definitely hear something. She turned to Nathan's side of the bed. Empty.

Okay, he couldn't sleep, so he'd gone downstairs. She could barely hear the music, so he was being considerate, keeping it low, probably doing paperwork in the office.

Even as she told herself this, though, she kept envisioning the knife. The big butcher's knife that seemed to have come from nowhere.

Nonsense. Her sister *had* given them a new set, and Nathan did most of the cooking, so it wasn't surprising that she hadn't recognized it. But as hard as she tried to convince herself, she just kept seeing Nathan standing in the twilight, sharpening that knife, the *skritch-skritch* getting louder, the blade getting sharper.

Damn her sister. And not for the knives, either. Last time they'd been up, her sister and boyfriend had insisted on picking the night's video. *The Shining*. New caretaker at inn is possessed by a murderous ghost and hacks up his wife. There was a reason Tanya didn't watch horror movies, and now she remembered why.

She turned on the bedside lamp, then pushed out of bed and flicked on the overhead light. The hall one went on, too. So did the one leading downstairs. Just being careful, of course. You never knew where a stray hammer or board could be lying around.

As she descended the stairs, the music got louder, the thump of the bass and the wail of the singer. Seventies' heavy-metal music. Hadn't the Rowe kid—? She squeezed her eyes shut and forced the thought out. Like she'd know seventies heavy metal from modern stuff anyway. And hadn't Nathan picked up that new AC/DC disk last month? *Before* they came to live here. He was probably listening to that, not realizing how loud it was.

When she got downstairs, though, she could feel the bass vibrating through the floorboards. Great. He couldn't sleep, so he was poking through those boxes in the basement.

Boxes belonging to the Rowe family. To the Rowe kid.

Oh, please. The Rowes had been gone for almost thirty years. Anything in the basement would belong to the Sullivans, a lovely old couple now living in Florida.

On the way to the basement, Tanya passed the kitchen. She stopped. She looked at the drawer where Nathan kept the knife, then walked over and opened it. Just taking a look, seeing if she remembered her sister giving it to them, not making sure it was still there. It was. And it still didn't look familiar.

She started to leave, then went back, took out the knife, wrapped it in a dishtowel, and stuck it under the sink. And, yes, she felt like an idiot. But she felt relief even more.

She slipped down to the basement, praying she wouldn't find Nathan sitting on the floor, staring into nothing, nodding to voices she couldn't hear. Again, she felt foolish for thinking it, and again she felt relief when she heard him digging through boxes, and more relief yet when she walked in and he looked up, grinning sheepishly like a kid caught sneaking into his Christmas presents.

"Caught me," he said. "Was it the music? I thought I had it low enough."

She followed his gaze and a chill ran through her. Across the room was a record player, an album spinning on the turntable, more stacked on the floor.

"Found it down here with the albums. Been a while since you've seen one of those, I bet."

"Was it...his? The Rowe boy?"

Nathan frowned, as if it hadn't occurred to him. "Could be, I guess. I didn't think of that."

He walked over and shut the player off. Tanya picked up an album. Initials had been scrawled in black marker in the corner. T. R. What was the Rowe boy's name? She didn't know and couldn't bring herself to ask Nathan, would rather believe he didn't know, either.

She glanced at him. "Are you okay?"

"Sure. I think I napped this afternoon, while you were out. Couldn't get to sleep."

"And otherwise...?"

He looked at her, trying to figure out what she meant, but what could she say? *Have you had the feeling of being not yourself lately? Hearing voices telling you to murder your family?*

She had to laugh at that. Yes, it was a ragged laugh, a little unsure of itself; but a laugh nonetheless. No more horror movies for her, however much her sister pleaded.

"Are you okay?" Nathan asked.

She nodded. "Just tired."

"I don't doubt it, the way you've been going. Come on. Let's get up to bed." He grinned. "See if I can't help us both get to sleep."

The next day, she was in the office, adding her first bookings to the ledger when she saw the folder pushed off to the side, the one Nathan had compiled on the Rowe murders. She'd set it down that day and never picked it up again. She could tell herself she'd simply forgotten, but she was never that careless. She hadn't read it because her newly traitorous imagination didn't need any more grist for its mill.

But now she thought of that album cover in the basement. Those initials. If it didn't belong to the Rowe boy, then this was an easy way to confirm that and set her mind at ease.

The first report was right there on top, the names listed, the family first, then the housekeeper, Madelyn Levy, and finally, the supposed killer, seventeen-year-old Timothy Rowe.

Tanya sucked in a deep breath, then chastised herself. What did that prove? She'd known he listened to that kind of music, and that's all Nathan had been doing—listening to it, not sharpening a knife, laughing maniacally.

Was it so surprising that the Rowes' things were still down there? Who else would claim them? The Sullivans had been over fifty when they moved in—maybe they'd never ventured down into the basement. There had certainly been enough room to store things upstairs.

And speaking of the Sullivans, they'd lived in this house for twenty-five years. If it was haunted, would they have stayed so long?

If it was *haunted*? Was she really considering the possibility? She squeezed her eyes shut. She was not that kind of person. She would not become that kind of person. She was rational and logical, and until she saw something that couldn't be explained by simple common sense, she was sending her imagination to the corner for a time-out.

The image made her smile a little, enough to settle back and read the article, determined now to prove her fancies wrong. She found her proof in the next paragraph, where it said that Timothy Rowe shot his father. *Shot.* No big, scary butcher—

Her gaze stuttered on the rest of the line. She went back to the beginning, rereading. Timothy Rowe had apparently started his rampage by shooting his father, then continued on to brutally murder the rest of his family with a ten-inch kitchen carving knife.

And what did that prove? Did she think Nathan had dug up the murder weapon with those old LPs? Of course not. A few lines down, it said that both the gun and knife had been recovered.

What if Nathan bought a matching one? Compelled to reenact—

She pressed her fists against her eyes. Nathan possessed by a killer teen, plotting to kill her? Was she losing her mind? It was Nathan—the same good-natured, carefree guy she'd lived with for ten years. Other than a few bouts of confusion, he was his usual self, and those bouts were cause for a doctor's appointment, not paranoia.

She skimmed through the rest of the articles. Nothing new there, just the tale retold again and again, until—the suspect dead—the story died a natural death, relegated to being a skeleton in the town's closet.

The last page was a memorial published on the first anniversary of the killings, with all the photos of the victims. Tanya glanced at the family photo and was about to close the folder when her gaze lit on the picture of the housekeeper: Madelyn Levy.

When Nathan came in a few minutes later, she was still staring at the picture.

"Hey, hon. What's wrong?"

"I—" She pointed at the housekeeper's photo. "I've seen this woman. She—she was outside, when we were looking at the house. She was picking raspberries."

The corners of Nathan's mouth twitched, as if he was expecting—hoping—that she was making a bad joke. When her gaze met his, the smile vanished and he took the folder from her hands, then sat on the edge of the desk.

"I think we should consider selling," he said.

"Wh-what? No. I—"

"This place is getting to you. Maybe—I don't know. Maybe there is something. Those workers certainly thought so. Some people could be more susceptible—"

She jerked up straight. "I am not susceptible—"

"You lost a job you loved. You left your home, your family, gave up everything to start over, and now it's not going the way you dreamed. You're under a lot of stress and it's only going to get worse when we open."

He took her hands and tugged her up, his arms going around her. "The guy who owns the Beamsville bed-and-breakfast has been asking about this place. He'd been eyeing it before, but with all the work it needed, it was too much for him. Now he's seen what we've done and, well, he's interested. Very interested. You wouldn't be giving up; you'd be renovating an old place and flipping it for a profit. Nothing wrong with that."

She stood. "No. I'm being silly, and I'm not giving in. We have two weeks until opening, and there's a lot of work to be done."

She turned back to her paperwork. He sighed and left the room.

It got worse after that, as if in refusing to leave, she'd issued a challenge to whatever lived there. She'd now stopped laughing when she caught herself referring to the spirits as if they were real. They were. She'd come to accept that. Seeing the housekeeper's picture had exploded the last obstacle. She'd wanted a haunted house and she'd gotten it.

For the last two nights, she'd woken to find herself alone in bed. Both times, Nathan had been downstairs listening to that damned music. The first time, he'd been digging through the boxes, wide awake, blaming insomnia. But last night...

Last night, she'd gone down to find him talking to someone. She'd tried to listen, but he was doing more listening than talking himself, and she caught only a few *um-hmms* and *okays* before he'd apparently woken up, startled and confused. They'd made an appointment to see the doctor after that. An appointment that was still a week away, which didn't do Tanya any good now, sitting awake in bed alone on the third night, listening to the strains of distant music.

She forced herself to lie back down. Just ignore it. Call the doctor in the morning, tell him Nathan would take any cancellation.

But lying down didn't mean falling asleep. As she lay there, staring at the ceiling, she made a decision. Nathan was right. There was no shame in flipping the house for a profit. Tell their friends and family they'd decided small-town life wasn't for them. Smile coyly when asked how much they'd made on the deal.

No shame in that. None at all. No one ever needed to know what had driven her from this house.

She closed her eyes and was actually on the verge of drifting off when she heard Nathan's footsteps climbing the basement stairs. Coming to bed? She hoped so, but she could still hear the boom and wail of the music. Nathan's steps creaked across the first level. A door opened. Then the squeak of a cupboard door. A *kitchen* cupboard door.

Grabbing something to eat before going back downstairs.

Only he didn't go downstairs. His footsteps headed upstairs.

He's coming up to bed—just forgot to turn off the music.

All very logical, but logical explanations didn't work for Tanya anymore. She got out of bed and went into the dark hall. She reached for the light switch, but stopped. She didn't dare announce herself like that.

Clinging to the shadows, she crept along the wall until she could make out the top of Nathan's blond head as he slowly climbed the stairs. Her gaze dropped, waiting for his hands to come into view.

A flash of silver winked in the pale glow of a nightlight. Her breath caught. She forced herself to stay still just a moment longer, to be sure, and then she saw it, the knife gripped in his hand, the angry set of his expression, the emptiness in his eyes, and she turned and fled.

A room. Any room. Just get into one, lock the door, and climb over the balcony.

The first one she tried was locked. She wrenched on the doorknob, certain she was wrong.

"Mom?" Nathan said, his voice gruff, unrecognizable. "Are you up here, Mom?"

Tanya turned. She looked down the row of doors. All closed. Only theirs was open, at the end. She ran for it as Nathan's footsteps thumped behind her.

She dashed into the room, slammed the door, and locked it. As she raced for the balcony, she heard the knob turn behind her. Then the creak of the door opening. But that couldn't be. She'd locked—

Tanya glanced over her shoulder and saw Nathan, his face twisted with rage.

"Hello, Mom. I have something for you."

Tanya grabbed the balcony door. It was already cracked open, since Nathan always insisted on fresh air. She ran out onto the balcony and looked down to the concrete patio twenty feet below. No way she could jump that, not without breaking both legs, and then she'd be trapped. Maybe if she could hang from it, then drop—

THE URBAN FANTASY ANTHOLOGY

Nathan stepped onto the balcony. Tanya backed up. She called his name, begged him to snap out of it, but he just kept coming, kept smiling, knife raised. She backed up, leaning against the railing.

"Nathan. Plea—"

There was a tremendous crack, and the railing gave way. She felt herself falling, dropping backward so fast that she didn't have time to twist, to scream, and then—

Nothing.

Nathan escorted the innkeeper from Beamsville to the door.

"You folks did an incredible job," the man said. "But I really do hate to take advantage of a tragedy..."

Nathan managed a wan smile. "You'd be doing me a favor. The sooner I can get away, the happier I'll be. Every time I drive in, I see that balcony, and I—" His voice hitched. "I keep asking myself why she went out there. I know she loved the view; she must have woken up and seen the moon and wanted a better look." He shook his head. "I meant to fix that balcony. We did the others, but she said ours could wait, and now..."

The man laid a hand on Nathan's shoulder. "Let me talk to my real estate agent and I'll get an offer drawn up, see if I can't take this place off your hands."

"Thank you."

Nathan closed the door and took a deep breath. He was making good use of those community-theater skills, but he really hoped he didn't have to keep this up much longer.

He headed into the office, giving it yet another once-over, making sure he'd gotten rid of all the evidence. He'd already checked, twice, but he couldn't be too careful.

There wasn't much to hide. The old woman had been an actor friend of one of his theater buddies, and even if she came forward, what of it? Tanya had wanted a haunted house and he'd hired her to indulge his wife's fancy.

Adding the woman's photo to the article had been simple Photoshop work, the files—paper and electronic—long gone now. The workmen really had been scared off by the haunting, which he'd orchestrated. The only person who knew about his "bouts" was Tanya. And he'd been very careful with the balcony, loosening the nails just enough that her weight would rip them from the rotting wood.

Killing Tanya hadn't been his original intention. But when she'd refused to leave, he'd been almost relieved. As if he didn't mind having to fall back on the more permanent solution, get the insurance money as well as the inheritance, go back home, hook up with Denise again—if she'd still have him—and open the kind of business he wanted. There'd been no chance of that while Tanya was alive. Her money. Her rules. Always.

He opened the basement door, stepped down, and almost went flying, his foot sending a hammer clunking down a few stairs. He retrieved it, wondering how it got there, then shoved it into his back pocket and—

The ring of the phone stopped his descent. He headed back up to answer it.

"Restrictions?" Nathan bellowed into the phone. "What do you mean *restrictions*? How long—?"

He paused.

"A year? I have to live here a year?"

Pause.

"Look, can't there be an exception under the circumstances? My wife died in this house. I need to get out of here."

Tanya stepped up behind Nathan and watched the hair on his neck rise. He rubbed it down and absently looked over his shoulder, then returned to his conversation. She stepped back, caught a glimpse of the hammer in his pocket, and sighed. So much for that idea. But she had plenty more, and it didn't sound like Nathan was leaving anytime soon.

She slid up behind him, arms going around his waist, smiling as he jumped and looked around. Her house might not have been haunted when she'd bought it. But it was now.

She's My Witch
Norman Partridge

We parked in the old cemetery that night, the Ford coupe I'd boosted up in Fresno wedged so tight between a couple of crumbling mausoleums that we could barely open one door. It seemed we'd spent the entire summer that way—sitting in one stolen car or another, talking or making out while we listened to the latest rhythm 'n' blues tunes on KTCB. Shari liked the old cemetery because it was real quiet. No one else ever came there, even in the daytime. As for me, I'd gotten used to the place. I wasn't crazy about it, but I was crazy about Shari.

That summer it was like no one else existed. The rest of the world couldn't touch us.

"Tonight's no different," I said. "Whatever's gonna happen later...well, it's just gonna happen, however it does."

Shari's hand slipped out of mine, just seemed to melt away. Her gaze was welded to the dash, like if she squinted real hard she'd actually be able to *see* LaVern Baker through the radio.

She wouldn't look at me at all, and I don't think she really heard the music, either. "I don't know," was all she said. And then she shook her head, her dark hair washing over her face like a silent wave.

I couldn't see her face at all, and I couldn't stand to be apart from her that way. Sitting there in a stolen car with my girl, her hair as black as night, her dress just as black...and having her whisper those three words in the darkness, like she didn't have any faith in me—in *us*—at all.

Those three words parting the only lips I wanted to kiss. And Shari not even looking at me when she said them, afraid that I'd see her doubts hiding in her eyes.

My girl, sitting there in a boosted Ford parked in her favorite place in the world, trembling, like she'd rather be somewhere else. *Anywhere* else. And who could blame her? Christ, with the things she'd discovered that summer, she could have had anyone. Sticking with me was just crazy, just—

Unsure, I reached out, my hand barely brushing her bare shoulder, traveling that delicate ridge of collarbone, exploring her slender and perfect neck. My fingers drifted through her hair, my movements surer now—I gotta admit it did something to me, just like always. I found her chin and gently turned her head in my direction, brushing that midnight hair over one shoulder.

There were those beautiful eyes of hers, alive with mysteries she could never share. Those full lips, containing all those secrets that she would never speak. Like I said, it did something to me. Just like always. I moved in to kiss her, and she didn't move away. It didn't start out like much of a kiss, but it shook me up the way I hoped it would.

When it was over, I really had the itch. I wanted her more than ever.

One look, and I knew that she felt the same way. A tear ran down one smooth marble cheek. I wiped it away, and it smeared on my callused fingers, and I found myself wishing that I could crush it in my fist.

She said, "I just want everything to stay the way it is."

"Don't worry, little darlin'," I said, trying to sound more confident than I was. "Tonight it's you and me. Just like it's been all summer, ever since you and me became an *us*. Those jerks are in for a big surprise." I slipped one hand around the back of her neck, but not in a rough way, and with the other I twisted the rearview in her direction. "Just look at you, Shari. You're not the same girl you were when school let out."

Shari stared at her reflection. She didn't blink once, and a shiver rocketed over my spine like someone was stepping on my grave.

"No," she said finally. "I'm not the same person. This place...and you...you've given me so much, Johnny."

She pushed the mirror away, looking at the cemetery through the mosaic of kamikaze bugs plastered to the old Ford's windshield. Low fog bathed the ring of tombstones where she'd danced a couple of nights back with nothing covering that beautiful marble skin of hers but the blood of a black cat. I wanted to tell her that everything was going to be okay, but I could see that she was spooked, just as spooked as the first time she visited the cemetery. That was back when she was just a scared kid in hand-me-downs who'd been broken by other kids because she couldn't bear to look anyone in the eye, before the black dress and the red lipstick, before I took to parking boosted cars in the long shadows between two jagged mausoleums, before all the secret kisses and all the things that went with them.

So much had passed between us that summer. We'd made a world of our own, and no one else knew anything about it. But with school ready to start up, our world was going to change. We'd have to face those other people again. I thought I had it all figured out. But with Shari so rattled and uncertain, I couldn't help but worry.

Her voice trembled. "Sometimes...this summer..." she began. "It just doesn't seem real. I keep thinking I'll wake up and it will have all been a dream. I keep thinking that maybe I'm imagining you.... I always had a crush on you, y'know? And I keep thinking that I'll wake up, and I'll be back in school with all those people, and you'll be here...."

I nodded. She took my hand then, her fingernails digging into my palm like little knives. I couldn't help but shiver; she couldn't seem to let go. Her face had disappeared in the darkness—there was just a little razor cut of a moon in the sky, and the night was coming on hard, clouds blanketing the stars.

"I keep staring at that moon," she said. "I keep thinking that it looks like a sickle."

She couldn't stop shaking. "I'm afraid the moon's going to slice down out of the sky, Johnny," she said, her fingers locked in mine. "I'm afraid it's going to cut us to pieces."

The carhop's roller skates made an icy little rumbling sound as she drifted across the parking lot, away from the stolen Ford.

When she was out of sight, I lifted the Coke off of the little metal tray and handed it to Shari. Then I reached under the seat and found the cardboard box. Inside was a Revell model kit that I'd swiped from a hobby shop in Fresno the same night I boosted the Ford. I slipped the lid off of the box, revealing a miniature '48 Chevy.

"Wow." Shari smiled. "It looks just like it."

"Yeah, I'm a real artist." I wasn't bragging. I'd done a good job. Customized it just right. Two-tone paint-job—turquoise and black. Every detail reproduced, right down to the miniature tornado swirling on the hood.

I handed the model to Shari, then rummaged through the unused parts in the bottom of the box until I found the decal sheet. I traded her the sheet for the Coke. She ran her fingers over the decals, whispering a few words.

I knew better than to listen. Instead I stared between a couple of dead moths splattered on the windshield, studying a turquoise-and-black '48 Chevy parked over by the bowling alley.

Shari dipped the decal sheet into the Coke. She let it sit for a minute, until the decals started to drift away from the backing.

There were two license plate decals. She attached one of them to a blank plastic plate glued to the trunk of the model.

The other floated on the surface of a Coca-Cola ice-floe. Shari stared down at it as she took the glass from my hand, then glanced over at the Chevy parked by the bowling alley.

"You promise not to blink, right?" she asked. "I mean, you're not going to get distracted by a carhop who's a dead ringer for Anita Ekberg or anything, are you?"

When the girl you love asks you something like that, you've got to laugh. "Baby, I'm just like The Flamingos," I said, and then I sang the rest of it—"*I only have eyes for you*."

Shari hustled on over there. My ears were treated to the sweet little staccato rhythm of her high heels on blacktop, but my eyes got the better part of the deal when she bent low behind the '48, her tight dress riding up over firm thighs.

The fingers of one hand dipped into the Coke. Then she reached out, kind of tenderly, the way she sometimes did when she ran a finger over my lips. But her finger only traveled the length of the Chevy's license plate, leaving behind a decal from a Revell model kit.

And then the two of them showed up, right on cue. Slammed out of the bowling alley like they owned the world, swaggered across the parking lot.

Shari barely had a chance to straighten up. They both saw her at the same time, saw that black dress hiked up to the limit, that red lipstick, saw everything through a testosterone haze.

Nick Bradley was the smarter of the two. He got his mouth open first, saying, "You like the ride, huh, honey? You maybe wanna go for a ride?"

"Course she wants to go for a ride." Marty Hyde's brain had finally kicked into gear. "But it's *my* ride, and I got the keys and the master switch." Marty jingled his car keys as punctuation, shoving Nick with one shoulder, Nick stumbling in spite of himself. "We don't have to make it a party," Marty added. "Unless you want it that way, angel."

Shari looked both of them dead in the eye. She refused to blink, and they... well, I'm sure the idiots wanted to blink, but they just *couldn't*.

Nick caught Shari's thought-wave first. He laughed, shaking his head. "Naw," he said. "*Naw!* It can't be!"

Marty caught up. "Sharon? Sharon Heep? Is that really you?"

Shari's eyes were daggers now. The corners of her mouth were playing with a smile, but just playing. And then she batted her eyelashes—a wicked twitch. Stirred the straw in the Coke and took a dainty sip....

"It is her!" Nick slapped Marty on the back. "It *is* the Heepster! Jesus, Marty, it looks like old Sharon's been to charm school this summer!"

"*Slut school*, more like it," Marty replied, ever the quick wit. "Hey, c'mon Sharon. Let's go for a ride, just the three of us. Let's see what you've learned this summer."

I said, "You guys got room for one more?"

Nick and Marty whirled. They hadn't heard me coming.

Once again, Nick caught on first. "Johnny!" He gasped, a look of horror crossing his face. "No...it can't be—"

Marty cut in with the clincher: "Christ, Johnny...you're dead!"

I nodded, flicking open the switchblade that Nick had buried in my guts back in June.

They froze—eyeballing the knife, their faces pasty-white—so I decided to help them out. "Let me steer you fellas in the right direction," I offered. "This is the part where you're supposed to run for your lives."

"Don't confuse them, Johnny," Shari said. "Don't be so literal."

"Sorry, fellas." I snapped the blade closed. "I mean, you don't have to *run* run—you can take the car."

Nick and Marty just stood there, staring at us as we returned to the Ford.

"Man, can you believe that they're so stupid?" I said.

Shari took my hand. "Believe it, Daddy-o."

Behind us, the Chevy's engine finally rumbled alive.

Four new tires burned rubber.

Nick and Marty were gone.

Pretty soon, they'd be the *gonest*.

"What was that junk you put in the Coke?" the carhop wanted to know.

Shari laughed. I didn't do a very good job of keeping a straight face, myself. But I did manage to set the model car on the serving tray.

"Decals," Shari explained between giggles.

"Yeah," I said. "We're a couple of hobbyists. We get together and build model cars. I guess we got a little sloppy tonight."

"It could have been worse." Shari's voice was suddenly real serious. "I mean, we could have gotten glue all over the French fries, or paint in the cheeseburgers, or something."

The carhop didn't seem to catch on. She frowned as she set a fresh Coke next to the model car. "Well, just don't do it again. Those darn *what-cha-ma-call-ems* are stuck to the glass. I bet it's going to take a razor blade to get 'em off. I mean, only a *gomer* would want to drink *Coke* out of a glass that says *Chevy*."

"Sorry," Shari said, and deep down I'll bet she really was sorry for putting the carhop to all that trouble.

The carhop skated away. We dug into our cheeseburgers, which hadn't even had a chance to get cold. Shari said, "I didn't think I'd ever want to eat again."

"You were really nervous, huh?"

"Are you kidding?" She swallowed another bite. "And it isn't like we're out of the woods yet."

"Sure it is."

She sighed. "C'mon, Johnny. We still have to go back to school. We still have to face everyone else."

"So what?"

"I mean, all the stories and everything...."

I shook my head. "It's like I said: This one little step, and it's all over. Nick and Marty were the biggest, toughest monkeys in that damn zoo. With them gone, it'll be easy."

"But what about you? Nick and Marty talked, y'know. I mean, I never would have found your grave if I hadn't listened to all the stories that were going around. And there'll be lots of questions when you show up again. Think about it, Johnny. You're going to have to explain things. Your parents are going to want to know what happened—"

"Those rummies?" My lips twisted into a smirk. "They'll be sorry to see me walk through the door. My old man will worry that I'll cut into the beer budget or something. Maybe I'll just stay in the boneyard. It's gotten so I kind of like it there."

"But everyone else—"

"Screw everyone else. Screw their questions. Who's gonna have the guts to ask 'em, anyhow? Who's gonna come up to a guy who's supposed to be dead and buried in an unmarked grave in the old cemetery...especially when the studs who supposedly gutted him and put him six feet under turn up dead? Who's gonna say a thing to that guy when he comes waltzing into school with a girl on his arm?"

Shari nodded. "Not just any girl. A *freak* who believed in ghosts and witches and things that go bump in the night. A *freak* who everyone laughed at." She took my hand. "Until she found someone who taught her to believe in herself."

"Yeah," I said, "but you had to dig me up to do it."

"Sometimes you have to be real desperate before you can really believe." She kissed me, a sweet schoolgirl peck on the cheek. "And, anyway," she added slyly, "some things are worth a little digging, y'know?"

We finished the cheeseburgers and drove back to the old cemetery, parking the stolen Ford between the same two broken-down mausoleums. Like I said, there was barely enough room to get one door open, so we both slipped out the driver's side. I left the radio on, because Dinah Washington was singing "My Man's an Undertaker." Somehow, it seemed appropriate.

There was a marble slab a few feet off. Spider-webbed with cracks, but pretty much level. I set the Chevy model on top of it. "I wonder where they are," Shari said.

"Let's find out." I knelt down, put my ear to the plastic hardtop and listened for a couple minutes while Shari paced back and forth between two granite tombstones.

"No clue where they are," I said finally, "but you should hear the idiots yelling at each other." I stood up, shaking my head, and winked at Shari. "I can't figure out what surprised them more—that I'd come back from the dead, or that you'd turned into such a dead solid knock-out."

"Real funny, Johnny."

"Yeah." I sat on the slab. "Sorry. But I gotta tell you, Shari—your legs really made an impression on them."

"Why, Johnny Benteen, you're such a card." She laughed. "I never would have guessed that a dead guy could possess such a lively sense of humor."

"Ouch. Score one for the sexpot sorceress."

"This is so weird."

"The weirdest."

"Let's get it over with."

"You want to do it?"

She turned away. "I don't even want to *watch*."

I slipped Nick's switchblade from my pocket. Flicked it open. Pressed the sharp metal point against the miniature tornado that swirled on the model's flimsy plastic hood.

"Look away, little darlin'," I said. "Look up at that pretty sickle of a moon."

Kitty's Zombie New Year
Carrie Vaughn

I'd refused to stay home alone on New Year's Eve. I wasn't going to be one of those angst-ridden losers stuck at home watching the ball drop in Times Square while sobbing into a pint of gourmet ice cream.

No, I was going to do it over at a friend's, in the middle of a party.

Matt, a guy from the radio station where I was a DJ, was having a wild party in his cramped apartment. Lots of booze, lots of music, and the TV blaring the Times Square special from New York—being in Denver, we'd get to celebrate New Year's a couple of times over. I wasn't going to come to the party, but he'd talked me into it. I didn't like crowds, which was why the late shift at the station suited me. But here I was, and it was just like I knew it would be: 10 pm, the ball dropped, and everyone except me had somebody to kiss. I gripped a tumbler filled with un-tasted rum and Coke and glowered at the television, wondering which well-preserved celebrity guest hosts were vampires, and which ones just had portraits in their attics that were looking particularly hideous.

It would happen all over again at midnight.

Sure enough, shortly after the festivities in New York City ended, the TV station announced it would re-broadcast everything at midnight.

An hour later, I'd decided to find Matt and tell him I was going home to wallow in ice cream after all, when a woman screamed. The room fell instantly quiet, and everyone looked toward the front door, where the sound had blasted.

The door stood open, and one of the crowd stared over the threshold, to another woman who stood motionless. A new guest had arrived and knocked, I assumed. But she just stood there, not coming inside, and the screamer stared at her, one hand on the doorknob and the other hand covering her mouth. The scene turned rather eerie and surreal. The seconds ticked by, no one said or did anything.

Matt, his black hair in a pony tail, pushed through the crowd to the door. The motion seemed out of place, chaotic. Still, the woman on the other side stood frozen, unmoving. I felt a sinking feeling in my gut.

Matt turned around and called, "Kitty!"

Sinking feeling confirmed.

I made my own way to the door, shouldering around people. By the time I reached Matt, the woman who'd answered the door had edged away to take shelter in her boyfriend's arms. Matt turned to me, dumbstruck.

The woman outside was of average height, though she slumped, her shoulders rolled forward as if she was too tired to hold herself up. Her head tilted to one side. She might have been a normal twenty-something, recent college grad, in worn jeans, an oversized blue T-shirt, and canvas sneakers. Her light hair was loose and stringy, like it hadn't been washed in a couple of weeks.

I glanced at Matt.

"What's wrong with her?" he said.

"What makes you think I know?"

"Because you know all about freaky shit." Ah, yes. He was referring to my call-in radio show about the supernatural. That made me an expert, even when I didn't know a thing.

"Do you know her?"

"No, I don't." He turned back to the room, to the dozens of faces staring back at him, round-eyed. "Hey, does anybody know who this is?"

The crowd collectively pressed back from the door, away from the strangeness.

"Maybe it's drugs." I called to her, "Hey."

She didn't move, didn't blink, didn't flinch. Her expression was slack, completely blank. She might have been asleep, except her eyes were open, staring straight ahead. They were dull, almost like a film covered them. Her mouth was open a little.

I waved my hand in front of her face, which seemed like a really clichéd thing to do. She didn't respond. Her skin was terribly pale, clammy-looking, and I couldn't bring myself to touch her. I didn't know what I would do if she felt cold and dead.

Matt said, "Geez, she's like some kind of zombie."

Oh, no. No way. But the word clicked. It was a place to start, at least.

Someone behind us said, "I thought zombies, like, attacked people and ate brains and stuff."

I shook my head. "That's horror movie zombies. Not voodoo slave zombies."

"So you do know what's going on?" Matt said hopefully.

"Not yet. I think you should call 911."

He winced and scrubbed his hand through his hair. "But if it's a zombie, if she's dead an ambulance isn't—"

"Call an ambulance." He nodded and grabbed his cell phone off the coffee table. "And I'm going to use your computer."

I did what any self-respecting American in this day and age would do in such a situation: I searched the Internet for zombies.

I couldn't say it was particularly useful. A frighteningly large number of the sites that came up belonged to survivalist groups planning for the great zombie infestation that would bring civilization collapsing around our ears. They helpfully informed a casual reader such as myself that the government was ill-prepared to handle the magnitude of the disaster that would wreak itself upon the country when the horrible zombie-virus mutation swept through the population. We must be prepared to defend ourselves against the flesh-eating hordes bent on our destruction.

This was a movie synopsis, not data, and while fascinating, it wasn't helpful.

A bunch of articles on voodoo and Haitian folklore seemed mildly more useful, but even those were contradictory: the true believers in magic arguing with the hardened scientists, and even the scientists argued among themselves about whether the legends sprang from the use of certain drugs or from profound psychological disorders.

I'd seen enough wild stories play out in my time that I couldn't discount any of these alternatives. These days, magic and science were converging on one another.

Someone was selling zombie powders on eBay. They even came with an instruction booklet. That might be fun to bid on just to say I'd done it. Even if I did, the instruction book that might have some insight on the problem wouldn't get here in time.

Something most of the articles mentioned: stories said that the taste of salt would revive a zombie. Revived them out of what, and into what, no one seemed to agree on. If they weren't really dead but comatose, the person would be restored. If they were honest-to-God walking dead, they'd be released from servitude and make their way back to their graves.

I went to the kitchen and found a salt shaker.

If she really was a zombie, she couldn't have just shown up here. She had either come here for a specific reason, there had to be some connection. She was here to scare someone, which meant someone here had to know her. Nobody was volunteering any information.

Maybe she could tell me herself.

Finally, I had to touch her, in order to get the salt into her mouth. I put my hand on her shoulder. She swayed enough that I thought she might fall over, so I pulled away. A moment later, she steadied, remaining upright. I could probably push her forward, guide her, and make her walk like a puppet.

I shivered.

Swallowing back a lump of bile threatening to climb my throat, I held her chin, tipping her head back. Her skin was waxen, neither warm nor cold. Her muscles were limp, perfectly relaxed. Or dead. I tried not to think of it. She'd been drugged. That was the theory I was going for. Praying for, rather.

"What are you doing?" Matt said.

"Never mind. Did you call the ambulance?"

"They should be here any minute."

I sprinkled a few shakes of salt into her mouth.

I had to tip her head forward and close her mouth for her because she couldn't do it herself. And if she couldn't do that, she surely couldn't swallow. None of the information said she had to swallow the salt, just taste it. In cultures around the world salt had magical properties. It was a ward against evil, protection against fairies, a treasure as great as gold. It seemed so common and innocuous now. Hard to believe it could do anything besides liven up a basket of french fries.

Her eyes moved.

The film, the dullness went away, and her gaze focused. It flickered, as if searching or confused.

Fear tightened her features. Her shoulders bunched, and her fingers clenched into claws. She screamed.

She let out a wail of anguish, bone-leaching in its intensity. A couple of yelps of shock answered from within the apartment. Her face melted into an expression of despair, lips pulled back in a frown, eyes red and wincing. But she didn't cry.

Reaching forward with those crooked fingers, she took a stumbling step forward. My heart racing, my nausea growing, I hurried out of her way. Another step followed, clumsy and unsure. She was like a toddler who'd just learned to walk. This was the slow, shuffling gait of a zombie in every B-grade horror movie I'd ever seen. The salt hadn't cured her; it had just woken her up.

She stumbled forward, step by step, reaching. People scrambled out of her way.

She didn't seem hungry. That look of utter pain and sadness remained locked on her features. She looked as if her heart had been torn out and smashed into pieces.

Her gaze searched wildly, desperately.

I ran in front of her, blocking her path. "Hey—can you hear me?" I waved my arms, trying to catch her attention. She didn't seem to notice, but she shifted, angling around me. So I tried again. "Who are you? Can you tell me your name? How did this happen?"

Her gaze had focused on something behind me. When I got in front of her, she looked right through me and kept going like I wasn't there. I turned to find what had caught her attention.

A man and woman sat wedged together in a secondhand armchair, looking like a Mack truck was about to run them down. The zombie woman shuffled toward them. Now that I was out of the way, she reached toward them, arms rigid and trembling. She moaned—she might have been trying to speak, but she couldn't shape her mouth right. She was like an infant who desperately wanted something but didn't have the words to say it. She was an infant in the body of an adult.

And what she wanted was the man in the chair.

A few steps away, her moaning turned into a wail. The woman in the chair screamed and fell over the arm to get away. The man wasn't that nimble, or he was frozen in place.

The zombie wobbled on her next step, then fell to her knees, but that didn't stop her reaching. She was close enough to grab his feet. Those clawlike hands clenched on his ankles, and she tried to pull herself forward, dragging herself on the carpet, still moaning.

The man shrieked and kicked at her, yanking his legs away and trying to curl up in the chair.

"Stop it!" I screamed at him, rushing forward to put myself between them.

She was sprawled on the floor now, crying gut-wrenching sobs. I held her shoulders and pulled her back from the chair, laying her on her back. Her arms still reached, but the rest of her body had become limp, out of her control.

"Matt, get a pillow and a blanket." He ran to the bedroom to get them. That was all I could think—try to make her comfortable. When were those paramedics going to get here?

I looked at the guy in the chair. Like the rest of the people at the party, he was twenty-something. Thin and generically cute, he had shaggy dark hair, a preppy button-up shirt, and gray trousers. I wouldn't have picked him out of the crowd.

"Who are you?" I said.

"C-Carson."

He even had a preppy name to go with the ensemble. I glanced at the woman who was with him. Huddled behind the armchair, she was starting to peer out. She had dyed black hair, a tiny nose stud, and a tight dress. More like the kind of crowd Matt hung out with. I wouldn't have put her and Carson together. Maybe they both thought they were slumming.

"Do you know her?" I asked him, nodding at the zombie woman on the floor.

He shook his head quickly, pressing himself even further back in the chair. He was sweating. Carson was about to lose it.

Matt returned and helped me fit the pillow under her head and spread the blanket over her. He, too, was beginning to see her as someone who was sick—not a monster.

"You're lying," I said. "She obviously knows you. Who is she?"

"I don't know, I don't know!"

"Matt, who is this guy?"

Matt glanced at him. "Just met him tonight. He's Trish's new boyfriend."

"Trish?" I said to the woman behind the armchair.

"I—I don't know. At least, I'm not sure. I never met her, but I think...I think she's his ex-girlfriend. Beth, I think. But Carson, you told me she moved away—"

Carson, staring at the woman on the floor, looked like he was about to have a screaming fit. He was still shaking his head.

I was ready to throttle him. I wanted an explanation. Maybe he didn't really know. But if he was lying..."Carson!"

He flinched at my shout.

Sirens sounded down the street, coming closer. The paramedics. I hoped they could help her, but the sick feeling in my stomach hadn't gone away.

"I'll meet them on the street," Matt said, running out.

"Beth," I said to the woman. I caught her hands, managed to pull them down so they were resting on her chest. I murmured at her, and she quieted. Her skin color hadn't gotten any better. She didn't feel cold as death, but she felt cool. The salt hadn't sent her back to any grave, and it hadn't revived her. I wasn't sure she could be revived.

A moment later, a couple of uniformed paramedics carrying equipment entered, followed by Matt. The living room should have felt crowded, but apparently as soon as the door cleared, most of the guests had fled. God, what a way to kill a party.

The paramedics came straight toward Beth. I got out of the way. They immediately knelt by her, checked her pulse, shined a light in her eyes. I breathed a little easier. Finally, someone was doing something useful.

"What happened?" one of them asked.

How did I explain this? *She's a zombie.* That wasn't going to work, because I didn't think she was one anymore. *She was a zombie* didn't sound any better.

"She was going to leave," Carson said, suddenly, softly. Responding to the authority of the uniform, maybe. He stared at her, unable to look away. He spoke as if in a trance. "I didn't want her to go. She asked me to come with her, to Seattle—but I didn't want to do that either. I wanted her to stay with me. So I...this stuff, this powder. It would make her do anything I wanted. I used it. But it...changed her. She wasn't the same. She—was like that. Dead almost. I left her, but she followed. She kept following me—"

"Call it poisoning," said one paramedic to the other.

"Where did you get this powder?" I said.

"Some guy on the Internet."

I wanted to kill him. Wanted to put my hands around his throat and kill him.

"Kitty—" Matt said. I took a breath. Calmed down.

"Any idea what was in this powder?" one of the paramedics said, sounding like he was repressing as much anger as I was.

Carson shook his head.

"Try tetrodotoxin," I said. "Induces a deathlike coma. Also causes brain damage. Irreparable brain damage."

Grimacing, the paramedic said, "We won't be able to check that until we get her to the hospital. I don't see any ID on her. I'm going to call in the cops, see if they've had a missing persons report on her. And to see what they want to do with him."

Carson flinched at his glare.

Trish backed away. "If I tried to break up with you—would you have done that to me too?" Her mouth twisted with unspoken accusations. Then, she fled.

Carson thought he'd make his own zombie slave girlfriend, then somehow wasn't satisfied at the results. She probably wasn't real good in bed. He'd probably done it, too—had sex with Beth's brain-damaged, comatose body. The cops couldn't get here fast enough, in my opinion.

"There's two parts to it," I said. "The powder creates the zombie. But then there's the spell to bind her to you, to bind the slave to the master. Some kind of object with meaning, a receptacle for the soul. You have it. That's why she followed you. That's why she wouldn't stay away." The salt hadn't broken that bond. She'd regained her will—but the damage was too great for her to do anything with it. She knew enough to recognize him and what he'd done to her, but could only cry out helplessly.

He reached into his pocket, pulled something out. He opened his fist to reveal what.

A diamond engagement ring lay in his palm.

Beth reacted, arcing her back, flailing, moaning. The paramedics freaked, pinned her arms, jabbed her with a hypodermic. She settled again, whimpering softly.

I took the ring from Carson. He glared at me, the first time he'd really looked at me. I didn't see remorse in his eyes. Only fear. Like Victor Frankenstein, he'd created a monster and all he could do when confronted with it was cringe in terror.

"Matt, you have a string or a shoelace or something?"

"Yeah, sure."

He came back with a bootlace fresh out of the package. I put the ring on it, knotted it, and slipped it over Beth's head. "Can you make sure this stays with her?" I asked the paramedics. They nodded.

This was half-science, half-magic. If the ring really did hold Beth's soul, maybe it would help. If it didn't help—well, at least Carson wouldn't have it anymore.

The cops came and took statements from all of us, including the paramedics, then took Carson away. The paramedics took Beth away; the ambulance siren howled down the street, away.

Finally, when Matt and I were alone among the remains of his disaster of a party, I started crying. "How could he do that? How could he even think it? She was probably this wonderful, beautiful, independent woman, and he destroyed—"

Matt had poured two glasses of champagne. He handed me one.

"Happy New Year, Kitty." He pointed at the clock on the microwave. 12:03.

Crap. I missed it. I started crying harder.

Matt, my friend, hugged me. So once again, I didn't get a New Year's kiss. This year, I didn't mind.

Seeing Eye
Patricia Briggs

The doorbell rang.

That was the problem with her business. Too many people thought that they could approach her at any time. Even oh dark thirty even though her hours were posted clearly on her door and on her website.

Of course answering the door would be something to do other than sit in her study shivering in the dark. Not that her world was ever anything but dark. It was one of the reasons she hated bad dreams—she had no way of turning on the light. Bad dreams that held warnings of things to come were the worst.

The doorbell rang again.

She slept—or tried to—the same hours as most people. Kept steady business hours too. Something that she had no trouble making clear to those morons who woke her up in the middle of the night. They came to see Glenda the Good Witch, but after midnight they found the Wicked Witch of the West and left quaking in fear of flying monkeys.

Whoever was at the door would have no reason to suspect how grateful she was for the interruption of her thoughts.

The doorbell began a steady throbbing beat, ring-long, ring-short, ring-short, ring-long and she grew a lot less grateful. To heck with flying monkeys, *she* was going to turn whoever it was into a frog. She shoved her concealing glasses on her face and stomped out the hall to her front door. No matter that most of the good transmutation spells had been lost with the Coranda family in the seventeenth century—rude people needed to be turned into frogs. Or pigs.

She jerked open the door and slapped the offending hand on her doorbell. She even got out a "stop that" before the force of his spirit hit her like a physical blow. Her nose told her, belatedly, that he was sweaty as if he'd been jogging.

Her other senses told her that he was something *other*.

Not that she'd expected him to be human. Unlike other witches, she didn't advertise and so seldom had mundane customers unless their needs disturbed her sleep and she set out one of her "find me" spells to speak to them—she knew when they were coming.

"Ms Keller," he growled. "I need to speak to you." At least he'd quit ringing the bell.

She let her left eyebrow slide up her forehead until it would be visible above her glasses. "Polite people come between the hours of eight in the morning and seven at night," she informed him. Werewolf, she decided. If he really lost his temper she might have trouble, but she thought he was desperate, not angry—though with a wolf, the two states could be interchanged with remarkable speed. "Rude people get sent on their way."

"Tomorrow morning might be too late," he said—and then added the bit that kept her from slamming the door in his face. "Alan Choo gave me your address, said you were the only one he knew with enough moxie to defy them."

She should shut the door in his face—not even a werewolf could get through her portal if she didn't want him to. But...*them*. Her dream tonight and for the past weeks had been about *them*, about *him* again. Portents, her instincts had told her, not just nightmares. The time had come at last. No. She wasn't grateful to him at all.

"Did Alan tell you to say it in those words?"

"Yes, ma'am." His temper was still there, but restrained and under control. It hadn't been aimed at her anyway, she thought, only fury born of frustration and fear. She knew how that felt.

She centered herself and asked the questions he'd expect. "Who am I supposed to be defying?"

And he gave her the answer she expected in return. "Something called Samhain's Coven."

Moira took a tighter hold on the door. "I see."

It wasn't really a coven. No matter what the popular literature said, it had been a long time since a real coven had been possible. Covens had thirteen members, no member related to any other to the sixth generation. Each family amassed its own specialty spells, and a coven of thirteen benefitted from all of those differing magics. But after most of the witchblood families had been wiped out by fighting amongst themselves, covens became a thing of the past. What few families remained (and there weren't thirteen, not if you didn't count the Russians or the Chinese who kept to their own ways) had a bone-deep antipathy for the other survivors.

Kouros changed the rules to suit the new times. His coven had between ten and thirteen members...he had a distressing tendency to burn out his followers. The current bunch descended from only three families that she knew of, and most of them weren't properly trained—children following their leader.

Samhain wasn't up to the tricks of the old covens, but they were scary enough even the local vampires walked softly around them, and Seattle, with its overcast skies, had a relatively large seethe of vampires. Samhain's master had approached Moira about joining them when she was thirteen. She'd refused and made her refusal stick at some cost to all the parties involved.

"What does Samhain have to do with a werewolf?" she asked.

"I think they have my brother."

"Another werewolf?" It wasn't unheard of for brothers to be werewolves, especially since the Marrok, He-Who-Ruled-the-Wolves, began Changing people with more care than had been the usual custom. But it wasn't at all common either. Surviving the Change, even with the safeguards the Marrok could manage, was still, she understood, nowhere near a certainty.

"No," he took a deep breath. "Not a werewolf. Human. He has the *sight*. Choo says he thinks that's why they took him."

"Your brother is a witch?"

The fabric of his shirt rustled with his shrug, telling her that he wasn't as tall as he felt to her. Only a little above average instead of a seven foot giant. Good to know.

"I don't know enough about witches to know—" he said. "Jon gets hunches. Takes a walk just at the right time to find five dollars someone dropped, picks the right lottery number to win ten bucks. That kind of thing. Nothing big, nothing anyone would have noticed if my grandma hadn't had it stronger."

The *sight* was one of those general terms that told Moira precisely nothing. It could mean anything from a little fae blood in the family tree or full-blown witchblood. His brother's lack of power wouldn't mean he wasn't a witch—the magic sang weaker in the men. But fae or witchblood, Alan Choo had been right about it being something that would attract Samhain's attention. She rubbed her cheekbone even though she knew the ache was a phantom pain touch wouldn't alter.

Samhain. Did she have a choice? In her dreams she died.

She could feel the intensity of the wolf's regard, strengthening as her silence continued. Then he told her the final straw that broke her resistance. "Jon's a cop—undercover—so I doubt your coven knows it. If his body turns up, though, there will be an investigation. I'll see to it that the witchcraft angle gets explored thoroughly. They might listen to a werewolf who tells them that witches might be a little more than the turbaned fortune-teller."

Blackmail galled him, she could tell—but he wasn't bluffing. He must love his brother.

She only had a touch of empathy and it came and went. It seemed to be pretty focused on this werewolf tonight, though.

If she didn't help him, his brother would die at Samhain's hands and his blood would be on her as well. If it cost her death, as her dreams warned her, perhaps that was justice served.

"Come in," Moira said, hearing the grudge in her voice. He'd think it was her reaction to the threat—and the police poking about the coven would end badly for all concerned.

But it wasn't his threat that moved her. She took care of the people in her neighborhood, that was her job. The police she saw as brothers-in-arms. If she could help one, it was her duty to do so. Even if it was her life for his.

"You'll have to wait until I get my coffee," she told him, and her mother's ghost forced the next bit of politeness out of her. "Would you like a cup?"

"No. There's no time."

He said that as if he had some idea about it—maybe the *sight* hadn't passed him by either.

"We have until tomorrow night if Samhain has him." She turned on her heel and left him to follow her or not, saying over her shoulder, "Unless they took him because he saw something. In which case he probably is already dead. Either way there's time for coffee."

He closed the door with deliberate softness and followed her. "Tomorrow's Halloween. Samhain."

"Kouros isn't Wiccan, anymore than he is Greek, but he apes both for his followers," she told him as she continued deeper into her apartment. She remembered to turn on the hall light—not that he'd need it, being a wolf. It just seemed courteous: allies should show each other courtesy. "Like a magician playing slight of hand he pulls upon myth, religion and anything else he can to keep them in thrall. Samhain, the time not the coven, has power for the fae, for Wicca, for witches. Kouros uses it to cement his own, and killing someone with a bit of power generates more strength than killing a stray dog and bothers him about as much."

"Kouros?" He said it as if it solved some puzzle, but it must not have been important because he continued with no more than a breath of pause. "I thought witches were all women?" He followed her into the kitchen and stood too close behind her. If he were to attack, she wouldn't have time to ready a spell.

But he wouldn't attack, her death wouldn't come at his hands tonight.

The kitchen lights were where she remembered them and she had to take it on faith that she was turning them on and not off, she could never remember which way the switch worked. He didn't say anything so she must have been right.

She always left her coffeepot primed for mornings, so all she had to do was push the button and it began gurgling in promise of coffee soon.

"Um," she said, remembering he'd asked her a question. His closeness distracted her—and not for the reasons it should. "Women tend to be more powerful witches, but you can make up for lack of talent with enough death and pain. Someone else's, of course, if you're a black practitioner like Kouros."

"What are you?" he asked, sniffing at her. His breath tickled the back of her neck—wolves, she'd noticed before, have a somewhat different idea of personal space than she did.

Her machine began dribbling coffee out into the carafe at last, giving her an excuse to step away. "Didn't Alan tell you? I'm a witch."

He followed; his nose touched her where his breath had sensitized her flesh and she probably had goose flesh on her toes from the zing that he sent through her. "My pack has a witch we pay to clean up messes. You don't smell like a witch."

He probably didn't mean anything by it, he was just being a wolf. She stepped out of his reach in the pretense of getting a coffee cup, or rather he allowed her to escape.

Alan was right, she needed to get out more. She hadn't so much as dated in... well a long time. The last man's reaction to seeing what she'd done to herself was something she didn't want to repeat.

This man smelled good, even with the smell of his sweat teasing her nose. He felt strong and warm, promising to be the strength and safety that she'd never had outside of her own two hands. Dominant wolves took care of their pack—doubtless something she'd picked up on. And then there was the possibility of death hovering over her.

Whatever the ultimate cause, his nearness and the light touch of breath on her skin sparked her interest in a way that she knew he'd have picked up on. You can't hide sexual interest from something that can trail a hummingbird on the wing. Neither of them needed the complication of sex interfering in urgent business, even assuming he'd be willing.

"Witchcraft gains power from death and pain. From sacrifice and sacrificing," she told him coolly, pouring coffee in two mugs with steady hands. She was an expert in sacrifice. Not sleeping with a strange werewolf who showed up on her doorstep didn't even register in her scale.

She drank coffee black so that was how she fixed it, holding the second cup out to him. "Evil leaves a psychic stench behind. Maybe a wolf nose can pick up on it. I don't know, not being a werewolf, myself. There's milk in the fridge and sugar in the cupboard in front of you if you'd like."

She wasn't at all what Tom had expected. Their pack's hired witch was a motherly woman of indeterminate years who wore swami robes in bright hues and smelled strongly of patchouli and old blood that didn't quite mask something bitter and dark. When he'd played her Jon's message, she'd hung up the phone and refused to answer it again.

By the time he'd driven to her house, it was shut up and locked with no one inside. That was his first clue that this Samhain Coven might be even more of a problem than he'd thought and his worry had risen to fever pitch. He'd gone down to the underpass where his brother had been living and used his nose through the parks and other places his brother had drifted through. But wherever they were holding Jon (and he refused to believe that he was dead) it wasn't anywhere near where they kidnaped him.

His alpha didn't like pack members concerning themselves with matters outside of the pack ("Your only family is your pack, son"). Tom didn't even bother contacting him. He'd gone to Choo instead. The Emerald City Pack's only submissive wolf, Alan worked as an herbalist and knew almost everyone in the supernatural world of Seattle. When he told Alan about the message Jon had left on his phone, Alan had written this woman's name and address and handed it to him. He'd have thought it was a joke but Alan had better taste than that. So Tom had gone looking for a witch named Wendy—Wendy Moira Keller.

He'd been disappointed at his first look. Wendy the witch was five foot nothing with rich curves in all the right places and feathery black hair that must have been dyed because only black labs and cats are that black. The stupid wraparound mirrored glasses kept him from guessing her age exactly, but he'd bet she wasn't yet thirty. No woman over thirty would be caught dead in those glasses. The cop in him wondered if she was covering up bruises—but he didn't smell a male in the living-scents in the house.

She wore a gray t-shirt without a bra and black pajama pants with white skull-and-crossbones wearing red bows. But despite all that he saw no piercings or tattoos—like she'd approached Mall-Goth culture, but only so far. She smelled of fresh flowers and mint. Her apartment was decorated with a minimal of furniture and a mishmash of colors that didn't quite fit together.

He didn't scare her.

Tom scared everyone—and he had even before their pack had a run-in with a bunch of fae a few years ago. His face had gotten cut up pretty badly with some sort of magical knife and hadn't healed right afterward. The scars made him look almost as dangerous as he was. People walked warily around him.

Not only wasn't she scared, but she didn't even bother to hide her irritation at being woken up. He stalked her and all she'd felt was a flash of sexual awareness that had come and gone so swiftly that if he'd been younger he might have missed it.

Either she was stupid or she was powerful. Since Alan had sent him here, he was betting on powerful. He hoped she was powerful.

He didn't want the coffee, but he took it when she handed to him. It was black and stronger that he usually drank it, but it tasted good. "So why don't you smell like other witches?"

"Like Kouros, I'm not Wiccan," she told him, "but 'an it harm none' seems like a good way to live to me."

White witch.

He knew that Wiccans consider themselves witches—and some of them had enough witchblood to make it so. But witches, the real thing, weren't witches because of what they believed, but because of genetic heritage. A witch was born a witch and studied to become a better one. But for witches, real power came from blood and death—mostly other people's blood and death.

White witches, especially those outside of Wicca (where numbers meant safety), were weak and valuable sacrifices for black witches who didn't have their scruples. As Wendy the Witch had noted—witches seemed to have a real preference for killing their own.

He sipped at his coffee and asked, "So how have you managed without ending up as bits and pieces in someone else's cauldron?"

She snorted a laugh and set her coffee down abruptly. Grabbing a paper towel off its holder she held it to her face as she gasped and choked coffee, looking suddenly a lot less than thirty. When she was finished she said, "That's awesome. Bits and pieces. I'll have to remember that."

Still grinning she picked up the coffee again. He wished he could see her eyes, because he was pretty sure that whatever humor she'd felt was only surface deep.

"I tell you what," she said, "why don't you tell me who you are and what you know. That way I can tell you if I can help you or not."

"Fair enough," he said. The coffee was strong and he could feel it and the four other cups he'd had since midnight settle in his bones with caffeine's untrustworthy gift of nervous energy.

"I'm Tom Franklin and I'm second in the Emerald City Pack." She wasn't surprised by that. She'd known what he was as soon as she opened her door. "My brother Jon is a cop and a damn fine one. He's been on the Seattle PD for nearly twenty years and for the last six months he's been undercover as a street person. He was sent as part of a drug task force: there's been some nasty shit out on the street lately and he's been looking for it."

Wendy Moira Keller leaned back against the cabinets with a sigh. "I'd like to say that no witch would mess with drugs. Not from moral principals, mind you, witches, for the most part, don't have moral principles. But drugs are too likely to attract unwanted attention. We never have been as deep in secrecy as you wolves used to be, not when witches sometimes crop up in mundane families—we need to be part of society enough that they can find us. Mostly people think we're a bunch of harmless charlatans—trafficking in drugs would change all that for the worse. But the Samhain bunch is powerful enough that no one wants to face them—and Kouros is arrogant and crazy. He likes money and there is at least one herbalist in his followers who could manufacture some really odd stuff."

He shrugged. "I don't know. I'm interested in finding my brother, not in finding out if witches are selling drugs. It sounded to me like the drugs had nothing to do with my brother's kidnaping. Let me play Jon's call and you make the determination." He pulled out his cell phone and played the message for her.

It had come from a payphone. There weren't many of them left, as cell phones had made it less profitable to keep repairing the damage of vandals. But there was no mistaking the characteristic static and hiss as his brother talked very quietly into the mouthpiece.

Tom had called in favors and found the phone Jon had used, but the people who took his brother were impossible to pick out from the scents of the hundreds of people who had been there since the last rain—and his brother's scent stopped right at the payphone, outside of a battered convenience store. Stopped as if they'd teleported him to another planet—or, more prosaically, thrown him in a car.

Jon's voice, smoker-dark though he'd never touched tobacco or any of its relatives, slid through the apartment. "Look, Tom. My gut told me to call you tonight—and I listen to my gut. I've been hearing something on the street about a freaky group calling themselves Samhain—" He spelled it, to be sure Tom got it right. "Last few days I've had a couple of people following me that might be part of Samhain. No one wants to talk about 'em much. The streets are afraid of these..."

He didn't know if the witch could hear the rest. He'd been a wolf for twenty years and more so his judgment about what human senses were good for was pretty much gone.

He could hear the girl's sweet voice clearly though. "Lucky Jon?" she asked. "Lucky Jon, who are you calling? Let's hang it up, now." A pause, then the girl spoke into the phone, "Hello?" Another pause. "It's an answering machine, I think. No worries."

At the same time, a male, probably young, was saying in a rapid, rabid flow of sound, "I feel it...Doncha feel it? I feel it in him. This is the one. He'll do for Kouros." Then there was a soft click as the call ended.

The last fifty times he'd heard the recording he couldn't make out the last word. But with the information the witch had given him, he understood it just fine this time.

He looked at Choo's witch but he couldn't tell what she thought. Somewhere she'd learned to discipline her emotions so he could only smell the strong ones—like the flash of desire she'd felt as he'd smelled the back of her neck. Even in this situation it had been enough to raise a thread of interest. Maybe after they got his brother back they could do something about that interest. In the...

"How much of the last did you hear, Wendy?" he asked.

"Don't call me Wendy," she snapped. "It's Moira. No one called me Wendy except my mom and she's been dead a long time."

"Fine," he snapped back before he could control himself. He was tired and worried, but he could do better than that. He tightened his control and softened his voice. "Did you hear the guy? The one who said that he felt *it* in him—meaning my brother, I think. And that he would do for Kouros?"

"No. Or at least not well enough to catch his words. But I know the woman's voice. You're right, it was Samhain." Though he couldn't feel anything from her, her knuckles were white on the coffee cup.

"You need a Finder and I can't do that anymore. Wait," she held up a hand before he could say anything. "I'm not saying I won't help you, just that it could be a lot simpler. Kouros moves all the time. Did you trace the call? It sounded like a payphone to me."

"I found the phone booth he called from, but I couldn't find anything except that he'd been there." He tapped his nose, then glanced at her dark glasses and said, "I could smell him there and back trail him, but I couldn't trail him out. They transported him somehow."

"They don't know that he's a cop, or that his brother is a werewolf."

"He doesn't carry ID with him while he's undercover. I don't see how anyone would know I was his brother. Unless he told them, and he wouldn't."

"Good," she said. "They won't expect you. That'll help."

"So do you know a Finder I can go to?"

She shook her head. "Not one who will help you against Samhain. Anyone, *anyone* who makes a move against them is punished in some rather spectacular ways." He saw her consider sharing one or two of them with him and discard it. She didn't want him scared off. Not that he could be, not with Jon's life at stake. But it was interesting that she hadn't tried.

"If you take me to where they stole him, maybe I can find something they left behind, something to use to find them."

Tom frowned at her. She didn't know his brother, he hadn't mentioned money and he was getting the feeling that she could care less if he called in the authorities. "So if Samhain is so all powerful, how come you, a white witch, is willing to buck them?"

"You're a cop, too, aren't you?" She finished her coffee, but if she was waiting for a reaction, she wasn't going to get one. He'd seen the "all-knowing" witch act before. Her lips turned up as she set the empty cup on the counter. "It's not magic. Cops are easy to spot—suspicious is your middle name. Fair enough."

She pulled off her glasses and he saw that he'd been wrong. He'd been pretty sure she was blind—the other reason women wore wraparound sunglasses at night. And she was. But that wasn't why she wore the sunglasses.

Her left eye was Swamp Thing-green without pupil or white. Her right eye was gone and it looked as though it had been removed by someone who wasn't too good with a knife. It was horrible—and he'd seen some horrible things.

"Sacrifice is good for power," she said again. "But it works best if you can manage to make the sacrifice your own."

Jesus. She'd done it to herself.

She might not be able to see him, but she read his reaction just fine. She smiled tightly. "There were some extenuating circumstances," she continued. "You aren't going to see witches cutting off their fingers to power their spells— it doesn't work that way. But this worked for me," she tapped the scar tissue around her right eye. "Kouros did the other one first. That's why I'm willing to take them on. I've done it before and survived—and I still owe them a few." She replaced her sunglasses and he watched her relax as they settled into place.

Tom Franklin hadn't brought a car and, for obvious reasons, *she* didn't drive. He said the phone was only a couple of miles from her apartment and neither wanted to wait around for a cab. So they walked. She felt his start of surprise when she tucked her arm in his but he didn't object. At least he didn't jump away from her and say, "ick," like the last person who'd seen what she'd done to herself.

"You'll have to tell me when we come to curbs or if there's something in the way," she told him. "Or you can amuse yourself when I fall on my face. I can find my way around my apartment, but out here I'm at your mercy."

He said, with sober humor, "I imagine watching you trip over a few curbs would be a good way to get you to help Jon. Why don't you get a guide dog?"

"Small apartments aren't a good place for big dogs," she told him. "It's not fair to the dog."

They walked a few blocks in silence, the rain drizzling unhappily down the back of her neck and soaking the bottoms of the jeans she'd put on before they started out. It didn't always rain in Seattle, despite its reputation. He guided her as if he'd done it before, unobtrusively but clearly, as if they were waltzing instead of walking down the street. She relaxed and walked faster.

"Wendy." He broke the companionable silence with the voice of One Who Suddenly Comprehends. "It's worse than I thought. I was stuck on Casper the Friendly Ghost and Wendy the Good Little Witch. But Wendy Moira...I bet it's Wendy Moira Angela, isn't it."

She gave him a mock scowl. "I don't have a kiss for you and I can't fly, not even with fairy dust. And I *hate Peter Pan*, the play, and all the movies."

His arm moved and she could tell he was laughing to himself. "I bet."

"It could be worse, Toto," she told him. "I could belong to the Emerald City Pack."

He laughed out loud at that, a softer sound that she'd thought he'd have from the rough grumble of his voice. "You know, I've never thought of it that way. It seemed logical, Seattle being the Emerald City."

She might have said something, but he suddenly picked up his pace like a hunting dog spotting his prey. She kept her hand tight on his arm and did her best to keep up. He stopped at last. "Here."

She felt his tension, the desire for action of some sort. Hopefully she'd be able to provide him the opportunity. She released his arm and stepped to the side.

"All right," she told him, falling into the comfortable patter she adopted with most of her clients—erasing the odd intimacy that had sprung up between them. "I know the girl on your brother's phone—her name used to be Molly, but I think she goes by something like Spearmint or Peppermint, something -mint. I'm going to call for things that belong to her—a hair, a cigarette—anything will do. You'll have to do the looking. Whatever it is will glow, but it might be very small, easy to overlook."

"What if I don't see anything?"

"Then they didn't leave anything behind and I'll figure out something else to try."

She set aside her worries, shedding them like a duck would shed the cool Seattle rain. Closing her senses to the outside world, she reached into her well of power and drew out a bucketful and threw it out in a circle around her as she called to the essence that was Molly. She hadn't done this spell since she could see out of both eyes—but there was no reason she couldn't do it now. Once learned, spells came to her hand like trained spaniels and this one was no exception.

"What do you see?" she asked. The vibration of power warmed her against the cold fall drizzle that began to fall. There was something here, she could feel it.

"Nothing." His voice told her that he'd put a lot of hope into this working.

"There's something," she said, sensations crawling up her arms and over her shoulders. She held out her right hand, her left being otherwise occupied with the workings of her spell. "Touching me might help you see."

Warm flooded her as his hand touched hers...and she could see the faint traces Molly had left behind. She froze.

"Moira?"

She couldn't see anything else. Just bright bits of pink light sparkling from the ground, giving her a little bit of idea what the landscape looked like. She let go of his hand and the light disappeared, leaving her in darkness again.

"Did you see anything?" she asked, her voice hoarse. The oddity of seeing anything...she craved it too much and it made her wary because she didn't know how it worked.

"No."

He wanted his brother and she wanted to see. Just for a moment. She held her hand out. "Touch me, again."

...and the sparkles returned like glitter scattered in front of her. Small bits of skin and hair, too small for what she needed. But there was something...

She followed the glittering trail and, as if it had been hidden, a small wad of something blazed like a bonfire.

"Is there a wall just to our right?" she asked.

"A building and an alley." His voice was tight, but she ignored it. She had other business first.

They'd waited for Tom's brother in the alley. Maybe Jon came to the payphone here often.

She led Tom to the blaze and bent to pick up it up: soft and sticky, gum. Better, she thought, better than she could have hoped. Saliva would make a stronger guide than hair or fingernails. She released his hand reluctantly.

"What did you find?"

"Molly's gum." She allowed her magic to loosen the last spell and slide back to her, hissing as the power warmed her skin almost to the point of burning. The next spell would be easier, even if it might eventually need more power. Sympathetic magic—which used the connections between like things—was one of those affinities that ran through her father's bloodlines into her.

But before she tried any more magic, she needed to figure out what he'd done to her spell. How touching him allowed her to *see*.

She looked unearthly. A violent wind he had not felt, not even when she'd fastened on to his hand with fierce strength, had blown her hair away from her face. The skin on her hands was reddened, as if she held them too close to a fire. He wanted to soothe them—but he firmly intended never to touch her again.

He had no idea what she'd done to him while she held on to him and made his body burn and tremble. He didn't like surprises and she'd told him that he would have to look, not that she'd use him to *see*. He especially didn't like it that as long as she was touching him, he hadn't wanted her to let him go.

Witches gather more power from hurting those with magic, she'd said... more or less. People just like him—but it hadn't hurt, not that he'd noticed.

He wasn't afraid of her, not really. Witch or not she was no match for him. Even in human form it would be only a matter of moments before he broke her human-fragile body. But if she was using him...

"Why are you helping me?" he asked as he had earlier, but the question seemed more important now. He'd known what she was, but witch meant something different to him now. He knew enough about witches not to ask the obvious question though, like what it was she'd done to him. Witches, in his experience, were secretive about their spells—like junkyard dogs are secretive about their bones.

She'd taken something from him by using him that way...broken the trust he'd felt building between them. He needed to reestablish what he could expect out of her. Needed to know exactly what she was getting him into, beyond rescuing his brother. Witches are not altruistic. "What do you want out of this? Revenge for your blindness?"

She watched him...appeared to watch him anyway as she considered his question. There hadn't been many people who could lie to Tom before he Changed—cops learn all about lying the first year on the job. Afterwards...he could smell a lie a mile away an hour before it was spoken.

"Andy Choo sent you," she said finally. "That's one. Your brother's a policeman, and an investigation into his death might be awkward. That's two. He takes risks to help people he doesn't know, it's only right someone return the favor. That's three."

They weren't lies, but they weren't everything either. Her face was very still, as if the magic she'd worked had changed her view of him, too.

Then she tilted her head sideways and said in a totally different voice, hesitant and raw. "Sins of the fathers."

Here was absolute truth. Obscure as hell, but truth. "Sins of the fathers?"

"Kouros's real name is Lin Keller, though he hasn't used it in twenty years or more."

"He's your father." And then he added two and two. "Your *father* is running Samhain's Coven?" Her father had ruined her eye and—Tom could read between the lines—caused her to ruin the other? Her own father?

She drew in a deep breath—and for a moment he was afraid she was going to cry or something. But a stray gust of air brought the scent of her to him and he realized she was angry. It tasted like a werewolf's rage, wild and biting.

"I am not a part of it," she said, her voice a half octave lower than it had been. "I'm not bringing you to his lair so he can dine upon werewolf, too. I am here because some jerk made me feel sorry for him. I am here because I want both he and his brother out of my hair and safely out of the hands of my rat-bastard father so I won't have their deaths on my conscience, too."

Someone else might have been scared of her, she being a witch and all. Tom wanted to apologize—and he couldn't remember the last time that impulse had touched him. It was even more amazing because he wasn't at fault: she'd misunderstood him. Maybe she'd picked up on how appalled he was that her own father had maimed her—he hadn't been implying she was one of them.

He didn't apologize, though, or explain himself. People said things when they were mad that they wouldn't tell you otherwise.

"What was it you did to me?"

"Did to you?" Arctic ice might be warmer.

"When you were looking for the gum. It felt like you hit me with a bolt of lightning." He was damned if he'd tell her everything he felt.

Her right eyebrow peaked out above her sunglasses. Interest replaced coldness. "You felt like I was doing something to you?" And then she held out her left hand. "Take my hand."

He looked at it.

After a moment she smiled. He didn't know she had a smile like that in her. Bright and cheerful and sudden. Knowing. As if she had gained every thought that passed through his head. Her anger, the misunderstanding between them was gone as if it had never been.

"I don't know what happened," she told him gently. "Let me try re-creating it and maybe I can tell you."

He gave her his hand. Instead of taking it, she put only two fingers on his palm. She stepped closer to him, dropped her head so he could see her scalp gleaming pale underneath her dark hair. The magic that touched him this time was gentler, sparklers instead of fireworks—and she jerked her fingers away as if his hand were a hot potato.

"What the heck..." She rubbed her hands on her arms with nervous speed.

"What?"

"You weren't acting as my focus, I can tell you that much."

"So what was going on?"

She shook her head, clearly uncomfortable. "I think I was using you to *see*. I shouldn't be able to do that."

He found himself smiling grimly. "So I'm your seeing-eye wolf?"

"I don't know."

He recognized her panic, having seen it in his own mirror upon occasion. It was always frightening when something you thought was firmly under control broke free to run where it would. With him it was the wolf.

Something resettled in his gut. She hadn't done it on purpose, she wasn't using him.

"Is it harmful to me?"

She frowned. "Did it hurt?"

"No."

"Either time?"

"Neither time."

"Then it didn't harm you."

"All right," he said. "Where do we go from here?"

She opened her right hand, the one with the gum in it. "Not us. Me. This is going to show us where Molly is—and Molly will know where your brother is."

She closed her fingers, turned her hand palm down, then turned in a slow circle. She hit a break in the pavement and he grabbed her before she could do more than stumble. His hand touched her wrist and she turned her hand to grab him, as the kick of power flowed through his body once more.

"They're in a boat," she told him, and went limp in his arms.

She awoke with the familiar headache that usually accompanied the overuse of magic, and absolutely no idea of where she was. It smelled wrong to be her apartment, but she was lying on a couch with a blanket covering her.

Panic rose in her chest—sometimes she hated being blind.

"Back in the land of the living?"

"Tom?"

He must have heard the distress in her voice because when he spoke again, he was much closer and his voice was softer. "You're on a couch in my apartment. We were as close to mine as we were to yours, and I knew I could get us into my apartment. Yours is probably sealed with hocus-pocus. Are you all right?"

She sat up and put her feet on the floor and her erstwhile bed proved itself to be a couch. "Do you have something with sugar in it? Sweet tea or fruit juice?"

"Hot cocoa or tea," he told her.

"Tea."

He must have had water already hot because he was quickly back with a hot cup. She drank the sweet stuff down as fast as she could and the heat did as much as the sugar to clear her headache.

"Sorry," she said.

"For what, exactly," he said.

"For using you. I think you don't have any barriers," she told him slowly. "We all have safeguards, walls that keep out intruders. It's what keeps us safe."

In his silence she heard him consider that.

"So, I'm vulnerable to witches?"

She didn't know what to do with her empty cup, so she set it on the couch beside her. Then she used her left hand, her seeking hand, to *look* at him again.

"No, I don't think so. Your barriers seem solid…even stronger than usual as I'd expect from a wolf as far up the command structure as you are. I think you are only vulnerable to me."

"Which means?"

"Which means when I touch you I can see magic through your eyes…with practice I might even be able just to see. It means that you can feed my magic with your skin." She swallowed. "You're not going to like this."

"Tell me."

"You are acting like my familiar." She couldn't feel a thing from him. "If I had a familiar."

Floor boards creaked under his feet as his weight shifted. His shoulder brushed her as he picked up the empty cup. She heard him walk away from her and set the cup on a hard surface. "Do you need more tea?"

"No," she said, needing, suddenly to be in a familiar place. Somewhere she wasn't so dependent upon him. "I'm fine. If you would call me a taxi, I'd appreciate it." She stood up, too. Then realized she had no idea where the door was or what obstacles might be hiding on the floor. In her own apartment, redolent with her magic, she was never so vulnerable.

"Can you find my brother?"

She hadn't heard him move, not a creak, not a breath, but his voice told her he was no more than a few inches from her. Disoriented and vulnerable, she was afraid of him for the first time.

He took a big step away from her. "I'm not going to hurt you."

"Sorry," she told him. "You startled me. Do we still have the gum?"

"Yes. You said she was on a boat."

She'd forgotten, but as soon as he said it, she could picture it in her head. That hadn't been the way the spell was supposed to work. It was more of a "hot and cold" spell, but she could still see the boat in her mind's eye.

Nothing had really changed, except that she'd used someone without asking. There was still a policeman to be saved and her father to kill.

"If we still have the gum, I can find Molly—the girl on your brother's phone call."

"I have a buddy whose boat we can borrow."

"All right," she told him after a moment. "Do you have some aspirin?"

She hated boating. The rocking motion disrupted her sense of direction, the engine's roar obscured softer sounds, and the scent of the ocean covered the subtler scents she used to negotiate everyday life. Worse than all of that, though, was the thought of trying to swim without knowing where she was going. The damp air chilled her already cold skin.

"Which direction?" said Tom over the sound of the engine.

His presence shouldn't have made her feel better—werewolves couldn't swim at all—but it did. She pointed with the hand that held the gum. "Not far now," she warned him.

"There's a private dock about a half mile up the coast. Looks like it's been here awhile," he told me. "There's a boat—*The Tern*, the bird."

It felt right. "I think that must be it."

There were other boats on the water, she could hear them. "What time is it?"

"About ten in the morning. We're passing the boat right now."

Molly's traces, left on the gum, pulled toward its source, tugging Moira's hand toward the back of the boat. "That's it."

"There's a park with docks about a mile back," he said and the boat tilted to the side. "We'll go tie up there and come back on foot."

But when he'd tied the boat up, he changed his mind. "Why don't you stay here and let me check this out?"

Moira rubbed her hands together. It bothered her to have her magic doing something it wasn't supposed to be and she'd let it throw her off her game: time to collect herself. She gave him a sultry smile. "Poor blind girl," she said. "Must be kept out of danger, do you think?" She turned a hand palm up and heard the whoosh of flame as it caught fire. "You'll need me when you find Molly—you may be a werewolf, but she's a witch who looks like a pretty young thing." She snuffed the flame and dusted off her hands. "Besides, she's afraid of me. She'll tell me where your brother is."

She didn't let him know how grateful she was for the help he gave her exiting the boat. When this night was over he'd go back to his life and she to hers. If she wanted to keep him—she knew that he wouldn't want to be kept by her. She was a witch and ugly with scars of the past.

Besides, if her dreams were right, she wouldn't survive to see nightfall.

She threaded through the dense underbrush as if she could see every hanging branch, one hand on his back and her other held out in front of her. He wondered if she was using magic to see.

She wasn't using him. Her hand in the middle of his back was warm and light, but his flannel shirt was between it and skin. Probably she was reading his body language and using her upraised hand as an insurance policy against low-hanging branches.

They followed a half-overgrown path that had been trod out a hundred feet or so from the coast, which was obscured by ferns and underbrush. He kept his ears tuned so if they started heading away from the ocean he'd know it.

The Tern had been moored in a small natural harbor on a battered dock next to the remains of a boathouse. A private property rather than the public dock he'd used.

They'd traveled north and were somewhere not too far from Everett by his reckoning. He wasn't terribly surprised when their path ended in a brand-new eight-foot chain-link fence. Someone had a goldmine on their hands and they were waiting to sell it to some developer when the price was right. Until then they'd try to keep out the riffraff.

He helped Moira over the fence, mostly a matter of whispering a few directions until she found the top of it. He waited until she was over and then vaulted over himself.

The path that they'd been following continued on, though not nearly as well-traveled as it had been before the fence. A quarter-mile of blackberry brambles ended abruptly in thigh-deep, damp grasslands that might once have been a lawn. He stopped before they left the cover of the bushes, sinking down to rest on his heels.

"There's a burnt-out house here," he told Moira who had ducked down when he did. "It must have burned down a couple of years ago because I don't smell it."

"Hidden," she commented.

"Someone's had tents up here," he told her. "And I see the remnants of a camp fire."

"Can you see the boat from here?"

"No, but there's a path I think should lead down to the water. I think this is the place."

She pulled her hand away from his arm. "Can you go check it out without being seen?"

"It would be easier if I do it as a wolf," Tom admitted. "But I don't dare. We might have to make a quick getaway and it'll be a while before I can shift back to human." He hoped Jon would be healthy enough to pilot in an emergency—but he didn't like to make plans that depended upon an unknown. Moira wasn't going to be piloting a boat anywhere.

"Wait," she told him. She murmured a few words and then put her cold fingers against his throat. A sudden shock, like a static charge on steroids, hit him and when it was over her fingers were hot on his pulse. "You aren't invisible, but it'll make people want to overlook you."

He pulled out his HK and checked the magazine before sliding it back in. The big gun fit his hand like a glove. He believed in using weapons, guns or fangs, whatever got the job done.

"It won't take me long."

"If you don't go you'll never get back," she told him and gave him a gentle push. "I can take care of myself."

It didn't sit right with him, leaving her alone in the territory of his enemies, but common sense said he'd have a better chance of roaming unseen. And no one tackled a witch lightly—not even other witches.

Spell or no, he slid through the wet overgrown trees like a shadow, crouching to minimize his silhouette and avoiding anything likely to crunch. One thing living in Seattle did was minimize the number of things that could crunch under your foot—all the leaves were wet and moldy without a noise to be had.

The boat was there, bobbing gently in the water. Empty. He closed his eyes and let the morning air tell him all it could.

His brother had been in the boat. There had been others, too—Tom memorized their scent. If anything happened to Jon he'd track them down and kill them, one by one. Once he had them, he let his nose lead him to Jon.

He found blood where Jon had scraped against a tree, crushed plants where his brother had tried to get away and rolled around in the mud with another man. Or maybe he'd just been laying a trail for Tom. Jon knew Tom would come for him—that's what family did.

The path the kidnappers took paralleled the waterfront for a while and then headed inland, but not for the burnt-out house. Someone had found a better hide-out. Nearly hidden under a shelter of trees, a small barn nestled snugly amidst broken pieces of corral fencing. Its silvered sides bore only a hint of red paint, but the aluminum roof, though covered with moss, was undamaged.

And his brother was there. He couldn't quite hear what Jon was saying, but he recognized his voice...and the slurring rapid rhythm of his schizophrenic-mimicry. If Jon was acting, he was all right. The relief of that settled in his spine and steadied his nerves.

All he needed to do was get his witch...movement caught his attention and he dropped to the ground and froze, hidden by wet grass and weeds.

Moira wasn't surprised when they found her—ten in the morning isn't a good time to hide. It was one of the young ones—she could tell by the surprised squeal and the rapid thud of footsteps as he ran for help.

Of course if she'd really been trying to hide, she might have managed it. But it had occurred to her, sometime after Tom left, that if she wanted to find Samhain—the easiest thing might be to let them find her. So she set about attracting their attention.

If they found her, it would unnerve them. They knew she worked alone. Her arrival here would puzzle them, but they wouldn't look for anyone else—leaving Tom as her secret weapon.

Magic calls to magic, unless the witch takes pains to hide it, so any of them should have been able to feel the flames that danced over her hands. It had taken them longer than she expected. While she waited for the boy to return, she found a sharp-edged rock and put it in her pocket. She folded her legs and let the coolness of the damp earth flow through her.

She didn't hear him come, but she knew by his silence who the young covenist had run to.

"Hello, Father," she told him, rising to her feet. "We have much to talk about."

She didn't look like a captive, Tom thought, watching Moira walk to the barn as if she'd been there before, though she might have been following the sullen-looking, half-grown boy who stalked through the grass ahead of her. A tall man followed them both, his hungry eyes on Moira's back.

His wolf recognized another dominant male with a snarl, while Tom thought that the man was too young to have a grown daughter. But there was no one else this could be than Lin Keller—that predator was not a man who followed anyone or allowed anyone around him who might challenge him. He'd seen an Alpha or two like that.

Tom watched them until they disappeared into the barn.

It hurt to imagine she might have betrayed him—as if there were some bond between them, though he hadn't known her a full day. Part of him would not believe it. He remembered her indignation when she thought he believed she was part of Samhain and it comforted him.

It didn't matter, couldn't matter. Not yet. Saving Jon mattered and the rest would wait. His witch was captured or had betrayed him. Either way it was time to let the wolf free.

The Change hurt, but experience meant he made no sound as his bones rearranged themselves and his muscles stretched and slithered to adjust to his new shape. It took fifteen minutes of agony before he rose on four paws, a snarl fixed on his muzzle—ready to kill someone. Anyone.

Instead he stalked like a ghost to the barn where his witch waited. He rejected the door they'd used, but prowled around the side where four stall doors awaited. Two of them were broken with missing boards, one of the openings was big enough for him to slide through.

The interior of the barn was dark and the stall's half-walls blocked his view of the main section where his quarry waited. Jon was still going strong, a wild ranting conversation with no one about the Old Testament, complete with quotes. Tom knew a lot of them himself.

"Killing things again, Father?" said Moira's cool disapproving voice, cutting through Jon's soliloquy.

And suddenly Tom could breathe again. They'd found her somehow, Samhain's Coven had, but she wasn't one of them.

"So judgmental." Tom had expected something...bigger from the man's voice. His own Alpha, for instance, could have made a living as a televangelist with his raw fire-and-brimstone voice. This man sounded like an accountant.

"Kill her. You have to kill her before she destroys us—I have seen it." It was the girl from Jon's message, Molly.

"You couldn't see your way out of a paper bag, Molly," said Moira. "Not that you're wrong, of course."

There were other people in the barn, Tom could smell them, but they stayed quiet.

"You aren't going to kill me," said Kouros. "If you could have done that you'd have done it before now. Which brings me to my point, why are you here?"

"To stop you from killing this man," Moira told him.

"I've killed men before—and you haven't stopped me. What is so special about this one?"

Moira felt the burden of all those deaths upon her shoulders. He was right. She could have killed him before—before he'd killed anyone else.

"This one has a brother," she said.

She felt Tom's presence in the barn, but her look-past-me spell must have still been working because no one seemed to notice. And any witch with a modicum of sensitivity to auras would have felt him. His brother was a faint trace to her left—which his constant stream of words made far more clear than her magic was able to.

Her father she could only follow from his voice.

There were other people in the structure—she hadn't quite decided what the cavernous building was: probably a barn, given the dirt floor and faint odor of cow—but she couldn't pinpoint them either. She knew where Molly was, though. And Molly was the important one, Kouros's right hand.

"Someone *paid* you to go up against me?" Her father's voice was faintly incredulous. "Against us?"

Then he did something, made some gesture. She wouldn't have known except for Molly's sigh of relief. So she didn't feel too badly when she tied Molly's essence, through the gum she still held, into her shield.

When the coven's magic hit the shield, it was Molly who took the damage. Who died. Molly, her little sister whose presence she could no longer feel.

Someone, a young man, screamed Molly's coven name—Mentha. And there was a flurry of movement where Moira had last sensed her.

Moira dropped the now-useless bit of gum on the ground.

"Oh you'll pay for that," breathed her father. "Pay in pain and power until there is nothing left of you."

Someone sent power her way, but it wasn't a concerted spell from the coven and it slid off her protections without harm. Unlike the fist that struck her in the face, driving her glasses into her nose and knocking her to the ground—her father's fist. She'd recognize the weight of it anywhere.

Unsure of where her enemies were, she stayed where she was, listening. But she didn't hear Tom, he was just suddenly there. And the circle of growing terror that spread around him—of all the emotions possible, it was fear that she could sense most often—told her he was in his lupine form. It must have been impressive.

"Your victim has a brother," she told her father again, knowing he'd hear the smugness in her tones. "And you've made him very angry."

The beast beside her roared. Someone screamed...even witches are afraid of monsters.

The coven broke. Children most of them, they broke and ran. Molly's death, followed by a beast out of their worst nightmares, was more than they could face, partially trained, deliberately crippled fodder for her father that they were.

Tom growled, the sound finding a silent echo in her own chest as if he were a bass drum. He moved, a swift silent predator, and someone who hadn't run died. Tom's brother, she noticed, had fallen entirely silent.

"A werewolf," breathed Kouros. "Oh, now there is a worthy kill." But she felt his terror and knew he'd attack Tom before he took care of her.

She reached out with her left hand, intending to spread her own defenses to the wolf—though that would leave them too thin to be very effective—but she hadn't counted on the odd effect he had on her magic. On her.

Her father's spell—a vile thing that would have induced terrible pain and permanently damaged Tom had it hit—connected just after she touched the wolf. And for a moment, maybe a whole breath, nothing happened.

Then she felt every hair under her hand stand to attention and Tom made an odd sound and power swept through her from him—all the magic Kouros had sent—and it filled her well to overflowing.

And she could see. For the first time since she'd been thirteen she could see.

She stood up, shedding broken pieces of sunglasses to the ground. The wolf beside her was huge, chocolate-brown, and easily tall enough to leave her hand on his shoulder as she came to her feet. A silvery scar curled around his snarling muzzle. His eyes were yellow-brown and cold. A sweeping glance showed her two dead bodies, one burnt the other savaged; a very dirty, hairy man tied to a post with his hands behind his back, who could only be Tom's brother Jon.

And her father, looking much younger than she remembered him. No wonder he went for teens to populate his *coven*—he was stealing their youth as well as their magic. A coven should be a meeting of equals, not a feeding trough for a single greedy witch.

She looked at him and saw that he was afraid. He should be. The werewolf had frightened him, too, no matter how calm he'd sounded. He'd used all of his magic to power his spell—he'd left himself defenseless. And now he was afraid of her.

Just as she had dreamed. She pulled the stone out of her pocket—and it seemed to her that she had all the time in the world to use it—and cut her right hand open. Then she pointed it, her bloody hand of power at him.

"*By the blood we share,*" she whispered and felt the magic gather. "*Blood follows blood.*"

"You'll die, too," Kouros said frantically as if she didn't know.

Before she spoke the last word she lifted her other hand from Tom's soft fur that none of this magic should fall to him. And as soon as she did, she could no longer see. But she wouldn't be blind for long.

Tom started moving before her fingers left him, knocking into her with his hip and spoiling her aim. Her magic flooded through him, hitting him instead of the one she'd aimed all that power at. The wolf let it sizzle through his bones and returned it to her, clean.

Pleasant as that was, he didn't let it distract him from his goal. He was moving so fast that the man was still looking at Moira when the wolf landed on him.

Die, he thought as he buried his fangs in Kouros's throat, drinking his blood and his death in one delicious mouthful of flesh. This one had moved against the wolf's family, against the wolf's witch. Satisfaction made the meat even sweeter.

"Tom?" Moira sounded lost.

"Tom's fine," answered his brother's rusty voice, he'd talked himself hoarse. "You just sit there until he calms down a little. You all right, lady?"

Tom lifted his head and looked at his witch. She was huddled on the ground looking small and lost, her scarred face bared for all the world to see. She looked fragile, but Tom knew better and Jon would learn.

As the dead man under his claws had learned. Kouros died knowing she would have killed him.

He had been willing to give her that kill—but not if it meant her death. So Tom had the double satisfaction of saving her and killing the man. He went back to his meal.

"Tom, stop that," Jon said. "Ick. I know you aren't hungry. Stop it now."

"Is Kouros dead?" His witch sounded shaken up.

"As dead as anyone I've seen," said Jon. "Look, Tom. I appreciate the sentiment, I've wanted to do that anytime this last day. But I'd like to get out of here before some of those kids decide to come back while I'm still tied up." He paused. "Your lady needs to get out of here."

Tom hesitated, but Jon was right. He wasn't hungry anymore and it was time to take his family home.

Hit
Bruce McAllister

"If life is a 'divine comedy,' as many insist it is, who has the last laugh?"

I'm given the assignment by an angel—I mean that, an angel—one wearing a high-end Armani suit with an Ermenegildo Zegna tie. A loud red one. Why red? To project confidence? Hell, I don't know. I'm having lunch at Parlami's, a mediocre bistro on Melrose where I met my first ex, when in he walks with what looks like a musical instrument case—French horn or tiny tuba, I'm thinking—and sits down. We do the usual disbelief dialogue from the movies: He announces he's an angel. I say, "You're kidding." He says, "No. Really." I ask for proof. He says, "Look at my eyes," and I do. His pupils are missing. "So?" I say. "That's easy with contacts." So he makes the butter melt on the plate just by looking at it, and I say, "Any demon could do that." He says, "Sure, but let's cut the bullshit, Anthony. God's got something He wants you to do, and if you'll take the job, He'll forgive everything." I shrug and tell him, "Okay, okay. I believe. Now what?" Everyone wants to be forgiven, and it's already sounding like any other contract.

He reaches for the case, opens it right there (no one's watching—not even the two undercover narcs—the angel makes sure of that) and hands it to me. It's got a brand-new crossbow in it. Then he tells me what I need to do to be forgiven.

"God wants you to kill the oldest vampire."

"Why?" I ask and can see him fight to keep those pupilless eyes from rolling. Even angels feel boredom, contempt, things like that, I'm thinking, and that makes it all that more convincing.

"Because He can't do it."

"And why is that?" I'm getting braver. Maybe they do need me. I'm good—one of the three best repairmen west of Vegas, just like my sainted dad was—and maybe guys who say yes to things like this aren't all that common.

"Because the fellow—the oldest bloodsucker—is the son of...well, you know..."

"No, I don't."

"Does 'The Prince of Lies' ring a bell?"

"Oh." I'm quiet for a second. Then I get it. It's like the mob and the police back in my uncle's day in Jersey. You don't take out the don because then maybe they take out your chief.

I ask him if this is the reasoning.

The contempt drops a notch, but holds. "No, but close enough."

"And where do I do it?"

"The Vatican."

"The Holy City?"

"Yes."

"Big place, but doesn't have to be tricky." I'd killed men with a wide range of appliance—the angel knew that—and suddenly this wasn't sounding any trickier. Crossbow. Composite frame, wooden arrows—darts—whatever they're called. One to the heart. I'd seen enough movies and TV.

"Well," he says, "maybe. But most of the Jesuits there are vampires too."

"Oh."

"That's the bad news. The good news is they're pissed at him—the oldest vampire, I mean. They think he wants to turn mortal. He's taken up with some twenty-eight-year-old bambina who knows almost as many languages as he does—a Vatican interpreter—and they've got this place in Siena—Tuscany, no less—and he hasn't bitten her, and it's been making the Brothers, his great-great-great-grandchildren, nervous for about a month now. Handle it right and she just might help you even if they don't."

"You serious?"

"Yes."

"Why?"

"Because she wants to be one, too—she's very Euro-goth—you know the type—and he just won't bite her."

No, I don't know the type, but I say, "She's that vindictive?"

"What woman isn't?"

This sounds awfully sexist for an angel, but I don't argue. Maybe angels get dumped too.

"Does he really?" I ask.

"Does he really what?"

"Want to be mortal again."

"He never was mortal."

"He was born that way?"

The eyes—which suddenly have pupils now, majorly dark blue ones—are starting to roll again. "What do you think? Son of You-Know-Who—who's not exactly happy with the traditional wine and wafer thing, but likes the idea of blood and immortality."

"Makes sense," I say, eyeing the narcs, who are eyeing two Fairfax High girls, "but why does God need someone to kill him if he wants to flip?"

He takes a breath. What an idiot, the pupils say. "Remember when China tried to give Taiwan a pair of pandas?"

I'm impressed. This guy's up on earthly news. "No."

"Taiwan couldn't take them."

"Why not?"

He takes another breath and I hear him counting to ten.

"Okay, okay," I say. "I get it. If they took the pandas, they were in bed with China. They'd have to make nice with them. You accept cute cuddly creatures from someone and it looks like love, right?"

"Basically."

"If You-Know-Who's son flips—goes mortal—God has to accept him."

"Right."

"And that throws everything off. No balance. No order. Chaos and eventually, well, Hell?"

The angel nods, grateful, I can tell, that I'm no stupider than I am.

I think for a moment.

"How many arrows do I get?"

I think he'll laugh, but he doesn't.

"Three."

"Three?" I don't like the feeling suddenly. It's like some Bible story where the guy gets screwed so that God can make some point about fatherly love or other form of sacrifice. Nice for God's message. Bad for the guy.

"It's a holy number," he adds.

"I get that," I say, "but I don't think so. Not three."

"That's all you get."

"What makes you think three will do it—even if they're all heart shots?"

"You only need one."

The bad feeling jumps a notch.

"Why?"

He looks at me and blinks. Then nods. "Well, each has a point made from a piece of the Cross, Mr. Pagano. We were lucky to get even that much. It's hidden under three floors and four tons of tiles in Jerusalem, you know."

"What is?"

"The Cross. You know which one."

I blink. "Right. That's the last thing he needs in the heart."

"Right."

"So all I've got to do is hit the right spot."

"Yes."

"Which means I need practice. How much time do I have?"

"A week."

I take a breath. "I'm assuming you—and He—know a few good crossbow schools, ones with weekly rates."

"We've got special tutors for that."

I'm afraid to ask. "And what do these tutors usually do?"

"Kill vampires."

"And you need me when you've got a team of them?"

"He'd spot them a mile away. They're his kids, you might say. He's been around 2000 years and he's had kids and his kids have had kids—in the way that they have them—you know, the biting and sucking thing—and they can sense each other a mile away. These kids—the ones working for us—are ones who've come over. Know what I mean?"

"And they weren't enough to throw off the—the 'balance.'"

Now he laughs. "No, they're little fish. Know what I mean?"

I don't really, but I nod. He's beginning to sound like my other uncle—Gian Felice—the one from Teaneck, the one with adenoids. *Know what I mean?*

I go home to my overpriced stucco shack in Sherman Oaks and to my girlfriend, who's got cheekbones like a runway model and lips that make men beg, but wears enough lipstick to stop a truck, and in any case is sick and tired of what I do for a living and probably has a right to be. I should know something besides killing people, even if they're people the police don't mind having dead and I'm as good at it as my father wanted me to be. It's too easy making excuses. Like a pool hustler who never leaves the back room. You start to think it's the whole world.

She can tell from my face that I've had one of those meetings. She shakes her head and says, "How much?"

"I'm doing it for free."

'No, Anthony, you're not."

"I am."

"Are you trying to get me to go to bed with your brother? He'd like that. Or Aaron, that guy at the gym? Or do you just want me to go live with my sister?"

She can be a real harpy.

"No," I tell her, and mean it.

"You must really hate me."

"I don't hate you, Mandy. I wouldn't put up with your temper tantrums if I hated you." The words are starting to hurt—the ones she's using and the ones I'm using. I do love her, I'm telling myself. I wouldn't live with her if I didn't love her, would I?

"And I live on what while you're away, Anthony?"

"I'll sell the XKE?"

"To who?"

"My cousin. He wants it. He's wanted it for years."

She looks at me for a moment and I see a flicker of— kindness. "You in trouble?"

"No."

"Then you're lying or you're crazy but anyway it comes down to the same thing: You don't love me. If you did, you'd take care of me. I'm moving out tomorrow, Anthony Pagano, and I'm taking the Jag."

"Please...."

"If you'll charge."

"I can't."

"You are in trouble."

"No."

How do you tell her you've got to kill a man who isn't really a man but wants to be one, and that if you do God will forgive you all the other killings?

She heads to the bedroom to start packing.

I get the case out, open it, touch the marbleized surface of the thing, and hope to hell that God wants a horny assassin because I'm certainly not seeing any action this night or any other before I leave for Rome, and action does help steady my finger. Which Mandy knows. Which every woman I've ever been with knows.

When I get up the next morning, she's gone. The note on the bathroom mirror, in slashes of that lipstick of hers, says, "I hope you miss my body so bad you can't walk or shoot straight, Anthony."

We do the instruction at a dead-grass firing range in Topanga Canyon. My tutor is a no-nonsense kid—maybe twenty—with Chinese characters tattooed around his neck like a dog collar, naked eyebrows, pierced tongue, nose, lower lip. He's serious and strict, but seems happy enough for a vampire killer. He picks me up in his Tundra and on the way to the canyon, three manikins (that holy number) bouncing in the truck bed, he says, "Yeah, I like it—even if it's not what you'd think from a *Buffy* rerun or a John Carpenter flick—you know, like that one shot in Mexico. More like CSI—not the Bruckheimer, but the Discovery Channel. Same way that being an investigative journalist isn't as much fun as you think it'll be—at least that's what I hear. All those hours Googling the public record. In my line of work, it's the tracking and casing and light-weapons prep. But you know more about that than I do, Mr. Pagano. Wasn't your dad—"

"Sounds like you've been to college, Kurt," I say.

"A year at a community college—that's it. But I'm a reader. Always have been."

How do you answer that? I've read maybe a dozen books in my life, all of them short and necessary, and I'm sitting with this kid who reads probably three fat ones a week. Not only is he more literate than I am, he's going to teach *me* how to kill—something I really thought I knew how to do.

"Don't worry," he says. "You'll pick it up. Your—shall we say 'previous training and experience'—should make up for your age, slower reflexes, *you* know."

What can I say? I've got fifteen years on him and we both know it. My reflexes *are* slower than his.

As we hit the Ventura Freeway, he tells me what I'm packing. "In the case beside you, Mr. Pagano, you've got a Horton Legend HD with a Talon Ultra-Light trigger, DP2 CamoTuff limbs, SpeedMax riser, alloy cams, Microflight arrow groove, and Dial-a-Range trajectory compensator—with LS MX aluminum arrows and Hunter Elite 3-arrow quivers. How does that make you feel?"

"Just wonderful," I tell him.

The firing range is upscale and very hip. There are dozens of trophy wives and starlets wearing $300 Scala baseball caps, newsboy caps, and sun visors. There are almost as many very metro guys wearing $600 aviator shades and designer jungle cammies. And all of them are learning Personal Protection under the tutelage of guys who are about as savvy about what they're doing as the ordinary gym trainer. They're all trying their best to hit fancy bull's-eye, GAG, PMT, and other tactical targets made for pros, but I'm looking like an even bigger idiot trying to hit, with my handfuls of little crossbow darts, the manikins the kid has lined up for me at fifty yards. The other shooters keep rubbernecking to get a look at us. The kid stares them down and they look away. If they only knew.

"Do the arrows made from the other material—" I begin. "Do they—uh—act…?" I ask.

"Arrows with wood made from the Cross act the same," the kid says, very professional. "We balance them the way we'd balance any arrow."

"When it hits—"

"When it hits a vampire, I'm sure it doesn't feel like ordinary wood. I've never taken one myself."

"Glad to hear it."

"Actually, someone did try an arrow once. Deer bow. Two inches off the mark. I've got a scar. Want to see it?"

"Not really. How would it feel to *us*?"

"You mean mortals?"

"Right."

"It would probably hurt like hell, and if you happened to die I doubt it would get you a free pass to Heaven."

"That's too bad."

"Isn't it."

When I've filled the manikins with ten quivers' worth of arrows and my heart-shot rate is a sad 10 percent, we quit for the day. It's getting close to sunset, one of those gorgeous smoggy ones. The other shooters have hit the road in their Escalades, H3s, and Land Sharks, and the kid is acting distracted.

"Date?"

"What?"

"You know. Two people. Dinner and a movie. Clubbing. Whatever."

"You could say that. But it's a threesome. Can't stand the guy—he's a Red-State crewcut ex-Delta-Forcer—but the girl, she's so hot she'll melt your belt buckle."

He can tell I'm not following.

"A job. It'll take the three of us about three hours. You know, holy number."

"Yeah, I know."

"Two Hollywood producers. Both vampires. They've got two very sexy, very cool low-budget vampire flicks—ones where the vampires win because, hey, if you're cool and sexy you should win, right?—in post-production, two more in production and three in development. These flicks will seduce too many teens to the Dark Side, He says, so He wants us to take out their makers. They'll be having late poolside dinner at Blue-on-Blue tonight. We'll be interrupting it."

"I see," I say. I'm staring at him and he beats me to it.

"You want to know what we eat if we can't drink blood."

"Yes, I do."

"We eat what you eat. We don't need blood since we came over."

"Which means you don't—how to put it?—you don't perpetuate the species."

"Right."

"Which can't make the elders very happy."

"No, it can't."

By the end of the sixth day my heart-shot rate is 80 percent and the kid's nodding, doing a dance move or two in his tight black jeans, and saying "You're the man, Anthony. You're the man." I shouldn't admit it, but what he thinks does matter.

When I get there, courtesy of Alitalia (the angel won't pay for Lufthansa), the city of Siena, in lovely Tuscany, country of my forefathers, is a mess. It's just after the horserace, the one where a dozen riders—each of them repping a neighborhood known for an animal (snail, dolphin, goose—you get the picture)—beat each other silly with little riding crops to impress their local Madonna. There's trash everywhere. I've got the crossbow in its case, and a kid on a Vespa tries to grab it as he sails by, but I'm ready. I know kids—I was one once—and I nail him with a kick to his knee. The Vespa skids and he flies into a fountain not far away. The fountain is a big sea shell—a scallop—which I know from reading my *Fodor's* must be this neighborhood's emblem for the race. He gets up, crying, gives me the *va-funcu* with his arm and fist, and screams something in native Sienese—which isn't at all the Italian I grew up with but which I'm sure means, "I'm going to tell my dad and brothers, you asshole!"

The apartment is not in the Neighborhood of the Scallop, but in the Neighborhood of the Salmon, and the girl who answers the door is stunning. Tall. The kind of blonde who tans better than a commercial. Eyes like shattered glass, long legs, cute little dimple in her chin. I don't see how he can keep his teeth off her.

This is Euro-goth? I don't think so.

"So you're the one," she says. Her English is perfect, just enough accent to make it sexy.

"Yeah. Anthony Pagano." I stick out my hand. She doesn't take it.

"Giovanna," she says. "Giovanna Musetti. And that's what you're going to do it with?" She gestures with her head at my case. She can't take her eyes off it.

"Yeah."

"Please don't do it," she says suddenly.

I don't know what to say.

"You're supposed to want him dead."

She looks at me like I'm crazy.

"Why would I want him dead?"

"Because you want him to bite you—because you want to be one too—and he—he won't oblige."

"Who told you that?"

"The—the angel who hired me."

"I know that angel. He was here. He interviewed me."

"You don't want him dead?"

"Of course not. I love him."

I sit down on the sofa. They've got a nice place. Maybe they enjoy the horseraces. Even if they don't, the tourists aren't so bad off-season according to *Fodor's*. And maybe when you're the oldest vampire, you don't have to obey the no-daylight rule. Maybe you get to walk around in the day—in a nice, clean, modern medieval city—maybe one you knew when you were only a thousand years old and it was being built and a lot trashier—and feel pretty mortal and normal. Who knows?

"Why did my employer get it wrong?"

She's got the same look the angel did. "The angel didn't get it wrong, Mr. Pagano. He *lied*."

"Why?" I'm thinking: Angels are allowed to do that? Lie? Sure, if God wants them to.

"Why?" I ask again.

"I don't know. That's one of the things I love about Frank—"

"Your man's name is Frank?"

"It is now. That's what he's gone by for the last hundred years, he says, and I believe him. That's one of the things I love."

"What?"

"That he doesn't lie. That he doesn't need to. He's seen it all. He's had all the power you could want and he doesn't want it anymore. He's bitten so many people he lost count after a century, and he doesn't want to do it anymore. He's tired of living the lie any vampire has to live. He's very human in his heart, Mr. Pagano—in his soul—so human you wouldn't believe it—and he's tired of doing his father's bidding, the darkness, the blasphemy, all of that. I don't think he was ever really into it, but he had to do it. He was his father's son, so he had to do it. Carry on the tradition—the business. Do you know what that's like?"

"Yes. I do."

I'm starting to like her, of course—really like her. She's great eye candy, but it isn't just that. The more she talks, the more I like what's inside. She understands—she understands the mortal human heart.

THE URBAN FANTASY ANTHOLOGY

"But I'm supposed to kill him," I say.

"Why?"

"Because of—because of 'balance.'"

"What?"

"That's what my employer said. Even though Frank wants to flip, and you'd think that would be a plus, it wouldn't be. It would throw things off."

"You really believe that, Anthony?"

Now we're on first-name basis, and I don't mind.

I don't say a thing for a second.

"I don't know."

"It sounds wrong, doesn't it."

"Yeah, it does."

We sit silent for a while. I'm looking at her hard, too interested, so I make myself look away.

"Do I make you self-conscious?" she asks gently.

That turns me red. "It's not you. It's me. You look awfully good. It's just me."

"That's sweet." Now she's doing the looking away, cheeks a little red, and when she looks back, she says, "Any idea why God would *really* want him killed?"

"None whatsoever."

"But you've still got to do it."

"There was this promise."

"I know."

"You do?"

"Sure. If you do it, He'll forgive everything. They offered me that too if I helped you."

"And you said no?"

"Yes."

She loves this guy—this vampire—this son of You-Know-Who—so much she'll turn down an offer like that? Now I'm *really* looking at her. She's not just beautiful, she's got *coglioni*. She'll stand up to God for love.

I'm thinking these things and also wondering whether the angel lied about her because maybe she stiffed him. Because *he's* the vindictive one.

"There's nothing I can say to stop you?" she's asking. She doesn't say "nothing

I can *do*." She says "nothing I can *say*," and that's all the difference in the world.

"Wish there were, but there isn't. Where is he?"

"You know."

"Yeah, I guess I do. He's in the Vatican somewhere trying to convince those Jesuit vampires that it's okay if he turns."

"That's where he said he was going when he left a week ago, so I'm sure it's true. Like I said, he—"

"Never lies. I know."

I get up.

"I'm sorry."

"Me too."

I'm depressed when I get to Rome and not because the city is big and noisy and feels like L.A. (My dad's people were from Calabria and they never had a good thing to say about *Romani*, so I'm biased.) It's because—well, just because. But when I reach the Vatican, I feel a lot better. Now this—this is beautiful. St. Peter's. The church, the square, marble everywhere, sunlight blinding you like the flashlight of God. Even the silly little Fiats going round and round the circle like they're trapped and can't get off are nice.

He's not going to be in the basilica, I know. That's where the Pope is—that new strict guy, Benedict—and it's visiting day, dispensations, blessings, the rest. I don't even try to go through the main Vatican doorway on the opposite side. Too many tourists there, too. Instead I go to a side entrance, Via Gerini, where there's no one. Construction cones, sidewalk repair, a big door with carvings on it. Why this entrance, I don't know. Just a hunch.

I know God can open any door for me that He wants to, so if my hunch is right why isn't the door opening? Maybe there'll be a mark on the right door—you know, a shadow that looks like the face of Our Lady, or the number 333, something—but before I can check the door for a sign, something starts flapping above my head and scares the shit out of me. I think it's a bat at first— that would make sense—but it's just a pigeon. No, a dove. Doves are smaller and pigeons aren't this white.

I know my employer thinks I'm slow, but a *white dove*?

The idiot bird keeps flapping two feet from my head and now I see it—a twig of something in its beak. I don't want to know.

The bird flies off, stops, hovers, and waits. I'm supposed to follow, so I do.

The door it's stopped at is the third one down from mine, of course. No face of Our Lady on it, but when I step up to it, it of course clicks and swings open.

We go through the next doorway, and the next, and the next, seven doorways in all—from a library to a little museum, then another library, then an office, then an archive with messy files, then a bigger museum. Some of the rooms are empty—of people, I mean—and some aren't, and when they're not, the people, some in suits or dresses and some in clerical outfits—give me a look like, "Well, he certainly seems to know where he's going with his musical instrument. Perhaps they're having chamber music with *espresso* for *gli ufficiali*. And of course that can't really be a pure white dove with an olive twig in its beak flapping in front of him, so everything's just fine. *Buon giorno, Signore.*"

When the bird stops for good, hovering madly, it's a really big door and it doesn't open right off. But I know this is it—that my guy is on the other side. Whatever he's doing, he's there and I'd better get ready. He's a vampire. Maybe he's confused—maybe he doesn't want to be one any longer—but he's still got, according to the angel, superhuman strength and super-senses and the rest.

When the door opens—without the slightest sound, I note—I'm looking down this spiral staircase into a gorgeous little chapel. Sunlight is coming through the stained-glass windows, so there's got to be a courtyard or something just outside, and the frescoes on the ceiling look like real Michelangelos. Big muscles. Those steroid bodies.

The bird has flown to the ceiling and is perched on a balustrade, waiting for the big event, but that's not how I know the guy I'm looking down at is Frank. It isn't even that he's got that distinguished-gentleman look that old vampires have in the movies. It's what he's doing that tells me.

He's kneeling in front of the altar, in front of this big golden crucifix with an especially bloody Jesus, and he's very uncomfortable doing it. Even at this distance I can tell he's shaking. He's got his hands out in prayer and can barely keep them together. He's jerking like he's being electrocuted. He's got his eyes on the crucifix, and when he speaks, it's loud and his voice jerks too. It sounds confessional—the tone is right—but it's not English and it's not Italian. It may not even be Latin, and why should it be? He's been around a long time and probably knows the original.

I'm thinking the stained-glass light is playing tricks on me, but it's not. There really *is* a blue light moving around his hands, his face, his pants legs—blue fire—and this, I see now, it's what's making him jerk.

He's got to be in pain. I mean, here in a chapel—in front of an altar—sunlight coming through the windows—making about the biggest confession any guy has ever made. Painful as hell, but he's doing it, and suddenly I know why she loves him. Hell, *anyone* would.

Without knowing it I've unpacked my crossbow and have it up and ready. This is what God wants, so I probably get some help doing it. I'm shaking too, but go ahead and aim the thing. *I need forgiveness, too, you know*, I want to tell him. You can't bank your immortal soul, no, but you do get to spend it a lot longer.

I put my finger on the trigger, but don't pull it yet. I want to keep thinking.

No, I don't. I don't want to keep thinking at all.

I lower the crossbow and the moment I do I hear a sound from the back of the chapel where the main door's got to be, and I crane my neck to see.

It's the main door, all right. Heads are peeking in. They're wearing black and I think to myself: *Curious priests. That's all.* But the door opens up more and three of them—that holy number—step in real quiet. They're wearing funny Jesuit collars—the ones the angel mentioned—and they don't look curious. They look like they know exactly what they're doing, and they look very unhappy.

Vampires have this sixth sense, I know. One of them looks up at me suddenly, smiles this funny smile, and I see sharp little teeth.

He says something to the other two and heads toward me. When he's halfway up the staircase I shoot him. I must have my heart in it because the arrow nearly goes through him, but that's not what really bothers him. It's the *wood*. There's an explosion of sparks, the same blue fire, and a hole opens up in his chest, grows, and in no time at all he's just not there anymore.

Frank has turned around to look, but he's dazed, all that confessing, hands in prayer position and shaking wildly, and he obviously doesn't get what's happening. The other two Jesuits are heading up the stairs now, and I nail them with my last two arrows.

The dove has dropped like a stone from its perch and is flapping hysterically in front of me, like *Wrong vampires! Wrong vampires!* I'm tired of its flapping, so I brush it away, turn and leave, and if it takes me (which it will) a whole day to get out of the Vatican without that dove to lead me and make doors open magically, okay. When you're really depressed, it's hard to give a shit about anything.

Two days later I'm back at Parlami's. I haven't showered. I look like hell. I've still got the case with me. God knows why.

I've had two martinis and when I look up, there he is. I'm not surprised, but I sigh anyway. I'm not looking forward to this.

"So you didn't do it," he says.

"You know I didn't, asshole."

"Yes, I do. Word does get out when the spiritual configuration of the universe doesn't shift the way He'd like it to."

I want to hit his baby-smooth face, his perfect nose and collagen lips, but I don't have the energy.

"So what happens now?" I ask.

"You really don't know?"

"No."

He shakes his head. Same look of contempt.

"I guess you wouldn't."

He takes a deep breath.

"Well, the Jesuits did it for you. They killed him last night."

"What?"

"They've got crossbows too. Where do you think we got the idea?"

"Same wood?"

"Of course. They handle it with special gloves."

"Why?"

"Why kill him? Same line of thought. If he flips, things get thrown off balance. Order is important for them, too, you know. Mortals are the same way, you may have noticed. You all need order. Throw things off and you go crazy. That's why you'll put up with despots—even choose them over more benign and loving leaders—just so you don't have to worry. Disorder makes for a lot of worry, Anthony."

"You already knew it?"

"Knew what?"

"That I wouldn't do it and the Jesuits would instead."

"Yes."

"Then why send me?"

Again the look, the sigh. "Ah. Think hard."

I do, and, miracle of miracles, I see it.

"Giovanna is free now," I say.

"Yes. Frank, bless his immortal soul—which God has indeed agreed to do—is gone in flesh."

"So He wants me to hook up with her?"

The angel nods. "Of course."

"Why?"

"Because she'll love you—*really* love you, innocent that you are—just the way she loved him."

"That's it?"

"Not exactly... Because she'll love you, you'll have to stop. You'll have to stop killing people, Anthony. It's just not right."

"No, I won't."

"Yes, you will."

"Don't think so."

"But you will—because, whether you know it yet or not, you love her, too."

What do you say to that?

The angel's gotten up, straightened his red Zegna, picked up the case, and is ready to leave.

"By the way," he adds, "He says He forgives you anyway."

I nod, tired as hell. "I figured that."

"You're catching on."

"About time," I say.

"He said that too."

"And the whole 'balance' thing—"

"What do *you* think?"

Pure bullshit is what I'm thinking.

"You got it," he says, reading my mind because angels can do that.

Twenty-four hours later I'm back in Siena, shaved and showered, and she doesn't seem surprised to see me. She's been grieving—that's obvious. Red eyes. Perfect hair tussled, a mess. She's been debriefed by the angel—that I can tell—and I don't know whether she's got a problem with the Plan or not, or even whether there is a Plan. The angel may have been lying about that too. But when she says quietly, "Hello, Anthony," and gives me a shy smile, I *know*—and my heart starts flapping like that idiot bird.

Boobs
Suzy McKee Charnas

The thing is, it's like your brain wants to go on thinking about the miserable history mid-term you have to take tomorrow, but your body takes over. And what a body! You can see in the dark and run like the wind and leap parked cars in a single bound.

Of course you pay for it the next morning (but it's worth it). I always wake up stiff and sore, with dirty hands and feet and face, and I have to jump in the shower fast so Hilda won't see me like that.

Not that she would know what it was about, but why take chances? So I pretend it's the other thing that's bothering me. So she goes, "Come on, sweetie, everybody gets cramps, that's no reason to go around moaning and groaning. What are you doing, trying to get out of going to school just because you've got your period?"

If I didn't like Hilda, which I do even though she is only a stepmother instead of my real mother, I would show her something that would keep me out of school forever, and it's not fake, either.

But there are plenty of people I'd rather show that to.

I already showed that dork Billy Linden.

"Hey, Boobs!" he goes, in the hall right outside homeroom. A lot of kids laughed, naturally, though Rita Frye called him an asshole.

Billy is the one that started it, sort of, because he always started everything, him with his big mouth. At the beginning of term, he came barreling down on me hollering, "Hey, look at Bornstein, something musta happened to her over the summer! What happened to Bornstein? Hey, everybody, look at Boobs Bornstein!"

He made a grab at my chest, and I socked him in the shoulder, and he punched me in the face, which made me dizzy and shocked and made me cry, too, in front of everybody.

I mean, I always used to wrestle and fight with the boys, being that I was strong for a girl. All of a sudden it was different. He hit me hard, to really hurt, and the shock sort of got me in the pit of my stomach and made me feel nauseous, too, as well as mad and embarrassed to death.

I had to go home with a bloody nose and lie with my head back and ice wrapped in a towel on my face and dripping down into my hair.

Hilda sat on the couch next to me and patted my arm. She goes, "I'm sorry about this, honey, but really, you have to learn it sometime. You're all growing up and the boys are getting stronger than you'll ever be. If you fight with boys, you're bound to get hurt. You have to find other ways to handle them."

To make things worse, the next morning I started to bleed down there, which Hilda had explained carefully to me a couple of times, so at least I knew what was going on. Hilda really tried hard without being icky about it, but I hated when she talked about how it was all part of these exciting changes in my body that are so important and how terrific it is to "become a young woman."

Sure. The whole thing was so messy and disgusting, worse than she had said, worse than I could imagine, with these black clots of gunk coming out in a smear of pink blood—I thought I would throw up. That's just the lining of your uterus, Hilda said. Big deal. It was still gross.

And plus, the smell.

Hilda tried to make me feel better, she really did. She said we should "mark the occasion" like primitive people do, so it's something special, not just a nasty thing that just sort of falls on you.

So we decided to put poor old Pinkie away, my stuffed dog that I've slept with since I was three. Pinkie is bald and sort of hard and lumpy since he got put in the washing machine by mistake, and you would never know he was all soft plush when he was new, or even that he was pink.

Last time my friend Gerry-Anne came over, before the summer, she saw Pinkie laying on my pillow and though she didn't say anything, I could tell she was thinking that was kind of babyish. So I'd been thinking about not keeping Pinkie around any more.

Hilda and I made him this nice box lined with pretty scraps from her quilting class, and I thanked him out loud for being my friend for so many years, and we put him up in the closet, on the top shelf.

I felt bad about it, but if Gerry-Anne decided I was too babyish to be friends with any more, I could end up with no friends at all. When you have never been popular since the time you were skinny and fast and everybody wanted you on their team, you have that kind of thing on your mind.

Hilda and Dad made me go to school the next morning so nobody would think I was scared of Billy Linden (which I was) or that he could keep me away just by being such a dork.

Everybody kept sneaking funny looks at me and whispering, and I was sure it was because I couldn't help walking funny with the pad between my legs and they could smell what was happening, which as far as I knew hadn't happened to anybody else in Eight A yet. Just like nobody else in the whole grade had anything real in their stupid training bras except me, thanks a lot!

Anyway I stayed away from everybody as much as I could and wouldn't talk to Gerry-Anne, even, because I was scared she would ask me why I walked funny and smelled bad.

Billy Linden avoided me just like everybody else, except one of his stupid buddies purposely bumped into me so I stumbled into Billy on the lunch-line. Billy turns around and goes, real loud, "Hey, Boobs, when did you start wearing black-and-blue makeup?"

I didn't give him the satisfaction of knowing that he had actually broken my nose, which the doctor said. Good thing they don't have to bandage you up for that. Billy would have been hollering up a storm about how I had my nose in a sling as well as my boobs.

That night I got up after I was supposed to be asleep and took off my underpants and T-shirt that I sleep in and stood looking at myself in the mirror. I didn't need to turn a light on. The moon was full and it was shining right into my bedroom through the big dormer window.

I crossed my arms and pinched myself hard to sort of punish my body for what it was doing to me.

As if that could make it stop.

No wonder Edie Siler starved herself to death in the tenth grade! I understood her perfectly. She was trying to keep her body down, keep it normal-looking, thin and strong, like I was too, back when I looked like a person, not a cartoon that somebody would call "Boobs."

And then something warm trickled in a little line down the inside of my leg, and I knew it was blood and I couldn't stand it any more. I pressed my thighs

THE URBAN FANTASY ANTHOLOGY

together and shut my eyes hard, and I did something.

I mean I felt it happening. I felt myself shrink down to a hard core of sort of cold fire inside my bones, and all the flesh part, the muscles and the squishy insides and the skin, went sort of glowing and free-floating, all shining with moonlight, and I felt a sort of shifting and balance-changing going on.

I thought I was fainting on account of my stupid period. So I turned around and threw myself on my bed, only by the time I hit it, I knew something was seriously wrong.

For one thing, my nose and my head were crammed with these crazy, rich sensations that it took me a second to even figure out were smells, they were so much stronger than any smells I'd ever smelled. And they were—I don't know—interesting instead of just stinky, even the rotten ones.

I opened my mouth to get the smells a little better, and heard myself panting in a funny way as if I'd been running, which I hadn't, and then there was this long part of my face sticking out and something moving there—my tongue.

I was licking my chops.

Well, there was this moment of complete and utter panic. I tore around the room whining and panting and hearing my toenails clicking on the floorboards, and then I huddled down and crouched in the corner because I was scared Dad and Hilda would hear me and come to find out what was making all this racket.

Because I could hear them. I could hear their bed creak when one of them turned over, and Dad's breath whistling a little in an almost-snore, and I could smell them too, each one with a perfectly clear bunch of smells, kind of like those desserts of mixed ice cream flavors they call a medley.

My body was twitching and jumping with fear and energy, and my room— it's a converted attic-space, wide but with a ceiling that's low in places—my room felt like a jail. And plus, I was terrified of catching a glimpse of myself in the mirror. I had a pretty good idea of what I would see, and I didn't want to see it.

Besides, I had to pee, and I couldn't face trying to deal with the toilet in the state I was in.

So I eased the bedroom door open with my shoulder and nearly fell down the stairs trying to work them with four legs and thinking about it, instead of letting my body just do it. I put my hands on the front door to open it, but my hands weren't hands, they were paws with long knobby toes covered in fur, and the toes had thick black claws sticking out of the ends of them.

The pit of my stomach sort of exploded with horror, and I yelled. It came out this wavery "woooo" noise that echoed eerily in my skullbones.

Upstairs, Hilda goes, "Jack, what was that?" I bolted for the basement as I heard Dad hit the floor of their bedroom.

The basement door slips its latch all the time, so I just shoved it open and down I went, doing better on the stairs this time because I was too scared to think. I spent the rest of the night down there, moaning to myself (which meant whining through my nose, really) and trotting around rubbing against the walls trying to rub off this crazy shape I had, or just moving around because I couldn't sit still. The place was thick with stinks and these slow-swirling currents of hot and cold air. I couldn't handle all the input.

As for having to pee, in the end I managed to sort of hike my butt up over the edge of the slop-sink by Dad's workbench and let go in there. The only problem was that I couldn't turn the taps on to rinse out the smell because of my paws.

Then about three a.m. I woke up from a doze curled up on a bare place on the floor where the spiders weren't so likely to walk, and I couldn't see a thing or smell anything much either, so I knew I was okay again even before I checked and found fingers on my hands again instead of claws.

I zipped upstairs and stood under the shower so long that Hilda yelled at me for using up the hot water when she had a load of wash to do. I was only trying to steam the stiffness out of my muscles, but I couldn't tell her that.

It was really weird to just dress and go to school after a night like that. One good thing, I had stopped bleeding after only one day, which Hilda said wasn't so strange for the first time. So it had to be the huge greenish bruise on my face from Billy's punch that everybody kept staring at.

That and the usual thing, of course. Well, why not? They didn't know I'd spent the night as a wolf.

So Fat Joey grabbed my book bag in the hallway outside the Science lab and tossed it to some kid from Eight B. I had to run after them to get it back, which of course was set up so the boys could cheer the jouncing of my boobs under my shirt.

I was so mad I almost caught Fat Joey, except I was afraid if I grabbed him, maybe he would sock me like Billy had.

Dad had told me, Don't let it get you, kid, all boys are jerks at that age.

Hilda had been saying all summer, Look, it doesn't do any good to walk around all hunched up with your arms crossed, you should just throw your shoulders back and walk like a proud person who's pleased that she's growing up. You're just a little early, that's all, and I bet the other girls are secretly envious of you, with their cute little training bras, for Chrissake, as if there was something that needed to be trained.

It's okay for her, she's not in school, and she doesn't remember what it's like.

So I quit running and walked after Joey until the bell rang, and then I got my book bag back from the bushes outside where he threw it. I was crying a little, and I ducked into the girls' room.

Stacey Buhl was in there doing her lipstick like usual and wouldn't talk to me like usual, but Rita came bustling in and said somebody should off that dumb dork Joey, except of course it was really Billy that put him up to it. Like usual.

Rita is okay except she's an outsider herself, being that her kid brother has AIDS, and lots of kids' parents don't think she should even be in the school. So I don't hang around with her a lot. I've got enough trouble, and anyway I was late for Math.

I had to talk to somebody, though. After school I told Gerry-Anne, who's been my best friend on and off since Fourth Grade. She was off at the moment, but I found her in the library and told her I'd had a weird dream about being a wolf. She wants to be a psychiatrist like her mother, so of course she listened.

She told me I was nuts. That was a big help.

That night I made sure the back door wasn't exactly closed, and then I got in bed with no clothes on—imagine turning in to a wolf in your underpants and T-shirt!—and just shivered, waiting for something to happen.

The moon came up and shone in my window, and I changed again, just like before, which is not one bit like how it is in the movies—all struggling and screaming and bones snapping with horrible cracking and tearing noises, just the way I guess you would imagine it to be, if you knew it had to be done by building special machines to do that for the camera and make it look real: if you were a special-effects man, instead of a werewolf.

For me, it didn't have to look real, it was real. It was this melting and drifting thing, which I got sort of excited by it this time. I mean it felt—interesting. Like something I was doing, instead of just another dumb body-mess happening to me because some brainless hormones said so.

I must have made a noise. Hilda came upstairs to the door of my bedroom, but luckily she didn't come in. She's tall, and my ceiling is low for her, so she often talks to me from the landing.

Anyway I'd heard her coming, so I was in my bed with my whole head shoved under my pillows, praying frantically that nothing showed.

I could smell her, it was the wildest thing—her own smell, sort of sweaty but sweet, and then on top of it her perfume, like an ice-pick stuck up my nose. I didn't actually hear a word she said, I was too scared, and also I had this ripply shaking feeling inside me, a high that was only partly terror.

See, I realized all of a sudden, with this big blossom of surprise, that I didn't have to be scared of Hilda or anybody. I was strong, my wolf-body was strong, and anyhow one clear look at me and she would drop dead.

What a relief, though, when she went away. I was dying to get out from under the weight of the covers, and besides I had to sneeze. Also I recognized that part of the energy roaring around inside me was hunger.

They went to bed—I heard their voices even in their bedroom, though not exactly what they said, which was fine. The words weren't important any more, I could tell more from the tone of what they were saying.

Like I knew they were going to do it, and I was right. I could hear them messing around right through the walls, which was also something new, and I have never been so embarrassed in my life. I couldn't even put my hands over my ears, because my hands were paws.

So while I was waiting for them to go to sleep, I looked myself over in the big mirror on my closet door.

There was this big wolf head with a long slim muzzle and a thick ruff around my neck. The ruff stood up as I growled and backed up a little.

Which was silly of course, there was no wolf in the bedroom with me. But I was all strung out, I guess, and one wolf, me in my wolf-body, was as much as I could handle the idea of, let alone two wolves, me and my reflection.

After that first shock, it was great. I kept turning one way and another for different views.

I was thin, with these long, slender legs, but strong, you could see the muscles, and feet a little bigger than I would have picked. But I'll take four big

THE URBAN FANTASY ANTHOLOGY

feet over two big boobs any day.

My face was terrific, with jaggedy white ripsaw teeth and eyes that were small and clear and gleaming in the moonlight. The tail was a little bizarre, but I got used to it, and actually it had a nice plumey shape. My shoulders were big and covered with long, glossy-looking fur, and I had this neat coloring, dark on the back and a sort of melting silver on my front and underparts.

The thing was, though, my tongue, hanging out. I had a lot of trouble with that, it looked gross and silly at the same time. I mean, that was my tongue, about a foot long and neatly draped over the points of my bottom canines. That was when I realized that I didn't have a whole lot of expressions to use, not with that face, which was more like a mask.

But it was alive, it was my face, those were my own long black lips that my tongue licked.

No doubt about it, this was me. I was a werewolf, like in movies they show over Halloween weekend. But it wasn't anything like your ugly movie werewolf that's just some guy loaded up with pounds and pounds of makeup. I was gorgeous.

I didn't want to just hang around admiring myself in the mirror, though. I couldn't stand being cooped up in that stuffy, smell-crowded room.

When everything else settled down and I could hear Dad and Hilda breathing the way people do when they're asleep, I snuck out.

The dark wasn't very dark to me, and the cold felt sharp like vinegar, but not in a hurting way. Everyplace I went, there were these currents like waves in the air, and I could draw them through my long wolf nose and roll the smell of them over the back of my tongue. It was like a whole different world, with bright sounds everywhere and rich, strong smells.

And I could run.

I started running because a car came by while I was sniffing at the garbage bags on the curb, and I was really scared of being seen in the headlights. So I took off down the dirt alley between our house and the Morrisons' next door, and holy cow, I could tear along with hardly a sound, I could jump their picket fence without even thinking about it. My back legs were like steel springs and I came down solid and square on four legs with almost no shock at all, let alone worrying about losing my balance or turning an ankle.

Man, I could run through that chilly air all thick and moisty with smells, I could almost fly. It was like last year, when I didn't have boobs bouncing and yanking in front even when I'm only walking fast.

Just two rows of neat little bumps down the curve of my belly. I sat down and looked.

I tore open garbage bags to find out about the smells in them, but I didn't eat anything from them. I wasn't about to chow down on other people's stale hotdog-ends and pizza crusts and fat and bones scraped off their plates and all mixed in with mashed potatoes and stuff.

When I found places where dogs had stopped and made their mark, I squatted down and pissed there too, right on top, I just wiped them out.

I bounded across that enormous lawn around the Wanscombe place, where nobody but the Oriental gardener ever sets foot, and walked up the back and over the top of their BMW, leaving big fat pawprints all over it. Nobody saw me, nobody heard me, I was a shadow.

Well, except for the dogs, of course.

There was a lot of barking when I went by, real hysterics which at first made me really scared. But then I popped out of an alley up on Ridge Road, right in front of about six dogs that run together. Their owners let them out all night and don't care if they get hit by a car.

They'd been trotting along with the wind behind them, checking the garbage set out for pickup the next morning. When they saw me, one of them let out a yelp of surprise, and they all skidded to a stop.

Six of them. I was scared. I growled.

The dogs turned fast, banging into each other in their hurry, and trotted away.

I don't know what they would have done if they met a real wolf, but I was something special, I guess.

I followed them.

They scattered and ran.

I ran too, and this was a different kind of running. I mean, I stretched, and I raced, and there was this joy. I chased one of them.

Zig, zag, this little terrier-kind of dog tried to cut left and dive under the gate of somebody's front walk, all without a sound—he was running too hard to yell, and I was happy running quiet.

Just before he could ooze under the gate, I caught up with him and without thinking I grabbed the back of his neck and pulled him off his feet and gave him a shake as hard as I could, from side to side.

I felt his neck crack, the sound vibrated through all the bones of my face.

I picked him up in my mouth, and it was like he hardly weighed a thing. I trotted away holding him up off the ground, and under a bush in Baker's Park I held him down with my paws and bit into his belly, that was still warm and quivering.

Like I said, I was hungry.

The blood gave me this rush like you wouldn't believe. I stood there a minute looking around and licking my lips, just sort of panting and tasting the taste because I was stunned by it, it was like eating honey or the best chocolate malted you ever had.

So I put my head down and chomped that little dog like shoving your face into a pizza and inhaling it. God, I was starved, so I didn't mind that the meat was tough and rank-tasting after that first wonderful bite. I even licked blood off the ground after, never mind the grit mixed in.

I ate two more dogs that night, one that was tied up on a clothesline in a cruddy yard full of rusted-out car parts down on the South side, and one fat old yellow dog out snuffling around on his own and way too slow. He tasted pretty bad and by then I was feeling full, so I left a lot.

I strolled around the park, shoving the swings with my big black wolf nose, and I found the bench where Mr. Granby sits and feeds the pigeons every day, never mind that nobody else wants the dirty birds around crapping on their cars. I took a dump there, right where he sits.

Then I gave the setting moon a goodnight, which came out quavery and wild, "Loo-loo-loo!" And I loped toward home, springing off the thick pads of my paws and letting my tongue loll out and feeling generally super.

I slipped inside and trotted upstairs, and in my room I stopped to look at myself in the mirror.

As gorgeous as before, and only a few dabs of blood on me, which I took time to lick off. I did get a little worried—I mean, suppose that was it, suppose having killed and eaten what I'd killed in my wolf shape, I was stuck in this shape forever? Like, if you wander into a fairy castle and eat or drink anything, that's it, you can't ever leave. Suppose when the morning came I didn't change back?

Well, there wasn't much I could do about that one way or the other, and to tell the truth, I felt like I wouldn't mind; it had been worth it.

When I was nice and clean, including licking off my own bottom which seemed like a perfectly normal and nice thing to do at the time, I jumped up on the bed, curled up, and corked right off. When I woke up with the sun in my eyes, there I was, my own self again.

It was very strange, grabbing breakfast and wearing my old sweatshirt that wallowed all over me so I didn't stick out so much, while Hilda yawned and shuffled around in her robe and slippers and acted like her and Dad hadn't been doing it last night, which I knew different.

And plus, it was perfectly clear that she didn't have a clue about what I had been doing, which gave me a strange feeling.

One of the things about growing up which they're careful not to tell you is, you start having more things you don't talk to your parents about. And I had a doozie.

Hilda goes, "What's the matter, are you off Sugar Pops now? Honestly, Kelsey, I can't keep up with you! And why can't you wear something nicer than that old shirt to school? Oh, I get it; disguise, right?"

She sighed and looked at me kind of sad but smiling, her hands on her hips. "Kelsey, Kelsey," she goes, "if only I'd had half of what you've got when I was a girl—I was as flat as an ironing board, and it made me so miserable, I can't tell you."

She's real thin and neat-looking, so what does she know about it? But she meant well, and anyhow I was feeling so good I didn't argue.

I didn't change my shirt, though.

That night I didn't turn into a wolf. I laid there waiting, but though the moon came up, nothing happened no matter how hard I tried, and after a while I went and looked out the window and realized that the moon wasn't really full any more, it was getting smaller.

I wasn't so much relieved as sorry. I bought a calendar at the school book sale two weeks later, and I checked the full moon nights coming up and waited anxiously to see what happened.

Meantime, things rolled along as usual. I got a rash of zits on my chin. I would look in the mirror and think about my wolf-face, that had beautiful sleek fur instead of zits.

Zits and all I went to Angela Durkin's party, and the next day Billy Linden told everybody that I went in one of the bedrooms at Angela's and made out with him, which I did not. But since no grown-ups were home and Fat Joey brought grass to the party, most of the kids were stoned and didn't know who did what or where anyhow.

As a matter of fact, Billy once actually did get a girl in Seven B high one time out in his parents' garage and him and two of his friends did it to her while she was zonked out of her mind, or anyway they said they did, and she was too embarrassed to say anything one way or another, and a little while later she changed schools.

How I know about it as the same way everybody else does, which is because Billy was the biggest boaster in the whole school, and you could never tell if he was lying or not.

So I guess it wasn't so surprising that some people believed what Billy said about me. Gerry-Anne quit talking to me after that. Meantime, Hilda got pregnant.

This turned into a huge discussion about how Hilda had been worried about her biological clock so she and Dad had decided to have a kid, and I shouldn't mind, it would be fun for me and good preparation for being a mother myself later on, when I found some nice guy and got married.

Sure. Great preparation. Like Mary O'Hare in my class, who gets to change her baby sister's diapers all the time, yick. She jokes about it, but you can tell she really hates it. Now it looked like it was my turn coming up, as usual.

The only thing that made life bearable was my secret.

"You're laid back today," Devon Brown said to me in the lunchroom one day after Billy had been specially obnoxious, trying to flick rolled up bits of bread from his table so they would land on my chest. Devon was sitting with me because he was bad at French, my only good subject, and I was helping him out with some verbs. I guess he wanted to know why I wasn't upset because of Billy picking on me. He goes, "How come?"

"That's a secret," I said, thinking about what Devon would say if he knew a werewolf was helping him with his French: loup, manger.

He goes, "What secret?" Devon has freckles and is actually kind of cute-looking.

"A secret," I go, "so I can't tell you, dummy."

He looks real superior and he goes, "Well, it can't be much of a secret, because girls can't keep secrets, everybody knows that."

Sure, like that kid Sara in Eight B who it turned out her own father had been molesting her for years, but she never told anybody until some psychologist caught on from some tests we all had to take in seventh grade. Up 'til then, Sara kept her secret fine.

And I kept mine, marking off the days on the calendar. The only part I didn't look forward to was having a period again, which last time came right before the change.

When the time came, I got crampy and more zits popped out on my face, but I didn't have a period.

I changed, though.

The next morning they were talking in school about a couple of prize miniature schnauzers at the Wanscombes that had been hauled out of their yard by somebody and killed, and almost nothing left of them.

Well, my stomach turned a little when I heard some kids describing what Mr. Wanscombe had found over in Baker's Park, "the remains," as people said. I felt a little guilty, too, because Mrs. Wanscombe really loved those little dogs, which somehow I didn't think about at all when I was a wolf the night before, trotting around hungry in the moonlight.

I knew those schnauzers personally, so I was sorry, even if they were irritating little mutts that made a lot of noise.

But heck, the Wanscombes shouldn't have left them out all night in the cold. Anyhow, they were rich, they could buy new ones if they wanted.

Still and all, though. I mean, dogs are just dumb animals. If they're mean, it's because they're wired that way or somebody made them mean, they can't help it. They can't just decide to be nice, like a person can. And plus, they don't taste so great, I think because they put so much junk in commercial dog-foods—anti-worm medicine and ashes and ground up fish, stuff like that. Ick.

In fact after the second schnauzer I had felt sort of sick and I didn't sleep real well that night. So I was not in a great mood to start with; and that was the day that my new brassiere disappeared while I was in gym. Later on I got passed a note telling me where to find it: stapled to the bulletin board outside the Principal's office, where everybody could see that I was trying a bra with an underwire.

Naturally, it had to be Stacey Buhl that grabbed my bra while I was changing for gym and my back was turned, since she was now hanging out with Billy and his friends.

Billy went around all day making bets at the top of his lungs on how soon I would be wearing a D-cup.

Stacey didn't matter, she was just a jerk. Billy mattered.

He had wrecked me in that school forever, with his nasty mind and his big, fat mouth. I was past crying or fighting and getting punched out. I was boiling, I had had enough crap from him, and I had an idea.

I followed Billy home and waited on his porch until his mom came home and she made him come down and talk to me. He stood in the doorway and talked through the screen door, eating a banana and lounging around like he didn't have a care in the world.

So he goes, "Watcha want, Boobs?"

I stammered a lot, being I was so nervous about telling such big lies, but that probably made me sound more believable.

I told him that I would make a deal with him: I would meet him that night in Baker's Park, late, and take off my shirt and bra and let him do whatever he wanted with my boobs if that would satisfy his curiosity and he would find somebody else to pick on and leave me alone.

"What?" he said, staring at my chest with his mouth open. His voice squeaked and he was practically drooling on the floor. He couldn't believe his good luck.

I said the same thing over again.

He almost came out onto the porch to try it right then and there. "Well, shit," he goes, lowering his voice a lot, "why didn't you say something before? You really mean it?"

I go, "Sure," though I couldn't look at him.

After a minute he goes, "Okay, it's a deal. Listen, Kelsey, if you like it, can we, uh, do it again, you know?"

I go, "Sure. But Billy, one thing: this is a secret, between just you and me. If you tell anybody, if there's just one other person hanging around out there tonight—"

"Oh, no," he goes, real fast, "I won't say a thing to anybody, honest. Not a word, I promise!"

Not until afterward, of course, was what he meant, which if there was one thing Billy Linden couldn't do, it was to keep quiet if he knew something bad about another person.

"You're gonna like it, I know you are," he goes, speaking strictly for himself as usual. "Jeez, I can't believe this!"

But he did, the dork.

I couldn't eat much for dinner that night, I was too excited, and I went upstairs early—to do homework, I told Dad and Hilda.

Then I waited for the moon, and when it came, I changed.

Billy was in the park. I caught a whiff of him, very sweaty and excited, but I stayed cool. I snuck around for a while, as quiet as I could—which was real quiet—making sure none of his stupid friends were lurking around. I mean, I wouldn't have trusted his promise for a million dollars.

I passed up half a hamburger lying in the gutter where somebody had parked for lunch next to Baker's Park. My mouth watered, but I didn't want to spoil my appetite. I was hungry and happy, sort of singing inside my own head, "Shoo, fly, pie, and an apple-pan-dowdie . . ."

Without any sound, of course.

Billy had been sitting on a bench, his hands in his pockets, twisting around to look this way and that way, watching for me—my human self—to come join him. He had a jacket on, being it was very chilly out.

Which he didn't stop to think that maybe a sane person wouldn't be crazy enough to sit out there and take off her top leaving her naked skin bare to the breeze. But that was Billy all right, totally fixed on his own greedy self without a single thought for somebody else. I bet all he could think about was what a great scam this was, to feel up old Boobs in the park and then crow about it all over school.

Now he was walking around the park, kicking at the sprinkler-heads and glancing up every once in a while, frowning and looking sulky.

I could see he was starting to think that I might stand him up. Maybe he even suspected that old Boobs was lurking around watching him and laughing to herself because he had fallen for a trick. Maybe old Boobs had even brought some kids from school with her to see what a jerk he was.

Actually that would have been pretty good, except Billy probably would have broken my nose for me again, or worse, if I'd tried it.

"Kelsey?" he goes, sounding mad.

I didn't want him stomping off home in a huff. I moved up closer, and I let the bushes swish a little around my shoulders.

He goes, "Hey, Kelse, it's late, where've you been?"

I listen to the words, but mostly I listen to the little thread of worry flickering in his voice, low and high, high and low, as he tried to figure out what was going on.

I let out the whisper of a growl.

He stood real still, staring at the bushes, and he goes, "That you, Kelse? Answer me."

I was wild inside. I couldn't wait another second. I tore through the bushes and leaped for him, flying.

He stumbled backward with a squawk—"What!"—jerking his hands up in front of his face, and he was just sucking in a big breath to yell with when I hit him like a demo-derby truck.

I jammed my nose past his feeble claws and chomped down hard on his face.

No sound came out of him except this wet, thick gurgle, which I could more taste than hear because the sound came right into my mouth with the gush of his blood and the hot mess of meat and skin that I tore away and swallowed.

He thrashed around, hitting at me, but I hardly felt anything through my fur. I mean, he wasn't so big and strong laying there on the ground with me straddling him all lean and wiry with wolf-muscle. And plus, he was in shock. I got a strong whiff from below as he let go of everything right into his pants.

Dogs were barking, but so many people around Baker's Park have dogs to scare away burglars, and the dogs make such a racket all the time, that nobody pays any attention. I wasn't worried. Anyway, I was too busy to care.

I nosed in under what was left of Billy's jaw and I bit his throat out.

Now let him go around telling lies about people.

His clothes were a lot of trouble and I really missed having hands. I managed to drag his shirt out of his belt with my teeth, though, and it was easy to tear his belly open. Pretty messy, but once I got in there, it was better than Thanksgiving dinner. Who would think that somebody as horrible as Billy Linden could taste so *good*?

He was barely moving by then, and I quit thinking about him as Billy

Linden any more. I quit thinking at all, I just pushed my muzzle in and pulled out delicious, steaming chunks and ate until I was picking at tidbits, and everything was getting cold.

On the way home I saw a police car cruising the neighborhood the way they do sometimes. I hid in the shadows and of course they never saw me.

There was a lot of washing up to do that night, and when Hilda saw my sheets in the morning she shook her head. She goes, "You should be more careful about keeping track of your period so as not to get caught by surprise like this."

Everybody in school knew something had happened to Billy Linden, but it wasn't until the day after that they got the word. Kids stood around in little huddles trading rumors about how some wild animal had chewed Billy up. I would walk up and listen in and add a really gross remark or two, part of the game of thrilling each other green and nauseous with made-up details to see who would upchuck first.

Not me, though it was a near thing. I mean, when somebody went on about how Billy's whole head was gnawed down to the skull and they didn't even know who he was except from the bus pass in his wallet, I got a little urpy. It's amazing the things people will dream up.

But when I thought about what I had actually done to Billy, I had to smile. And it felt totally wonderful to walk through the halls without having anybody yelling, "Hey, Boobs!"

There are people who just plain do not deserve to live. And the same goes for Fat Joey, if he doesn't quit crowding me in science lab, trying to get a feel.

One funny thing, though, I don't get periods at all any more. I get a little crampy, and my breasts get sore, and I break out more than usual—and then instead of bleeding, I change.

Which is fine with me, though I take a lot more care now about how I hunt on my wolf nights. I stay away from Baker's Park. The suburbs go on for miles and miles, and there are lots of places I can hunt and still get home by morning. A running wolf can cover a lot of ground.

And I make sure I make my kills where I can eat in private, so no cop car can catch me unawares, which could easily have happened that night when I killed Billy, I was so deep into the eating thing that first time. I look around a lot more now when I'm on a kill, I keep watch.

Good thing it's only once a month this happens, and only a couple of nights. "The Full Moon Killer" has the whole state up in arms and terrified as it is. Eventually I guess I'll have to go somewhere else, which I'm not looking forward to at all. If I can just last until I can have a car of my own, life will get a lot easier.

Meantime, some wolf nights I don't even feel like hunting. Mostly I'm not as hungry as I was those first times. I think I must have been storing up my appetite for a long time. Sometimes now I just prowl around, and I run, boy do I run. If I am hungry, sometimes I eat garbage instead of killing somebody. It's no fun, but you do get a taste for it. I don't mind garbage as long as once in a while I can have the real thing fresh-killed, nice and wet. People can be awfully nasty, but they sure taste sweet.

I do pick and choose, though. I look for people sneaking around in the middle of the night, like Billy waiting in the park that time. I figure they've got to be out looking for trouble at that hour, so whose fault is it if they find it? I have done a lot more for the burglary problem around Baker's Park than a hundred dumb "watchdogs," believe me.

Gerry-Anne is not only talking to me again, she has invited me to go on a double-date with her. Some guy she met at a party invited her, and he has a friend. They're both from Fawcett Junior High across town, which will be a nice change. I was nervous, but finally I said yes. We're going to the movies next weekend. My first real date! I am still pretty nervous, to tell the truth.

For New Year's, I have made two solemn vows.

One is that on this date I will not worry about my chest, I will not be self-conscious, even if the guy stares.

The other is, I'll never eat another dog.

Farewell, My Zombie
Francesca Lia Block

They call a male P.I. a private Dick. So what would they call me? Not a C word or a V word, that would be much too offensive. There are plenty of Dicks but no Vaginas walking around. That just wouldn't be right, now would it? Maybe my title would be Jane. Private Jane. Dick and Jane. Makes you wonder why Jane hasn't been used as a nickname for female genitalia before. Better than a lot of them. Men have a nicer selection.

It was one of those warm L.A. autumn days when you felt guilty if you were at the beach while other people were working or freezing their asses off somewhere, and even more guilty if you were sitting in an office letting your life slip away. That's what I was doing. Sitting in my office with my black-booted feet up on the table (even though it was too hot for boots), staring at the window, wondering why I wasn't at the beach. But I knew why. The beach made me think of Max. I tried to distract myself by poking around some paranormal activity websites on the Mac. There was an extended family in the Midwest who ghost hunted together. They had a disclaimer on their site that they could turn down any job that felt too dangerous. The woman kept spelling the word "were" like "where" and "You're" like "your." That happened so much online I wondered if someone had officially changed it and not told me.

That was when I got the call.

"Merritt," I said.

"Jane Merritt?" the caller asked.

"Speaking."

"Sorry, I...I need some help."

"That's what we're here for. You'll just need to come in and fill out some forms."

There was a silence on the line and for a second I thought the call had dropped.

"Hello?"

"Uh, yeah. Thanks. Sorry."

"So when would you like to come in? Everything perfectly confidential, of course."

"Thanks. Sorry. It's about my father."

"I see. Yes."

"He's a monster."

I waited for the giggling on the other end. She was obviously very young. I got calls like this all the time. Curious teens with too much time on their hands.

No giggling.

"I mean really," she said. "A real monster."

Then she hung up.

No one else called that day. Business had been slow. I left the office early and stopped at the West L.A. Trader Joe's for a few groceries. Bagels, cream cheese, apples, celery, the cheapest Pinot Noir I could find and a tub of cat cookies, plus a can of food for David. I wanted to buy myself flowers because that's what all the women's magazines tell you to do when you haven't been fucked in too long, but I decided not to waste the money. There was a big bouquet of fourteen white roses with a pink cast. They looked pretty good but I knew they'd blow up in a few days in this weather, petals loosening from their cluster and drifting to the floor. Besides, roses were another thing that reminded me of Max.

I went home and watched CNN while David and I ate dinner. Bad news as usual. The economy, disasters, war. Not to mention global warming and assorted acts of violence. It was like a horror movie, really. I drank the whole bottle of wine. Then I took a bath and went to bed. I had really weird dreams about letting Max go by himself on a train at night and then realizing what I had done and not being able to get anyone to understand why I was so upset when he didn't come home. Dreams are cruel; they won't let you forget.

Coco Hart came to see me about a week later. She was a beautiful girl in a private school uniform skirt and blouse and a ratty sweatshirt that was too hot for the weather. Her long hair up in a ponytail and makeup so lightly and carefully applied that only the most discerning eyes would notice it there. She looked perfectly well-adjusted but her fingernails were bitten down so far that it hurt to look at them.

"I called you," she said after she'd introduced herself. Her eyes darted around the room trying to find clues. I don't have any in this tiny, dingy office. Not even a photo of Max. I had to hide it in a drawer.

"About your father?"

She nodded.

"Is he hurting you?"

"No," she said. "Sorry. It's not that."

"You can tell me. I'm here to help."

"Thank you. You were the only woman I could find. Well except that one who tries to entrap the guys by wearing wigs in their favorite color."

People always mention her when they come to see me. I'm nothing like that Amazon. Just cause we are both Janes.

"So why not her?"

"I heard that interview with you."

There's only been one. It was in conjunction with the new *X-Files* movie. The local news compared me to Fox Mulder because of my interest in the paranormal. I expected business to boom after that but it didn't. In L.A. you have to look like a movie star with big tits or be a guy to make it big in this business. I'm neither.

In the interview I talked a little about some weird, dark stuff, the kind of thing teenagers and *X-Files* fans eat up. But most teens aren't going around hiring a P.I. and the *X-Files* fans would rather watch David Duchovny reruns. Like the famous female P.I. who wears the wigs, he has a lot more sex appeal than I do.

Coco put her hand to her mouth as if she were about to chew on what was left of her nails, then thought better of it and folded her hands tightly in her plaid-skirted lap. She looked out at the sunny fall day. The leaves on the tree outside my window looked like they were on fire. I didn't know what kind of tree it was. I wondered why Coco was here and not at some mall with her friends or something.

She took some crumpled bills out of her sweatshirt pocket and put them on the table.

"That's all I have," she said. "But I'll get more."

"And you want me to do what exactly?"

"Oh. Uh. Sorry." She hesitated. "Do you believe in zombies?" she said, finally.

Fuck.

Sorry, but I am not going to pretend to you that I am normal. I am not normal in any way. Yes I shop at Trader Joe's and watch CNN, get my hair cut on a regular basis, shower and use deodorant. I wear my dark hair scraped back in a tight bun like I did on the force, and dress in flat-front black trousers and white stretch button-down shirts from the Limited and black heels or flats or boots from Macy's.

When I got out of the hospital they let me live in the trailer in the backyard of what used to be my home. I can see my old house through the trailer window. It is a long, low structure painted avocado green. My ex and I were always planning on repainting it but we never got around to that. Then Kimmy came and picked the green. It looks nasty, even monstrous in certain lights. I planted the roses in the garden but I've stopped trying to take care of them. Once Kimmy came out while I was watering and weeding. I said, "Sorry," and scuttled back into my trailer. The roses remind me.

At night I stay up watching the windows of my old bedroom until the lights go out.

I went into this work because I didn't know what else to do. I thought it would help me forget to get up every day and go to my little office on Washington. It helps me forget that I was ever Max's mom but it makes me remember the hospital and the doctor's face, as I sit here waiting for someone who really needs me to come in.

I mostly just follow cheating husbands and wives. Once I followed a woman who was engaged to two men at the same time. The guy that hired me was so upset he started crying in my office. Then he wanted me to dress up like her and fuck him. That was the most eventful case I'd handled so far. But the thing that happened with Max made me open to the possibility of stuff that wasn't so easy to understand.

Coco told me that her father had been behaving very strangely. She'd seen him eating flesh in big, gross, salivating bites and it didn't look like cow, pig, goat, lamb, chicken or turkey. Let's just say that. And he never spoke anymore. After his stroke he shambled around the house with these heavy steps just staring at the floor. He grumbled and grimaced and that was all. His skin was a weird shade of greenish white and once when he was asleep she'd felt for a pulse and there wasn't one there. He smelled bad, too.

I said, "Sorry, but I have to ask you something. What makes you think he's one of the undead though? I mean, how do you think this could have happened?"

Coco's father was a car salesman in Van Nuys. He'd done pretty well for himself selling SUVs until people stopped being able to afford gas at almost five dollars a gallon. The stress was too much for him. While waiting for the electric car to return he'd had a stroke and almost died. Well, according to Coco there was no almost involved.

"When he came back from the hospital," Coco said. "He just wasn't the same."

"What was he like before?" I asked.

"Well, kind of like now. Except I recognized the meat he ate and he had better skin tone and a pulse. And...sorry, but... he didn't smell so bad."

I tried not to say, "Ouch. Harsh." I was trying to behave with some decorum.

"You sound very angry at your father," I said, recalling a psych class I'd taken in junior college.

"Sorry. My father is all right. Well, he was. Before he turned into a monster. I mean, he's a Republican. He voted for George W. And he's against women's right to choose. He still supports the war. But he'd never lay a hand on me, you know. But I'm worried about what he's doing to other people. Where he like, gets his dinner and that kind of thing."

"Why didn't you go to the police?" I asked."

"Um, I think you know why. Sorry..."

"So you came to me."

"Well," she said, "Not everyone's kid gets stolen by zombies. I mean, I saw it on YouTube."

Okay, sorry, it's true. The thing I'm known for is about Max and the Zombies.

I wasn't really interviewed by the local news. I made a video for YouTube and posted it, talking about what happened. That's how Coco had found me. Not the guy whose fiancée was cheating on him; he got my name out of the phone book.

See, people think my kid got sick and died but I know better. No one wants to talk about it because they're afraid everyone will think they are crazy. Or maybe because they're afraid of even worse consequences.

"What do you want me to do?" I asked Coco.

"Would you please pretend you're a customer and check him out?" she asked. "They have really good deals on Escalades now," she added.

"I ride a bike."

I borrowed Daniel's car and went to the car dealership where Coco's dad worked. They hired him back part time after the stroke. It was night and the cars glowed surreally in the fluorescent lights. The air smelled obscenely of flowers and motor oil.

Mr. Hart lumbered out toward me, tucking his shirt into his pants. He had a large belly and stiff legs and arms. His skin did have an unhealthy sheen to it.

"How can I help you, young lady?" he groaned. A foul, sulfur smell emitted itself from his body. "We have some great deals on SUVs tonight. What are you driving?"

"A bike," I said.

He looked at me dully. "Thinking of upgrading then?"

"You don't sell any electric cars?" I asked.

"No. Why? You do a lot of driving?"

"Not so much. I'm concerned about the environment."

"Global warming? Sweetheart, that's a myth they created to scare you, believe me. No such thing. God knows what He's doing."

I smoothed back my hair. It was unnaturally hot for an October evening. There was something hellish about that kind of heat this time of year. I thought of the ice floes melting at the North Pole and the polar bears dying. I was sweating uncomfortably and I was afraid I might be staining my white blouse. I used deodorant but I had stopped wearing antiperspirant because of the link between aluminum and Alzheimer's. Not that I cared. Alzheimer's might actually be all right. You stagger around in a state of detachment and forgetting.

There are certain things I can't forget, no matter how hard I try. No matter how many photographs I hide or how much zombie research I do, they pop into my mind when I least expect them.

Max used to ask me, "Mommy, when is the Earth going to explode? When is the sun going to burn us up?" Once he said, "Mommy, will you hold me from the time the Earth was made until it ends?"

"Yes, honey," I said. "I will hold you forever."

He curled up into my arms, his delicately-boned, dusty-brown feet tucked up on my lap. His eyes were big and brown with eyelashes that all the nurses in the hospital said they wanted.

"It's not fair," they cooed.

Of course, it was more than fair. The other stuff was what wasn't fair.

"How about a Prius?" I asked Mr. Hart.

"How about a Hummer? Owned by a little old lady from Pasadena. Almost no mileage."

"I'll think about it," I said. "Sorry," I said. And left.

There is a proliferation of zombies around lately, let me tell you.

My ex Daniel's girlfriend Kimmy is not behaving at all normally, even for a stressed-out, middle-aged, hyperactive kickboxing instructor dame. She drones on and on about herself and is unable to ask anyone questions about how they are doing. She wears the same rapacious grin frozen on her face at all times, even when she is angry. She talks loudly and proudly at all social gatherings about how she had tumors in her uterus and can no longer have any more children. (I know Daniel finds this perversely comforting; no chance of any more children means no chance of any more tragedies for him.) She never lets anyone see her eat, not even Daniel. (He told me this; I think even he is worried.) While she cooks his dinner she tells him she caught a bite at the gym and that she doesn't digest food well after four p.m. She walks with jerky movements and snaps her gum spastically and calls everyone dude. Do you see?

In addition there is that presidential candidate and his running mate. I believe they have been bitten. Look at their glassy eyes. Listen to their hollow voices—hers more shrill, but hollow still. Read about their policies to destroy nature and take away women's rights, gay rights. I can just imagine them hunting people out of helicopters and gnawing on someone's thighbone with gristle between their teeth.

I remember that doctor at the hospital where Max was. He strolled out into the waiting room and tried to take my hand but I wouldn't let him touch me. His skin was greenish white under the fluorescence and his legs and arms were stiff.

When I saw him I knew. I thought it was going to be like on TV where they say, "I'm sorry."

I didn't want to hear those words from him. So I said them first.

"I'm sorry!" I screamed. I fell to my knees. "I'm so so sorry."

Zombies are reanimated corpses. I looked it up online. It said that if there is an invasion find a shopping mall or grocery store and barricade yourself inside. Then you will have plenty of supplies until you can come up with a plan.

I called Coco.

"Yes, I think you're right."

"What?"

"He seems to be what you say he is."

"Thanks for...Sorry... Um. What should we do about it?"

"Come meet me," I said. "But try not to say sorry so much."

"Sorry. I mean..."

"It's okay. I do it too. You're very polite. Most people in L.A. don't say thank you so much either."

"Oh. Sorry. We're from Florida?"

I should be the one saying sorry.

Okay, so I'm not a legitimate P.I. My ex, Daniel, rented this office for me. It's on Washington next to a store that sells knives and other exotic weaponry. The rent was so cheap. Daniel thought it might help me after what happened with Max. He thought it would be good for me to have some place to go to every day, something to get dressed for. Kind of like playing office when you're a kid.

Okay, so I hadn't really had any clients except for Coco, but hell, at least I had her. The guy with the cheating fiancée—I made him up. But not Coco. Not the zombie father. I would never lie to you about zombies.

Coco came in wearing a pair of skinny jeans, black-and-white-checked Vans slip-on sneakers and the same oversized sweatshirt with the sleeves pulled down over her hands. She looked like a typical teenager except that her face had a very serious expression. She kept the sleeves of her sweatshirt bunched in her hand while she gnawed on her fingers. She wasn't even pretending that she didn't bite her nails this time.

"Thank you for looking into this."

"You're welcome."

"What are we going to do?" she asked me. "What did you do before?"

"You can't panic," I said. "But at the same time you must be vigilant not to get bitten."

She nodded. "He hasn't tried that."

"What precautionary actions are you taking?" I asked her.

"I have a secret hideaway stashed with water and food supplies," she told me.

"That's good."

"And I sleep with my door locked."

"Good."

Then she said, "Can I ask you something?"

I knew what was coming.

"Would you write on my arm?" She shoved up her sweatshirt sleeve and stuck out her bare forearm. There were raised white scars running horizontally just above her wrists.

I was wrong. I hadn't expected that question nor had I expected the scars. It took me a moment to talk. "What do you mean? I asked.

"With a Sharpie. I think it will help me to be brave. If you write a message."

I had no idea what to write but I took the Sharpie she handed me and opened it. It smelled like chemicals. It smelled like back-to-school and summer sport's camp when I had to write Max's name on his baseball hat and backpack and lunch box. A bunch of lunchboxes were recalled because of lead content. I wondered what other dangerous substances lurked in products for children.

There were carcinogens in things that seemed perfectly innocuous, like bubble bath and hot dogs.

"I don't think Sharpie is good for your skin," I told Coco. "It doesn't say non-toxic. It's permanent."

"Exactly."

She was still holding her arm out so I wrote, "Farewell my Zombie," She smiled with satisfaction and pulled her sleeve down over it.

"Don't let your father see," I said.

She nodded.

"What happened? To your wrist."

"When I was a baby I got really sick," she said. "I'm better now. But I had to take all this medication and get all these treatments that really fucked me up. Sorry. Messed me up. I'd survived all that but my life at home sucked and I didn't want to live anymore."

I suddenly wished I'd insisted on using non-toxic marker on her arm. "I understand," I said. "But you can't give up now. I mean, really. You can't."

She looked at me blankly.

"Okay?"

"Okay," she said. Then: "Can I ask you something else?"

Here it was.

"What really happened with your son?" she said, just as I thought she would.

I hadn't talked about it in so long.

"Everyone thought he had a brain tumor," I said. "But it wasn't like that. It wasn't like that at all. They wanted him and they got him. So that's why I'm here. In case I can help anyone else."

Coco reached out and gently touched my hand. "Sorry but...do you think, maybe, you just might not want to look at what really happened?"

I jumped as if she'd slapped me. "Get out please," I said.

"Oh! Sorry! I'm so sorry, Miss Merritt. I didn't mean to upset you."

The thing is, maybe Coco's right. Maybe Max really did have cancer. Maybe Coco had cancer and recovered and then wished she hadn't. Maybe her father isn't a zombie but maybe he did lay a hand on her. Maybe there's no such thing as global warming and it's okay to drive an Escalade but I don't think so. Maybe people are just out there trying to scare us. Hmmm. Maybe the presidential candidate and his running mate are not trying to eat us up. Maybe I'm crazy; maybe I'm perfectly sane. Who knows?

Well, baby, I know this. Today I am going to shut the office and ride my bike (because who wants to take a chance on making that hole in the ozone bigger, just in case) down Washington to the beach. I am going to take off my shoes and walk on the wet sand. I am going to eat my cheese sandwich and watch the sun set like a beautiful apocalypse. Maybe I'll even build a sandcastle. Those are the things you and I used to do. That is why I haven't been to the beach in all these years. But today at sunset I am going to close my eyes and I am going to remember every little thing I can about you. From your eyelashes clumped with salt water, to the sand under your fingernails, to the little curled shells of your toes. I am going to remember all our days at the beach and the way you used to burrow into my arms when you were cold and the way, when you were a little older, you used to pick roses from the garden for me, in spite of the thorns.

I am going to apologize to Coco when she comes back but I am not going to apologize to any more zombies. I am going to find out some more details and if a zombie or cancer or whatever you want to call it threatens Coco Hart or any kids I know I am going to kick that motherfucker zombie's ass.

I miss you, baby. But it's better than forgetting.

Noir Fantasy

We Are Not a Club, But We Sometimes Share a Room

Joe R. Lansdale

Nothing is new under the sun.

Urban Fantasy is not new, but the recognition of it as a commercial genre is. Actually, it hasn't been that long ago that horror fiction of any kind, though it existed of course, was not a commercial genre.

There were bestselling authors who wrote some horror stories, Ira Levin, William Blatty, and Tom Tryon come to mind, but there wasn't a long chain of horror novels being trumpeted, and though there were exceptions, most that were written appeared in small presses, or as original paperbacks. It was the same for short stories, though they had an even lower profile.

It wasn't until the popularity of Stephen King that horror became an actual commercial label, both for novels and short stories; mostly the former.

In spite of its immense popularity in the '80s, it faded dramatically in the early '90s, came back in the late '90s, disappeared again, rather quickly, and is now on the scene again, wearing a variety of festive party hats.

I admit up front, and quickly, that I am not a proponent of isolationist fiction. Meaning, by my definition, a kind of story that not only fits a specific genre, or a subset of that genre, but is damn proud of it to the point of inclusion and exclusion.

These distinctions are okay, and necessary to some degree, but what I dislike are the hard and fast rules. There are no rules. There's fiction. There are story tellers. And the rest is hair splitting.

It's not my purpose here to round up these stories and brand them. They can be tagged to some degree, but they are not confined by the tag. The authors that wrote these stories all have tales here that loosely—and I will emphasize that word, loosely—fall into a collection box. But the authors themselves are not bound by it, and have written many stories outside this narrow definition.

These kinds of stories have ancestors. There were many writers who opened the lid on this box for the rest of us, and most of those writers were writers who, like those in this volume, were not restricted by it. They knew how to go their own way.

Fritz Leiber is a good example, and he could also be said to be someone who wrote Urban Fantasy/Horror when it wasn't cool. He was there before most anyone. His short stories "Smoke Ghost" and "The Automatic Pistol" are good examples of the general type of fiction gathered here, though these are mutations and hybrids of his pioneering. The connection with Leiber is this: The fiction has the stink of the urban about it, same as many of his stories, either because they take place in the city, or display the weaknesses of humanity in large numbers and close quarters. The terror is often due to the actions of people: pollution, street crime, over population, dehumanization, and so on. What supernatural elements there are, are dragged out of the haunted house and into the tract house and walk-up apartment, or they take place in the wasteland of some horrid aftermath brought on by the mistakes of civilization.

This section of stories owes less to *Buffy the Vampire Slayer* and more to noir and writers who tripped the dark fantastic with gleeful enthusiasm. Influences come from authors outside of horror, like Raymond Chandler, Dashiell Hammett, James Cain, Ernest Hemingway, and Flannery O'Connor, and many others. I'm not suggesting that all the writers here are directly influenced by these writers, only that the type of fiction they write owes a measure of its existence to it, as surely as it does to horror and fantasy writers.

Whatever the individual writer's influences are, in this collection, each of them has put their spin on the work, given it a piece of themselves; something created by their experience, personality, geography, etc.

But there is no doubt that writers of the fantastic are the most important forerunners here. Among those writers, along with Fritz Leiber, is Robert Nathan, someone nearly forgotten these days, best known for *A Portrait of Jennie*, who blazed a trail for so many others, including Jack Finney. There is also Ray Bradbury.

Ray Bradbury's impact is impossible to measure. It goes off the scale, especially fiction written in his darker days—collections like *Dark Carnival* and the novels *Something Wicked This Way Comes* and *Fahrenheit 451*. Bradbury had the ability to see strangeness in the most common of things. His stories are indebted more to the rural and small town tradition than the urban, but it would be remiss not to mention him. He may in fact be the most responsible for making fantasy stories legitimate.

Richard Matheson's impact on this particular kind of tale is even stronger. His *The Shrinking Man* takes place in suburbia, and deals with threats of pollution via insecticide, something that causes the hero of the novel, after many adventures, to shrink, and shrink, until he is literally one with the universe. Matheson's book is in the same school as Leiber's short stories, or even Jack Finney's classic novel *The Body Snatchers*, which is as much about depersonalization as it is a Cold War allegory, though the author always denied the latter. Matheson and Finney both explain their stories with science fictional tropes, but their creations feel and taste more like horror or fantasy than science fiction.

Matheson's incredible novel, *I Am Legend*, is also a forerunner of the yarns here. Influenced to a great degree by noir, as well as science fiction, fantasy, and horror, specifically stories about vampires, he managed to write not only a crackerjack tale, but a claustrophobic novel of paranoia and loneliness that has yet to be surpassed. Every few years it is rediscovered, and its influence is immeasurable. *I Am Legend* is a wonderful book, a masterpiece, no matter what sticker you glue to it, and it will continue to influence. The DNA is strong in this one, my friends. Take for example *Night of the Living Dead* and its many sequels and the films and stories it has influenced. Not only were Romero's zombies inspired by Matheson's creation, there have been at least three films directly based on the novel, and a horde of others that lie within its shadow. The same goes for fiction.

And we can't forget Harlan Ellison (not that he would let you), who has put his personal touch on so many urban fantasies and has influenced a horde of writers.

There was also Henry Kuttner, and Cyril Kornbluth, and Cordwainer Smith. They donated many of their ingredients to the literary stews brewed by future writers, and they too have helped shape this specific branch of the field. This is just the beginning of the list of writers who are owed their due for opening the way for the stories in this book. It would take a book just to list them.

It seems that now the time is right for this kind of story to be truly popular. An audience has gradually been inoculated to embrace these tales, where in the past most of these writers were read by a small group of rabidly dedicated fans. With fantastic imagery so much a part of modern-day life, with television channels devoted to science fiction and fantasy, horror and the weird, with commercials using fantastic themes and spending more money to present them than was spent on entire films of this nature in the past, the rarity that was once fantastic fandom is no more.

It's gone mainstream.

Will it last?

Maybe not as Urban Fantasy or Horror, but tales of this nature will endure in one form or another. The stories in this collection will certainly reveal that. They are unusually good, and though they fit the Urban Fantasy/Horror mold, they can also fit numerous other molds; they are like living organisms that can shift shape and mutate. I am proud of this assembly, and in the end, it doesn't really matter what you call them.

A brand name is just a nice way to put a book together. It appeals to those who want to at least know whose backyard they have crept into. Nothing wrong with that.

But it's like *Enter the Dragon* when Bruce Lee points to the heavens, and his student looks at the tip of his finger. There's more out there than just the tip of the finger, my friends.

I don't want to be someone who is trying to minimize readership by denying people their labels, but neither do I want to be part of directing fiction, as if the stories are cows, through a chute and into the slaughterhouse. The more something can be identified, the more likely it will soon contain sick cows, and pretty soon the whole group is diseased and has to be put down.

It's happened to Splatterpunk and Cyberpunk and Gothic-Romance, and so on.

But if you use the label as a general guide, then so be it. If it makes you happy, I won't kick. What you have here are stories that are created from many genres and non-genres. Add to this literary fiction, as well as cult writers, experimental writers, and the influence of film and radio shows and comic books and music, and you have...Well, you have these magnificent peculiarities.

I suppose I must step forward and own up to the fact that I have a story among them. I was one of the writers the publisher felt had opened these gates wider, behind the great writers mentioned previously, of course.

If that's true, I didn't know I was doing it, and if it bothers you that I'm also an editor and have a story in this grouping, then skip mine and read the others.

Like the cliché sports quote: "I'm just happy to be here."

These stories are all trips into a world of strange magic, places where you have not been. Once you come back from your journey, you're unlikely to forget the voyage any time soon.

Take photographs while you're there, maybe a few notes.

No, better yet, just read the stories again when the mood hits you. They are worlds that you can revisit, without need of luggage or plane fare.

Go visit them often.

They are way worth it, even if the terrain is a little weird and maybe even scary.

The White Man
Thomas M. Disch

> If human testimony, taken with every care and solemnity, judicially, before commissions innumerable, each consisting of many members, all chosen for integrity and intelligence, and constituting reports more voluminous perhaps than exist upon any other class of cases, is worth anything, it is difficult to deny, or even to doubt the existence of such a phenomenon as the vampire.
>
> "Carmilla"
> —J. Sheridan Le Fanu

It was the general understanding that the world was falling apart in all directions. Bad things had happened and worse were on the way. Everyone understood that—the rich and the poor, old and young (although for the young it might be more dimly sensed, an intuition). But they also understood that there was nothing much anyone could do about it, and so you concentrated on having some fun while there was any left to have. Tawana chewed kwash, which the family grew in the backyard alongside the house, in among the big old rhubarb plants. Once they had tried to eat the rhubarb, but Tawana had to spit it out—and a lucky thing, too, because later on she learned that rhubarb is poison.

The kwash helped if you were hungry (and Tawana was hungry even when her stomach was full) but it could mess up your thinking at the same time. Once in the third grade when she was transferred to a different school closer to downtown and had missed the regular bus, she set off by herself on foot, chewing kwash, and the police picked her up, crying and shoeless, out near the old airport. She had no idea how she'd got there, or lost her shoes. That's the sort of thing the kwash could do, especially if you were just a kid. You got lost without even knowing it.

Anyhow, she was in high school now and the whole system had changed. First when there was the Faith Initiative, she'd gone to a Catholic school, where boys and girls were in the same room all day and things were very strict. You couldn't say a word without raising your hand, or wear your own clothes, only the same old blue uniform every day. But that lasted less than a year. Then the public schools got special teachers for the Somali kids with Intensive English programs, and Tawana and her sisters got vouchers to attend Diversitas, a charter school in what used to be a parking garage in downtown Minneapolis near the old football stadium that they were tearing down. Diversitas is the Latin word for Diversity, and all cultures were respected there. You could have your own prayer rug, or chant, or meditate. It was the complete opposite of Our Lady of Mercy, where everybody had to do everything at the same time, all together. How could you call that freedom of religion? Plus, you could wear pretty much anything you wanted at Diversitas, except for any kind of jewelry that was potentially dangerous. There were even prizes for the best outfits of the week, which Tawana won when she was in the sixth grade. The prize-winning outfit was a Swahili Ceremonial Robe with a matching turban that she'd designed herself with duct tape. Ms. McLeod asked her to wear it to the assembly when the prizes were given out, but that wasn't possible since the towels had had to be returned to their container in the bathroom. She wasn't in fact Swahili, but at that point not many people (including Tawana) knew the difference between Somalia and other parts of Africa. At the assembly, instead of Tawana wearing the actual robe, they had shown a picture from the video on the school's surveillance camera. Up on the screen Tawana's smile must have been six feet from side to side. She was self conscious about her teeth for the next week (kwash tends to darken teeth.)

Ms. McLeod had printed out a small picture from the same surveillance tape showing Tawana in her prize-winning outfit, all gleaming white with fuzzy pink flowers. But in the background of that picture there was another figure in white, a man. And no one who looked at the picture had any idea who he might have been. He wasn't one of the teachers, he wasn't in maintenance, and parents rarely visited the school in the daytime. At night there were remedial classes for adult refugees in the basement classrooms, and slams and concerts, sometimes, in the auditorium.

Tawana studied his face a lot, as though it were a puzzle to be solved. Who might he be, that white man, and why was he there at her ceremony? She taped the picture on the inside of the door of her hall locker, underneath the magnetic To Do list with its three immaculately empty categories: Shopping, School, Sports. Then one day it wasn't there. The picture had been removed from her locker. Nothing else had been taken, just that picture of Tawana in her robe and the white man behind her.

That was the last year there were summer vacations, After that you had to go to school all the time. Everybody bitched about it, but Tawana wondered if the complainers weren't secretly glad if only because of the breakfast and lunch programs. With the new year-round schedule there was also a new music and dance teacher, Mr. Furbush, with a beard that had bleached tips. He taught junior high how to do ancient Egyptian dances, a couple of them really exhausting, but he was cute. Some kids said he was having a love affair with Ms. McLeod, but others said no, he was gay.

On a Thursday afternoon late in August of that same summer, when Tawana had already been home from school for an hour or so, the doorbell rang. Then it rang a second time, and third time. Anyone who wanted to visit the family would usually just walk in the house, so the doorbell served mainly as a warning system. But Tawana was at home by herself and she thought what if it was a package and there had to be someone to sign for it?

So she went to the door, but it wasn't a package, it was a man in a white shirt and a blue tie lugging a satchel full of papers. "Are you Miss Makwinja?" he asked Tawana. She should have known better than to admit that's who she was, but she said, yes, that was her name. Then he showed her a badge that said he was an agent for the Census Bureau and he just barged into the house and took a seat in the middle of the twins' futon and started asking her questions. He wanted to know the name of everyone in the family, and how it was spelled and how old they all were and where they were born and their religion and did they have a job. An endless stream of questions, and it was no use saying you didn't know, cause then he would tell her to make a guess. He had a thermos bottle hanging off the side of his knapsack, all beaded with sweat the same as his forehead. The drops would run down the sides of the bottle and down his forehead and his cheeks in zig-zags like the mice trying to escape from the laboratory in her brother's video game. "I have to do my homework now," she told him. "That's fine," he said and just sat there. Then after they both sat there a while, not budging, he said, "Oh, I have some other questions here about the house itself. Is there a bathroom?" Tawana nodded. "More than one bathroom?" "I don't know," she said, and suddenly she needed to go to the bathroom herself. But the man wouldn't leave, and wouldn't stop asking his questions. It was like going to the emergency room and having to undress.

And then she realized that she had seen him before this. He was the man behind her in the picture. The picture someone had taken from her locker. The man she had dreamed of again and again.

She got up off the futon and went to stand on the other side of the wooden trunk with the twins' clothes in it. "What did you say your name was?" she asked warily.

"I don't think I did. We're not required to give out our names, you know. My shield number is K-384." He tapped the little plastic badge pinned to his white shirt.

"You know *our* names."

"True. I do. But that's what I'm paid for." And then he smiled this terrible smile, the smile she'd seen in stores and offices and hospitals all her life, without every realizing what it meant. It was the smile of an enemy, of someone sworn to kill her. Not right this moment, but someday maybe years later, someday for sure. He didn't know it yet himself, but Tawana did, because she sometimes had psychic powers. She could look into the future and know what other people were thinking. Not their ideas necessarily, but their feelings. Her mother had had the same gift before she died.

"Well," the white man said, standing up, with a different smile, "thank you for your time." He neatened his papers into a single sheaf and stuffed them back in his satchel.

Someday, somewhere, she would see him again. It was written in the Book of Fate.

All that was just before Lionel got in trouble with the INS and disappeared. Lionel had been the family's main source of unvouchered income, and his absence was a source of deep regret, not just for Lucy and the twins, but all of them. No more pizzas, no more hmong take-out. It was back to beans and rice, canned peas and stewed tomatoes. The cable company took away all the good channels and there was nothing to look at but Tier One, with the law and shopping channels and really dumb cartoons. Tawana got very depressed and even developed suicidal tendencies, which she reported to the school medical officer, who prescribed some purple pills as big as your thumb. But they didn't help much more than a jaw of kwash.

Then Lucy fell in love with a Mexican Kawasaki dealer called Super Hombre and moved to Shakopee, leaving the twins temporarily with the family at the 26th Ave. N.E. house. Except it turned out not to be that temporary. Super Hombre's Kawasaki dealership was all pretend. The bikes in the show window weren't for sale, they were just parked there to make it look like a real business. Super Hombre was charged with sale and possession of a controlled substance, and Lucy was caught in the larger sting and got five to seven. Minnesota had become very strict about even minor felonies.

Without Lucy to look after them, the niños became Tawana's responsibility, which was a drag not just in the practical sense that it meant curtailing her various extracurricular activities—the Drama Club, Muslim Sisterhood, Mall Minders—but because it was so embarrassing. She was at an age when she might have had niños of her own but instead she'd preserved her chastity. And all for nothing because here she was just the same, wheeling the niños back and forth from day care, changing diapers, screaming at them to shut the fuck up. But she never smacked them, which was more than you could say for Lionel or Lucy. Super Hombre had been a pretty good care provider, too, when he had to, except the once when he laid into Kenny with his belt. But Kenny had been asking for it, and Super Hombre was stoned.

The worst thing about being a substitute mom were the trips to the County Health Center. Why couldn't people be counted on to look after their kids without a lot of government bureaucrats sticking their noses into it? All the paperwork, not to mention the shots every time there was some new national amber alert. Or the blood draws! What were they all about? If they did find out you were a carrier, what were they going to do about it anyhow? Empty out all the bad blood and pump you full of a new supply, like bringing a car in for a change of oil?

Basically Tawana just did not like needles and syringes. The sight of her own blood snaking into the little clouded plastic tube and slowly filling one cylinder after another made her sick. She would have nightmares. Sometimes just the sight of a smear of strawberry jam on one of the twin's bibs would register as a bloodstain, and she would feel a chill through her whole body, like diving into a pool. She *hated* needles. She hated the Health Center. She hated every store and streetlight along the way to the Health Center. And most of all she hated the personnel. Nurse Lundgren with his phony smile. Nurse Richardson with her orange hair piled up in an enormous bun. Doctor Shen.

But if someone didn't take the twins in to the Health Center, then there would be Inspectors coming round to the house, perhaps even the INS. And more papers to fill out. And the possibility that the niños would be taken off to foster care and the child care stipends suspended or even cancelled. So someone had to get them in to the Health Center and that someone was the person in the family with the least clout. Tawana.

Thanksgiving was the big holiday of the year for the Makwinjas, because of the turkeys. Back in the '90s when the first Somalis had come to Minnesota, their grandfather among them, they'd all been employed by E.G. Harris, the biggest turkey processor in the country. Tawana had seen photographs of the gigantic batteries where the turkeys were grown. They looked like palaces for some Arabian sheik, if you didn't know what they really were. One of the bonuses for E.G. Harris employees to this day was a supersized frozen bird on Thanksgiving and another at Christmas, along with an instruction DVD on making the most of turkey leftovers. There were still two members of the family working for E.G. Harris, so well into February there was plenty of turkey left for turkey pot pie, turkey noodle casserole, and turkey up the ass (which was what Lucy used to call turkey a la king).

The older members of the family, who could still remember what life had been like in Somalia, had a different attitude toward all the food in America than Tawana and her sisters and cousins. Their lives revolved around cooking and grocery shopping and food vouchers. So when the neighborhood Stop 'N' Shop was shut down and CVS took over the building, the older Makwinja women were out on the picket line every day to protest and chant and chain themselves to the awnings. (They were the only exterior elements that anything *could* be chained to: the doors didn't have knobs or handles.) Of course, the protests didn't accomplish anything. In due course CVS moved in, and once people realized there was nowhere else for fourteen blocks to buy basics like Coke and canned soup and toilet paper they started shopping there. One of the last things that Tawana ever heard her grandfather say was after his first visit to the new CVS to fill his prescription for his diabetes medicine. "You know what," he said, "this city is getting to be more like Mogadishu every day." Aunt Bima protested vehemently, saying there was no resemblance at all, that Minneapolis was all clean and modern, while Mogadishu had always been a dump. "You think I'm blind?" Grandpa asked. "You think I'm stupid?" Then he just clamped his jaw shut and refused to argue. A week later he was dead. An embolism.

Half a block from the CVS, what used to be a store selling mattresses and pine furniture had subdivided into an All-Faiths Pentecostal Tabernacle (upstairs) and (downstairs) the Northeast Minneapolis Arts Cooperative. There was a sign over the entrance (which was always padlocked) that said "IRON Y MONGERS" and under that what looked almost like an advertisement from *People* or *GQ* showing four fashion models with big dopey grins under a slogan in mustard-yellow letters: "WELL-DRESSED PEOPLE WEAR CLEAN CLOTHES." In the display windows on either side of the locked door were mannikins dressed entirely in white. The two male mannikins sported white tuxedos and there were a number of female mannikins in stiff sheer white dresses and veils like bridal gowns but sexy. There were bouquets of paper flowers in white vases, and a bookcase full of books all painted white—like the hands and faces of the mannikins. The paint had been applied as carefully as makeup. The mannikins' eyes were realistically blue or green and their lips were bright red, even the two men.

The first time she saw them Tawana thought the mannikins were funny, that the paint on their faces was like the makeup on clowns. But then, walking by the windows a few days later, during a late afternoon snow flurry, she was creeped out. The mannikins seemed half-alive, and threatening. Then, on a later visit, Tawana started feeling angry, as though the display in the windows was somehow a slur directed at herself and her family and all the African Americans in the neighborhood, at everyone who had to walk past the store (which wasn't really a store, since it was always closed) and look at the mannikins with their bright red lips and idiot grins. Why would anyone ever go to the trouble to fix up a window like that? They weren't selling the clothes. You couldn't go inside. If there was a joke, Tawana didn't get it.

She began to dream about the two mannikins in the tuxedos. In her dream they were alive but mannikins at the same time. She was pushing the twins in their stroller along 27th Avenue, and the two men, with their white faces and red lips, were following her, talking to each other in whispers and snickering. When Tawana walked faster, so would they, and when she paused at every curb to lift or lower the wheels of the stroller, the two men would pause too. She realized they were following her in order to learn where she lived, that's why they always kept their distance.

The man in charge of the All-Faiths Pentecostal Tabernacle was a Christian minister by the name of Gospel Blantyre Blount, D.D., and he came from Malawi. "Malawi," the Reverend Blount explained to the seventh grade class visiting the Tabernacle on the second Tuesday of Brotherhood Month, "is a narrow strip of land in the middle of Africa, in the middle of four Z's. To the west is Zambia and Zimbabwe, and to the east is Tanzania and Mozambique. I come from the town of Chiradzulu, which you may have read about or even seen on the news. The people there are mostly Zulus, and famous for being tall. Like me. How tall do you think I am?"

No one raised a hand.

"Don't be shy, children," said Ms. McLeod, who was wearing a traditional Zulu headress and several enormous copper earrings. "Take a guess. Jeffrey."

Jeffrey squirmed. "Six foot," he hazarded.

"Six foot, ten inches," said Reverend Blount, getting up off his stool and demonstrating his full height, and an imposing gut as well. "And I'm the short guy in the family."

This was greeted by respectful, muted laughter.

"Anyone here ever been to Africa?" Reverend Blount asked, in a rumbling, friendly voice, like the voice in the Verizon ads.

"I have!" said Tawana.

"Oh, Tawana, you have not!" Ms. McLeod protested with a rattle of earrings.

"I was born here in Minneapolis, but my family is from Somalia."

Reverend Blount nodded his head gravely. "I've been there. Somalia's a beautiful nation. But they got problems there. Just like Malawi, they got problems."

"Gospel," Ms. McLeod said, "you promised. We can't get into that with the children."

"Okay. But let me ask: how many of you kids has been baptized?"

Six of the children raised their hands. Jeffrey, who hadn't, explained: "We're Muslim, the rest of us."

"The reason I asked, is in the Tabernacle here we don't think someone is a 'kid' if they been baptized. So the baptized are free to listen or not, as they choose."

"Gospel, this is not a religious matter."

"But what if it is? What it is, for sure, is a matter of life and death. And it's in the *newspapers*. I can show you! Right here." He took a piece of paper from an inside pocket of his dashiki, unfolded it, and held it up for the visitors to see. "This is from the *New York Times*, Tuesday, January 14, 2003. Not that long ago, huh? And what it tells about is the *vampires* in Malawi. Let me just read you what it says at the end of the article, okay?

> In these impoverished rural communities [they're talking about Malawi], which lack electricity, running water, adequate food, education and medical care, peasant farmers are accustomed to being battered by forces they cannot control or fully understand. The sun burns crops, leaving fields withered and families hungry. Rains drown chickens and wash away huts, leaving people homeless. Newborn babies die despite the wails of their mothers and the powerful prayers of their elders.
>
> People here believe in an invisible God, but also in malevolent forces—witches who change into hyenas, people who can destroy their enemies by harnessing floods. So the notion of vampires does not seem farfetched.

Rev. Blount laid the paper down on the pulpit and slammed his hand down over it, as though he were nailing it down. "And I'll just add this. It especially don't seem farfetched if you seen them with your own eyes! If you had neighbors who was vampires. If you seen the syringes they left behind them when they was all full of blood and sleepy. Cause that's what these vampires use nowadays. They don't have sharp teeth like cats or wolves, they got syringes! And they know how to use them as well as any nurse at the hospital. Real fast and neat, they don't leave a drop of blood showing, just slide it in and slip it out." He pantomimed the vampires' expertise.

"Gospel, I'm sorry," Ms. McLeod admonished, "we are going to have to leave. Right now. Children, put your coats on. The Reverend is getting into matters that we had agreed we wouldn't discuss in the context of Brotherhood Month."

"Vampires are real, kids," Reverend Blount boomed out, sounding more like Verizon than ever. "They are real, and they are living here in Minneapolis! If you just look around you will see them in their white suits and their white dresses. And they are laughing at you cause you can't see what's there right under your nose."

Before she got up from her folding chair to follow Ms. McLeod out of the tabernacle, Tawana took one of the bulletins from the stack on the window sill next to her. It was the first time in her life that she had taken up any kind of reading matter without being told to. Maybe she wasn't a kid any more. Maybe the words of Gospel Blantyre Blount, D.D., had been the water of her baptism, just like they'd talked about at the Catholic school. They said if you were baptized and you died your flesh would be raised incorruptible. That's how she felt leaving the All-Faith Tabernacle, incorruptible.

In April the Governor declared the ten counties of the Metro area a Disaster Area and called in the National Guard to help where the roads were washed away and in those areas that had security problems, especially East St. Paul and Duluth, where there had been massive demonstrations and looting. In Shakopee, six African-American teenagers were killed when their Dodge Ram pickup was swept off Route 19 by the reborn Brown Beaver River. An estimated twelve thousand acres of productive farmland were lost in that single inundation, and the President (who had vetoed the Emergency Land Reclamation Act) was widely blamed for the damage sustained throughout the state.

Despite all these tragedies there hadn't been one school day canceled at

Diversitas, though the bus service was now optional and rather expensive. Morning after soggy morning Tawana had trudged through the slush and the puddles in her leaky Nikes, which she had thrown such a scene to get when Aunt Bima had wanted to get her a cheaper alternative at the Mall of America. Now Tawana had no one but herself to blame for her misery, which made it a lot more of a misery than it would otherwise have been.

It was only the left Nike that leaked, so if she were careful where she stepped, her foot would stay dry for the whole thirty-four blocks she had to walk. Sometimes, if it wasn't raining too hard, she'd take a slightly longer route that passed by the CVS and other stores that had awnings she could walk under, making an umbrella unnecessary. Tawana hated umbrellas.

That longer route also took her past the All-Faiths Tabernacle and the Northeast Minneapolis Arts Cooperative on the ground floor.

There, on the day after the Governor's declaration, the "Well-Dressed People" display had been taken down and a new display mounted. The sign this time said:

ENTERTAINMENT IS FUN—
FOR THE WHOLE FAMILY!

The same white-faced mannikins, in the same white clothes, were seated in front of an old-fashioned tv set with a dinky screen, and gazing at a tape loop that showed a part of a movie that they had all had to watch at school in the film appreciation class. You could hear the music over an invisible speaker: "I'm singing in the rain, just singing in the rain. I'm singing and dancing in the rain!" The same snippet of the song over and over as the man on the tv whirled with his umbrella about a lamp post and splashed in the puddles on the street. Maybe it was supposed to be fun, like the sign in the window said, but it only made Tawana feel more miserably wet.

The next day it drizzled, and the same actor (Gene Kelly it said at one point in the loop) was still whirling around the same lamp pole to the same music. Then, to Tawana's astonishment, a door opened behind the tv set and a real man (but dressed in a white suit like the mannikins) stepped into the imaginary room behind the window. Tawana knew him. It was Mr. Forbush who had been the music and dance teacher at Diversitas two years earlier. His hair was shorter now and dyed bright gold. When he saw Tawana staring at him, he tipped his head to the side, and smiled, and wiggled his fingers to say hello. Then he turned round to get hold of a gigantic, bright yellow baby chick, which he positioned next to the mannikins so it, too, would be looking at *Singin' in the Rain*.

When Mr. Forbush was satisfied with the baby chick's positioning he began to fluff up its fake feathers with a battery-powered hair dryer. From time to time, when he saw Tawana still standing there under the awning, wavering between amusement and suspicion, he would aim the blow dryer at his own mop of wispy golden curls.

"Well, hello there," said a man's voice that seemed strangely familiar. "I believe we've met before."

Tawana looked to the side, where the Reverend Gospel Blantyre Blount, D.D. was standing in a black dashiki in the shadows of the entrance to the Tabernacle.

"You're Tawana, aren't you?"

She nodded.

"Would you like something to eat, Tawana?"

She nodded again and followed the minister up the dark stairway, leaving Gene Kelly singing and spinning around in the endless rain.

Rev. Blount poured some milk powder into a big mug and stirred it up with water from a plastic bottle, added a spoonful of Swiss Miss Diet Cocoa, and put the mug into a microwave to cook. After the bell dinged, he took it out and set it front of Tawana on what would have been the kitchen table if this were a kitchen. It was more like an office or a library, with piles of paper on the table, and two desks, lots of bookcases. There was also a sink in one corner with a bathroom cabinet over it and a pile of firewood though nowhere to burn any of it. A pair of windows let in some light from the back alley, but not a lot, since they were covered by pink plastic shower curtains, which were drawn almost closed so you could only get a peek at the back alley and the rain coming down.

"Nothing like a hot cup of cocoa on a rainy day," Rev. Blount declared in his booming voice. Tawana concurred with a wary nod, and lifted the brim of the cup to her lips. It was more lukewarm than hot, but even so she did not take a sip.

"I'll bet you're wondering why I called you here."

"You didn't call me here," Tawana said matter-of-factly. "I was looking at the crazy stuff inside that window downstairs."

"Well, I *was* calling, sending out a mental signal, and you *are* here, so figure that out. But you're right about that window. It's crazy, or something worse. Aren't you going to drink that cocoa?"

Tawana took a sip and then an actual swallow. Before she set the mug back down she'd drunk down half the cocoa in it. All the while Rev. Gospel Blantyre Blount kept his eyes fixed on her like a teacher expecting an answer to a question.

Finally he said, "It's the vampires, isn't it? You want to know about the vampires."

"I didn't say that."

"But that's what you was thinking." His large eyes narrowed to a sly knowing slit.

Tawana hooked her finger into the handle of the mug. It *was* the vampires. Ever since she'd read the stuff in the church bulletin that she'd taken home she'd wanted to know more than just what was there in writing, most of it taken out of newspapers. She wanted the whole truth, the truth that didn't get into newspapers.

"You actually saw then yourself, the vampires?"

Rev. Blount nodded. His eyes looked sad, the lids all droopy, with yellowish scuzz in the corners. From time to time he'd wipe the scuzz away with a fingertip, but it would be there again within a few blinks.

"What'd they look like?"

"Just the same as people you see on the street. Tall mostly, but then that's so for most us Malawis. They always wear white. That's how they get their name in Bantu. The White Man is what we call a vampire. It's not the same as calling someone a white man over here, though most vampires do have white skin. Not all, but the overwhelming majority."

Tawana pondered this. In the one movie she had ever seen about her own native country of Somalia she had noticed the same thing. All the American soldiers who went into the city of Mogadishu to kill the people there were white with one exception. That one black soldier didn't have a name that she could remember but she remembered him more clearly than all the white soldiers, because he behaved just the way they did, as though they'd turned him into one of them. If there could be black soldiers like him, why not black vampires?

"I saw the movie," she said, by way of offering her own credentials. And added (thinking he might not know which movie), "The one in black and white."

"Dracula!" said the Reverend Blount. "Yeah, that is one kind of vampire all right. With those teeth. Don't mess with that mother. But the White Man is a different kind of vampire. He don't bite into your neck and suck the blood out, which must be a trickier business than they let on in the old movie. No, the White Man uses modern technology. He's got syringes. You know, like at the doctor's office. Big ones. He jabs them in anywheres, sometimes in the neck, or in the arm, wherever. Then when the thing is filled up with blood he takes off the full test tube-thing and wiggles in an empty one. As many times as he needs to. Sometimes he'll take all the blood they got, if he's hungry. Other times, but not that often, he'll only take a sip. Like you, with that cocoa. That's how new vampires get created. Cause there is some vampire blood inside the syringe and it gets into the victim's bloodstream and turns them into vampires themselves. AIDS works just the same. You know about AIDS?"

Tawana nodded. "We have to study it at school. And you can't share needles."

"True! Especially with the White Man."

Tawana had a feeling she wasn't being told the whole story, just the way grown-ups never tell you the whole story about sex. Usually you had to listen to them when they thought you weren't there. Then you found out.

"The vampire you saw," she said, shifting directions, "was it just one? And was it a man or a woman?"

"Good question!" Rev. Blount said approvingly. "Because there can be lady vampires. Not as many as the men but a lot. And to answer your question, the only ones I ever saw for sure was men. But I have met some ladies I thought might of been vampires—black ladies!—but I cleared out before I could find out for certain. If I hadn't of I might not be here now."

Tawana felt frustrated. Rev. Blount answered her questions honestly enough, but even so he seemed kind of...slippery. He wasn't telling her the *details*.

"You want to know the exact details, don't you?" he asked, reading her mind. "Okay, here's what happened. This was back in 1997 and I was studying theology at the All-Faith Mission and Theological Seminary in Blantyre, which is the city in Malawi that has had the biggest vampire problem but which is also my middle name because I was born there. Well, one day Dr. Hopkins who runs the Mission assembled all the seminarians to the hall and told us we would be welcoming a guest from the United Nations health service, and he would be testing us for AIDS! Dr.Hopkins said how we should be cooperative and let the man from the UN do his job, because it was a humanitarian mission the same as ours, and there had to be someone to set an example. The health service, it seems, was having a problem with cooperation. People in Malawi don't like a stranger coming and sticking needles into them."

"I hate needles," Tawana declared fervently.

"Well, we all hate needles, sister. And why us? we had to wonder. Of course, at that time, no one in Blantyre really believed in AIDS. People got sick, yes, and they died, some of them, but there can be other explanations for that. Most people in Malawi thought AIDS was witchcraft. A witch can put a spell on someone and that someone starts feeling bad and he can't...do whatever he used to. And dies. Only this wasn't any ordinary kind of witchcraft."

"It was the White Man!"

Rev. Blount nodded gravely. "Exactly. Only we didn't know that then. So we agreed to go along with what Dr. Hopkins was asking us to do, and this 'guest' came to the Seminary and we all lined up and let him take our blood. Only *I* refused to let him have any of mine, cause I had a funny feeling about the whole thing. Well, some time went by, and we more or less forgot about the visit we had. But then the guest returned, and talked to Dr. Hopkins, and then he talked with four of the seminarians. But I think there was more than talk that went on. It was like he'd drained the blood right out of them. They were dead before they died. And within a month's time they was genuinely dead, all four of them. It was all hushed up, but I was one of the people Dr. Hopkins asked to clean up their rooms after. And you know what I found? Syringes. I showed them to Dr. Hopkins, but he said just get rid of them, that is nothing to do with the Seminary. Well, what was it then? I wondered. They wasn't taking drugs in the Seminary. I don't think so! It wasn't AIDS, not them boys."

"It was the White Man," Tawana said.

Rev. Blount nodded. "It was the White Man. He tasted the different kinds of blood we sent him, and those boys had the taste the White Man liked best. So he kept coming back for more. And once a vampire has had his first taste, there's nothing you can do to stop him coming back for more. That old movie had it right there. I don't know how the vampires got to them, but those four boys sure as hell didn't commit suicide, which was what some of them at the Seminary was insinuating. Their whole religion is against suicide. No. No. The White Man got them, plain and simple."

"Tawana!" Ms. McLeod exclaimed with her customary excess of gusto. "Come in, come in!" The school's principal placed her wire-framed reading glasses atop a stack of multiple-choice Personnel Evaluation forms that had occupied the same corner of her desk since the start of the spring quarter, an emblem of her supervisory status and a clear sign that her rank as principal set her apart from graders of papers and monitors of lunch rooms.

Tawana entered the Principal's office holding up the yellow slip that had summoned her from Numerical Thinking, her last class before lunch.

"Is this your essay, Tawana?" Ms. McLeod asked, producing three pages of ruled paper. The title—OUR SOMALI BROTHERS AND SISTERS: A Minnesota Perspective—was written with orange magic marker in letters two inches high. Under it, on a more modest scale, was the author's name, Tawana Makwinja.

"Yes, Ms. McLeod."

"And the assignment was to write a letter about your family's cultural heritage. Is that right?"

Tawana dipped her head in agreement.

"Would you," purred Ms. McLeod, handing the paper to Tawana "read it aloud—so I can hear it in the author's own voice?"

Tawana looked down at the paper, then up at Ms. McLeod, whose thin, plucked eyebrows were lifted high to pantomime attentiveness and curiosity. "Just begin at the beginning."

Tawana began to read from her essay:

> It is difficult to determine exactly the number of Somalis living in the Twin Cities. Minnesota Department of Human Services has estimated as many as 15,000, but the Somalia Council of Minnesota maintains that these figures are greatly inflated. Over 95% of Somali people in Minnesota are refugees. Many Somalis in Minnesota are single women with five or more children,

because so many men were killed in the war.

According to Mohammed Essa, director of the Somali Community in Minnesota, the role of women as authority figures in U.S. society is different from Somalia where few women work outside the home and men do not take instruction from women. For instance, the two sexes do not shake hands. Somalis practice corporal punishment, and many complain that the child protection workers are too quick to take away their children.

Somali religious tradition requires female circumcision at the youngest possible age, in order in ensure a woman's virginity, to increase a man's sexual pleasure, and promote marital fidelity. However, this practice is outlawed in Minnesota. Before the circumcision of an infant daughter there is a 40-day period called the "afartanbah," followed by important celebrations attended by friends and family members that involve the killing of a goat.

Somalis are proud of their heritage and lineage. Children and family are deeply valued by Somalis, who favor large families. Seven or more children are common. Due to resettlement and the inability to keep families together in refugee situations, few Somali children in Minnesota live with both parents. The availability of culturally appropriate childcare is a major issue in Minnesota.

Tawana looked up cautiously, as after a sustained punishment. Ms. McLeod had made her read the whole thing out loud. She would rather have been whipped with a belt.

"Thank you, Tawana," said Ms. McLeod, reaching out to take back the essay. "There were a *few* pronunciation problems along the way, but that often happens when we read words we know only from books. I'm sure you know what all the words *mean*, don't you?"

Tawana nodded, glowering.

"This one, for instance—'corporal'? What kind of punishment might that be? Hmm? Or 'lineage'? Why exactly is that a source of pride, Tawana?"

Ms. McLeod went on with word after word. It really was not fair. Tawana wasn't stupid, but Ms. McLeod was trying to make her look stupid. Making her read her essay aloud had been a trap.

"Have *you* ever attended an 'afartanbah,' Tawana?"

Tawana raised her eyes in despair. What kind of question was that! "What is a… the word you said?"

"You answered that question in your own essay, Tawana. It is a celebration forty days after the birth of a baby sister. Have you had such a celebration at your home, where there was goat?"

"Who eats goats in Minnesota?" Tawana protested. "You can't get goats with food stamps. I don't even *like* goat!"

With a thin smile Ms. McLeod conceded defeat in that line of interrogation and shifted back to pedagogic mode. "I want you to understand, Tawana, that there is nothing *wrong* with quoting from legitimate sources. All scholars do that. But note that I said 'sources,' plural. To copy out someone else's work word for word is not scholarship, it is plagiarism, and that is simply against all the rules. Students are expelled from university classes for doing what you have done. So you will have to write your essay over, from scratch, and not just copy out …this!" She produced a print-out of the same study from the Center for Cross-Cultural Health, "Somali Culture in Minnesota," that the school librarian had called up on the Internet for Tawana's use.

"That was the bad news," said Ms. McLeod with a sympathetic smile. "The *good* news is that you have really lovely handwriting!"

"I do?"

"Indeed. Firm, well-rounded, but not…childish. I don't know where you developed such a hand—not here at Diversitas, I'm sorry to say. The emphasis here has never been on fine penmanship."

"The nuns taught the Palmer Method at my last school."

"Well, you must have been one of their best students. Now, penmanship is a genuine skill. And anyone with a skill is in a position to earn money! How would you like a *job*, Miss Makwinja?"

Tawana regarded the Principal with ill-concealed dismay. "A job? But I'm just…a kid."

"Oh, I don't mean to send you off to a nine-to-five, full-time place of employment. No, this would be a part-time job, but it would pay more than you would earn by babysitting. And you could work as much or as little as you like, if you do a good job."

"What would I have to do?"

"Just copy out the words of a letter with your clear, bold penmanship. We can have an audition for the job right now. Here is the text of the letter I want you to copy. And here is the stationery to write on. You should be able to fit the whole letter on a single page, if you use both sides of the paper. Don't rush. Make it as neat as your essay."

Tawana regarded the letterhead on the stationery:

Holy Angels School of Nursing and Widwifery
4217 Ralph Bunche Boulevard
Kampala
Uganda, East Africa.

"Here." Ms. McLeod placed a fat fountain pen on top of the Holy Angels stationery. "A real pen always makes a better impression than ballpoint."

Tawana began to copy the letter, neatly and accurately, including all its mistakes.

Dear friend in Christ's Name,

I send you warm greeting hoping you are in a good-sounding health. I am so happy to write to you and I cry for your spiritual kindness to rescue me from this distressed moment.

I am Elesi Kuseliwa, a girl of 18 years old, and a first born in a family of 4 children. We are orphans.

I completed Ordinary level in 2003 and in 2004 I joined the above-mentioned school and took a course in midwifery. Unfortunately in October both our parents perished in a car accident on their way from church. We were left helpless in agony without any one to console or to take care of us. Life is difficult and unbearable.

This is my last and final year to complete my course of study. We study three terms a year and each term I am supposed to pay 450 UK pounds. The total fee for the year is 1350 pounds. I humbly request you to sympathize and become my sponsor so

I may complete my course and to take my family responsibilities, most importantly, paying school fees for my younger sisters.

Enclosed is a photocopy of my end of third term school report. I pray and await your kind and caring response.

Yours faithfully,
Elisi Kuseliwa

"Very good," said Ms. McLeod, when she had looked over the finished copy. "That took you just a little over fifteen minutes, which means that in an hour you should be able to make four copies just like this. Now I understand that girls your age can earn as much as two-fifty at babysitting. I'll do better than that. I'll pay four dollars an hour. Or one dollar for each letter you copy. Do we have a deal?"

What could Tawana say but yes.

Tawana still had one friend left from when she'd gone to Our Lady of Mercy, Patricia Brown. That was not her Somali name, of course. She'd become Patricia Brown when her mother died and she was adopted into the Brown family. She was a quiet, plodding bully of a girl, already two hundred pounds when Tawana had met her in fourth grade, and now lighting up the screen on the scale at 253. Tawana had won her friendship by patiently listening to Patricia's ceaseless complainings about her foster parents, her siblings, her teachers, and her classmates at Our Lady of Mercy, a skill she had learned from having sat still for Lucy's long whines and Grandpa's rants. In exchange for her nods and murmers Tawana was able to see shows on the Browns' tv that Tawana couldn't get at home. That is how Tawana (and Patricia as well) came to be a fan of *Buffy the Vampire Slayer*.

At first the later afternoon reruns had been as hard to understand as if you arrived at a stranger's house in the middle of a complicated family quarrel that had been going on for years. You couldn't tell who was right and who was wrong. Or in this case who was the vampire and who wasn't. Buffy herself definitely wasn't, but she had her own superhuman powers. When she wanted to she could zap one of the vampires to the other side of the room with just a tap of her finger. Sometimes she would walk up to a vampire and start talking to him and then without a word of warning whack him through the heart with a wooden stake. But other times, confusingly, she would fall in love with some guy who would turn out to be a vampire, but that didn't stop their being in love.

Patricia said there was a simple explanation. The vampires were able to confuse people by their good looks, and Buffy would eventually realize the mistake she was making with Spike and whack him just like the others. Tawana was not so sure. Spike might be a vampire but he seemed to really love Buffy. Also, he looked a lot like Mr. Forbush, with the same bleached hair and thin face and sarcastic smile. Though, as Patricia had pointed out, what did that have to do with anything! It was all just a story like *Days of Our Lives*, only more so since it was about vampires and vampires are only make-believe. Tawana did not tell Patricia about the real vampires in Malawi. Everything that she had learned about the White Man was between her and Rev. Gospel Blount.

But in the course of watching many episodes of *Buffy* and thinking them over and discussing them with other kids at Diversitas. Tawana developed a much broader understanding of the nature of vampires and the powers they possessed than you could get from an out-of-date movie like *Dracula*. Or even from reading books, though Tawana had never actually tried to do that. She was not much interested in books. Even their smell could get her feeling queasy.

The main thing to be learned was that here in America just the same as in Rev. Blount's native land of Malawi there were vampires everywhere. Most people had no idea who the vampires were, but a few special individuals like Buffy, or Tawana, could recognize a vampire from the kind of fire that would flash from their eyes, or by other subtle signs.

The vampires in Minneapolis were usually white, and tended to be on the thin side, and older, especially the men. And they would watch you when they thought you weren't looking. If you caught them at it, they would tilt their head backwards and pretend to be staring at the ceiling.

A lot of what people thought of as the drug problem was actually vampires. That was how they kept themselves out of the news. All the people who died from a so-called drug overdose? It was usually vampires.

Then one day in May toward the end of seventh grade Tawana developed a major insight into vampires that was all her own. She was in the Browns' living room with Patricia and her younger brother Michael watching a rerun of *Buffy* that they all had seen before. Patricia and Michael were sitting side by side in the glider, spaced out on Michael's medication, and Tawana was sitting behind them, keeping the glider rocking real slow with her toe, the same as if they were the twins in their stroller. Instead of looking at the story on the tv Tawana's attention was fixed on the big statue of Jesus on the wall. There were silver spikes through his hands and feet, and his naked body was twisting around and his neck stretched up, trying to escape the crucifix. Tawana realized that Jesus looked exactly like one of the vampires when Buffy had pounded a wooden stake into him. Their skin was the same clouded white, the same expression on their faces, a kind of holy pain. Not only that but with Jesus, the same as with vampires, you might think you had killed him but then a day or two later he wasn't in the coffin where you thought. He was out on the street again, alive.

Jesus had been the first White Man!

Tawana kept rocking the two Brown children, and sneaking sideways glances at the crucifix, and wondering who in the world she could ever tell about her incredible insight, which kept making more and more sense.

The priests, the nuns, the missionaries! Hospitals and health clincs. The crucifixes in everybody's homes, just like the story of Moses when the Jews in Egypt marked their doors with blood to keep out the Angel of Death!

Everything was starting to connect. Here in America and there in Africa, for centuries and centuries, it was all the same ancient never-ending struggle of good against evil, human against vampire, Black against White.

On July 3, in preparation for the holidays, the Northeast Minneapolis Arts Cooperative once again changed its window display in the store that was never open underneath the All-Faiths Tabernacle. The old ENTERTAINMENT IS FUN—FOR THE WHOLE FAMILY! sign wasn't taken down. Instead WAR was pasted over ENTERTAINMENT, and the mannikins who had been sitting around the imaginary living room watching Gene Kelly on tv had been dismembered, their detached limbs and white clothes scattered around a cemetery made of cardboard tombstones and spray-on cobwebs. A big flag rippled in a breeze supplied by a standing fan at the side of the window, while the hidden sound system played the Jimi Hendrix version of the "Star-Spangled Banner."

Tawana's first reaction, as for the earlier displays, was a perplexed indignation, a sense of having been personally violated without knowing exactly how. But now that she had become more adept at unriddling such conundrums the basic meaning of the display in the window slowly became clear like a face on tv emerging from the green and grey sprinkles of static. This was the cemetery that the vampires lived in, only they weren't home. The White Man was hunting for more victims. The limbs beside the gravestones were the remnants of some earlier feast.

It actually helped to know what the real situation was. When there is a definite danger it is possible to act. Tawana went round to the back of the building. The Arts Cooperative people always used their back door and kept their front door locked, and Rev. Blount did just the opposite. There was no doorbell, so Tawana knocked.

Mr. Forbush answered the inner door and stood behind the patched and sagging screen, blinking. "Yes?" he asked, stupid with sleep.

"Mr. Forbush, can I come in and talk with you?" When he seemed uncertain, she added, "It's about Rev. Blount, upstairs."

Tawana knew from Rev. Blount there were problems between the Arts Cooperative, who owned the building, and the Tabernacle, which was behind in its rent and taking its landlord to court for harrassment and other reasons. And sure enough Mr. Forbush forgot his suspicions and invited Tawana inside.

She was in a space almost as jumbled and crazy as the shop window out front, with some of the walls torn down, and drywall partitions painted to look like pictures, and rugs on top of rugs and piles of gigantic pillows and other piles of cardboard and plastic boxes and not much real furniture anywhere. Tawana had never been anywhere vampires lived, and this was nothing like she would have expected. She was fascinated, and a little dazed.

"What are you looking for?" Mr. Forbush asked. "The bathroom?"

"Are we by ourselves?" Tawana asked, running her fingers across the top of the gas stove as though it were a piano.

Before he could answer, the phone rang. All the tension inside of Tawana relaxed away like a puff of smoke. The ring of the phone was the sound of heaven answering her prayers. Mr. Forbush swiveled round in the pile of cushions he'd settle down on, reaching for a cell phone on top of the CD player that sat on the bare floor.

Tawana grabbed hold of the cast iron frying pan on the back burner of the stove, and before there was any answer to Mr. Forbush's "Hello?" she had knocked him over the head. The first blow didn't kill him, or the second. But they were solid enough that he was never able to fight back. He groaned some and waved his arms, but that did nothing to keep Tawana from slaying him.

Outside, along the driveway, there was an old, old wooden fence that hadn't been painted for years. That provided the stake she needed. She didn't even have to sharpen the end of it. She drove it through his heart with the same frying pan she'd used to smash his head in. She was amazed at the amount of blood that spilled out into the pile of pillows. Perhaps he had been feasting through the night.

There was no use trying to mop the floor, no way to hide the body. But she did change out of her bloody clothes, and found a white dress that must have belonged to one of the mannikins. She wore that to go home in, with her own dirty clothes stuffed in a plastic bag from CVS.

Mr. Forbush's death received a good deal of attention on WCCO and the other news programs, and Rev. Blount was often on the tv to answer questions and deny reports. But no charges were every brought against him, or against any other suspect. However, it was not possible, after so much media attention, to deny that Minneapolis had a vampire problem just the same as Malawi. There were many who believed that Mr. Forbush had been a vampire, or at least had been associating with vampires, on the principle that where there is smoke there is fire. It was discovered by a reporter on the *Star* that the Arts Cooperative was a legal fiction designed to help Mr. Forbush evade state and local taxes, that he was, in effect, the sole owner, having inherited the property after the bankruptcy of his father's mattress store and the man's subsequent suicide. It was rumored that the father's death might not have been a suicide, and that he had been the first victim of the vampires—or, alternatively, that he had been the first of the vampires.

None of these stories ever received official media attention, but they were circulated widely enough that the All-Faiths Pentecostal Tabernacle became a big success story in the Twin Cities' Somali-American community. Rev. Blount received a special award for his contributions to Interfaith Dialogue from the Neighborhood Development Association, and even after the protests that followed the "Mall of America Massacre" and the effort by the police to close down the Tabernacle, he was saluted as a local hero and a possible candidate for the State Senate.

Tawana was never to enjoy the same celebrity status, though as a member of All-Faiths' choir she had her share of the general good fortune, including her own brief moment of glory in the spotlight. It was during the NBC Special Report, *The Vampires of Minnesota*. She was in her red and white choir robes, standing outside the Tabernacle after a Sunday service. The camera had been pressed up to her face, close enough to kiss, and she'd stared right into it, no smile on her lips, completely serious, and said, "They said it could never happen here. They said it might happen somewhere *primitive* and *backwards* like Malawi, but never in Minneapolis."

Then she just lowered her eyes and turned her head sideways, and they started to roll the credits.

Gestella
Susan Palwick

Time's the problem. Time and arithmetic. You've known from the beginning that the numbers would cause trouble, but you were much younger then— much, much younger—and far less wise. And there's culture shock, too. Where you come from, it's okay for women to have wrinkles. Where you come from, youth's not the only commodity.

You met Jonathan back home. Call it a forest somewhere, near an Alp. Call it a village on the edge of the woods. Call it old. You weren't old, then: you were fourteen on two feet and a mere two years old on four, although already fully grown. Your kind are fully grown at two years, on four feet. And experienced: oh, yes. You knew how to howl at the moon. You knew what to do when somebody howled back. If your four-footed form hadn't been sterile, you'd have had litters by then—but it was, and on two feet, you'd been just smart enough, or lucky enough, to avoid continuing your line.

But it wasn't as if you hadn't had plenty of opportunities, enthusiastically taken. Jonathan liked that. A lot. Jonathan was older than you were: thirty-five, then. Jonathan loved fucking a girl who looked fourteen and acted older, who acted feral, who *was* feral for three to five days a month, centered on the full moon. Jonathan didn't mind the mess that went with it, either: all that fur, say, sprouting at one end of the process and shedding on the other, or the aches and pains from various joints pivoting, changing shape, redistributing weight, or your poor gums bleeding all the time from the monthly growth and recession of your fangs. "At least that's the only blood," he told you, sometime during that first year.

You remember this very clearly: you were roughly halfway through the four-to-two transition, and Jonathan was sitting next to you in bed, massaging your sore shoulder blades as you sipped mint tea with hands still nearly as clumsy as paws, hands like mittens. Jonathan had just filled two hot water bottles, one for your aching tailbone and one for your aching knees. Now you know he wanted to get you in shape for a major sportfuck—he loved sex even more than usual, after you'd just changed back—but at the time, you thought he was a real prince, the kind of prince girls like you weren't supposed to be allowed to get, and a stab of pain shot through you at his words. "I didn't kill anything," you told him, your lower lip trembling. "I didn't even hunt."

"Gestella, darling, I know. That wasn't what I meant." He stroked your hair. He'd been feeding you raw meat during the four-foot phase, but not anything you'd killed yourself. He'd taught you to eat little pieces out of his hand, gently, without biting him. He'd taught you to wag your tail, and he was teaching you to chase a ball, because that's what good four-foots did where he came from. "I was talking about—"

"Normal women," you told him. "The ones who bleed so they can have babies. You shouldn't make fun of them. They're lucky." You like children and puppies; you're good with them, gentle. You know it's unwise for you to have any of your own, but you can't help but watch them, wistfully.

"I don't want kids," he says. "I had that operation. I told you."

"Are you sure it took?" you ask. You're still very young. You've never known anyone who's had an operation like that, and you're worried about whether Jonathan really understands your condition. Most people don't. Most people think all kinds of crazy things. Your condition isn't communicable, for instance, by biting or any other way, but it is hereditary, which is why it's good that you've been so smart and lucky, even if you're just fourteen.

Well, no, not fourteen anymore. It's about halfway through Jonathan's year of folklore research—he's already promised not to write you up for any of the journals, and keeps assuring you he won't tell anybody, although later you'll realize that's for his protection, not yours—so that would make you, oh, seventeen or eighteen. Jonathan's still thirty-five. At the end of the year, when he flies you back to the United States with him so the two of you can get married, he'll be thirty-six. You'll be twenty-one on two feet, three years old on four.

Seven to one. That's the ratio. You've made sure Jonathan understands this. "Oh, sure," he says. "Just like for dogs. One year is seven human years. Everybody knows that. But how can it be a problem, darling, when we love each other so much?" And even though you aren't fourteen anymore, you're still young enough to believe him.

At first it's fun. The secret's a bond between you, a game. You speak in code. Jonathan splits your name in half, calling you Jessie on four feet and Stella on two. You're Stella to all his friends, and most of them don't even know that he has a dog one week a month. The two of you scrupulously avoid scheduling social commitments for the week of the full moon, but no one seems to notice the pattern, and if anyone does notice, no one cares. Occasionally someone you know sees Jessie, when you and Jonathan are out in the park playing with balls, and Jonathan always says that he's taking care of his sister's dog while she's away on business. His sister travels a lot, he explains. Oh, no, Stella doesn't mind, but she's always been a bit nervous around dogs—even though Jessie's such a *good* dog—so she stays home during the walks.

Sometimes strangers come up, shyly. "What a beautiful dog!" they say. "What a *big* dog!" "What kind of dog is that?"

"A Husky-wolfhound cross," Jonathan says airily. Most people accept this. Most people know as much about dogs as dogs know about the space shuttle.

Some people know better, though. Some people look at you, and frown a little, and say, "Looks like a wolf to me. Is she part wolf?"

"Could be," Jonathan always says with a shrug, his tone as breezy as ever. And he spins a little story about how his sister adopted you from the pound because you were the runt of the litter and no one else wanted you, and now look at you! No one would ever take you for a runt now! And the strangers smile and look encouraged and pat you on the head, because they like stories about dogs being rescued from the pound.

You sit and down and stay during these conversations; you do whatever Jonathan says. You wag your tail and cock your head and act charming. You let people scratch you behind the ears. You're a *good* dog. The other dogs in the park, who know more about their own species than most people do, aren't fooled by any of this; you make them nervous, and they tend to avoid you, or to act supremely submissive if avoidance isn't possible. They grovel on their bellies, on their backs; they crawl away backwards, whining.

Jonathan loves this. Jonathan loves it that you're the alpha with the other dogs—and, of course, he loves it that he's your alpha. Because that's another thing people don't understand about your condition: they think you're vicious, a ravening beast, a fanged monster from hell. In fact, you're no more bloodthirsty than any dog not trained to mayhem. You haven't been trained to mayhem: you've been trained to chase balls. You're a pack animal, an animal who craves hierarchy, and you, Jessie, are a one-man dog. Your man's Jonathan. You adore him. You'd do anything for him, even let strangers who wouldn't know a wolf from a wolfhound scratch you behind the ears.

The only fight you and Jonathan have, that first year in the States, is about the collar. Jonathan insists that Jessie wear a collar. "Otherwise," he says, "I could be fined." There are policemen in the park. Jessie needs a collar and an ID tag and rabies shots.

"Jessie," you say on two feet, "needs no such thing." You, Stella, are bristling as you say this, even though you don't have fur at the moment. "Jonathan," you tell him, "ID tags are for dogs who wander. Jessie will never leave your side, unless you throw a ball for her. And I'm not going to get rabies. All I eat is Alpo, not dead raccoons: How am I going to get rabies?"

"It's the law," he says gently. "It's not worth the risk, Stella."

And then he comes and rubs your head and shoulders *that* way, the way you've never been able to resist, and soon the two of you are in bed having a lovely sportfuck, and somehow by the end of the evening, Jonathan's won. Well, of course he has: he's the alpha.

So the next time you're on four feet, Jonathan puts a strong chain choke collar and an ID tag around your neck, and then you go to the vet and get your shots. You don't like the vet's office much, because it smells of too much fear and pain, but the people there pat you and give you milk bones and tell you how beautiful you are, and the vet's hands are gentle and kind.

The vet likes dogs. She also knows wolves from wolfhounds. She looks at you, hard, and then looks at Jonathan. "A gray wolf?" she asks.

"I don't know," says Jonathan. "She could be a hybrid."

"She doesn't look like a hybrid to me." So Jonathan launches into his breezy story about how you were the runt of the litter at the pound: you wag your tail and lick the vet's hand and act utterly adoring.

The vet's not having any of it. She strokes your head; her hands are kind, but she smells disgusted. "Mr. Argent, gray wolves are endangered."

"At least one of her parents was a dog," Jonathan says. He's starting to sweat.

"Now, *she* doesn't look endangered, does she?"

"There are laws about keeping exotics as pets," the vet says. She's still stroking your head; you're still wagging your tail, but now you start to whine, because the vet smells angry and Jonathan smells afraid. "Especially endangered exotics."

"She's a dog," Jonathan says.

"If she's a dog," the vet says, "may I ask why you haven't had her spayed?"

Jonathan splutters. "Ex*cuse* me?"

"You got her from the pound. Do you know how animals wind up at the pound, Mr. Argent? They land there because people breed them and then don't want to take care of all those puppies or kittens. They land there—"

"We're here for a rabies shot," Jonathan says. "Can we get our rabies shot, please?"

"Mr. Argent, there are regulations about breeding endangered species—"

"I understand that," Jonathan says. "There are also regulations about rabies shots. If you don't give my *dog* her rabies shot—"

The vet shakes her head, but she gives you the rabies shot, and then Jonathan gets you out of there, fast. "Bitch," he says on the way home. He's shaking. "Animal-rights fascist bitch! Who the hell does she think she is?"

She thinks she's a vet. She thinks she's somebody who's supposed to take care of animals. You can't say any of this, because you're on four legs. You lie in the back seat of the car, on the special sheepskin cover Jonathan bought to protect the upholstery from your fur, and whine. You're scared. You liked the vet, but you're afraid of what she might do. She doesn't understand your condition; how could she?

The following week, after you're fully changed back, there's a knock at the door while Jonathan's at work. You put down your copy of *Elle* and pad, barefooted, over to the door. You open it to find a woman in uniform; a white truck with "Animal Control" written on it is parked in the driveway.

"Good morning," the officer says. "We've received a report that there may be an exotic animal on this property. May I come in, please?"

"Of course," you tell her. You let her in. You offer her coffee, which she doesn't want, and you tell her that there aren't any exotic animals here. You invite her to look around and see for herself.

Of course there's no sign of a dog, but she's not satisfied. "According to our records, Jonathan Argent of this address had a dog vaccinated last Saturday.

We've been told that the dog looked very much like a wolf. Can you tell me where that dog is now?"

"We don't have her anymore," you say. "She got loose and jumped the fence on Monday. It's a shame: she was a lovely animal."

The animal-control lady scowls. "Did she have ID?"

"Of course," you say. "A collar with tags. If you find her, you'll call us, won't you?"

She's looking at you, hard, as hard as the vet did. "Of course. We recommend that you check the pound at least every few days, too. And you might want to put up flyers, put an ad in the paper."

"Thank you," you tell her. "We'll do that." She leaves; you go back to reading *Elle*, secure in the knowledge that your collar's tucked into your underwear drawer upstairs and that Jessie will never show up at the pound.

Jonathan's incensed when he hears about this. He reels off a string of curses about the vet. "Do you think you could rip her throat out?" he asks.

"No," you say, annoyed. "I don't want to, Jonathan. I liked her. She's doing her job. Wolves don't just attack people: you know better than that. And it wouldn't be smart even if I wanted to: it would just mean people would have to track me down and kill me. Now look, relax. We'll go to a different vet next time, that's all."

"We'll do better than that," Jonathan says. "We'll move."

So you move to the next county over, to a larger house with a larger yard. There's even some wild land nearby, forest and meadows, and that's where you and Jonathan go for walks now. When it's time for your rabies shot the following year, you go to a male vet, an older man who's been recommended by some friends of friends of Jonathan's, people who do a lot of hunting. This vet raises his eyebrows when he sees you. "She's quite large," he says pleasantly. "Fish and Wildlife might be interested in such a large dog. Her size will add another, oh, hundred dollars to the bill, Johnny."

"I see." Jonathan's voice is icy. You growl, and the vet laughs.

"Loyal, isn't she? You're planning to breed her, of course."

"Of course," Jonathan snaps.

"Lucrative business, that. Her pups will pay for her rabies shot, believe me. Do you have a sire lined up?"

"Not yet." Jonathan sounds like he's strangling.

The vet strokes your shoulders. You don't like his hands. You don't like the way he touches you. You growl again, and again the vet laughs. "Well, give me a call when she goes into heat. I know some people who might be interested."

"Slimy bastard," Jonathan says when you're back home again. "You didn't like him, Jessie, did you? I'm sorry."

You lick his hand. The important thing is that you have your rabies shot, that your license is up to date, that this vet won't be reporting you to Animal Control. You're legal. You're a *good* dog.

You're a good wife, too. As Stella, you cook for Jonathan, clean for him, shop. You practice your English while devouring *Cosmopolitan* and *Martha Stewart Living*, in addition to *Elle*. You can't work or go to school, because the week of the full moon would keep getting in the way, but you keep yourself busy. You learn to drive and you learn to entertain; you learn to shave your legs and pluck your eyebrows, to mask your natural odor with harsh chemicals, to walk in high heels. You learn the artful uses of cosmetics and clothing, so that you'll be even more beautiful than you are *au naturel*. You're stunning: everyone says so, tall and slim with long silver hair and pale, piercing blue eyes. Your skin's smooth, your complexion flawless, your muscles lean and taut: you're a good cook, a great fuck, the perfect trophy wife. But of course, during that first year, while Jonathan's thirty-six going on thirty-seven, you're only twenty-one going on twenty-eight. You can keep the accelerated aging from showing: you eat right, get plenty of exercise, become even more skillful with the cosmetics. You and Jonathan are blissfully happy, and his colleagues, the old fogies in the Anthropology Department, are jealous. They stare at you when they think no one's looking. "They'd all love to fuck you," Jonathan gloats after every party, and after every party, he does just that.

Most of Jonathan's colleagues are men. Most of their wives don't like you, although a few make resolute efforts to be friendly, to ask you to lunch. Twenty-one going on twenty-eight, you wonder if they somehow sense that you aren't one of them, that there's another side to you, one with four feet. Later you'll realize that even if they knew about Jessie, they couldn't hate and fear you anymore than they already do. They fear you because you're young, because you're beautiful and speak English with an exotic accent, because their husbands can't stop staring at you. They know their husbands want to fuck you. The wives may not be young and beautiful any more, but they're no fools. They lost the luxury of innocence when they lost their smooth skin and flawless complexions.

The only person who asks you to lunch and seems to mean it is Diane Harvey. She's forty-five, with thin gray hair and a wide face that's always smiling. She runs her own computer repair business, and she doesn't hate you. This may be related to the fact that her husband Glen never stares at you, never gets too close to you during conversation; he seems to have no desire to fuck you at all. He looks at Diane the way all the other men look at you: as if she's the most desirable creature on earth, as if just being in the same room with her renders him scarcely able to breathe. He adores his wife, even though they've been married for fifteen years, even though he's five years younger than she is and handsome enough to seduce a younger, more beautiful woman. Jonathan says that Glen must stay with Diane for her salary, which is considerably more than his. You think Jonathan's wrong; you think Glen stays with Diane for herself.

Over lunch, as you gnaw an overcooked steak in a bland fern bar, all glass and wood, Diane asks you kindly when you last saw your family, if you're homesick, whether you and Jonathan have any plans to visit Europe again soon. These questions bring a lump to your throat, because Diane's the only one who's ever asked them. You don't, in fact, miss your family—the parents who taught you to hunt, who taught you the dangers of continuing the line, or the siblings with whom you tussled and fought over scraps of meat—because you've transferred all your loyalty to Jonathan. But two is an awfully small pack, and you're starting to wish Jonathan hadn't had that operation. You're starting to wish you could continue the line, even though you know it would be a foolish thing to do. You wonder if that's why your parents mated, even though they knew the dangers.

"I miss the smells back home," you tell Diane, and immediately you blush, because it seems like such a strange thing to say, and you desperately want this kind woman to like you. As much as you love Jonathan, you yearn for someone else to talk to.

But Diane doesn't think it's strange. "Yes," she says, nodding, and tells you about how homesick she still gets for her grandmother's kitchen, which had a signature smell for each season: basil and tomatoes in the summer, apples in the fall, nutmeg and cinnamon in winter, thyme and lavender in the spring. She tells you that she's growing thyme and lavender in her own garden; she tells you about her tomatoes.

She asks you if you garden. You say no. In truth, you're not a big fan of vegetables, although you enjoy the smell of flowers, because you enjoy the smell of almost anything. Even on two legs, you have a far better sense of smell than most people do; you live in a world rich with aroma, and even the scents most people consider noxious are interesting to you. As you sit in the sterile fern bar, which smells only of burned meat and rancid grease and the harsh chemicals the people around you have put on their skin and hair, you realize that you really do miss the smells of home, where even the gardens smell older and wilder than the woods and meadows here.

You tell Diane, shyly, that you'd like to learn to garden. Could she teach you?

So she does. One Saturday afternoon, much to Jonathan's bemusement, Diane comes over with topsoil and trowels and flower seeds, and the two of you measure out a plot in the backyard, and plant and water and get dirt under your nails, and it's quite wonderful, really, about the best fun you've had on two legs, aside from sportfucks with Jonathan. Over dinner, after Diane's left, you try to tell Jonathan how much fun it was, but he doesn't seem particularly interested. He's glad you had a good time, but really, he doesn't want to hear about seeds. He wants to go upstairs and have sex.

So you do.

Afterwards, you go through all of your old issues of *Martha Stewart Living*, looking for gardening tips.

You're ecstatic. You have a hobby now, something you can talk to the other wives about. Surely some of them garden. Maybe, now, they won't hate you. So at the next party, you chatter brightly about gardening, but somehow all the wives are still across the room, huddled around a table, occasionally glaring in your direction, while the men cluster around you, their eyes bright, nodding eagerly at your descriptions of weeds and aphids.

You know something's wrong here. Men don't like gardening, do they? Jonathan certainly doesn't. Finally one of the wives, a tall blonde with a tennis tan and good bones, stalks over and pulls her husband away by the sleeve. "Time to go home now," she tells him, and curls her lip at you.

You know that look. You know a snarl when you see it, even if the wife's too civilized to produce an actual growl.

You ask Diane about this the following week, while you're in her garden, admiring her tomato plants. "Why do they hate me?" you ask Diane.

"Oh, Stella," she says, and sighs. "You really don't know, do you?" You shake your head, and she goes on. "They hate you because you're young and beautiful, even though that's not your fault. The ones who have to work hate you because you don't, and the ones who don't have to work, whose husbands support them, hate you because they're afraid their husbands will leave them for younger, more beautiful women. Do you understand?"

You don't, not really, even though you're now twenty-eight going on thirty-five. "Their husbands can't leave them for me," you tell Diane. "I'm married to Jonathan. I don't *want* any of their husbands." But even as you say it, you know that's not the point.

A few weeks later, you learn that the tall blonde's husband has indeed left her, for an aerobics instructor twenty years his junior. "He showed me a picture," Jonathan says, laughing. "She's a big-hair bimbo. She's not *half* as beautiful as you are."

"What does that have to do with it?" you ask him. You're angry, and you aren't sure why. You barely know the blonde, and it's not as if she's been nice to you. "His poor wife! That was a terrible thing for him to do!"

"Of course it was," Jonathan says soothingly.

"Would you leave me if I wasn't beautiful anymore?" you ask him.

"Nonsense, Stella. You'll always be beautiful."

But that's when Jonathan's going on thirty-eight and you're going on thirty-five. The following year, the balance begins to shift. He's going on thirty-nine; you're going on forty-two. You take exquisite care of yourself, and really, you're as beautiful as ever, but there are a few wrinkles now, and it takes hours of crunches to keep your stomach as flat as it used to be.

Doing crunches, weeding in the garden, you have plenty of time to think. In a year, two at the most, you'll be old enough to be Jonathan's mother, and you're starting to think he might not like that. And you've already gotten wind of catty faculty-wife gossip about how quickly you're showing your age. The faculty wives see every wrinkle, even through artfully applied cosmetics.

During that thirty-five to forty-two year, Diane and her husband move away, so now you have no one with whom to discuss your wrinkles or the catty faculty wives. You don't want to talk to Jonathan about any of it. He still tells you how beautiful you are, and you still have satisfying sportfucks. You don't want to give him any ideas about declining desirability.

You do a lot of gardening that year: flowers—especially roses—and herbs, and some tomatoes in honor of Diane, and because Jonathan likes them. Your best times are the two-foot times in the garden and the four-foot times in the forest, and you think it's no coincidence that both of these involve digging around in the dirt. You write long letters to Diane, on e-mail or, sometimes, when you're saying something you don't want Jonathan to find on the computer, on old-fashioned paper. Diane doesn't have much time to write back, but does send the occasional e-mail note, the even rarer postcard. You read a lot, too, everything you can find: newspapers and novels and political analysis, literary criticism, true crime, ethnographic studies. You startle some of Jonathan's colleagues by casually dropping odd bits of information about their field, about other fields, about fields they've never heard of: forensic geography, agricultural ethics, poststructuralist mining. You think it's no coincidence that the obscure disciplines you're most interested in involve digging around in the dirt.

Some of Jonathan's colleagues begin to comment not only on your beauty, but on your intelligence. Some of them back away a little bit. Some of the wives, although not many, become a little friendlier, and you start going out to lunch again, although not with anyone you like as much as Diane.

The following year, the trouble starts. Jonathan's going on forty; you're going on forty-nine. You both work out a lot; you both eat right. But Jonathan's hardly wrinkled at all yet, and your wrinkles are getting harder to hide. Your stomach refuses to stay completely flat no matter how many crunches you do; you've developed the merest hint of cottage-cheese thighs. You forego your old look, the slinky, skin-tight look, for long flowing skirts and dresses, accented with plenty of silver. You're going for exotic, elegant, and you're getting there just fine; heads still turn to follow you in the supermarket. But the sportfucks are less frequent, and you don't know how much of this is normal aging and how much is lack of interest on Jonathan's part. He doesn't seem quite as enthusiastic as he once did. He no longer brings you herbal tea and hot water bottles during your transitions; the walks in the woods are a little shorter than they used to be, the ball-throwing sessions in the meadows more perfunctory.

And then one of your new friends, over lunch, asks you tactfully if anything's wrong, if you're ill, because, well, you don't look quite yourself. Even as you assure her that you're fine, you know she means that you look a lot older than you did last year.

At home, you try to discuss this with Jonathan. "We knew it would be a problem eventually," you tell him. "I'm afraid that other people are going to notice, that someone's going to figure it out—"

"Stella, sweetheart, no one's going to figure it out." He's annoyed, impatient. "Even if they think you're aging unusually quickly, they won't make the leap to Jessie. It's not in their worldview. It wouldn't occur to them even if you were aging a hundred years for every one of theirs. They'd just think you had some unfortunate metabolic condition, that's all."

Which, in a manner of speaking, you do. You wince. It's been five weeks since the last sportfuck. "Does it bother you that I look older?" you ask Jonathan.

"Of *course* not, Stella!" But since he rolls his eyes when he says this, you're not reassured. You can tell from his voice that he doesn't want to be having this conversation, that he wants to be somewhere else, maybe watching TV. You recognize that tone. You've heard Jonathan's colleagues use it on their wives, usually while staring at you.

You get through the year. You increase your workout schedule, mine *Cosmo* for bedroom tricks to pique Jonathan's flagging interest, consider and reject liposuction for your thighs. You wish you could have a facelift, but the recovery period's a bit too long, and you're not sure how it would work with your transitions. You read and read and read, and command an increasingly subtle grasp of the implications of, the interconnections between, different areas of knowledge: ecotourism, Third-World famine relief, art history, automobile design. Your lunchtime conversations become richer, your friendships with the faculty wives more genuine.

You know that your growing wisdom is the benefit of aging, the compensation for your wrinkles and for your fading—although fading slowly, as yet—beauty.

You also know that Jonathan didn't marry you for wisdom.

And now it's the following year, the year you're old enough to be Jonathan's mother, although an unwed teenage one: you're going on fifty-six while he's going on forty-one. Your silver hair's losing its luster, becoming merely gray. Sportfucks coincide, more or less, with major national holidays. Your thighs begin to jiggle when you walk, so you go ahead and have the liposuction, but Jonathan doesn't seem to notice anything but the outrageous cost of the procedure.

You redecorate the house. You take up painting, with enough success to sell some pieces in a local gallery. You start writing a book about gardening as a cure for ecotourism and agricultural abuses, and you negotiate a contract with a prestigious university press. Jonathan doesn't pay much attention to any of this. You're starting to think that Jonathan would only pay attention to a full-fledged Lon Chaney imitation, complete with bloody fangs, but if that was ever in your nature, it certainly isn't now. Jonathan and Martha Stewart have civilized you.

On four legs, you're still magnificent, eliciting exclamations of wonder from other pet owners when you meet them in the woods. But Jonathan hardly ever plays ball in the meadow with you anymore; sometimes he doesn't even take you to the forest. Your walks, once measured in hours and miles, now clock in at minutes and suburban blocks. Sometimes Jonathan doesn't even walk you. Sometimes he just shoos you out into the backyard to do your business. He never cleans up after you, either. You have to do that yourself, scooping old poop after you've returned to two legs.

A few times you yell at Jonathan about this, but he just walks away, even more annoyed than usual. You know you have to do something to remind him that he loves you, or loved you once; you know you have to do something to reinsert yourself into his field of vision. But you can't imagine what. You've already tried everything you can think of.

There are nights when you cry yourself to sleep. Once, Jonathan would have held you; now he rolls over, turning his back to you, and scoots to the farthest edge of the mattress.

During that terrible time, the two of you go to a faculty party. There's a new professor there, a female professor, the first one the Anthropology Department has hired in ten years. She's in her twenties, with long black hair and perfect skin, and the men cluster around her the way they used to cluster around you.

Jonathan's one of them.

Standing with the other wives, pretending to talk about new films, you watch Jonathan's face. He's rapt, attentive, totally focused on the lovely young woman, who's talking about her research into ritual scarification in New Guinea. You see Jonathan's eyes stray surreptitiously, when he thinks no one will notice, to her breasts, her thighs, her ass.

You know Jonathan wants to fuck her. And you know it's not her fault, any more than it was ever yours. She can't help being young and pretty. But you hate her anyway. Over the next few days, you discover that what you hate most, hate even more than Jonathan wanting to fuck this young woman, is what your hate is doing to you: to your dreams, to your insides. The hate's your problem, you know; it's not Jonathan's fault, any more than his lust for the young professor is hers. But you can't seem to get rid of it, and you can sense it making your wrinkles deeper, shriveling you as if you're a piece of newspaper thrown into a fire.

You write Diane a long, anguished letter about as much of this as you can safely tell her. Of course, since she hasn't been around for a few years, she doesn't know how much older you look, so you simply say that you think Jonathan's fallen out of love with you since you're over forty now. You write the letter on paper, and send it through the mail.

Diane writes back, and not a postcard this time: she sends five single-spaced pages. She says that Jonathan's probably going through a midlife crisis. She agrees that his treatment of you is, in her words, "barbaric." "Stella, you're a beautiful, brilliant, accomplished woman. I've never known anyone who's grown so much, or in such interesting ways, in such a short time. If Jonathan doesn't appreciate that, then he's an ass, and maybe it's time to ask yourself if you'd be happier elsewhere. I hate to recommend divorce, but I also hate to see you suffering so much. The problem, of course, is economic: Can you support yourself if you leave? Is Jonathan likely to be reliable with alimony? At least— small comfort, I know—there are no children who need to be considered in all this. I'm assuming that you've already tried couples therapy. If you haven't, you should."

This letter plunges you into despair. No, Jonathan isn't likely to be reliable with alimony. Jonathan isn't likely to agree to couples therapy, either. Some of your lunchtime friends have gone that route, and the only way they ever got their husbands into the therapist's office was by threatening divorce on the spot. If you tried this, it would be a hollow threat. Your unfortunate metabolic condition won't allow you to hold any kind of normal job, and your writing and painting income won't support you, and Jonathan knows all that as well as you do. And your continued safety's in his hands. If he exposed you—

You shudder. In the old country, the stories ran to peasants with torches. Here, you know, laboratories and scalpels would be more likely. Neither option's attractive.

You go to the art museum, because the bright, high, echoing rooms have always made it easier for you to think. You wander among abstract sculpture and impressionist paintings, among still lifes and landscapes, among portraits. One of the portraits is of an old woman. She has white hair and many wrinkles; her shoulders stoop as she pours a cup of tea. The flowers on the china are the same pale, luminous blue as her eyes, which are, you realize, the same blue as your own.

The painting takes your breath away. This old woman is beautiful. You know the painter, a nineteenth-century English duke, thought so too.

You know Jonathan wouldn't.

You decide, once again, to try to talk to Jonathan. You make him his favorite meal, serve him his favorite wine, wear your most becoming outfit, gray silk with heavy silver jewelry. Your silver hair and blue eyes gleam in the candlelight, and the candlelight, you know, hides your wrinkles.

This kind of production, at least, Jonathan still notices. When he comes into the dining room for dinner, he looks at you and raises his eyebrows. "What's the occasion?"

"The occasion's that I'm worried," you tell him. You tell him how much it hurts you when he turns away from your tears. You tell him how much you miss the sportfucks. You tell him that since you clean up his messes more than three weeks out of every month, he can damn well clean up yours when you're on four legs. And you tell him that if he doesn't love you anymore, doesn't want you anymore, you'll leave. You'll go back home, to the village on the edge of the forest near an Alp, and try to make a life for yourself.

"Oh, Stella," he says. "Of course I still love you!" You can't tell if he sounds impatient or contrite, and it terrifies you that you might not know the difference. "How could you even *think* of leaving me? After everything I've given you, everything I've done for you—"

"That's been changing," you tell him, your throat raw. "The changes are the *problem*. Jonathan—"

"I can't believe you'd try to hurt me like this! I can't believe—"

"Jonathan, I'm *not* trying to hurt you! I'm reacting to the fact that you're hurting me! Are you going to stop hurting me, or not?"

He glares at you, pouting, and it strikes you that after all, he's very young, much younger than you are. "Do you have any idea how ungrateful you're being? Not many men would put up with a woman like you!"

"*Jonathan!*"

"I mean, do you have any idea how hard it's been for *me*? All the secrecy, all the lying, having to walk the damn dog—"

"You used to enjoy walking the damn dog." You struggle to control your breathing, struggle not to cry. "All right, look, you've made yourself clear. I'll leave. I'll go home."

"You'll do no such thing!"

You close your eyes. "Then what do you want me to do? Stay here, knowing you hate me?"

"I don't hate you! You hate me! If you didn't hate me, you wouldn't be threatening to leave!" He gets up and throws his napkin down on the table; it lands in the gravy boat. Before leaving the room, he turns and says, "I'm sleeping in the guestroom tonight."

"Fine," you tell him dully. He leaves, and you discover that you're trembling, shaking the way a terrier would, or a poodle. Not a wolf.

Well. He's made himself very plain. You get up, clear away the uneaten dinner you spent all afternoon cooking, and go upstairs to your bedroom. Yours, now: not Jonathan's anymore. You change into jeans and a sweatshirt. You think about taking a hot bath, because all your bones ache, but if you allow yourself to relax into warm water, you'll fall apart; you'll dissolve into tears, and there are things you have to do. Your bones aren't aching just because your marriage has ended; they're aching because the transition is coming up, and you need to make plans before it starts.

So you go into your study, turn on the computer, call up an Internet travel agency. You book a flight back home for ten days from today, when you'll definitely be back on two feet again. You charge the ticket to your credit card. The bill will arrive here in another month, but by then you'll be long gone. Let Jonathan pay it.

Money. You have to think about how you'll make money, how much money you'll take with you—but you can't think about it now. Booking the flight has hit you like a blow. Tomorrow, when Jonathan's at work, you'll call Diane and ask her advice on all of this. You'll tell her you're going home. She'll probably ask you to come stay with her, but you can't, because of the transitions. Diane, of all the people you know, might understand, but you can't imagine summoning the energy to explain.

It takes all the energy you have to get yourself out of the study, back into your bedroom. You cry yourself to sleep, and this time Jonathan's not even across the mattress from you. You find yourself wondering if you should have handled the dinner conversation differently, if you should have kept yourself from yelling at him about the turds in the yard, if you should have tried to seduce him first, if—

The ifs could go on forever. You know that. You think about going home. You wonder if you'll still know anyone there. You realize how much you'll miss your garden, and you start crying again.

Tomorrow, first thing, you'll call Diane.

But when tomorrow comes, you can barely get out of bed. The transition has arrived early, and it's a horrible one, the worst ever. You're in so much pain you can hardly move. You're in so much pain that you moan aloud, but if Jonathan hears, he doesn't come in. During the brief pain-free intervals when you can think lucidly, you're grateful that you booked your flight as soon as you did. And then you realize that the bedroom door is closed, and that Jessie won't be able to open it herself. You need to get out of bed. You need to open the door.

You can't. The transition's too far advanced. It's never been this fast; that must be why it hurts so much. But the pain, paradoxically, makes the transition seem longer than a normal one, rather than shorter. You moan, and whimper, and lose all track of time, and finally howl, and then, blessedly, the transition's over. You're on four feet.

You can get out of bed now, and you do, but you can't leave the room. You howl, but if Jonathan's here, if he hears you, he doesn't come.

There's no food in the room. You left the master bathroom toilet seat up, by chance, so there's water, full of interesting smells. That's good. And there are shoes to chew on, but they offer neither nourishment nor any real comfort. You're hungry. You're lonely. You're afraid. You can smell Jonathan in the room—in the shoes, in the sheets, in the clothing in the closet—but Jonathan himself won't come, no matter how much you howl.

And then, finally, the door opens. It's Jonathan. "Jessie," he says. "Poor Jessie. You must be so hungry; I'm sorry." He's carrying your leash; he takes your collar out of your underwear drawer and puts it on you and attaches the leash, and you think you're going for a walk now. You're ecstatic. Jonathan's going to walk you again. Jonathan still loves you.

"Let's go outside, Jess," he says, and you dutifully trot down the stairs to the front door. But instead he says, "Jessie, this way. Come on, girl," and leads you on your leash to the family room at the back of the house, to the sliding glass doors that open onto the back yard. You're confused, but you do what Jonathan says. You're desperate to please him. Even if he's no longer quite Stella's husband, he's still Jessie's alpha.

He leads you into the backyard. There's a metal pole in the middle of the backyard. That didn't used to be there. Your canine mind wonders if it's a new toy. You trot up and sniff it, cautiously, and as you do, Jonathan clips one end of your leash onto a ring in the top of the pole.

You yip in alarm. You can't move far; it's not that long a leash. You strain against the pole, the leash, the collar, but none of them give; the harder you pull, the harder the choke collar makes it for you to breathe. Jonathan's still next to you, stroking you, calm, reassuring. "It's okay, Jess. I'll bring you food and water, all right? You'll be fine out here. It's just for tonight. Tomorrow we'll go for a nice long walk, I promise."

Your ears perk up at "walk," but you still whimper. Jonathan brings your food and water bowls outside and puts them within reach.

You're so glad to have the food that you can't think about being lonely or afraid. You gobble your Alpo, and Jonathan strokes your fur and tells you what a good dog you are, what a beautiful dog, and you think maybe everything's going to be all right, because he hasn't stroked you this much in months, hasn't spent so much time talking to you, admiring you.

Then he goes inside again. You strain towards the house, as much as the choke collar will let you. You catch occasional glimpses of Jonathan, who seems to be cleaning. Here he is dusting the picture frames; here he is running the vacuum cleaner. Now he's cooking—beef stroganoff, you can smell it—and now he's lighting candles in the dining room.

You start to whimper. You whimper even more loudly when a car pulls into the driveway on the other side of the house, but you stop when you hear a female voice, because you want to hear what it says.

"...so terrible that your wife left you. You must be devastated."

"Yes, I am. But I'm sure she's back in Europe now, with her family. Here, let me show you the house." And when he shows her the family room, you see her: in her twenties, with long black hair and perfect skin. And you see how Jonathan looks at her, and you start to howl in earnest.

"*Jesus,*" Jonathan's guest says, peering out at you through the dusk. "What the hell *is* that? A wolf?"

"My sister's dog," Jonathan says. "Husky-wolfhound mix. I'm taking care of her while my sister's away on business. She can't hurt you: don't be afraid." And he touches the woman's shoulder to silence her fear, and she turns towards him, and they walk into the dining room. And then, after a while, the bedroom light flicks on, and you hear laughter and other noises, and you start to howl again.

You howl all night, but Jonathan doesn't come outside. The neighbors yell at Jonathan a few times—*Shut that dog up, goddammit!*—but Jonathan will never come outside again. You're going to die here, tethered to this stake.

But you don't. Towards dawn you finally stop howling; you curl up and sleep, exhausted, and when you wake up the sun's higher and Jonathan's coming through the open glass doors. He's carrying another dish of Alpo, and he smells of soap and shampoo. You can't smell the woman on him.

You growl anyway, because you're hurt and confused. "Jessie," he says. "Jessie, it's all right. Poor, beautiful Jessie. I've been mean to you, haven't I? I'm so sorry."

He does sound sorry, truly sorry. You eat the Alpo, and he strokes you, the same way he did last night, and then he unsnaps your leash from the pole and says, "Okay, Jess, through the gate into the driveway, okay? We're going for a ride."

You don't want to go for a ride. You want to go for a walk. Jonathan promised you a walk. You growl.

"Jessie! Into the car, *now*! We're going to another meadow, Jess. It's farther away than our old one, but someone told me he saw rabbits there, and he said it's really big. You'd like to explore a new place, wouldn't you?"

You don't want to go to a new meadow. You want to go to the old meadow, the one where you know the smell of every tree and rock. You growl again.

"Jessie, you're being a *very bad dog!* Now get in the car. Don't make me call Animal Control."

You whine. You're scared of Animal Control, the people who wanted to take you away so long ago, when you lived in that other county. You know that Animal Control kills a lot of animals, in that county and in this one, and if you die as a wolf, you'll stay a wolf. They'd never know about Stella. As Jessie, you'd have no way to protect yourself except your teeth, and that would only get you killed faster.

So you get into the car, although you're trembling.

In the car, Jonathan seems more cheerful. "Good Jessie. Good girl. We'll go to the new meadow and chase balls now, eh? It's a big meadow. You'll be able to run a long way." And he tosses a new tennis ball into the backseat, and you chew on it, happily, and the car drives along, traffic whizzing past. When you lift your head from chewing on the ball, you can see trees, so you put your head back down, satisfied, and resume chewing. And then the car stops, and Jonathan opens the door for you, and you hop out, holding your ball in your mouth.

This isn't a meadow. You're in the parking lot of a low concrete building that reeks of excrement and disinfectant and fear, *fear,* and from the building you hear barking and howling, screams of misery, and in the parking lot are parked two white Animal Control trucks.

You panic. You drop your tennis ball and try to run, but Jonathan has the leash, and he starts dragging you inside the building, and you can't breathe because of the choke collar. You cough, gasping, trying to howl. "Don't fight, Jessie. Don't fight me. Everything's all right."

Everything's not all right. You can smell Jonathan's desperation, can taste your own, and you should be stronger than he is but you can't breathe, and he's saying, "Jessie, don't bite me, it will be worse if you bite me, Jessie," and the screams of horror still swirl from the building and you're at the door now, someone's opened the door for Jonathan, someone says, "Let me help you with that dog," and you're scrabbling on the concrete, trying to dig your claws into the sidewalk just outside the door, but there's no purchase, and they've dragged you inside, onto the linoleum, and everywhere are the smells and sounds of terror. Above your own whimpering you hear Jonathan saying, "She jumped the fence and threatened my girlfriend, and then she tried to bite me, so I have no choice, it's such a shame, she's always been such a good dog, but in good conscience I can't—"

You start to howl, because he's lying, *lying*, you never did any of that!

Now you're surrounded by people, a man and two women, all wearing colorful cotton smocks that smell, although faintly, of dog shit and cat pee. They're putting a muzzle on you, and even though you can hardly think through your fear—and your pain, because Jonathan's walked back out the door, gotten into the car, and driven away, Jonathan's *left* you here—even with all of that, you know you don't dare bite or snap. You know your only hope is in being a good dog, in acting as submissive as possible. So you whimper, crawl along on your stomach, try to roll over on your back to show your belly, but you can't, because of the leash.

"Hey," one of the women says. The man's left. She bends down to stroke you. "Oh, God, she's so scared. Look at her."

"Poor thing," the other woman says. "She's *beautiful.*"

"I know."

"Looks like a wolf mix."

"I know." The first woman sighs and scratches your ears, and you whimper and wag your tail and try to lick her hand through the muzzle. Take me home, you'd tell her if you could talk. Take me home with you. You'll be my alpha, and I'll love you forever. I'm a *good* dog.

The woman who's scratching you says wistfully, "We could adopt her out in a minute, I bet."

"Not with that history. Not if she's a biter. Not even if we had room. You know that."

"I know." The voice is very quiet. "Wish I could take her myself, though."

"Take home a biter? Lily, you have kids!"

Lily sighs. "Yeah, I know. Makes me sick, that's all."

"You don't need to tell me that. Come on, let's get this over with. Did Mark go to get the room ready?"

"Yeah."

"Okay. What'd the owner say her name was?"

"Stella."

"Okay. Here, give me the leash. Stella, come. Come on, Stella."

The voice is sad, gentle, loving, and you want to follow it, but you fight every step, anyway, until Lily and her friend have to drag you past the cages of other dogs, who start barking and howling again, whose cries are pure terror, pure loss. You can hear cats grieving, somewhere else in the building, and you can smell the room at the end of the hall, the room to which you're getting inexorably closer. You smell the man named Mark behind the door, and you smell medicine, and you smell the fear of the animals who've been taken to that room before you. But overpowering everything else is the worst smell, the smell that makes you bare your teeth in the muzzle and pull against the choke collar and scrabble again, helplessly, for a purchase you can't get on the concrete floor: the pervasive, metallic stench of death.

The Coldest Girl in Coldtown
Holly Black

Matilda was drunk, but then she was always drunk anymore. Dizzy drunk. Stumbling drunk. Stupid drunk. Whatever kind of drunk she could get.

The man she stood with snaked his hand around her back, warm fingers digging into her side as he pulled her closer. He and his friend with the open-necked shirt grinned down at her like underage equaled dumb, and dumb equaled gullible enough to sleep with them.

She thought they might just be right.

"You want to have a party back at my place?" the man asked. He'd told her his name was Mark, but his friend kept slipping up and calling him by a name that started with a D. Maybe Dan or Dave. They had been smuggling her drinks from the bar whenever they went outside to smoke—drinks mixed sickly sweet that dripped down her throat like candy.

"Sure," she said, grinding her cigarette against the brick wall. She missed the hot ash in her hand, but concentrated on the alcoholic numbness turning her limbs to lead. Smiled. "Can we pick up more beer?"

They exchanged an obnoxious glance she pretended not to notice. The friend—he called himself Ben—looked at her glassy eyes and her cold-flushed cheeks. Her sloppy hair. He probably made guesses about a troubled home life. She hoped so.

"You're not going to get sick on us?" he asked. Just out of the hot bar, beads of sweat had collected in the hollow of his throat. The skin shimmered with each swallow.

She shook her head to stop staring. "I'm barely tipsy," she lied.

"I've got plenty of stuff back at my place," said MarkDanDave. *Mardave*, Matilda thought and giggled.

"Buy me a 40," she said. She knew it was stupid to go with them, but it was even stupider if she sobered up. "One of those wine coolers. They have them at the bodega on the corner. Otherwise, no party."

Both of the guys laughed. She tried to laugh with them even though she knew she wasn't included in the joke. She was the joke. The trashy little slut. The girl who can be bought for a big fat wine cooler and three cranberry-and-vodkas.

"Okay, okay," said Mardave.

They walked down the street and she found herself leaning easily into the heat of their bodies, inhaling the sweat and iron scent. It would be easy for her to close her eyes and pretend Mardave was someone else, someone she wanted to be touched by, but she wouldn't let herself soil her memories of Julian.

They passed by a store with flat-screens in the window, each one showing different channels. One streamed video from Coldtown—a girl who went by the name Demonia made some kind of deal with one of the stations to show what it was really like behind the gates. She filmed the Eternal Ball, a party that started in 1998 and had gone on ceaselessly ever since. In the background, girls and boys in rubber harnesses swung through the air. They stopped occasionally, opening what looked like a modded hospital tube stuck on the inside of their arms just below the crook of the elbow. They twisted a knob and spilled blood into little paper cups for the partygoers. A boy who looked to be about nine, wearing a string of glowing beads around his neck, gulped down the contents of one of the cups and then licked the paper with a tongue as red as his eyes. The camera angle changed suddenly, veering up, and the viewers saw the domed top of the hall, full of cracked windows through which you could glimpse the stars.

"I know where they are," Mardave said. "I can see that building from my apartment."

"Aren't you scared of living so close to the vampires?" she asked, a small smile pulling at the corners of her mouth.

"We'll protect you," said Ben, smiling back at her.

"We should do what other countries do and blow those corpses sky high," Mardave said.

Matilda bit her tongue not to point out that Europe's vampire hunting led to the highest levels of infection in the world. So many of Belgium's citizens were vampires that shops barely opened their doors until nightfall. The truce with Coldtown worked. Mostly.

She didn't care if Mardave hated vampires. She hated them too.

When they got to the store, she waited outside to avoid getting carded and lit another cigarette with Julian's silver lighter—the one she was going to give back to him in thirty-one days. Sitting down on the curb, she let the chill of the pavement deaden the backs of her thighs. Let it freeze her belly and frost her throat with ice that even liquor couldn't melt.

Hunger turned her stomach. She couldn't remember the last time she'd eaten anything solid without throwing it back up. Her mouth hungered for dark, rich feasts; her skin felt tight, like a seed thirsting to bloom. All she could trust herself to eat was smoke.

When she was a little girl, vampires had been costumes for Halloween. They were the bad guys in movies, plastic fangs and polyester capes. They were Muppets on television, endlessly counting.

Now she was the one who was counting. Fifty-seven days. Eighty-eight days. Eighty-eight nights.

"Matilda?"

She looked up and saw Dante saunter up to her, earbuds dangling out of his ears like he needed a soundtrack for everything he did. He wore a pair of skintight jeans and smoked a cigarette out of one of those long, movie-star holders. He looked pretentious as hell. "I'd almost given up on finding you."

"You should have started with the gutter," she said, gesturing to the wet, clogged tide beneath her feet. "I take my gutter-dwelling very seriously."

"*Seriously*." He pointed at her with the cigarette holder. "Even your mother thinks you're dead. Julian's crying over you."

Matilda looked down and picked at the thread of her jeans. It hurt to think about Julian while waiting for Mardave and Ben. She was disgusted with herself, and she could only guess how disgusted he'd be. "I got Cold," she said. "One of them bit me."

Dante nodded his head.

That's what they'd started calling it when the infection kicked in—Cold—because of how cold people's skin became after they were bitten. And because of the way the poison in their veins caused them to crave heat and blood. One taste of human blood and the infection mutated. It killed the host and then raised it back up again, colder than before. Cold through and through, forever and ever.

"I didn't think you'd be alive," he said.

She hadn't thought she'd make it this long either without giving in. But going it alone on the street was better than forcing her mother to choose between chaining her up in the basement or shipping her off to Coldtown. It was better, too, than taking the chance Matilda might get loose from the chains and attack people she loved. Stories like that were in the news all the time; almost as frequent as the ones about people who let vampires into their homes because they seemed so nice and clean-cut.

"Then what are you doing looking for me?" she asked. Dante had lived down the street from her family for years, but they didn't hang out. She'd wave to him as she mowed the lawn while he loaded his panel van with DJ equipment. He shouldn't have been here.

She looked back at the store window. Mardave and Ben were at the counter with a case of beer and her wine cooler. They were getting change from a clerk.

"I was hoping you, er, *wouldn't* be alive," Dante said. "You'd be more help if you were dead."

She stood up, stumbling slightly. "Well, screw you too."

It took eighty-eight days for the venom to sweat out a person's pores. She only had thirty-seven to go. Thirty-seven days to stay so drunk that she could ignore the buzz in her head that made her want to bite, rend, devour.

"That came out wrong," he said, taking a step toward her. Close enough that she felt the warmth of him radiating off him like licking tongues of flame. She shivered. Her veins sang with need.

"I can't help you," said Matilda. "Look, I can barely help myself. Whatever it is, I'm sorry. I can't. You have to get out of here."

"My sister Lydia and your boyfriend Julian are gone," Dante said. "Together. She's looking to get bitten. I don't know what he's looking for . . . but he's going to get hurt."

Matilda gaped at him as Mardave and Ben walked out of the store. Ben carried a box on his shoulder and a bag on his arm. "That guy bothering you?" he asked her.

"No," she said, then turned to Dante. "You better go."

"Wait," said Dante.

Matilda's stomach hurt. She was sobering up. The smell of blood seemed to float up from underneath their skin.

She reached into Ben's bag and grabbed a beer. She popped the top, licked off the foam. If she didn't get a lot drunker, she was going to attack someone.

"Jesus," Mardave said. "Slow down. What if someone sees you?"

She drank it in huge gulps, right there on the street. Ben laughed, but it wasn't a good laugh. He was laughing at the drunk.

"She's infected," Dante said.

Matilda whirled toward him, chucking the mostly empty can in his direction automatically. "Shut up, asshole."

"Feel her skin," Dante said. "Cold. She ran away from home when it happened, and no one's seen her since."

"I'm cold because it's cold out," she said.

She saw Ben's evaluation of her change from *damaged enough to sleep with strangers* to *dangerous enough to attack strangers*.

Mardave touched his hand gently to her arm. "Hey," he said.

She almost hissed with delight at the press of his hot fingers. She smiled up at him and hoped her eyes weren't as hungry as her skin. "I really like you."

He flinched. "Look, it's late. Maybe we could meet up another time." Then he backed away, which made her so angry that she bit the inside of her own cheek.

Her mouth flooded with the taste of copper and a red haze floated in front of her eyes.

Fifty-seven days ago, Matilda had been sober. She'd had a boyfriend named Julian, and they would dress up together in her bedroom. He liked to wear skinny ties and glittery eye shadow. She liked to wear vintage rock t-shirts and boots that laced up so high that they would constantly be late because they were busy tying them.

Matilda and Julian would dress up and prowl the streets and party at lockdown clubs that barred the doors from dusk to dawn. Matilda wasn't particularly careless; she was just careless enough.

She'd been at a friend's party. It had been stiflingly hot, and she was mad because Julian and Lydia were doing some dance thing from the musical they were in at school. Matilda just wanted to get some air. She opened a window and climbed out under the bobbing garland of garlic.

Another girl was already on the lawn. Matilda should have noticed that the girl's breath didn't crystallize in the air, but she didn't.

"Do you have a light?" the girl had asked.

Matilda did. She reached for Julian's lighter when the girl caught her arm and bent her backwards. Matilda's scream turned into a shocked cry when she felt the girl's cold mouth against her neck, the girl's cold fingers holding her off balance.

Then it was as though someone slid two shards of ice into her skin.

The spread of vampirism could be traced to one person—Caspar Morales. Films and books and television had started romanticizing vampires, and maybe it was only a matter of time before a vampire started romanticizing *himself*.

Crazy, romantic Caspar decided that he wouldn't kill his victims. He'd just drink a little blood and then move on, city to city. By the time other vampires caught up with him and ripped him to pieces, he'd infected hundreds of people. And those new vampires, with no idea how to prevent the spread, infected thousands.

When the first outbreak happened in Tokyo, it seemed like a journalist's prank. Then there was another outbreak in Hong Kong and another in San Francisco.

The military put up barricades around the area where the infection broke out. That was the way the first Coldtown was founded.

Matilda's body twitched involuntarily. She could feel the spasm start in the muscles of her back and move to her face. She wrapped her arms around herself to try and stop it, but her hands were shaking pretty hard. "You want my help, you better get me some booze."

"You're killing yourself," Dante said, shaking his head.

"I just need another drink," she said. "Then I'll be fine."

He shook his head. "You can't keep going like this. You can't just stay drunk to avoid your problems. I know, people do. It's a classic move, even, but I didn't figure you for fetishizing your own doom."

She started laughing. "You don't understand. When I'm wasted I don't crave blood. It's the only thing keeping me human."

"What?" He looked at Matilda like he couldn't quite make sense of her words.

"Let me spell it out: if you don't get me some alcohol, I am going to bite you."

"Oh." He fumbled for his wallet. "Oh. Okay."

Matilda had spent all the cash she'd brought with her in the first few weeks, so it'd been a long time since she could simply overpay some homeless guy to go into a liquor store and get her a fifth of vodka. She gulped gratefully from the bottle Dante gave her in a nearby alley.

A few moments later, warmth started to creep up from her belly, and her mouth felt like it was full of needles and Novocain.

"You okay?" he asked her.

"Better now," she said, her words slurring slightly. "But I still don't understand. Why do you need me to help you find Lydia and Julian?"

"Lydia got obsessed with becoming a vampire," Dante said, irritably brushing back the stray hair that fell across his face.

"Why?"

He shrugged. "She used to be really scared of vampires. When we were kids, she begged Mom to let her camp in the hallway because she wanted to sleep where there were no windows. But then I guess she started to be fascinated instead. She thinks that human annihilation is coming. She says that we all have to choose sides and she's already chosen."

"I'm not a vampire," Matilda said.

Dante gestured irritably with his cigarette holder. The cigarette had long burned out. He didn't look like his usual contemptuous self; he looked lost. "I know. I thought you would be. And—I don't know—you're on the street. Maybe you know more than the video feeds do about where someone might go to get themselves bitten."

Matilda thought about lying on the floor of Julian's parents' living room. They had been sweaty from dancing and kissed languidly. On the television, a list of missing people flashed. She had closed her eyes and kissed him again.

She nodded slowly. "I know a couple of places. Have you heard from her at all?"

He shook his head. "She won't take any of my calls, but she's been updating her blog. I'll show you."

He loaded it on his phone. The latest entry was titled: *I Need a Vampire*. Matilda scrolled down and read. Basically, it was Lydia's plea to be bitten. She wanted any vampires looking for victims to contact her. In the comments, someone suggested Coldtown and then another person commented in ALL CAPS to say that everyone knew that the vampires in Coldtown were careful to keep their food sources alive.

It was impossible to know which comments Lydia had read and which ones she believed.

Runaways went to Coldtown all the time, along with the sick, the sad, and the maudlin. There was supposed to be a constant party, theirs for the price of blood. But once they went inside, humans—even human children, even babies born in Coldtown—weren't allowed to leave. The National Guard patrolled the barbed-wire-wrapped and garlic-covered walls to make sure that Coldtown stayed contained.

People said that vampires found ways through the walls to the outside world. Maybe that was just a rumor, although Matilda remembered reading something online about a documentary that proved the truth. She hadn't seen it.

But everyone knew there was only one way to get out of Coldtown if you were still human. Your family had to be rich enough to hire a vampire hunter. Vampire hunters got money from the government for each vampire they put in Coldtown, but they could give up the cash reward in favor of a voucher for a single human's release. One vampire in, one human out.

There was a popular reality television series about one of the hunters, called *Hemlok*. Girls hung posters of him on the insides of their lockers, often right next to pictures of the vampires he hunted.

Most people didn't have the money to outbid the government for a hunter's services. Matilda didn't think that Dante's family did and knew Julian's didn't. Her only chance was to catch Lydia and Julian before they crossed over.

"What's with Julian?" Matilda asked. She'd been avoiding the question for hours as they walked through the alleys that grew progressively more empty the closer they got to the gates.

"What do you mean?" Dante was hunched over against the wind, his long, skinny frame offering little protection against the chill. Still, she knew he was warm underneath. Inside.

"Why did Julian go with her?" She tried to keep the hurt out of her voice.

She didn't think Dante would understand. He DJ'ed at a club in town and was rumored to see a different boy or girl every day of the week. The only person he actually seemed to care about was his sister.

Dante shrugged slim shoulders. "Maybe he was looking for you."

That was the answer she wanted to hear. She smiled and let herself imagine saving Julian right before he could enter Coldtown. He would tell her that he'd been coming to save her and then they'd laugh and she wouldn't bite him, no matter how warm his skin felt.

Dante snapped his fingers in front of Matilda and she stumbled.

"Hey," she said. "Drunk girl here. No messing with me."

He chuckled.

Matilda and Dante checked all the places she knew, all the places she'd slept on cardboard near runaways and begged for change. Dante had a picture of Lydia in his wallet, but no one who looked at it remembered her.

Finally, outside a bar, they bumped into a girl who said she'd seen Lydia and Julian. Dante traded her the rest of his pack of cigarettes for her story.

"They were headed for Coldtown," she said, lighting up. In the flickering flame of her lighter, Matilda noticed the shallow cuts along her wrists. "Said she was tired of waiting."

"What about the guy?" Matilda asked. She stared at the girl's dried garnet scabs. They looked like crusts of sugar, like the lines of salt left on the beach when the tide goes out. She wanted to lick them.

"He said his girlfriend was a vampire," said the girl, inhaling deeply. She blew out smoke and then started to cough.

"When was that?" Dante asked.

The girl shrugged her shoulders. "Just a couple of hours ago."

Dante took out his phone and pressed some buttons. "Load," he muttered. "Come on, *load*."

"What happened to your arms?" Matilda asked.

The girl shrugged again. "They bought some blood off me. Said that they might need it inside. They had a real professional setup too. Sharp razor and one of those glass bowls with the plastic lids."

Matilda's stomach clenched with hunger. She turned against the wall and breathed slowly. She needed a drink.

"Is something wrong with her?" the girl asked.

"Matilda," Dante said, and Matilda half-turned. He was holding out his phone. There was a new entry up on Lydia's blog, entitled: *One-Way Ticket to Coldtown*.

"You should post about it," Dante said. "On the message boards."

Matilda was sitting on the ground, picking at the brick wall to give her fingers something to do. Dante had massively overpaid for another bottle of vodka and was cradling it in a crinkled paper bag.

She frowned. "Post about what?"

"About the alcohol. About it helping you keep from turning."

"Where would I post about that?"

Dante twisted off the cap. The heat seemed to radiate off his skin as he swigged from the bottle. "There are forums for people who have to restrain someone for eighty-eight days. They hang out and exchange tips on straps and dealing with the begging for blood. Haven't you seen them?"

She shook her head. "I bet sedation's already a hot topic of discussion. I doubt I'd be telling them anything they don't already know."

He laughed, but it was a bitter laugh. "Then there's all the people who want to be vampires. The websites reminding all the corpsebait out there that being bitten by an infected person isn't enough; it has to be a vampire. The ones listing gimmicks to get vampires to notice you."

"Like what?"

"I dated a girl who cut thin lines on her thighs before she went out dancing so if there was a vampire in the club, it'd be drawn to her scent." Dante didn't look extravagant or affected anymore. He looked defeated.

Matilda smiled at him. "She was probably a better bet than me for getting you into Coldtown."

He returned the smile wanly. "The worst part is that Lydia's not going to get what she wants. She's going to become the human servant of some vampire who's going to make her a whole bunch of promises and never turn her. The last thing they need in Coldtown is new vampires."

Matilda imagined Lydia and Julian dancing at the endless Eternal Ball. She pictured them on the streets she'd seen in pictures uploaded to Facebook and Flickr, trying to trade a bowl full of blood for their own deaths.

When Dante passed the bottle to her, she pretended to swig. On the eve of her fifty-eighth day of being infected, Matilda started sobering up.

Crawling over, she straddled Dante's waist before he had a chance to shift positions. His mouth tasted like tobacco. When she pulled back from him, his eyes were wide with surprise, his pupils blown and black even in the dim streetlight.

"Matilda," he said and there was nothing in his voice but longing.

"If you really want your sister, I am going to need one more thing from you," she said.

His blood tasted like tears.

Matilda's skin felt like it had caught fire. She'd turned into lit paper, burning up. Curling into black ash.

She licked his neck over and over and over.

The gates of Coldtown were large and made of consecrated wood, barbed wire covering them like heavy, thorny vines. The guards slouched at their posts, guns over their shoulders, sharing a cigarette. The smell of percolating coffee wafted out of the guardhouse.

"Um, hello," Matilda said. Blood was still sticky where it half-dried around her mouth and on her neck. It had dribbled down her shirt, stiffening it nearly to cracking when she moved. Her body felt strange now that she was dying. Hot. More alive than it had in weeks.

Dante would be all right; she wasn't contagious and she didn't think she'd hurt him too badly. She hoped she hadn't hurt him too badly. She touched the phone in her pocket, his phone, the one she'd used to call 911 after she'd left him.

"Hello," she called to the guards again.

One turned. "Oh my god," he said and reached for his rifle.

"I'm here to turn in a vampire. For a voucher. I want to turn in a vampire in exchange for letting a human out of Coldtown."

"What vampire?" asked the other guard. He'd dropped the cigarette, but not stepped on the filter so that it just smoked on the asphalt.

"Me," said Matilda. "I want to turn in me."

They made her wait as her pulse thrummed slower and slower. She wasn't a vampire yet, and after a few phone calls, they discovered that technically she could only have the voucher after undeath. They did let her wash her face in the bathroom of the guardhouse and wring the thin cloth of her shirt until the water ran down the drain clear, instead of murky with blood.

When she looked into the mirror, her skin had unfamiliar purple shadows, like bruises. She was still staring at them when she stopped being able to catch her breath. The hollow feeling in her chest expanded and she found herself panicked, falling to her knees on the filthy tile floor. She died there, a moment later.

It didn't hurt as much as she'd worried it would. Like most things, the surprise was the worst part.

The guards released Matilda into Coldtown just a little before dawn. The world looked strange—everything had taken on a smudgy, silvery cast, like she was watching an old movie. Sometimes people's heads seemed to blur into black smears. Only one color was distinct—a pulsing, oozing color that seemed to glow from beneath skin.

Red.

Her teeth ached to look at it.

There was a silence inside her. No longer did she move to the rhythmic drumming of her heart. Her body felt strange, hard as marble, free of pain. She'd never realized how many small agonies were alive in the creak of her bones, the pull of muscle. Now, free of them, she felt like she was floating.

Matilda looked around with her strange new eyes. Everything was beautiful. And the light at the edge of the sky was the most beautiful thing of all.

"What are you doing?" a girl called from a doorway. She had long black hair, but her roots were growing in blonde. "Get in here! Are you crazy?"

In a daze, Matilda did as she was told. Everything smeared as she moved, like the world was painted in watercolors. The girl's pinkish-red face swirled along with it.

It was obvious the house had once been grand, but it looked like it'd been abandoned for a long time. Graffiti covered the peeling wallpaper and couches had been pushed up against the walls. A boy wearing jeans but no shirt was painting make-up onto a girl with stiff pink pigtails, while another girl in a retro polka-dotted dress pulled on mesh stockings.

In a corner, another boy—this one with glossy brown hair that fell to his waist—stacked jars of creamed corn into a precarious pyramid.

"What is this place?" Matilda asked.

The boy stacking the jars turned. "Look at her eyes. She's a vampire!" He didn't seem afraid, though; he seemed delighted.

"Get her into the cellar," one of the other girls said.

"Come on," said the black-haired girl and pulled Matilda toward a doorway. "You're fresh-made, right?"

"Yeah," Matilda said. Her tongue swept over her own sharp teeth. "I guess that's pretty obvious."

"Don't you know that vampires can't go outside in the daylight?" the girl asked, shaking her head. "The guards try that trick with every new vampire, but I never saw one almost fall for it."

"Oh, right," Matilda said. They went down the rickety steps to a filthy basement with a mattress on the floor underneath a single bulb. Crates of foodstuffs were shoved against the walls, and the high, small windows had been painted over with a tarry substance that let no light through.

The black-haired girl who'd waved her inside smiled. "We trade with the border guards. Black-market food, clothes, little luxuries like chocolate and cigarettes for some ass. Vampires don't own everything."

"And you're going to owe us for letting you stay the night," the boy said from the top of the stairs.

"I don't have anything," Matilda said. "I didn't bring any cans of food or whatever."

"You have to bite us."

"What?" Matilda asked.

"One of us," the girl said. "How about one of us? You can even pick which one."

"Why would you want me to do that?"

The girl's expression clearly said that Matilda was stupid. "Who doesn't want to live forever?"

I don't, Matilda wanted to say, but she swallowed the words. She could tell they already thought she didn't deserve to be a vampire. Besides, she wanted to taste blood. She wanted to taste the red, throbbing, pulsing insides of the girl in front of her. It wasn't the pain she'd felt when she was infected, the hunger that made her stomach clench, the craving for warmth. It was heady, greedy desire.

"Tomorrow," Matilda said. "When it's night again."

"Okay," the girl said, "but you promise, right? You'll turn one of us?"

"Yeah," said Matilda, numbly. It was hard to even wait that long.

She was relieved when they went upstairs, but less relieved when she heard something heavy slide in front of the basement door. She told herself that didn't matter. The only thing that mattered was getting through the day so that she could find Julian and Lydia.

She shook her head to clear it of thoughts of blood and turned on Dante's phone. Although she didn't expect it, a text message was waiting: *I cant tell if I luv u or if I want to kill u.*

Relief washed over her. Her mouth twisted into a smile and her newly sharp canines cut her lip. She winced. Dante was okay.

She opened up Lydia's blog and posted an anonymous message: *Tell Julian his girlfriend wants to see him . . . and you.*

Matilda made herself comfortable on the dirty mattress. She looked up at the rotted boards of the ceiling and thought of Julian. She had a single ticket out of Coldtown and two humans to rescue with it, but it was easy to picture herself saving Lydia as Julian valiantly offered to stay with her, even promised her his eternal devotion.

She licked her lips at the image. When she closed her eyes, all her imaginings drowned in a sea of red.

Waking at dusk, Matilda checked Lydia's blog. Lydia had posted a reply: *Meet us at the Festival of Sinners.*

Five kids sat at the top of the stairs, watching her with liquid eyes.

"Are you awake?" the black-haired girl asked. She seemed to pulse with color. Her moving mouth was hypnotic.

"Come here," Matilda said to her in a voice that seemed so distant that she was surprised to find it was her own. She hadn't meant to speak, hadn't meant to beckon the girl over to her.

"That's not fair," one of the boys called. "I was the one who said she owed us something. It should be me. You should pick me."

Matilda ignored him as the girl knelt down on the dirty mattress and swept aside her hair, baring a long, unmarked neck. She seemed dazzling, this creature

THE URBAN FANTASY ANTHOLOGY

of blood and breath, a fragile manikin as brittle as sticks.

Tiny golden hairs tickled Matilda's nose as she bit down.

And gulped.

Blood was heat and heart running-thrumming-beating through the fat roots of veins to drip syrup slow, spurting molten hot across tongue, mouth, teeth, chin.

Dimly, Matilda felt someone shoving her and someone else screaming, but it seemed distant and unimportant. Eventually the words became clearer.

"Stop," someone was screaming. "Stop!"

Hands dragged Matilda off the girl. Her neck was a glistening red mess. Gore stained the mattress and covered Matilda's hands and hair. The girl coughed, blood bubbles frothing on her lip, and then went abruptly silent.

"What did you do?" the boy wailed, cradling the girl's body. "She's dead. She's dead. You killed her."

Matilda backed away from the body. Her hand went automatically to her mouth, covering it. "I didn't mean to," she said.

"Maybe she'll be okay," said the other boy, his voice cracking. "We have to get bandages."

"She's *dead*," the boy holding the girl's body moaned.

A thin wail came from deep inside Matilda as she backed toward the stairs. Her belly felt full, distended. She wanted to be sick.

Another girl grabbed Matilda's arm. "Wait," the girl said, eyes wide and imploring. "You have to bite me next. You're full now so you won't have to hurt me—"

With a cry, Matilda tore herself free and ran up the stairs—if she went fast enough, maybe she could escape from herself.

By the time Matilda got to the Festival of Sinners, her mouth tasted metallic and she was numb with fear. She wasn't human, wasn't good, and wasn't sure what she might do next. She kept pawing at her shirt, as if that much blood could ever be wiped off, as if it hadn't already soaked down into her skin and her soiled insides.

The Festival was easy to find, even as confused as she was. People were happy to give her directions, apparently not bothered that she was drenched in blood. Their casual demeanor was horrifying, but not as horrifying as how much she already wanted to feed again.

On the way, she passed the Eternal Ball. Strobe lights lit up the remains of the windows along the dome, and a girl with blue hair in a dozen braids held up a video camera to interview three men dressed all in white with gleaming red eyes.

Vampires.

A ripple of fear passed through her. She reminded herself that there was nothing they could do to her. She was already like them. Already dead.

The Festival of Sinners was being held at a church with stained-glass windows painted black on the inside. The door, papered with pink-stenciled posters, was painted the same thick tarry black. Music thrummed from within and a few people sat on the steps, smoking and talking.

Matilda went inside.

A doorman pulled aside a velvet rope for her, letting her past a small line of people waiting to pay the cover charge. The rules were different for vampires, perhaps especially for vampires accessorizing their grungy attire with so much blood.

Matilda scanned the room. She didn't see Julian or Lydia, just a throng of dancers and a bar that served alcohol from vast copper distilling vats. It spilled into mismatched mugs. Then one of the people near the bar moved and Matilda saw Lydia and Julian. He was bending over her, shouting into her ear.

Matilda pushed her way through the crowd, until she was close enough to touch Julian's arm. She reached out, but couldn't quite bring herself to brush his skin with her foulness.

Julian looked up, startled. "Tilda?"

She snatched back her hand like she'd been about to touch fire.

"Tilda," he said. "What happened to you? Are you hurt?"

Matilda flinched, looking down at herself. "I . . ."

Lydia laughed. "She ate someone, moron."

"Tilda?" Julian asked.

"I'm sorry," Matilda said. There was so much she had to be sorry for, but at least he was here now. Julian would tell her what to do and how to turn herself back into something decent again. She would save Lydia and Julian would save her.

He touched her shoulder, let his hand rest gingerly on her blood-stiffened

THE URBAN FANTASY ANTHOLOGY

shirt. "We were looking for you everywhere." His gentle expression was tinged with terror; fear pulled his smile into something closer to a grimace.

"I wasn't in Coldtown," Matilda said. "I came here so that Lydia could leave. I have a pass."

"But I don't want to leave," said Lydia. "You understand that, right? I want what you have—eternal life."

"You're not infected," Matilda said. "You have to go. You can still be okay. Please, I need you to go."

"One pass?" Julian said, his eyes going to Lydia. Matilda saw the truth in the weight of that gaze—Julian had not come to Coldtown for Matilda. Even though she knew she didn't deserve him to think of her as anything but a monster, it hurt savagely.

"I'm not leaving," Lydia said, turning to Julian, pouting. "You said she wouldn't be like this."

"*I killed a girl,*" Matilda said. "I killed her. Do you understand that?"

"Who cares about some mortal girl?" Lydia tossed back her hair. In that moment, she reminded Matilda of her brother, pretentious Dante who'd turned out to be an actual nice guy. Just like sweet Lydia had turned out cruel.

"You're a girl," Matilda said. "You're mortal."

"I know that!" Lydia rolled her eyes. "I just mean that we don't care who you killed. Turn us and then we can kill lots of people."

"No," Matilda said, swallowing. She looked down, not wanting to hear what she was about to say. There was still a chance. "Look, I have the pass. If you don't want it, then Julian should take it and go. But I'm not turning you. I'm never turning you, understand."

"Julian doesn't want to leave," Lydia said. Her eyes looked bright and two feverish spots appeared on her cheeks. "Who are you to judge me anyway? You're the murderer."

Matilda took a step back. She desperately wanted Julian to say something in her defense or even to look at her, but his gaze remained steadfastly on Lydia.

"So neither one of you want the pass," Matilda said.

"Fuck you," spat Lydia.

Matilda turned away.

"Wait," Julian said. His voice sounded weak.

Matilda spun, unable to keep the hope off her face, and saw why Julian had called to her. Lydia stood behind him, a long knife to his throat.

"Turn me," Lydia said. "Turn me, or I'm going to kill him."

Julian's eyes were wide. He started to protest or beg or something and Lydia pressed the knife harder, silencing him.

People had stopped dancing nearby, backing away. One girl with red-glazed eyes stared hungrily at the knife.

"Turn me!" Lydia shouted. "I'm tired of waiting! I want my life to begin!"

"You won't be alive—" Matilda started.

"I'll be alive—more alive than ever. Just like you are."

"Okay," Matilda said softly. "Give me your wrist."

The crowd seemed to close in tighter, watching as Lydia held out her arm. Matilda crouched low, bending down over it.

"Take the knife away from his throat," Matilda said.

Lydia, all her attention on Matilda, let Julian go. He stumbled a little and pressed his fingers to his neck.

"I loved you," Julian shouted.

Matilda looked up to see that he wasn't speaking to her. She gave him a glittering smile and bit down on Lydia's wrist.

The girl screamed, but the scream was lost in Matilda's ears. Lost in the pulse of blood, the tide of gluttonous pleasure and the music throbbing around them like Lydia's slowing heartbeat.

Matilda sat on the blood-soaked mattress and turned on the video camera to check that the live feed was working.

Julian was gone. She'd given him the pass after stripping him of all his cash and credit cards; there was no point in trying to force Lydia to leave since she'd just come right back in. He'd made stammering apologies that Matilda ignored; then he fled for the gate. She didn't miss him. Her fantasy of Julian felt as ephemeral as her old life.

"It's working," one of the boys—Michael—said from the stairs, a computer cradled on his lap. Even though she'd killed one of them, they welcomed her back, eager enough for eternal life to risk more deaths. "You're streaming live video."

Matilda set the camera on the stack of crates, pointed toward her and the wall where she'd tied a gagged Lydia. The girl thrashed and kicked, but Matilda ignored her. She stepped in front of the camera and smiled.

My name is Matilda Green. I was born on April 10, 1997. I died on September 3, 2013. Please tell my mother I'm okay. And Dante, if you're watching this, I'm sorry.

You've probably seen lots of video feeds from inside Coldtown. I saw them too. Pictures of girls and boys grinding together in clubs or bleeding elegantly for their celebrity vampire masters. Here's what you never see. What I'm going to show you.

For eighty-eight days you are going to watch someone sweat out the infection. You are going to watch her beg and scream and cry. You're going to watch her throw up food and piss her pants and pass out. You're going to watch me feed her can after can of creamed corn. It's not going to be pretty.

You're going to watch me, too. I'm the kind of vampire that you'd be, one who's new at this and basically out of control. I've already killed someone and I can't guarantee I'm not going to do it again. I'm the one who infected this girl.

This is the real Coldtown.

I'm the real Coldtown.

You still want in?

Talking Back to the Moon
Steven R. Boyett

Out of the Santa Monica Mountains they walked south through the San Fernando Valley on the broken thoroughfare of I-5, threading their way among corroded cars and shattered pavement. Worn-down houses and burned-down condos and broken-fronted convenience stores to either side. The shorthaired girl sunbrowned and thin in baggy cargo shorts with bulging pockets, nylon backpack with toy figures dangling from the zipper pulls and a bedroll tied beneath. A worn and faded black babydoll tee shirt with a glittery rabbit iron-on gone dull in strips where the outer coating had peeled. Sheathed bowie knife half the length of her arm hanging from her cabled belt. Bright yellow wraparound sunglasses. Multicolored Adidas walking shoes and mismatched socks. A different color of nail polish flaking on each ragged nail. The centaur huge and gaunt beside her like a stick-figure drawing of a mythical centaur. Dark and angular and alert. Tapered head not much wider than the muscular stalk of neck. The mouth a line sawn into the dark face like a healing scar from ear to hard triangular ear. Javelin in extra-jointed hand and pannier occasionally clinking with the gait of his odd tricornered feet. Not hooves and not paws but something in between, as if some reptile had evolved to something equine.

The girl pulled a roadmap gone furry at the folds from its backpack pocket and turned her back to the wind and leafed through it without unfolding it. She looked south as if to match what she saw to what her map depicted.

Do cities all look the same to you? she said. I mean not the same, but like any one place you are, you can't tell where you are cause it looks like all the other places.

Don unnastan.

Yeah, okay. She folded the map and returned it to its backpack pocket and they resumed walking. Santa Ana winds sent ripples through the freeway grass.

She sat up in her sleeping bag. The faceless dark above her. The bowie handle in her hand. She hadn't been aware of reaching for it.

Chay stood watch near the vinecovered overpass support. They'd lit no fire and would not while they were in the Valley. Bottled water mixed into an MRE pouch was good enough for now.

She drank flat soda water and got out of her sleeping bag and went to pee. She came back and stood silent near Chay unmoving as some roadside sculpture. She set a hand against the centaur's flank. The pebbled hide warm. Neither of them spoke here where the underpass would echo and a normal voice could carry a quarter mile. The moon already set and concrete ghostly in the starlight. Nightsounds in the darkened world. Derelict cars on the freeway like foundered boats rotting on some bedroughted reef.

She moved her hand to her chest and closed her eyes. No moon out to call forth her former wildness. Was it there to answer, any part of it? Could it be restored? This is why we're heading south.

Next day Avy called lunch in Sunland and stood looking over the freeway railing at some old overgrown and half-collapsed warehouse district and ate rehydrated mac and cheese. Chay had killed a raccoon with a rock and as he dressed it with a filleting knife he asked her what it had felt like when she changed.

You'd get hungry as shit a couple days before, she said. Dad said it burned unbelievable calories when you turned.

Calree?

Like wood your body burns to keep it going. He said just changing could starve you to death if you didn't eat enough before. We used to have to stock up like crazy every month. And then after you changed you were starving again. I don't really remember much about what it was like after I changed or what I did or anything. It's like trying to remember when you were a baby or something. Like the parts of your brain that do the thinking and remembering aren't there any more. The human parts. But I remember being really hungry. Half our runs were looking for food.

Runs.

That's what we called it, because we'd just run and run. All over the hills up around where we were living. I remember it felt really good. Like this is what I'm made for. I can sort of remember stuff like that. Feelings. We'd hunt. Coyotes would run from us. Wolves would howl. We were like them but we weren't like them at all. They didn't know what to make of us. And the nights were bright because the moon was always full when we changed. And the moon was—

She stopped. Looking off the freeway into some invisible distance.

It was like you could hear it. Like the light made some kind of sound. The second it came up you knew it was there. You didn't have to see it. It didn't matter where you were. And it wasn't hearing really because it happened in your head. Like you felt it. The color and the light and the sound and the weight and it all just pulled at you. I really miss it.

The centaur swallowed the raccoon and the girl swabbed out her cup and tied her backpack and hoisted it. Come on, she said.

Late that afternoon they passed the Ventura Freeway connector and the 5 turned due south to parallel the sludge of the concrete-banked and -bedded Los Angeles River. Great berms of garbage and rusted frames of shopping carts half submerged in a kind of narrow bog. Miles of concrete embankment painted over with spraycans or brushes or rollers in a dense scrawl of pictoglyphs as if some dying race had struggled to reclaim the act of writing itself in order to set down some paltry hurried record that in all its myriad manifestations along this declining borderline of corralled waterway said entirely, I was here. We were here.

Downtown was a dozen miles away by the map. Full night would fall before they got there and there was no way in hell she was going into any downtown in the dark. They were passing the eastern end of the Hollywood Hills and all about their right side lay the wilded mass of what had once been Griffith Park. What remained of the Los Angeles Zoo just off the freeway somewhere in that thicket. The wasted sprawl of Glendale to their left.

They were in the shadow of the hills and dark would be upon them soon. She told Chay they should make camp soon and he said okay. Half a mile past the Colorado Boulevard exit they set up as they had the night before. Around them a stakebed truck with the wooden stakes collapsed, a phone company van with ladders on the roof, a FedEx tractor trailer, a rusteaten yellow schoolbus with steps caked and filthy past the foldback door aslant in its frame. Half the windowglass stove in. She did not look inside but instead folded down the back seat of a Scion and swept out the dirt and cobwebs and dead leaves with the edge of her hand and then unrolled her bedding there.

She ate her MRE directly from the foil pouch and cold. Chay taught her several words for things and tested her by saying them at random times and making her point to what they represented. She was wrong often as not. The guttural and phlegmy speech all but indistinguishable to her, one belch from the other. But Chay seemed to approve.

He left for his evening ritual while she ate her tasteless thirty-year-old cookie and downed it with bottled water. She thought about downtown and what might be there. She drew her bowie knife and practiced with it. A beautiful weapon for someone two feet taller than her. The handle banded with ebony, leather, and brass, brass-ended and with a curled brass fingerguard. The grip large in one hand and small in both. The blade itself looked a small companion to a cutlass, broad with a large and upswept cutting fore and curved cutback in the lead third. Both edges shaving sharp. Bloodlet on both sides alongside the thicker keel. The metal spotless and no rust anywhere. A deep cutaway blade trap just before the guard. The whole thing nearly a foot and a half long and heavy enough to tire her arm with wielding. You could hack off a branch with it, or an arm. The cutback gave authority to a backslash and made stabbing more effective. She loved the bowie even though it really was a lot of knife for her.

She sheathed the knife and gathered the empty MRE packets and carried them to a car a hundred yards away and threw them in. On the way back she walked slowly by the schoolbus and eyed it warily. The square blind windows necklaced in glass chunks. The chassis lowered on dryrotted tires. A faint urine stench as she passed downwind. The whole interior probably some massive rodent den.

The shadow of the hills stretched well across the Valley now. The breeze grew chill and she changed to her much-worn flannel hoodie. As dark came on, strange cries rose from the enjungled hillside. Shrieks and squawks and chittering. Sobbing peacocks and enraged macaws. Chittering monkeys and obscene toads. Once a roar and a trumpeted reply. In the hills coyotes barked accompaniment. Soon the whole was riotous and strange, a great odd menagerie settling in for the night. She was accustomed to odd animal noises and had slept outside nearly half her life yet she had never heard anything like it. She had no qualms concerning creatures out there hunting creatures. Often she'd been one of them. But some of these creatures sounded large and the sounds were mysterious and a little worrisome.

She turned to fetch more water from the pack she'd left in the lowered tailgate of the Scion and she stopped. A hyena stood watching her from the roof of that very car. Spotted like a leopard and built like a madman's nightmare of a dog, it appraised her steadily. Rear legs short and front long and all blackfooted. Close-set eyes and wide muzzle black.

She stared back only long enough to be sure it was not about to leap and then looked around for the others. It would call them soon and they would flank her. She saw nothing but continued to look because she would soon need shelter or a place where she could fight. She had broken her lifelong habit of noting what fully windowed cars or other protected spaces were at hand wherever she made camp and now here she stood and there stood the smartest and most remorseless predator she had seen aside from human being or centaur and more on the way. She had seen them bite through leg bones and they were better strategists than most people knew.

The decoy on the Scion roof was bristling at the mane now. Her head went low to just before her paws and she grinned down at the girl. Nothing but ten feet of air between those teeth and her.

Avy unsnapped the sheath strap and drew the bowie and grinned back and sang out a long fuuuck you. Then she glanced around once more and threw her head back and yelled Chay's name as loud as she could.

The hyena grunted softly several times and then began to whoop. Highpitched and upbending. Avy grabbed the bowie in two hands and felt herself relax. The wolf in her was gone but mind and body remembered.

She realized that she already knew where they'd be coming from and she turned toward the schoolbus and yelled Chay's name again as the clan leapt from the doorway one at a time. One looked out a broken window at her and lifted its nose to the air and withdrew and emerged in its turn a moment later. Now a dozen of them paced the road in strange half-upright postures, eyes on her and heads swiveling on long thick necks to stay in place as if on gimbals as their slopebacked bodies turned and turned impatiently. Each a match for her

THE URBAN FANTASY ANTHOLOGY

weight and probably her knife.

She yelled out again and this seemed to incite them. A group of three came toward her and another group of three moved to circle round behind her. Loping in their peculiar bearish gait and batlike faces stern. Grunting as if exasperated. The remaining six stayed where they were. These would rush to help if the others could not bring her down or they would rush to feed if she did fall. The two groups approaching would pause just long enough to take her measure and then come at her singly from either side, the first in front to busy her and the other behind to hamstring her. She had seen a group of less than this coordinate to bring down an armed man twice her weight and gut him with their teeth even as he grabbed at them and kicked and beat and looked on in flateyed voiceless terror. Unable even to scream because fascia and diaphragm had been torn through and bloodsoaked muzzles already worried at his guts.

The telephone company van was nearby and she sidled to it and stood with her back to it. The decoy on the Scion roof was puffed up now and whooping pure hilarity. The shag of her dun mane all on end. Avy kept her gaze fixed at a point between the two approaching groups and shifted her knife to her left hand and groped behind her with her right until she found the side door latch. She pulled and felt it disengage but nothing happened and she pulled harder and it moved but grudgingly. The rusted chassis becoming all of a piece. The flanking groups stopped ten feet away all of them whooping and appraising her and she knew she had only seconds before the first came at her. The door shrieked in its track and yielded a foot of entry that was all she needed. She kept the knifepoint to the fore and turned sideways and ducked into the van and hit the back of her head on the top of the frame hard enough to see pinprick explosions of light just as the first of them ran at her. She pulled the knife in after her and then pushed it out again as the hyena leapt to follow her in, and the hunter's jaws clamped on the blade entire. Their very force opening him up palate and tongue. The impact drove her back into the crowded van heaped with corroded gear. The upturned bowie point still lodged in the hyena's palate and the lower jaw snapping at the edge. Black eyes bright and fevered to get at her. The front paws scrabbled and she braced a hand behind her and pushed her upper body forward and then pushed the blade again. The creature laughed maniacally and tried to backpedal and she let it. The second attacker crowding the doorway now to snap beside the injured creature's bleeding snout. She jerked the handle left then right and the impaled head followed and she yanked back and the fingerguard caught the thick and bloodsoaked fangs to pull the animal toward her. She almost lost the knife in its head. She twisted the other way and pulled back and kicked out and the hyena backed out of the van. The second attacker snapped at her in the doorway now almost on top of the first and she rolled sideways and grabbed the door and slammed it against the fangbared muzzle and it laughed as had its partner. The muzzle withdrew and she shut the door completely and backed into the crowded van and looked around at where she'd make her stand. The sides arranged with arcane devices in decline on racks and stacked bins of cable and connector. Nowhere to go and nowhere to fight but also no room for their lethal teamwork. She shifted the knife to the other hand and wiped her palm against her pants and shifted the knife back as the next one leapt up on the snub hood and pulled itself up and looked at her in a kind of ludicrous surprise. It turned its head and whooped. She threw the nearest thing at hand, some metal box with dials, and it hit but all the animal did was flinch and then keep coming. A second leapt to knock glass chunks from the bottom of the windshield frame with its front paws and then leapt again to hook its paws on the cleared frame and haul itself in.

One at a time she had a chance but not if she waited. The first was between the bucket seats now and coming back and she swung another metal box by two feet of power cable and clouted the hyena on the muzzle and followed with a slash of the bowie that garroted the thing so fully that its head half peeled from its neck. Blood engulfed her knife hand and sprayed a bright graffiti on the close walls. The body fell kicking. The other already behind it and not even pausing to examine its fallen partner. She backslashed and nearly lost the heavy knife again for the warm blood covering her hand and again she swung the box on its cord but the swing had nothing behind it and the hit meant nothing. The teeth popped so close to her wrist she felt the wind of it. It was on her before she could swing again and her hands came up to ward the head and met its throat as it knocked her back amid the gear. Its hind legs scrabbling to drive itself into her and front paws digging at her chest for purchase enough to open her up. Her right hand gripped matted fur with the bowie handle pressed between and the blade flat against the neck and she could feel its breath rasp through its windpipe against her fingers and she smelled rank dead

THE URBAN FANTASY ANTHOLOGY

meat breath as it snapped above her straining to nod down toward her and she thought about the flat beseeching look in the eyes of the man she'd seen killed by this creature's kin and she yelled and let go the fur in her right hand to grip the knife as she pushed with the left and turned the edge toward the throat and brought the handle toward herself so hard the brass cap hit her just under the ribs and knocked the wind from her. The claws against her had no will behind them now and the shrill laugh had liquid in it and she was blinded by a gout of blood in one eye before her hands slipped in the blood now jetting from its severed jugular and windpipe. It fell whole atop her snapping still and gurgling. She cradled it like a crib toy until the legs stopped kicking and the teeth stopped popping beside her bloodsoaked face and then she shoved it boneless off and tried to stand and could not breathe.

Already another hung in the passenger window like some spectator that had wagered on the outcome. Avy wiped her hands and wiped her face but this only spread the blood around. A heavy smell of shit and iron in the van now. She tried to yell at her next combatant but the breath for it would not come. Sparkling black edged her vision. Not now. Fuck you. Not now.

She grabbed the gear rack with her free hand to hold herself up and stepped between the two dead hyenas and brought her knife toward the third at the window. Its claws scraped metal as it hoisted itself up. Blood flung from her hand as she beckoned it with the blade. Come on. It was halfway in the window like some horror being born into the van and she grabbed the bowie in both hands and crouched and then the hyena's head exploded. It dropped to drape across the windowframe like an empty duffel and the near eye hung down by the stalk against its muzzle like a grape on a vine.

At first she did not understand what she had seen and stood there waiting still to meet it. She heard loud trumpeting and wondered what other animal had come to join the fray and then knew what animal it was. The clan's calls changed from whoops to frenzied highpitched laughter and she stumbled forward past the bodies still warm at her feet, holding herself up with left hand braced against the rough and flaking wall. She readied the knife and leaned forward to look out the window and past the rock-killed body still kicking at the doorpanel as if caught in some primal dream of hunting. As perhaps it was. She sank to her knees with the breath still not coming. The window a yard away and beyond reach. She put a hand to her chest and realized some of the blood on her was hers. The hysterical cries intensified and she heard several thuds and then something in her gut unclenched and she drew a great long wheezing breath and fell backward into the van. Head pillowed upon the first of her slain predators.

Of course Chay had a first aid kit. Injuries among his kind were no different in nature or in treatment than injuries among her own.

He found her gear and moved her half a mile down the road and set her on a car roof where he could see her while he scouted the vicinity. He found a plastic gascan on a jeep with an inch of gas still in it and he used it and her mag bar to set a convertible ablaze by way of campfire and worklight. He set her upwind of it on her foam sleeping pad on the trunk of a car. She watched with odd dissociation as he bent to her and cut her shredded flannel hoodie from collar to hem with her Gerber knife. The fabric soaked through with her blood and her assailants' blood and already stiffening. He laid aside the parted halves and cocked his head and studied her. She looked scourged by a thin switch. Two narrow sets of three cuts each and many scratches ran from the inner swell of each small breast and between her ribs, down to midstomach. If she'd held the hyena two inches lower he'd have gutted her sure.

I never let anyone get this far with me, she said.

Don unnastan.

Nothing. Sorry. She turned her head and wondered if she would be sick. Her forehead felt hot. What's your word for ouch?

Chay opened a waterbottle and soaked a handtowel and started washing blood off her chest but pulled his hand back when she hissed.

Little softer please?

Yeh.

He swabbed more gently and then pulled back out of his own shadow and studied her wounds by firelight. Deepset eyes enshadowed and unreadable.

She leaned her head up to look even though it hurt.

It didn't feel that bad when it happened, she said.

Not tok, hokay?

Okay. Sorry. She let her head fall back. A shooting star segmented by his silhouette. The menagerie calls in the thick-growth hills subdued but still there. What's your word for sorry?

Don haff one. Affy quiet now.

He bent to the plastic tackle box repurposed as his first aid kit and came up with a glass pint flask of Stolichnaya half-full. He opened it and held her up with one hand across her shoulder blades and she felt the cuts bleeding again. He put the bottle in her hand. Drink, he said. One, two drink, yeh? He made two comical gunk-gunk swallows.

She sipped and then immediately coughed and tried to sit up and regretted that because it hurt like hell. Jesus effin, she said.

Affy drink.

Yeah yeah, okay. She pinched her nose and drank and took a breath and shivered and drank again. Oh man. People do this for fun?

Not jus yooman.

He set out gauze rolls and number four gauze pads in plastic packets and surgical tape and shortbladed scissors. He touched the bruise beneath her ribs already turning ugly and he cocked his head.

I hit myself with my fucking knife, she said. She laughed. You should see the other guy.

Affy cold?

Naw. Affy fine, dude.

He made sure her bowie knife was out of her reach and then he pointed to her right. She turned her head to look and he upended the bottle of Stoli on her wounds. Her yell would have put out a campfire. The surrounding nightsounds stopped altogether. She bucked and he held her down and then wiped away the bloody vodka with a new clean rag and then he dabbed the wounds and let them dry. He taped the edges of the gauze pads and aligned them on the open cuts and pressed down gently and then lifted her to wrap her chest in bands of gauze. He taped that off and stood looking down at her. She was breathing hard but made no other sound. He lowered her back down. The arboreal racket seeped back into the night.

He looked through her backpack and found her tee shirt but no other. He eased her up again and removed the cut and bloodsoaked flannel hoodie smelling of vodka and made her raise her arms and tried to put the tee shirt over them but had never done such a thing and could not sort it out. She leaned her weight back against his outspread hand and put the shirt on herself and he laid her back down. She asked if she could have another swallow and he gave her the bottle. She swigged and held it out to him. He capped it and put it away.

Make beddah?

Fuck no. Make not give a shit.

He draped her sleeping bag across her. The burning car already guttering. The night windy but not cool.

I'm sorry about your spear.

The centaur shrugged. Jus piece a pipe, yeh? Make anudduh one t'morrah.

She squinted. I'm goddamned if I understand you.

Sokay. Affy res now.

Okay.

The centaur cleaned her bowie knife and oiled his sharpening stone with a small metal bottle of 3-in-One oil and sharpened the knife, pushing the angled edge across the stone in sure deft strokes, one just like the other. He wiped the blade again and cleaned the slurry from the stone and put the stone away. He held the blade up and turned it before him. A big knife even in his own big hand. He returned it to its sheath and set it beside the girl. She was breathing evenly. He watched her a moment and then turned away.

I'm looking for my mom and dad, she said.

Affy leef dem?

She did not reply and he began repacking his first aid kit.

I think they left me, she said. I think I mighta seen em die.

He shut the plastic tacklebox and returned it to his pannier and began sorting this night's finds on his Shroud of Turin beach towel.

I need to find out. Alive or dead I need to know.

Know is beddah yeh.

Yeah.

Chay hep find. Now Affy res. Drink wadder too. Don be sick t'morrah.

Okey dokey.

He finished up his sorting and threw away half of it and threw out some of his previous kit to replace with the new and repacked the panniers and set them aside. He opened a bottled water and squeezed it into his gaping mouth.

I think you killed em, she said. Your people I mean. I think I saw it.

He threw the bloodsoaked handtowels and her shredded flannel and the waterbottle on the carfire. The fabrics flared pale blue and haloed and then began to smoke and pop as the waterbottle blackened and shriveled like some prehistoric insect carapace.

Only fair I guess. God knows I killed my share. Maybe someone's kid saw me, huh.

He looked at her. She lay on her back with her eyes closed. The sheathed bowie alongside. The waning firelight upon her.

Mebbe, he said.

That Avy's dead now though. I guess thass good but it don't feel good.

She let out a long breath.

Don't understand why you don't wanna kill me like all the others do.

The centaur watched her breathing lengthen and he took up his watch and said no more. After he was sure she was asleep he opened up the two English phrasebooks she had given him and began to read them in the waning light.

Trumpeting awoke her and her first thought was that Chay had made another musical javelin and was trying it out. She sat up and then hissed between her teeth and put her hand to her chest and felt the bandages beneath her shirt. She remembered all of it at once and could not believe she was not dead.

She braced a hand behind her and glared back at the day and shaded her eyes. The morning well advanced. Chay stood in the back of the stakebed truck with forelegs on the cab and looked down at something off the freeway.

She pulled out the neck of her shirt and looked down at herself. She let go the collar and lay back and thought about throwing up. Hell with that. She stood and staggered backward and leaned against the car she'd slept beside. She breathed deep and waited for the pinprick blackness to subside. Let's try that again. She straightened from the car and stood a moment and then took an experimental step. It didn't kill her so she took another one. She retrieved her bowie from beside the sleeping bag and took off her belt and put it on again with the knife at her hip. She walked around the charred remains of the convertible. Chay was watching her now but did not move to help her. She nodded at him and he beckoned her on. When she got to the stakebed he pointed off at whatever he was looking at and she started to climb up but when she put a hand on the open tailgate and lifted her leg she felt her cuts grow tight in their bandages.

Loud wet sneezing sounds from the aqueduct now. Chay motioned for her to come around to the front instead and she did.

Three elephants stood bathing themselves in the aqueduct. Two adults and a child. They lifted trunks from the sludgy water and curled them back over their heads and sprayed themselves, dark wet patches spreading in the wrinkled gray. She stared at them in no more wonder than she had when she'd first seen a unicorn. And no less. Both equally belonging to the world she knew, neither more preposterous than the other.

I've heard of these, she whispered to Chay. Are they smart like us?

Smot, he said. But not like us.

She wanted to push on but Chay would have none of it. He opened one of the phrasebooks and deftly turned the pages and pointed at lines.

That doesn't look good.

You need to rest.

This needs to be mended.

Please lie down.

I would like to see some dresses.

She turned from the phrasebook to look up at him. You'd like to see some dresses?

He pointed at her shirt. Affy cloze. Burn big one lass night, dis one no good now. Yeh?

We'll have to leave the freeway for that.

Sokay. Affy need res.

Would it do any good to argue?

They left the elephants to their bath.

It hurt to walk and he carried her. Across the southbound side, a short leap over the divider wall and across the northbound swath, then up what had been the northbound onramp from Los Feliz. They crossed the river above long concrete baffles in the sluggish water and she saw that half were clotted with accumulated trash and dead branches. A mushy shoreline of rotted leaves. Ahead another iteration of decaying cars, broken sidewalks, overgrowth, dead greenery, stripped billboards, angled telephone poles, drooping power lines, broken storefronts, sagging structures. Fire had not touched this area but earthquake had. Fallen awnings and collapsed apartment buildings in what had been mixed residential off the main thoroughfare. A tree growing in the middle of the weedy street, radiating rootcracks giving it the look of something that had punched through suddenly from below. Up ahead a shop door banged in the wind as it had for nearly thirty years. A gaunt coyote stepped out from a doorway and stopped in the road looking at them with its tongue dangling. As if it had run a long way to be here in time see them. They walked on past curbed cars rusting beside parking meters sprouting from the grass. Torn flaps curled from a billboard up ahead. COMING SOON discernible in the ragged strips remaining. Car wash, service station, fast food, repair shop. A garbage truck. Wind and crickets and that banging door.

They found an RV on a concrete pad alongside a house beneath a tubeframe plastic-sheeted structure that had collapsed on top of it. They pulled the covering partway back as if turning down bedding. The RV weathered but in good shape. The door was locked and Avy pried it open with a prybar and went inside. Must and cobwebs, a brittle dry feel. As if some untenanted sarcophagus beneath the desert floor had been exhumed and opened to admit air and light withheld for centuries. Kitchen, dual sink, two popouts, draw curtains, recliner, sofabed, queensize bed. Pots and pans and utensils. Maps. No food. She could not imagine this thing moving on the roads she traveled.

She leaned out the door. Chay stood in the grassy driveway studying the ruined neighborhood.

Okay, I'll sleep here tonight. But we head downtown tomorrow. Got it?

Yeh.

She took the prybar with her and they scavenged the neighborhood but found nothing useful. A shrunken skeleton wrapped in thin stretched mottled leather sagging on an 80d nail driven into a front door. One side of the head bashed in down to the zygomatic arch. Eyesockets ever regarding the wooden shingle hanging from its knobbed neck, the faded word LOOTER scribbled on it with a Sharpie. It did not look like the remains of a human being at all but like some kind of scarecrow patched together out of the hides of other animals and it hung there telling all the story it had left to tell.

They went back to the boulevard and started in on the stores. There were signs that people had lived in some but not in many years. More coyote and raccoon prints than shoeprints traced out in the dust and filled in again, outlines softened. Rat droppings everywhere and a few dark shops become pigeon roosts.

Chay took a ten-foot length of one-and-a-half-inch copper pipe from a plumbing supply. In a small dark room in back of a Mexican grocery Avy found a stand of lockers. Nothing in the unlocked ones and padlocks on the other two. She ran the prybar through the hasps and twisted and the lockers' metal tabs gave way after being wrenched back and forth a few times. Sneakers far too large for her, desiccated antiperspirants, a large tee shirt and an extra large sweatshirt. She flapped the shirts and stirred up dust that made her sneeze. She rolled them up and put them in her backpack left on the register conveyor belt and picked up the backpack by a strap and left the store through its smashed-in window.

Chay could not fit inside the RV so Avy sat on the tailgate of a junkfilled Toyota shortbed beside the all but invisible curb near the house, dangling her sneakers and kicking at weeds as Chay removed his first aid kit from his pannier and opened it. She took a deep breath and started to take off her shirt but blood had seeped through the bandages and stuck to it and she stopped and poured water on it and rubbed the fabric and then slowly peeled the shirt off and threw it into the truck bed. She looked down at the gauze strips. Russet blotches like some kind of mold. She felt behind her and pulled at the curling ends of surgical tape banding her. The odd sensation as her skin lifted up and the tape peeled from her. Dried blood cemented the gauze to her skin. She poured more water and rubbed gently and paid no attention to the pale red flowing down her belly to darken the waistband of her shorts. Then she pulled at the taped gauze strips and they sloughed off redbellied and dripping like interrupted leeches. The sudden air cold against the puckered cuts. A wisp of cotton stuck to one crusting edge and made a faint ripping sound as she pulled it free.

Most of the wounds were superficial cuts that would scab and itch and heal. The left claw had found more purchase in her right breast and cut deep. The wound was wet and felt hot to the touch, and the skin on either side was plumcolored and swollen. Her father had taught her about germs but she didn't understand it completely and wasn't sure she believed what she did. But she knew to bathe the wound with alcohol and keep it clean and covered.

She looked up. Chay stood before her with the bottle of Stoli and an unused shop rag taken from a plastic bag.

Yeah, okay, she said.

He poured vodka on the folded rag and bent to her. She looked at his alien face and clutched the edge of the tailgate and did not make a sound throughout. He set the vodka bottle down and re-dressed her wounds as before. It occurred to her as he worked that she had inflicted just this kind of injury and much worse among his kind without restraint or remorse and yet here she bore such wounds and he treated them. She shook her head. The symmetry of it too perfect. You would be a fool not to learn what lesson this is trying to teach you.

She wiped herself dry and put on her new sweatshirt and bunched the sleeves and rolled the wrists. Thanks, she said. She slid off the tailgate and eyed the bottle as he repacked his kit.

Are you gonna make another spear tonight?

Spear yeh.

Not gonna hunt?

He retrieved a phrasebook and quickly guided her through several pages.

Thank you, but I am not hungry now.

I will rest now.

Tomorrow will be another beautiful day.

She gave him back the phrasebook and grinned. Every bit as beautiful as today I'm sure, she said.

They did not light a fire but sat outside on the concrete pad before the RV. She had found a webbed folding chair and she sat spooning cold cheese tortellini from an MRE pouch and watching Chay organize tools on a sheet spread out before him, the nearer edge weighted down by the length of copper pipe. He picked up a hacksaw and cut two feet off the length at a sharp angle without a vice or any kind of clamp apart from his hand. He sawed a wedge into this angle cut to make two points one above the other like a gaping shark and then began to sharpen the whole of that end with rattail and barrel files.

Avy asked him the words for file and for copper and for saw. Then she asked if he would let her have the bottle of Stoli. He stopped filing and looked at her.

Affy need fuh wounds?

She tapped her forehead. For wounds. Definitely.

He turned the copper pipe before him and then set it down. He got out his bait box and handed her the Stoli pint. The bottle a third full. She thanked him and did not open it but set it aside.

Chay ran a long thumb along a tapering edge and took a file to the edge again.

Avy nodded at the forming spear. The spear's alive, right? You breathe life into it.

Breeve yeh.

But you throw em away and make new ones like they're waterbottles.

Yeh. Easy make.

But how can it be both? I mean, it's either a piece of pipe and you throw it away like it's nothing or it's alive and you take care of it and hate to see it get broken.

He patted his flat chest. Liff from heeyah, yeh? Breeve inta here. He patted the shaping weapon. Chay liff. Chay liff in heeyah. Yeh?

You put part of your life into the spear. Oh—that's why you play em, yeh? You're breathing life into them.

Yeh. Affy unnastan good yeh. Be like Chay peepah soon.

Did you just make a joke?

Choke yeh.

She laughed and then put a hand to her chest. Then she picked up the Stoli bottle and opened it and drank. It tasted as bad as it had the first time. She drank again.

He filed and tested edges and filed more. He put his lipless mouth to the blunt end and blew and the copper weapon thrummed. He puffed and the weapon tooted. He brought his mouth away and looked at it and patted it. Then he laid it on the sheet and opened up his paint box. Identical to his first aid box but for the color. He withdrew several yellow-labeled pint cans. 1 Shot lettering enamel. Brushes. A small flatbladed screwdriver. A pair of wooden chopsticks in a finegrained wooden slide-lid case patterned with darker woods. A particolored rag. A fitness magazine with half the pages torn out.

He pried off a can lid with the screwdriver and began stirring with a chopstick. He tore a page from the magazine and folded it and poured a circle of white paint on it and dipped his brush there and picked up the spear with the point near his face.

Avy took one more swallow from the Stoli bottle and recapped it and set it down near Chay. Then she picked up her bowie and her food wrappers and went down the street and threw the wrappers in a car and stood looking at it. Drunk and unaccountably disquieted.

When she got back Chay held up the spear for her to see the eyes he'd painted just before the main point taper.

That so it can see where it's going?

He nodded. See? he said. Affy unnastan.

Something woke her in the night. She lay listening and heard nothing that did not fit the night. She sat up and put a hand to her chest and felt the bandages and breathed a moment. The pale squares of shaded windows. The large soft bed. Sheets and a bedspread and pillows. Walls and roof. Comfortable and warm and so mistrusted by her.

She drew down the sheets and their rustle seemed loud. She eased out of bed and into her shoes. Socks already on. She picked up the bowie from where it leaned against the nightstand. The houselike vehicle creaking as she went to the door and opened it.

Chay was waiting there and he nodded at the moonlit road where wolves were nosing in the bed of the Toyota truck. They were northern gray wolves come down from the nearby hills to hunt and they had smelled her blood and vodka-soaked shirt from half a mile away. Their numbers flourished and their species no longer fragmented. These were quiet and curious and not at all tentative. They did not even look at Chay who stood armed ten yards from them. There were three of them and one picked up the shirt in its mouth and shook it from side to side as if breaking the neck of a rat and let it go to drape the side of the truck bed and another wolf picked it up and stood there holding it while the other two sniffed at it. One of them backed away and lifted a leg and pissed against the truck.

Avy stepped out into the night. The wolves stilled instantly and their fur went flat and they stood looking at her from the small and junkfilled bed of the truck. She stepped away from the RV and lowered her bowie to the ground and stood up without it. Chay looked at her but said nothing nor made move to stop her.

The gaunt wolves bathed in moonlight watched the girl approach. The leader's head lowered close to his paws. They smelled the blood on her. The same as on the shirt they'd found. She held her empty hands out wide and came on. The leader bristled but gave no other warning or motion.

She stopped in the sparse grass growing from the broken sidewalk. Not two yards from them wild and innate as they had been since before there were men to fear them or fires by which to tell stories of their prowess real or fanciful and their muzzles filled with the smell of her own blood. Yet not crazed. The night air cool and all around ensilvered by the moon's pale monochrome above the overhanging trees.

One of them gave a small yip and the leader turned and jumped from the tailgate like some kind of flowing liquid. The soft sure tap of its pads. It stood looking at her with ears high and muzzle raised and nape fur smoothing. The other two watching from the truck. Then it moved toward her in a kind of crouch as if easing under some low barrier. Avy turned to meet the soft approach. Held out an outspread hand and made no other motion. The wolf went still and stayed crouched low but not as if to pounce. The muzzle coming up to sniff. And then it batted her palm wetly and turned away and the others flowed from the truck to join it and trot away surefooted along the withering neighborhood and into their replevined world.

The girl watched them go and then looked at her palm. That cold wet touch a brand now in her heart. She looked up from her hand. The tatters of night sky visible through the overarching trees washed of stars by the full moon light. The moon that so recently had bound her to its cycle. The moon whose light had called her up from sleep.

On The Far Side of the Cadillac Desert with Dead Folks

Joe R. Lansdale

1

After a month's chase, Wayne caught up with Calhoun one night at a little honky-tonk called Rosalita's. It wasn't that Calhoun had finally gotten careless, it was just that he wasn't worried. He'd killed four bounty hunters so far, and Wayne knew a fifth didn't concern him.

The last bounty hunter had been the famous Pink Lady McGuire—one mean mama—three hundred pounds of rolling, ugly meat that carried a twelve-gauge Remington pump and a bad attitude. Story was, Calhoun jumped her from behind, cut her throat, and as a joke, fucked her before she bled to death. This not only proved to Wayne that Calhoun was a dangerous sonofabitch, it also proved he had bad taste.

Wayne stepped out of his '57 Chevy reproduction, pushed his hat back on his forehead, opened the trunk, and got the sawed-off double barrel and some shells out of there. He already had a .38 revolver in the holster at his side and a bowie knife in each boot, but when you went into a place like Rosalita's it was best to have plenty of backup.

Wayne put a handful of shotgun shells in his shirt pocket, snapped the flap over them, looked up at the red-and-blue neon sign that flashed ROSALITA'S: COLD BEER AND DEAD DANCING, found his center, as they say in Zen, and went on in.

He held the shotgun against his leg, and as it was dark in there and folks were busy with talk or drinks or dancing, no one noticed him or his artillery right off.

He spotted Calhoun's stocky, black-hatted self immediately. He was inside the dance cage with a dead buck-naked Mexican girl of about twelve. He was holding her tight around the waist with one hand and massaging her rubbery ass with the other like it was a pillow he was trying to shape. The dead girl's handless arms flailed on either side of Calhoun, and her little tits pressed to his thick chest. Her wire-muzzled face knocked repeatedly at his shoulder and drool whipped out of her mouth in thick spermy ropes, stuck to his shin, faded and left a patch of wetness.

For all Wayne knew, the girl was Calhoun's sister or daughter. It was that kind of place. The kind that had sprung up immediately after that stuff had gotten out of a lab upstate and filled the air with bacteria that brought dead humans back to life, made their basic motor functions work and made them hungry for human flesh; made it so if a man's wife, daughter, sister, or mother went belly up and he wanted to turn a few bucks, he might think: "Damn, that's tough about ole Betty Sue, but she's dead as hoot-owl shit and ain't gonna be needing nothing from here on out, and with them germs working around in her, she's just gonna pull herself out of the ground and cause me a problem. And the ground out back of the house is harder to dig than a calculus problem is to work, so I'll just toss her cold ass in the back of the pickup next to the chain saw and the barbed-wire roll, haul her across the border to sell her to the Meat Boys to sell to the tonics for dancing.

"It's a sad thing to sell one of your own, but shit, them's the breaks. I'll just stay out of the tonics until all the meat rots off her bones and they have to throw her away. That way I won't go in some place for a drink and see her up there shaking her dead tits and end up going sentimental and dewy-eyed in front of one of my buddies or some ole two-dollar gal."

This kind of thinking supplied the dancers. In other parts of the country, the dancers might be men or children, but here it was mostly women. Men were used for hunting and target practice.

The Meat Boys took the bodies, cut off the hands so they couldn't grab, ran screws through their jaws to fasten on wire muzzles so they couldn't bite, sold them to the honky-tonks about the time the germ started stirring.

Bar owners put them inside wire enclosures up front of their joints, staffed music, and men paid five dollars to get in there and grab them and make like they were dancing when all the women wanted to do was grab and bite, which, muzzled and handless, they could not do.

If a man liked his partner enough, he could pay more money and have her tied to a cot in the back and he could get on her and at some business. Didn't have to hear no arguments or buy presents or make promises or make them come. Just fuck and hike.

As long as the establishment sprayed the dead for maggots and kept them perfumed and didn't keep them so long hunks of meat came off on a man's dick, the customers were happy as flies on shit.

Wayne looked to see who might give him trouble, and figured everyone was a potential customer. The six foot two, two-hundred-fifty-pound bouncer being the most immediate concern.

But, there wasn't anything to do but to get on with things and handle problems when they came up. He went into the cage where Calhoun was dancing, shouldered through the other dancers and went for him.

Calhoun had his back to Wayne, and as the music was loud, Wayne didn't worry about going quietly. But Calhoun sensed him and turned with his hand full of a little .38.

Wayne clubbed Calhoun's arm with the barrel of the shotgun. The little gun flew out of Calhoun's hand and went skidding across the floor and clanked against the metal cage.

Calhoun wasn't outdone. He spun the dead girl in front of him and pulled a big pigsticker out of his boot and held it under the girl's armpit in a threatening manner, which with a knife that big was no feat.

Wayne shot the dead girl's left kneecap out from under her and she went down. Her armpit trapped Calhoun's knife. The other men deserted their partners and went over the wire netting like squirrels.

Before Calhoun could shake the girl loose, Wayne stepped in and hit him over the head with the barrel of the shotgun. Calhoun crumpled and the girl began to crawl about on the floor as if looking for lost contacts.

The bouncer came in behind Wayne, grabbed him under the arms and tried to slip a full nelson on him.

Wayne kicked back on the bouncer's shin and raked his boot down the man's instep and stomped his foot. The bouncer let go. Wayne turned and kicked him in the balls and hit him across the face with the shotgun.

The bouncer went down and didn't even look like he wanted up.

Wayne couldn't help but note he liked the music that was playing. When he turned he had someone to dance with.

Calhoun.

Calhoun charged him, hit Wayne in the belly with his head, knocked him over the bouncer. They tumbled to the floor and the shotgun went out of Wayne's hands and scraped across the floor and hit the crawling girl in the head. She didn't even notice, just kept snaking in circles, dragging her blasted leg behind her like a skin she was trying to shed.

The other women, partnerless, wandered about the cage. The music changed. Wayne didn't like this tune as well. Too slow. He bit Calhoun's earlobe off.

Calhoun screamed and they grappled around on the floor. Calhoun got his arm around Wayne's throat and tried to choke him to death.

Wayne coughed out the earlobe, lifted his leg and took the knife out of his boot. He brought it around and back and hit Calhoun in the temple with the hilt.

Calhoun let go of Wayne and rocked on his knees, then collapsed on top of him.

Wayne got out from under him and got up and kicked him in the head a few times. When he was finished, he put the bowie in its place, got Calhoun's .38 and the shotgun. To hell with the pigsticker.

A dead woman tried to grab him, and he shoved her away with a thrust of his palm. He got Calhoun by the collar, started pulling him toward the gate.

Faces were pressed against the wire, watching. It had been quite a show. A friendly cowboy type opened the gate for Wayne and the crowd parted as he pulled Calhoun by. One man felt helpful and chased after them and said, "Here's his hat, Mister," and dropped it on Calhoun's knee and it stayed there.

Outside, a professional drunk was standing between two cars taking a leak on the ground. As Wayne pulled Calhoun past, the drunk said, "Your buddy don't look so good."

"Look worse than that when I get him to Law Town," Wayne said.

Wayne stopped by the '57, emptied Calhoun's pistol and tossed it as far as he could, then took a few minutes to kick Calhoun in the ribs and ass. Calhoun grunted and farted, but didn't come to.

When Wayne's leg got tired, he put Calhoun in the passenger seat and handcuffed him to the door.

He went over to Calhoun's '62 Impala replica with the plastic bull horns mounted on the hood—which was how he had located him in the first place, by his well known car—and kicked the glass out of the window on the driver's side and used the shotgun to shoot the bull horns off. He took out his pistol and shot all the tires flat, pissed on the driver's door, and kicked a dent in it.

By then he was too tired to shit in the back seat, so he took some deep breaths and went back to the '57 and climbed in behind the wheel.

Reaching across Calhoun, he opened the glove box and got out one of his thin, black cigars and put it in his mouth.

He pushed the lighter in, and while he waited for it to heat up, he took the shotgun out of his lap and reloaded it.

A couple of men poked their heads outside of the tonk's door, and Wayne stuck the shotgun out the window and fired above their heads. They disappeared inside so fast they might have been an optical illusion.

Wayne put the lighter to his cigar, picked up the wanted poster he had on the seat, and set fire to it. He thought about putting it in Calhoun's lap as a joke, but didn't. He tossed the flaming poster out of the window.

He drove over close to the tonk and used the remaining shotgun load to shoot at the neon Rosalita's sign. Glass tinkled onto the tonk's roof and onto the gravel drive.

Now if he only had a dog to kick.

He drove away from there, bound for the Cadillac Desert, and finally Law Town on the other side.

2

The Cadillacs stretched for miles, providing the only shade in the desert. They were buried nose down at a slant, almost to the windshields, and Wayne could see skeletons of some of the drivers in the cars, either lodged behind the steering wheels or lying on the dashboards against the glass. The roof and hood guns had long since been removed and all the windows on the cars were rolled up, except for those that had been knocked out and vandalized by travelers, or dead folks looking for goodies.

The thought of being in one of those cars with the windows rolled up in all this heat made Wayne feel even more uncomfortable than he already was. Hot as it was, he was certain even the skeletons were sweating.

He finished pissing on the tire of the Chevy, saw the piss had almost dried. He shook the drops off, watched them fall and evaporate against the burning sand. Zipping up, he thought about Calhoun, and how when he'd pulled over earlier to let the sonofabitch take a leak, he'd seen there was a little metal ring through the head of his dick and a Texas emblem dangling from that. He could understand the Texas emblem, being from there himself, but he couldn't for the life of him imagine why a fella would do that to his general. Any idiot who would put a ring through the head of his pecker deserved to die, innocent or not.

Wayne took off his cowboy hat and rubbed the back of his neck and ran his hand over the top of his head and back again. The sweat on his fingers was thick as lube oil, and the thinning part of his hairline was tender; the heat was cooking the hell out of his scalp, even through the brown felt of his hat.

Before he put his hat on, the sweat on his fingers was dry. He broke open the shotgun, put the shells in his pocket, opened the Chevy's back door and tossed the shotgun on the floorboard.

He got in the front behind the wheel and the seat was hot as a griddle on his back and ass. The sun shone through the slightly tinted windows like a polished chrome hubcap; it forced him to squint.

Glancing over at Calhoun, he studied him. The fucker was asleep with his head thrown back and his black wilted hat hung precariously on his head—it looked jaunty almost. Sweat oozed down Calhoun's red face, flowed over his eyelids and around his neck, running in rivulets down the white seat covers, drying quickly. He had his left hand between his legs, clutching his balls, and his right was on the arm rest, which was the only place it could be since he was handcuffed to the door.

Wayne thought he ought to blow the bastard's brains out and tell God he died. The shithead certainly needed shooting, but Wayne didn't want to lose a thousand dollars off his reward. He needed every penny if he was going to get that wrecking yard he wanted. The yard was the dream that went before him like a carrot before a donkey, and he didn't want any more delays. If he never made another trip across this goddamn desert, that would suit him fine.

Pop would let him buy the place with the money he had now, and he could pay the rest out later. But that wasn't what he wanted to do. The bounty business had finally gone sour, and he wanted to do different. It wasn't any goddamn fun anymore. Just met the dick cheese of the earth. And when you ran the sonofabitches to ground and put the cuffs on them, you had to watch your ass 'til you got them turned in. Had to sleep with one eye open and a hand on your gun. It wasn't any way to live.

And he wanted a chance to do right by Pop. Pop had been like a father to him. When he was a kid and his mama was screwing the Mexicans across the border for the rent money, Pop would let him hang out in the yard and climb on the rusted cars and watch him fix the better ones, tune those babies so fine they purred like dick-whipped women.

When he was older, Pop would haul him to Galveston for the whores and out to the beach to take potshots at all the ugly, fucked-up critters swimming around in the Gulf. Sometimes he'd take him to Oklahoma for the Dead Roundup. It sure seemed to do the old fart good to whack those dead fuckers with a tire iron, smash their diseased brains so they'd lay down for good. And it was a challenge. 'Cause if one of those dead buddies bit you, you could put your head between your legs and kiss your rosy ass goodbye.

Wayne pulled out of his thoughts of Pop and the wrecking yard and turned on the stereo system. One of his favorite country-and-western tunes whispered at him. It was Billy Conteegas singing, and Wayne hummed along with the music as he drove into the welcome, if mostly ineffectual, shadows provided by the Cadillacs.

> My baby left me,
> She left me for a cow,
> But I don't give a flying fuck,
> She's gone radioactive now,
> Yeah, my baby left me,
> Left me for a six-tittied cow.

Just when Conteegas was getting to the good part, doing the trilling sound in his throat he was famous for, Calhoun opened his eyes and spoke up.

"Ain't it bad enough I got to put up with the fucking heat and your fucking humming without having to listen to that shit? Ain't you got no Hank Williams stuff, or maybe some of that nigger music they used to make? You know, where the coons harmonize and one of 'em sings like his nuts are cut off."

"You just don't know good music when you hear it, Calhoun."

Calhoun moved his free hand to his hatband, found one of his few remaining cigarettes and a match there. He struck the match on his knee, lit the smoke and coughed a few rounds. Wayne couldn't imagine how Calhoun could smoke in all this heat.

"Well, I may not know good music when I hear it, capon, but I damn sure know bad music when I hear it. And that's some bad music."

"You ain't got any kind of culture, Calhoun. You been too busy raping kids."

"Reckon a man has to have a hobby," Calhoun said, blowing smoke at Wayne. "Young pussy is mine. Besides, she wasn't in diapers. Couldn't find one that young. She was thirteen. You know what they say. If they're old enough to bleed, they're old enough to breed."

"How old they have to be for you to kill them?"

"She got loud."

"Change channels, Calhoun."

"Just passing the time of day, capon. Better watch yourself, bounty hunter, when you least expect it, I'll bash your head."

"You're gonna run your mouth one time too many, Calhoun, and when you do, you're gonna finish this ride in the trunk with ants crawling on you. You ain't so priceless I won't blow you away."

"You lucked out at the tonk, boy. But there's always tomorrow, and every day can't be like at Rosalita's."

Wayne smiled. "Trouble is, Calhoun, you're running out of tomorrows."

3

As they drove between the Cadillacs, the sky fading like a bad bulb, Wayne looked at the cars and tried to imagine what the Chevy-Cadillac Wars had been like, and why they had been fought in this miserable desert. He had heard it was a hell of a fight, and close, but the outcome had been Chevy's and now they were the only cars Detroit made. And as far as he was concerned, that was the only thing about Detroit that was worth a damn. Cars.

He felt that way about all cities. He'd just as soon lie down and let a diseased dog shit in his face than drive through one, let alone live in one.

Law Town being an exception. He'd go there. Not to live, but to give Calhoun to the authorities and pick up his reward. People in Law Town were always glad to see a criminal brought in. The public executions were popular and varied and supplied a steady income.

Last time he'd been to Law Town he'd bought a front-row ticket to one of the executions and watched a chronic shoplifter, a redheaded rat of a man, get pulled apart by being chained between two souped-up tractors. The execution itself was pretty brief, but there had been plenty of buildup with clowns and balloons and a big-tittied stripper who could swing her tits in either direction to boom-boom music.

Wayne had been put off by the whole thing. It wasn't organized enough and the drinks and food were expensive and the front-row seats were too close to the tractors. He had gotten to see that the redhead's insides were brighter than his hair, but some of the insides got sprinkled on his new shirt, and cold water or not, the spots hadn't come out. He had suggested to one of the management that they put up a big plastic shield so the front row wouldn't get splattered, but he doubted anything had come of it.

They drove until it was solid dark. Wayne stopped and fed Calhoun a stick of jerky and some water from his canteen. Then he handcuffed him to the front bumper of the Chevy.

"See any snakes, Gila monsters, scorpions, stuff like that," Wayne said, "yell out. Maybe I can get around here in time."

"I'd let the fuckers run up my asshole before I'd call you," Calhoun said.

Leaving Calhoun with his head resting on the bumper, Wayne climbed in the back seat of the Chevy and slept with one ear cocked and one eye open.

Before dawn Wayne got Calhoun loaded in the '57 and they started out. After a few minutes of sluicing through the early morning grayness, a wind started up. One of those weird desert winds that come out of nowhere. It carried grit through the air at the speed of bullets, hit the '57 with a sound like rabid cats scratching.

The sand tires crunched on through, and Wayne turned on the windshield blower, the sand wipers, and the head-beams, and kept on keeping on.

When it was time for the sun to come up, they couldn't see it. Too much sand. It was blowing harder than ever and the blowers and wipers couldn't handle it. It was piling up. Wayne couldn't even make out the Cadillacs anymore.

He was about to stop when a shadowy, whale-like shape crossed in front of him and he slammed on the brakes, giving the sand tires a workout. But it wasn't enough.

The '57 spun around and rammed the shape on Calhoun's side. Wayne heard Calhoun yell, then felt himself thrown against the door and his head smacked metal and the outside darkness was nothing compared to the darkness into which he descended.

4

Wayne rose out of it as quickly as he had gone down. Blood was trickling into his eyes from a slight forehead wound. He used his sleeve to wipe it away.

His first clear sight was of a face at the window on his side; a sallow, moon-terrain face with bulging eyes and an expression like an idiot contemplating Sanscrit. On the man's head was a strange, black hat with big round ears, and in the center of the hat, like a silver tumor, was the head of a large screw. Sand lashed at the face, imbedded in it, struck the unblinking eyes and made the round-eared hat flap. The man paid no attention. Though still dazed, Wayne knew why. The man was one of the dead folks.

Wayne looked in Calhoun's direction. Calhoun's door had been mashed in and the bending metal had pinched the handcuff attached to the arm rest in two. The blow had knocked Calhoun to the center of the seat. He was holding his hand in front of him, looking at the dangling cuff and chain as if it were a silver bracelet and a line of pearls.

Leaning over the hood, cleaning the sand away from the windshield with his hands, was another of the dead folks. He too was wearing one of the round-eared hats. He pressed a wrecked face to the clean spot and looked in at Calhoun. A string of snot-green saliva ran out of his mouth and onto the glass.

More sand was wiped away by others. Soon all the car's glass showed the pallid and rotting faces of the dead folks. They stared at Wayne and Calhoun as if they were two rare fish in an aquarium.

Wayne cocked back the hammer of the .38.

"What about me," Calhoun said. "What am I supposed to use?"

"Your charm," Wayne said, and at that moment, as if by signal, the dead folk faded away from the glass, leaving one man standing on the hood holding a baseball bat. He hit the glass and it went into a thousand little stars. The bat came again and the heavens fell and the stars rained down and the sand storm screamed in on Wayne and Calhoun.

The dead folks reappeared in full force. The one with the bat started though the hole in the windshield, heedless of the jags of glass that ripped his ragged clothes and tore his flesh like damp cardboard.

Wayne shot the batter through the head, and the man, finished, fell through, pinning Wayne's arm with his body.

Before Wayne could pull his gun free, a woman's hand reached through the hole and got hold of Wayne's collar. Other dead folks took to the glass and hammered it out with their feet and fist. Hands were all over Wayne; they felt dry and cool like leather seat covers. They pulled him over the steering wheel and dash and outside. The sand worked at his flesh like a cheese grater. He could hear Calhoun yelling, "Eat me, motherfuckers, eat me and choke."

They tossed Wayne on the hood of the '57. Faces leaned over him. Yellow teeth and toothless gums were very near. A road-kill odor washed through his nostrils. He thought: now the feeding frenzy begins. His only consolation was that there were so many dead folks, there wouldn't be enough of him left to come back from the dead. They'd probably have his brain for dessert.

But no. They picked him up and carried him off. Next thing he knew was a clearer view of the whale-shape the '57 had hit, and its color. It was a yellow school bus.

The door to the bus hissed open. The dead folks dumped Wayne inside on his belly and tossed his hat after him. They stepped back and the door closed, just missing Wayne's foot.

Wayne looked up and saw a man in the driver's seat smiling at him. It wasn't a dead man. Just fat and ugly. He was probably five feet tall and bald except for a fringe of hair around his shiny bald head the color of a shit ring in a toilet bowl. He had a nose so long and dark and malignant-looking it appeared as if it might fall off his face at any moment, like an overripe banana. He was wearing what Wayne first thought was a bathrobe, but proved to be a robe like that of a monk. It was old and tattered and moth-eaten and Wayne could see pale flesh through the holes. An odor wafted from the fat man that was somewhere between the smell of stale sweat, cheesy balls and an unwiped asshole.

"Good to see you," the fat man said.

"Charmed," Wayne said.

From the back of the bus came a strange, unidentifiable sound. Wayne poked his head around the seats for a look.

In the middle of the aisle, about halfway back, was a nun. Or sort of a nun. Her back was to him and she wore a black-and-white nun's habit. The part that covered her head was traditional, but from there down was quite a departure from the standard attire. The outfit was cut to the middle of her thigh and she wore black fishnet stockings and thick high heels. She was slim with good legs and a high little ass that, even under the circumstances, Wayne couldn't help but appreciate. She was moving one hand above her head as if sewing the air.

Sitting on the seats on either side of the aisle were dead folks. They all wore the round-eared hats, and they were responsible for the sound.

They were trying to sing.

He had never known dead folks to make any noise outside of grunts and groans, but here they were singing. A toneless sort of singing to be sure, some of the words garbled and some of the dead folks just opening and closing their mouths soundlessly, but, by golly, he recognized the tune. It was "Jesus Loves Me."

Wayne looked back at the fat man, let his hand ease down to the bowie in his right boot. The fat man produced a little .32 automatic from inside his robe and pointed it at Wayne.

"It's small caliber," the fat man said, "but I'm a real fine shot, and it makes a nice, little hole."

Wayne quit reaching in his boot.

"Oh, that's all right," said the fat man. "Take the knife out and put it on the floor in front of you and slide it to me. And while you're at it, I think I see the hilt of one in your other boot."

Wayne looked back. The way he had been thrown inside the bus had caused his pants legs to hike up over his boots, and the hilts of both his bowies were revealed. They might as well have had blinking lights on them.

It was shaping up to be a shitty day.

He slid the bowies to the fat man, who scooped them up nimbly and dumped them on the other side of his seat.

The bus door opened and Calhoun was tossed in on top of Wayne. Calhoun's hat followed after.

Wayne shrugged Calhoun off, recovered his hat, and put it on. Calhoun found his hat and did the same. They were still on their knees.

"Would you gentlemen mind moving to the center of the bus?"

Wayne led the way. Calhoun took note of the nun now, said, "Man, look at that ass."

The fat man called back to them. "Right there will do fine."

Wayne slid into the seat the fat man was indicating with a wave of the .32, and Calhoun slid in beside him. The dead folks entered now, filled the seats up front, leaving only a few stray seats in the middle empty.

Calhoun said, "What are those fuckers back there making that noise for?"

"They're singing," Wayne said. "Ain't you got no churchin'?"

"Say they are?" Calhoun turned to the nun and the dead folks and yelled, "Y'all know any Hank Williams?"

The nun did not turn and the dead folks did not quit their toneless singing.

"Guess not," Calhoun said. "Seems like all the good music's been forgotten."

The noise in the back of the bus ceased and the nun came over to look at Wayne and Calhoun. She was nice in front too. The outfit was cut from throat to crotch, laced with a ribbon, and it showed a lot of tit and some tight, thin, black panties that couldn't quite hold in her escaping pubic hair, which grew as thick and wild as kudzu. When Wayne managed to work his eyes up from that and look at her face, he saw she was dark-complected with eyes the color of coffee and lips made to chew on.

Calhoun never made it to the face. He didn't care about faces. He sniffed, said into her crotch, "Nice snatch."

The nun's left hand came around and smacked Calhoun on the side of the head.

He grabbed her wrist, said, "Nice arm, too."

The nun did a magic act with her right hand; it went behind her back and hiked up her outfit and came back with a double-barreled derringer. She pressed it against Calhoun's head.

Wayne bent forward, hoping she wouldn't shoot. At that range the bullet might go through Calhoun's head and hit him too.

"Can't miss," the nun said.

Calhoun smiled. "No you can't," he said, and let go of her arm.

She sat down across from them, smiled, and crossed her legs high. Wayne felt his Levi's snake swell and crawl against the inside of his thigh.

"Honey," Calhoun said, "you're almost worth taking a bullet for."

The nun didn't quit smiling. The bus cranked up. The sand blowers and wipers went to work, and the windshield turned blue, and a white dot moved on it between a series of smaller white dots.

Radar. Wayne had seen that sort of thing on desert vehicles. If he lived through this and got his car back, maybe he'd rig up something like that. And maybe not, he was sick of the desert.

Whatever, at the moment, future plans seemed a little out of place.

Then something else occurred to him. Radar. That meant these bastards had known they were coming and had pulled out in front of them on purpose.

He leaned over the seat and checked where he figured the '57 hit the bus. He didn't see a single dent. Armored, most likely. Most school buses were these days, and that's what this had been. It probably had bullet-proof glass and puncture-proof sand tires too. School buses had gone that way on account of the race riots and the sending of mutated calves to school just like they were humans. And because of the Codgers—old farts who believed kids ought to be fair game to adults for sexual purposes, or for knocking around when they wanted to let off some tension.

"How about unlocking this cuff?" Calhoun said. "It ain't for shit now anyway."

Wayne looked at the nun. "I'm going for the cuff key in my pants. Don't shoot."

Wayne fished it out, unlocked the cuff, and Calhoun let it slide to the floor. Wayne saw the nun was curious and he said, "I'm a bounty hunter. Help me get this man to Law Town and I could see you earn a little something for your troubles."

The woman shook her head.

"That's the spirit," Calhoun said. "I like a nun that minds her own business... You a real nun?"

She nodded.

"Always talk so much?"

Another nod.

Wayne said, "I've never seen a nun like you. Not dressed like that and with a gun."

"We are a small and special order," she said.

"You some kind of Sunday school teacher for these dead folks?"

"Sort of."

"But with them dead, ain't it kind of pointless? They ain't got no souls now, do they?"

"No, but their work adds to the glory of God."

"Their work?" Wayne looked at the dead folks sitting stiffly in their seats. He noted that one of them was about to lose a rotten ear. He sniffed. "They may be adding to the glory of God, but they don't do much for the air."

The nun reached into a pocket on her habit and took out two round objects. She tossed one to Calhoun, and one to Wayne. "Menthol lozenges. They help you stand the smell."

Wayne unwrapped the lozenge and sucked on it. It did help overpower the smell, but the menthol wasn't all that great either. It reminded him of being sick.

"What order are you?" Wayne asked.

"Jesus Loved Mary," the nun said.

"His mama?"

"Mary Magdalene. We think he fucked her. They were lovers. There's evidence in the scriptures. She was a harlot and we have modeled ourselves on her. She gave up that life and became a harlot for Jesus."

"Hate to break it to you, sister," Calhoun said, "but that do-gooder Jesus is as dead as a post. If you're waiting for him to slap the meat to you, that sweet thing of yours is going to dry up and blow away."

"Thanks for the news," the nun said. "But we don't fuck him in person. We fuck him in spirit. We let the spirit enter into men so they may take us in the fashion Jesus took Mary."

"No shit?"

"No shit."

"You know, I think I feel the old boy moving around inside me now. Why don't you shuck them drawers, honey, throw back in that seat there and let ole Calhoun give you a big load of Jesus."

Calhoun shifted in the nun's direction.

She pointed the derringer at him, said, "Stay where you are. If it were so, if you were full of Jesus, I would let you have me in a moment. But you're full of the Devil, not Jesus."

"Shit, sister, give ole Devil a break. He's a fun kind of guy. Let's you and me mount up... Well, be like that. But if you change your mind, I can get religion at a moment's notice. I dearly love to fuck. I've fucked...anything I could get my hands on but a parakeet, and I'd have fucked that little bitch if I could have found the hole."

"I've never known any dead folks to be trained," Wayne said, trying to get the nun talking in a direction that might help, a direction that would let him know what was going on and what sort of trouble he had fallen into.

"As I said, we are a very special order. Brother Lazarus," she waved a hand at the bus driver, and without looking he lifted a hand in acknowledgement, "is the founder. I don't think he'll mind if I tell his story, explain about us, what we do and why. It's important that we spread the word to the heathens."

"Don't call me no fucking heathen," Calhoun said. "This is heathen, riding 'round in a fucking bus with a bunch of stinking dead folks with funny hats on. Hell, they can't even carry a tune."

The nun ignored him. "Brother Lazarus was once known by another name, but that name no longer matters. He was a research scientist, and he was one of those who worked in the laboratory where the germs escaped into the air and made it so the dead could not truly die as long as they had an undamaged brain in their heads.

"Brother Lazarus was carrying a dish of the experiment, the germs, and as a joke, one of the lab assistants pretended to trip him, and he, not knowing it was a joke, dodged the assistant's leg and dropped the dish. In a moment, the air conditioning system had blown the germs throughout the research center. Someone opened a door, and the germs were loose on the world.

"Brother Lazarus was consumed by guilt. Not only because he dropped the dish, but because he helped create it in the first place. He quit his job at the laboratory, took to wandering the country. He came out here with nothing more than basic food, water and books. Among these books was the Bible, and the lost books of the Bible: the Apocrypha and the many cast-out chapters of the New Testament. As he studied, it occurred to him that these cast-out books actually belonged. He was able to interpret their higher meaning, and an angel came to him in a dream and told him of another book, and Brother Lazarus took up his pen and recorded the angel's words, direct from God, and in this book, all the mysteries were explained."

"Like screwing Jesus," Calhoun said.

"Like screwing Jesus, and not being afraid of words that mean sex. Not being afraid of seeing Jesus as both God and man. Seeing that sex, if meant for Christ and the opening of the mind, can be a thrilling and religious experience, not just the rutting of two savage animals.

"Brother Lazarus roamed the desert, the mountains, thinking of the things the Lord had revealed to him, and lo and behold, the Lord revealed yet another thing to him. Brother Lazarus found a great amusement park."

"Didn't know Jesus went in for rides and such," Calhoun said.

"It was long deserted. It had once been part of a place called Disneyland. Brother Lazarus knew of it. There had been several of these Disneylands built about the country, and this one had been in the midst of the Chevy-Cadillac Wars, and had been destroyed and sand had covered most of it."

The nun held out her arms. "And in this rubble, he saw a new beginning."

"Cool off, baby," Calhoun said, "before you have a stroke."

"He gathered to him men and women of a like mind and taught the gospel to them. The Old Testament. The New Testament. The Lost Books. And his own Book of Lazarus, for he had begun to call himself Lazarus. A symbolic name signifying a new beginning, a rising from the dead and coming to life and seeing things as they really are."

The nun moved her hands rapidly, expressively as she talked. Sweat beaded on her forehead and upper lip.

"So he returned to his skills as a scientist, but applied them to a higher purpose—God's purpose. And as Brother Lazarus, he realized the use of the dead. They could be taught to work and build a great monument to the glory of God. And this monument, this coed institution of monks and nuns would be called Jesus Land."

At the word "Jesus," the nun gave her voice an extra trill, and the dead folks, cued, said together, "Eees num be prased."

"How the hell did you train them dead folks?" Calhoun said. "Dog treats?"

"Science put to the use of our lord Jesus Christ, that's how. Brother Lazarus made a special device he could insert directly into the brains of dead folks, through the tops of their heads, and the device controls certain cravings. Makes them passive and responsive—at least to simple commands. With the regulator, as Brother Lazarus calls the device, we have been able to do much positive work with the dead."

"Where do you find these dead folks?" Wayne asked.

"We buy them from the Meat Boys. We save them from amoral purposes."

"They ought to be shot through the head and put in the goddamn ground," Wayne said.

"If our use of the regulator and the dead folks was merely to better ourselves, I would agree. But it is not. We do the Lord's work."

"Do the monks fuck the sisters?" Calhoun asked.

"When possessed by the Spirit of Christ. Yes."

"And I bet they get possessed a lot. Not a bad setup. Dead folks to do the work on the amusement park—"

"It isn't an amusement park now."

"—and plenty of free pussy. Sounds cozy. I like it. Old shithead up there's smarter than he looks."

"There is nothing selfish about our motives or those of Brother Lazarus. In fact, as penance for loosing the germ on the world in the first place, Brother Lazarus injected a virus into his nose. It is rotting slowly."

"Thought that was quite a snorkel he had on him," Wayne said.

"I take it back," Calhoun said. "He *is* as dumb as he looks."

"Why do the dead folks wear those silly hats?" Wayne asked.

"Brother Lazarus found a storeroom of them at the site of the old amusement park. They are mouse ears. They represent some cartoon animal that was popular once and part of Disneyland. Mickey Mouse, he was called. This way we know which dead folks are ours, and which ones are not controlled by our regulators. From time to time, stray dead folks wander into our area. Murder victims. Children abandoned in the desert. People crossing the desert who died of heat or illness. We've had some of the sisters and brothers attacked. The hats are a precaution."

"And what's the deal with us?" Wayne asked.

The nun smiled sweetly. "You, my children, are to add to the glory of God."

"Children?" Calhoun said. "You call an alligator a lizard, bitch?"

The nun slid back in the seat and rested the derringer in her lap. She pulled her legs into a cocked position, causing her panties to crease in the valley of her vagina; it looked like a nice place to visit, that valley.

Wayne turned from the beauty of it and put his head back and closed his eyes, pulled his hat down over them. There was nothing he could do at the moment, and since the nun was watching Calhoun for him, he'd sleep, store up and figure what to do next. If anything.

He drifted off to sleep wondering what the nun meant by, "You, my children, are to add to the glory of God."

He had a feeling that when he found out, he wasn't going to like it.

5

He awoke off and on and saw that the sunlight filtering through the storm had given everything a greenish color. Calhoun, seeing he was awake, said, "Ain't that a pretty color? I had a shirt that color once and liked it lots, but I got in a fight with this Mexican whore with a wooden leg over some money and she tore it. I punched that little bean bandit good."

"Thanks for sharing that," Wayne said, and went back to sleep.

Each time he awoke it was brighter, and finally he awoke to the sun going down and the storm having died out. But he didn't stay awake. He forced himself to close his eyes and store up more energy. To help him nod off he listened to the hum of the motor and thought about the wrecking yard and Pop and all the fun they could have, just drinking beer and playing cards and fucking the border women, and maybe some of those mutated cows they had over there for sale.

Nah. Nix the cows, or any of those genetically altered critters. A man had to draw the line somewhere, and he drew it at fucking critters, even if they had been bred so that they had human traits. You had to have some standards.

'Course, those standards had a way of eroding. He remembered when he said he'd only fuck the pretty ones. His last whore had been downright scary looking. If he didn't watch himself he'd be as bad as Calhoun, trying to find the hole in the parakeet.

He awoke to Calhoun's elbow in his ribs and the nun was standing beside their seat with the derringer. Wayne knew she hadn't slept, but she looked bright-eyed and bushy-tailed. She nodded toward their window, said, "Jesus Land."

She had put that special touch in her voice again, and the dead folks responded with, "Eees num be prased."

It was good and dark now, a crisp night with a big moon the color of hammered brass. The bus sailed across the white sand like a mystical schooner with a full wind in its sails. It went up an impossible hill toward what looked like an aurora borealis, then dove into an atomic rainbow of colors that filled the bus with fairy lights.

When Wayne's eyes became accustomed to the lights, and the bus took a right turn along a precarious curve, he glanced down into the valley. An aerial view couldn't have been any better than the view from his window.

Down there was a universe of polished metal and twisted neon. In the center of the valley was a great statue of Jesus crucified that must have been twenty-five stories high. Most of the body was made of bright metals and multicolored neon; and much of the light was coming from that. There was a crown of barbed wire wound several times around a chromium plate of a forehead and some rust-colored strands of neon hair. The savior's eyes were huge, green strobes that swung left and right with the precision of an oscillating fan. There was an ear-to-ear smile on the savior's face and the teeth were slats of sparkling metal with wide cavity-black gaps between them. The statue was equipped with a massive dick of polished, interwoven cables and coils of neon, the dick was thicker and more solid looking than the arthritic steel-tube legs on either side of it; the head of it was made of an enormous spotlight that pulsed the color of irritation.

The bus went around and around the valley, descending like a dead roach going down a slow drain, and finally the road rolled out straight and took them into Jesus Land.

They passed through the legs of Jesus, under the throbbing head of his cock, toward what looked like a small castle of polished gold bricks with an upright drawbridge inlayed with jewels.

The castle was only one of several tall structures that appeared to be made of rare metals and precious stones: gold, silver, emeralds, rubies, and sapphires. But the closer they got to the buildings, the less fine they looked and the more they looked like what they were: stucco, cardboard, phosphorescent paint, colored spotlights, and bands of neon.

Off to the left Wayne could see a long, open shed full of vehicles, most of them old school buses. And there were unlighted hovels made of tin and tar paper; homes for the dead, perhaps. Behind the shacks and the bus barn rose skeletal shapes that stretched tall and bleak against the sky and the candy-gem lights; shapes that looked like the bony remains of beached whales.

On the right, Wayne glimpsed a building with an open front that served as a stage. In front of the stage were chairs filled with monks and nuns. On the stage, six monks—one behind a drum set, one with a saxophone, the others with guitars—were blasting out a loud, rocking rhythm that made the bus shake. A nun with the front of her habit thrown open, her headpiece discarded, sang into a microphone with a voice like a suffering angel. The voice screeched out of the amplifiers and came in through the windows of the bus, crushing the sound of the engine. The nun crowed "Jesus" so long and hard it sounded like a plea from hell. Then she leapt up and came down doing the splits, the impact driving her back to her feet as if her ass had been loaded with springs.

"Bet that bitch can pick up a quarter with that thing," Calhoun said.

Brother Lazarus touched a button, the pseudo-jeweled drawbridge lowered over a narrow moat, and he drove them inside.

It wasn't as well lighted in there. The walls were bleak and gray. Brother Lazarus stopped the bus and got off, and another monk came on board. He was tall and thin and had crooked buck teeth that dented his bottom lip. He also had a twelve-gauge pump shotgun.

"This is Brother Fred," the nun said. "He'll be your tour guide."

Brother Fred forced Wayne and Calhoun off the bus, away from the dead folks in their mouse-ear hats and the nun in her tight, black panties, jabbed them along a dark corridor, up a swirl of stairs and down a longer corridor with open doors on either side and rooms filled with dark and light and spoiled meat and guts on hooks and skulls and bones lying about like discarded walnut shells and broken sticks; rooms full of dead folks (truly dead) stacked neat as firewood, and rooms full of stone shelves stuffed with beakers of fiery-red and sewer-green and sky-blue and piss-yellow liquids, as well as glass coils through which other colored fluids fled as if chased, smoked as if nervous, and ran into big flasks as if relieved; rooms with platforms and tables and boxes and stools and chairs covered with instruments or dead folks or dead-folk pieces or the asses of monks and nuns as they sat and held charts or tubes or body parts and frowned at them with concentration, lips pursed as if about to explode with some earth-shattering pronouncement; and finally they came to a little room with a tall, glassless window that looked out upon the bright, shiny mess that was Jesus Land.

The room was simple. Table, two chairs, two beds—one on either side of the room. The walls were stone and unadorned. To the right was a little bathroom without a door.

Wayne walked to the window and looked out at Jesus Land pulsing and thumping like a desperate heart. He listened to the music a moment, leaned over and stuck his head outside.

They were high up and there was nothing but a straight drop. If you jumped, you'd wind up with the heels of your boots under your tonsils.

Wayne let out a whistle in appreciation of the drop. Brother Fred thought it was a compliment for Jesus Land. He said, "It's a miracle, isn't it?"

"Miracle?" Calhoun said. "This goony light show? This ain't no miracle. This is for shit. Get that nun on the bus back there to bend over and shit a perfectly round turd through a hoop at twenty paces, and I'll call that a miracle, Mr. Fucked-up Teeth. But this Jesus Land crap is the dumbest fucking idea since dog sweaters.

"And look at this place. You could use some knickknacks or something in here. A picture of some ole naked gal doing a donkey, couple of pigs fucking. Anything. And a door on the shitter would be nice. I hate to be straining out a big one and know someone can look in on me. It ain't decent. A man ought to have his fucking grunts in private. This place reminds me of a motel I stayed at in Waco one night, and I made the goddamn manager give me my money back. The roaches in that shit hole were big enough to use the shower."

Brother Fred listened to all this without blinking an eye, as if seeing Calhoun talk was as amazing as seeing a frog sing. He said, "Sleep tight, don't let the bed bugs bite. Tomorrow you start to work."

"I don't want no fucking job," Calhoun said.

"Goodnight, children," Brother Fred said, and with that he closed the door and they heard it lock, loud and final as the clicking of the drop board on a gallows.

6

At dawn, Wayne got up and took a leak, went to the window to look out. The stage where the monks had played and the nun had jumped was empty. The skeletal shapes he had seen last night were tracks and frames from rides long abandoned. He had a sudden vision of Jesus and his disciples riding a roller coaster, their long hair and robes flapping in the wind.

THE URBAN FANTASY ANTHOLOGY

The large crucified Jesus looked unimpressive without its lights and night's mystery, like a whore in harsh sunlight with makeup gone and wig askew.

"Got any ideas how we're gonna get out of here?" Calhoun asked.

Wayne looked at Calhoun. He was sitting on the bed, pulling on his boots. Wayne shook his head.

"I could use a smoke. You know, I think we ought to work together. Then we can try to kill each other."

Unconsciously, Calhoun touched his ear where Wayne had bitten off the lobe.

"Wouldn't trust you as far as I could kick you," Wayne said.

"I hear that. But I give my word. And my word's something you can count on. I won't twist it."

Wayne studied Calhoun, thought: Well, there wasn't anything to lose. He'd just watch his ass.

"All right," Wayne said. "Give me your word you'll work with me on getting us out of this mess, and when we're good and free, and you say your word has gone far enough, we can settle up."

"Deal," Calhoun said, and offered his hand. Wayne looked at it.

"This seals it," Calhoun said.

Wayne took Calhoun's hand and they shook.

7

Moments later the door unlocked and a smiling monk with hair the color and texture of mold fuzz came in with Brother Fred, who still had his pump shotgun. There were two dead folks with them. A man and a woman. They wore torn clothes and the mouse-ear hats. Neither looked long dead or smelled particularly bad. Actually, the monks smelled worse.

Using the barrel of the shotgun, Brother Fred poked them down the hall to a room with metal tables and medical instruments.

Brother Lazarus was on the far side of one of the tables. He was smiling. His nose looked especially cancerous this morning. A white pustule the size of a thumb tip had taken up residence on the left side of his snout, and it looked like a pearl onion in a turd.

Nearby stood a nun. She was short with good, if skinny, legs, and she wore the same outfit as the nun on the bus. It looked more girlish on her, perhaps because she was thin and small-breasted. She had a nice face, and eyes that were all pupil. Wisps of blond hair crawled out around the edges of her headgear. She looked pale and weak, as if wearied to the bone. There was a birthmark on her right cheek that looked like a distant view of a small bird in flight.

"Good morning," Brother Lazarus said. "I hope you gentlemen slept well."

"What's this about work?" Wayne said.

"Work?" Brother Lazarus said.

"I described it to them that way," Brother Fred said. "Perhaps an impulsive description."

"I'll say," Brother Lazarus said. "No work here, gentlemen. You have my word on that. We do all the work. Lie on these tables and we'll take a sampling of your blood."

"Why?" Wayne said.

"Science," Brother Lazarus said. "I intend to find a cure for this germ that makes the dead come back to life, and to do that, I need living human beings to study. Sounds kind of mad scientist, doesn't it? But I assure you, you've nothing to lose but a few drops of blood. Well, maybe more than a few drops, but nothing serious."

"Use your own goddamn blood," Calhoun said.

"We do. But we're always looking for fresh specimens. Little here, little there. And if you don't do it, we'll kill you."

Calhoun spun and hit Brother Fred on the nose. It was a solid punch and Brother Fred hit the floor on his butt, but he hung onto the shotgun and pointed it up at Calhoun. "Go on," he said, his nose streaming blood. "Try that again."

Wayne flexed to help, but hesitated. He could kick Brother Fred in the head from where he was, but that might not keep him from shooting Calhoun, and there would go the extra reward money. And besides, he'd given his word to the bastard that they'd try to help each other survive until they got out of this.

The other monk clasped his hands and swung them into the side of Calhoun's head, knocking him down. Brother Fred got up, and while Calhoun was trying to rise, he hit him with the stock of the shotgun in the back of the head, hit him so hard it drove Calhoun's forehead into the floor. Calhoun rolled over on his side and lay there, his eyes fluttering like moth wings.

"Brother Fred, you must learn to turn the other cheek," Brother Lazarus said. "Now put this sack of shit on the table."

Brother Fred checked Wayne to see if he looked like trouble. Wayne put his hands in his pockets and smiled.

Brother Fred called the two dead folks over and had them put Calhoun on the table. Brother Lazarus strapped him down.

The nun brought a tray of needles, syringes, cotton and bottles over, put it down on the table next to Calhoun's head. Brother Lazarus rolled up Calhoun's sleeve and fixed up a needle and stuck it in Calhoun's arm, drew it full of blood. He stuck the needle through the rubber top of one of the bottles and shot the blood into that.

He looked at Wayne and said, "I hope you'll be less trouble."

"Do I get some orange juice and a little cracker afterwards?" Wayne said.

"You get to walk out without a knot on your head," Brother Lazarus said.

"Guess that'll have to do."

Wayne got on the table next to Calhoun and Brother Lazarus strapped him down. The nun brought the tray over and Brother Lazarus did to him what he had done to Calhoun. The nun stood over Wayne and looked down at his face. Wayne tried to read something in her features but couldn't find a clue.

When Brother Lazarus was finished he took hold of Wayne's chin and shook it. "My, but you two boys look healthy. But you can never be sure. We'll have to run the blood through some tests. Meantime, Sister Worth will run a few additional tests on you, and," he nodded at the unconscious Calhoun, "I'll see to your friend here."

"He's no friend of mine," Wayne said.

They took Wayne off the table, and Sister Worth and Brother Fred, and his shotgun, directed him down the hall into another room.

The room was lined with shelves that were lined with instruments and bottles. The lighting was poor, most of it coming through a slatted window, though there was an anemic yellow bulb overhead. Dust motes swam in the air.

In the center of the room on its rim was a great, spoked wheel. It had two straps well spaced at the top, and two more at the bottom. Beneath the bottom straps were blocks of wood. The wheel was attached in back to an upright metal bar that had switches and buttons all over it.

Brother Fred made Wayne strip and get on the wheel with his back to the hub and his feet on the blocks. Sister Worth strapped his ankles down tight, then he was made to put his hands up, and she strapped his wrists to the upper part of the wheel.

"I hope this hurts a lot," Brother Fred said.

"Wipe the blood off your face," Wayne said. "It makes you look silly."

Brother Fred made a gesture with his middle finger that wasn't religious and left the room.

8

Sister Worth touched a switch and the wheel began to spin, slowly at first, and the bad light came through the windows and poked through the rungs and the dust swam before his eyes and the wheel and its spokes threw twisting shadows on the wall.

As he went around, Wayne closed his eyes. It kept him from feeling so dizzy, especially on the down swings.

On a turn up, he opened his eyes and caught sight of Sister Worth standing in front of the wheel staring at him. He said, "Why?" and closed his eyes as the wheel dipped.

"Because Brother Lazarus says so," came the answer after such a long time Wayne had almost forgotten the question. Actually, he hadn't expected a response. He was surprised that such a thing had come out of his mouth, and he felt a little diminished for having asked.

He opened his eyes on another swing up, and she was moving behind the wheel, out of his line of vision. He heard a snick like a switch being flipped and lightning jumped through him and he screamed in spite of himself. A little fork of electricity licked out of his mouth like a reptile tongue tasting air.

Faster spun the wheel and the jolts came more often and he screamed less loud, and finally not at all. He was too numb. He was adrift in space wearing only his cowboy hat and boots, moving away from earth very fast. Floating all around him were wrecked cars. He looked and saw that one of them was his '57, and behind the steering wheel was Pop. Sitting beside the old man was a Mexican. Two more were in the back seat. They looked a little drunk.

One of the whores in back pulled up her dress and cocked it high up so he could see her pussy. It looked like that needed a shave.

He smiled and tried to go for it, but the '57 was moving away, swinging wide and turning its tail to him. He could see a face at the back window. Pop's face. He had crawled back there and was waving slowly and sadly. A whore pulled Pop from view.

The wrecked cars moved away too, as if caught in the vacuum of the '57's retreat. Wayne swam with his arms, kicked with his legs, trying to pursue the '57 and the wrecks. But he dangled where he was, like a moth pinned to a board. The cars moved out of sight and left him there with his arms and legs stretched out, spinning amidst an infinity of cold, uncaring stars.

"...how the tests are run...marks everything about you...charts it...EKG, brain waves, liver...everything...it hurts because Brother Lazarus wants it to...thinks I don't know these things...that I'm slow...slow, not stupid...smart really...used to be scientist...before the accident...Brother Lazarus is not holy...he's mad...made the wheel because of the Holy Inquisition...knows a lot about the Inquisition... thinks we need it again...for the likes of men you...the unholy, he says... But he just likes to hurt...I know."

Wayne opened his eyes. The wheel had stopped. Sister Worth was talking in her monotone, explaining the wheel. He remembered asking her, "Why" about three thousand years ago.

Sister Worth was staring at him again. She went away and he expected the wheel to start up, but when she returned, she had a long, narrow mirror under her arm. She put it against the wall across from him. She got on the wheel with him, her little feet on the wooden platforms beside his. She hiked up the bottom of her habit and pulled down her black panties. She put her face close to his, as if searching for something.

"He plans to take your body...piece by piece...blood, cells, brain, your cock... all of it... He wants to live forever."

She had her panties in her hand, and she tossed them. Wayne watched them fly up and flutter to the floor like a dying bat.

She took hold of his dick and pulled on it. Her palm was cold and he didn't feel his best, but he began to get hard. She put him between her legs and rubbed his dick between her thighs. They were as cold as her hands, and dry.

"I know him now...know what he's doing...the dead germ virus...he was trying to make something that would make him live forever...it made the dead come back...didn't keep the living alive, free of old age..."

His dick was throbbing now, in spite of the coolness of her body.

"He cuts up dead folks to learn...experiments on them...but the secret of eternal life is with the living...that's why he wants you...you're an outsider...those who live here he can...test...but he must keep them alive to do his bidding...not let them know how he really is...needs your insides and the other man's...he wants to be a God...flies high above us in a little plane and looks down... Likes to think he is the creator, I bet..."

"Plane?"

"Ultralight."

She pushed his cock inside her, and it was cold and dry in there, like liver left overnight on a drainboard. Still, he found himself ready. At this point, he would have gouged a hole in a turnip.

She kissed him on the ear and alongside the neck; cold little kisses, dry as toast.

"...thinks I don't know... But I know he doesn't love Jesus... He loves himself, and power... He's sad about his nose..."

"I bet."

"Did it in a moment of religious fervor...before he lost the belief... Now he wants to be what he was... A scientist. He wants to grow a new nose...know how...saw him grow a finger in a dish once...grew it from the skin off a knuckle of one of the brothers... He can do all kinds of things."

She was moving her hips now. He could see over her shoulder into the mirror against the wall. Could see her white ass rolling, the black habit hiked up above it, threatening to drop like a curtain. He began to thrust back, slowly, firmly.

She looked over her shoulder into the mirror, watching herself fuck him. There was a look more of study than rapture on her face.

"Want to feel alive," she said. "Feel a good, hard dick... Been too long."

"I'm doing the best I can," Wayne said. "This ain't the most romantic of spots."

"Push so I can feel it."

"Nice," Wayne said. He gave it everything he had. He was beginning to lose his erection. He felt as if he were auditioning for a job and not making the best of impressions. He felt like a knothole would be dissatisfied with him.

She got off of him and climbed down.

"Don't blame you," he said.

She went behind the wheel and touched some things on the upright. She mounted him again, hooked her ankles behind his. The wheel began to turn. Short electrical shocks leaped through him. They weren't as powerful as before. They were invigorating. When he kissed her it was like touching his tongue to a battery. It felt as if electricity was racing through his veins and flying out the head of his dick; he felt as if he might fill her with lightning instead of come.

The wheel creaked to a stop; it must have had a timer on it. They were upside down and Wayne could see their reflection in the mirror; they looked like two lizards fucking on a window pane.

He couldn't tell if she had finished or not, so he went ahead and got it over with. Without the electricity he was losing his desire. It hadn't been an A-one piece of ass, but hell, as Pop always said, "Worse pussy I ever had was good."

"They'll be coming back," she said. "Soon... Don't want them to find us like this...Other tests to do yet."

"Why did you do this?"

"I want out of the order... Want out of this desert... I want to live... And I want you to help me."

"I'm game, but the blood is rushing to my head and I'm getting dizzy. Maybe you ought to get off me."

After an eon she said, "I have a plan."

She untwined from him and went behind the wheel and hit a switch that turned Wayne upright. She touched another switch and he began to spin slowly, and while he spun and while lightning played inside him, she told him her plan.

9

"I think ole Brother Fred wants to fuck me," Calhoun said. "He keeps trying to get his finger up my asshole."

They were back in their room. Brother Fred had brought them back, making them carry their clothes, and now they were alone again, dressing.

"We're getting out of here," Wayne said. "The nun, Sister Worth, she's going to help."

"What's her angle?"

"She hates this place and wants my dick. Mostly, she hates this place."

"What's the plan?"

Wayne told him first what Brother Lazarus had planned. On the morrow he would have them brought to the room with the steel tables, and they would go on the tables, and if the tests had turned out good, they would be pronounced fit as fiddles and Brother Lazarus would strip the skin from their bodies, slowly, because according to Sister Worth he liked to do it that way, and he would drain their blood and percolate it into his formulas like coffee, cut their brains out and put them in vats and store their veins and organs in freezers.

All of this would be done in the name of God and Jesus Christ (Eees num be prased) under the guise of finding a cure for the dead folks germ. But it would all instead be for Brother Lazarus who wanted to have a new nose, fly his ultralight above Jesus Land, and live forever.

Sister Worth's plan was this:

She would be in the dissecting room. She would have guns hidden. She would make the first move, a distraction, then it was up to them.

"This time," Wayne said, "one of us has to get on top of that shotgun."

"You had your finger up your ass in there today, or we'd have had them."

"We're going to have surprise on our side this time. Real surprise. They won't be expecting Sister Worth. We can get up there on the roof and take off in that ultralight. When it runs out of gas we can walk, maybe get back to the '57 and hope it runs."

"We'll settle our score then. Whoever wins keeps the car and the split tail. As for tomorrow, I've got a little ace."

Calhoun pulled on his boots. He twisted the heel of one of them. It swung out and a little knife dropped into his hand. "It's sharp," Calhoun said. "I cut a Chinaman from gut to gill with it. It was easy as sliding a stick through fresh shit."

"Been nice if you'd had that ready today."

"I wanted to scout things out first. And to tell the truth, I thought one pop to Brother Fred's mouth and he'd be out of the picture."

"You hit him in the nose."

"Yeah, goddamn it, but I was aiming for his mouth."

10

Dawn and the room with the metal tables looked the same. No one had brought in a vase of flowers to brighten the place.

THE URBAN FANTASY ANTHOLOGY

Brother Lazarus's nose had changed however; there were two pearl onions nestled in it now.

Sister Worth, looking only a little more animated than yesterday, stood nearby. She was holding the tray with the instruments. This time the tray was full of scalpels. The light caught their edges and made them wink.

Brother Fred was standing behind Calhoun, and Brother Mold Fuzz was behind Wayne. They must have felt pretty confident today. They had dispensed with the dead folks.

Wayne looked at Sister Worth and thought maybe things were not good. Maybe she had lied to him in her slow talking way. Only wanted a little dick and wanted to keep it quiet. To do that, she might have promised anything. She might not care what Brother Lazarus did to them.

If it looked like a double cross, Wayne was going to go for it. If he had to jump right into the mouth of Brother Fred's shotgun. That was a better way to go than having the hide peeled from your body. The idea of Brother Lazarus and his ugly nose leaning over him did not appeal at all.

"It's so nice to see you," Brother Lazarus said. "I hope we'll have none of the unpleasantness of yesterday. Now, on the tables."

Wayne looked at Sister Worth. Her expression showed nothing. The only thing about her that looked alive was the bent wings of the bird birthmark on her cheek.

All right, Wayne thought, I'll go as far as the table, then I'm going to do something. Even if it's wrong.

He took a step forward, and Sister Worth flipped the contents of the tray into Brother Lazarus's face. A scalpel went into his nose and hung there. The tray and the rest of its contents hit the floor.

Before Brother Lazarus could yelp, Calhoun dropped and wheeled. He was under Brother Fred's shotgun and he used his forearm to drive the barrel upwards. The gun went off and peppered the ceiling. Plaster sprinkled down.

Calhoun had concealed the little knife in the palm of his hand and he brought it up and into Brother Fred's groin. The blade went through the robe and buried to the hilt.

The instant Calhoun made his move, Wayne brought his forearm back and around into Brother Mold Fuzz's throat, then turned and caught his head and jerked that down and kneed him a couple of times. He floored him by driving an elbow into the back of his neck.

Calhoun had the shotgun now, and Brother Fred was on the floor trying to pull the knife out of his balls. Calhoun blew Brother Fred's head off, then did the same for Brother Mold Fuzz.

Brother Lazarus, the scalpel hanging from his nose, tried to run for it, but he stepped on the tray and that sent him flying. He landed on his stomach. Calhoun took two deep steps and kicked him in the throat. Brother Lazarus made a sound like he was gargling and tried to get up.

Wayne helped him. He grabbed Brother Lazarus by the back of his robe and pulled him up, slammed him back against a table. The scalpel still dangled from the monk's nose. Wayne grabbed it and jerked, taking away a chunk of nose as he did. Brother Lazarus screamed.

Calhoun put the shotgun in Brother Lazarus's mouth and that made him stop screaming. Calhoun pumped the shotgun. He said, "Eat it," and pulled the trigger. Brother Lazarus's brains went out the back of his head riding on a chunk of skull. The brains and skull hit the table and sailed onto the floor like a plate of scrambled eggs pushed the length of a cafe counter.

Sister Worth had not moved. Wayne figured she had used all of her concentration to hit Brother Lazarus with the tray.

"You said you'd have guns," Wayne said to her.

She turned her back to him and lifted her habit. In a belt above her panties were two .38 revolvers. Wayne pulled them out and held one in each hand. "Two-Gun Wayne," he said.

"What about the ultralight?" Calhoun said. "We've made enough noise for a prison riot. We need to move."

Sister Worth turned to the door at the back of the room, and before she could say anything or lead, Wayne and Calhoun snapped to it and grabbed her and pushed her toward it.

There were stairs on the other side of the door and they took them two at a time. They went through a trap door and onto the roof and there, tied down with bungee straps to metal hoops, was the ultralight. It was blue-and-white canvas and metal rods, and strapped to either side of it was a twelve gauge pump and a bag of food and a canteen of water.

They unsnapped the roof straps and got in the two-seater and used the straps to fasten Sister Worth between them. It wasn't comfortable, but it was a ride.

They sat there. After a moment, Calhoun said, "Well?"

"Shit," Wayne said. "I can't fly this thing."

They looked at Sister Worth. She was staring at the controls.

"Say something, damn it," Wayne said.

"That's the switch," she said. "That stick...forward is up, back brings the nose down...side to side..."

"Got it."

"Well, shoot this bastard over the side," Calhoun said. Wayne cranked it, gave it the throttle. The machine rolled forward, wobbled.

"Too much weight," Wayne said.

"Throw the cunt over the side," Calhoun said.

"It's all or nothing," Wayne said. The ultralight continued to swing its tail left and right, but leveled off as they went over the edge.

They sailed for a hundred yards, made a mean curve Wayne couldn't fight, and fell straight away into the statue of Jesus, striking it in the head, right in the midst of the barbed wire crown. Spot lights shattered, metal groaned, the wire tangled in the nylon wings of the craft and held it. The head of Jesus nodded forward, popped off, and shot out on the electric cables inside like a jack-in-the-box. The cables pulled tight a hundred feet from the ground and worked the head and the craft like a yo-yo. Then the barbed wire crown unraveled and dropped the craft the rest of the way. It hit the ground with a crunch and a rip and a cloud of dust.

The head of Jesus bobbed above the shattered ultralight like a bird preparing to peck a worm.

11

Wayne crawled out of the wreckage and tried his legs. They worked.

Calhoun was on his feet cussing, unstrapping the shotguns and supplies.

Sister Worth lay in the midst of the wreck, the nylon and aluminum supports folded around her like butterfly wings.

Wayne started pulling the mess off of her. He saw that her leg was broken. A bone punched out of her thigh like a sharpened stick. There was no blood.

"Here comes the church social," Calhoun said.

The word was out about Brother Lazarus and the others. A horde of monks, nuns and dead folks were rushing over the drawbridge. Some of the nuns and monks had guns. All of the dead folks had clubs. The clergy was yelling.

Wayne nodded toward the bus barn, "Let's get a bus." Wayne picked up Sister Worth, cradled her in his arms, and made a run for it. Calhoun, carrying the guns and the supplies, passed them. He jumped through the open doorway of a bus and dropped out of sight. Wayne knew he was jerking wires loose, trying to hotwire them a ride. Wayne hoped he was good at it and fast.

When Wayne got to the bus, he laid Sister Worth down beside it and pulled the .38s and stood in front of her. If he was going down he wanted to go like Wild Bill Hickok: A blazing gun in either fist and a woman to protect.

Actually, he'd prefer the bus to start.

It did.

Calhoun jerked it in gear, backed it out and around in front of Wayne and Sister Worth. The monks and nuns had started firing and their rounds bounced off the side of the armored bus.

From inside Calhoun yelled, "Get the hell on."

Wayne stuck the guns in his belt, grabbed up Sister Worth and leapt inside. Calhoun jerked the bus forward and Wayne and Sister Worth went flying over a seat and into another.

"I thought you were leaving," Wayne said.

"I wanted to. But I gave my word."

Wayne stretched Sister Worth out on the seat and looked at her leg. After that tossing Calhoun had given them, the break was sticking out even more.

Calhoun closed the bus door and checked his wing-mirror. Nuns and monks and dead folks had piled into a couple of buses, and now the buses were pursuing them. One of them moved very fast, as if souped up.

"I probably got the granny of the bunch," Calhoun said. They climbed over a ridge of sand, then they were on the narrow road that wound itself upwards. Behind them, one of the buses had fallen back, maybe some kind of mechanical trouble. The other was gaining.

The road widened and Calhoun yelled, "I think this is what the fucker's been waiting for."

Even as Calhoun spoke, their pursuer put on a burst of speed and swung left and came up beside them, tried to swerve over and push them off the road, down into the deepening valley. But Calhoun fought the curves and didn't budge.

The other bus swung its door open and a nun, the very one who had been on the bus that brought them to Jesus Land, stood there with her legs spread wide, showing the black-pantied mound of her crotch. She had one arm bent around a seat post and was holding in both hands the ever-popular clergy tool, the twelve-gauge pump.

As they made a curve, the nun fired a round into the window next to Calhoun. The window made a cracking noise and thin, crooked lines spread in all directions, but the glass held.

She pumped a round into the chamber and fired again. Bullet proof or not, this time the front sheet of glass fell away. Another well-placed round and the rest of the glass would go and Calhoun could wave his head goodbye.

Wayne put his knees in a seat and got the window down. The nun saw him, whirled and fired. The shot was low and hit the bottom part of the window and starred it and pelleted the chassis.

Wayne stuck a .38 out of the window and fired as the nun was jacking another load into position. His shot hit her in the head and her right eye went big and wet, and she swung around on the pole and lost the shotgun. It went out the door. She clung there by the bend of her elbow for a moment, then her arm straightened and she fell outside. The bus ran over her and she popped red and juicy at both ends like a stomped jelly roll.

"Waste of good pussy," Calhoun said. He edged into the other bus, and it pushed back. But Calhoun pushed harder and made it hit the wall with a screech like a panther.

The bus came back and shoved Calhoun to the side of the cliff and honked twice for Jesus.

Calhoun down-shifted, let off the gas, allowed the other bus to soar past by half a length. Then he jerked the wheel so that he caught the rear of it and knocked it across the road. He speared it in the side with the nose of his bus and the other started to spin. It clipped the front of Calhoun's bus and peeled the bumper back. Calhoun braked and the other bus kept spinning. It spun off the road and down into the valley amidst a chorus of cries.

Thirty minutes later they reached the top of the canyon and were in the desert. The bus began to throw up smoke from the front and make a noise like a dog strangling on a chicken bone. Calhoun pulled over.

12

"Goddamn bumper got twisted under there and it's shredded the tire some," Calhoun said. "I think if we can peel the bumper off, there's enough of that tire to run on."

Wayne and Calhoun got hold of the bumper and pulled but it wouldn't come off. Not completely. Part of it had been creased, and that part finally gave way and broke off from the rest of it.

"That ought to be enough to keep from rubbing the tire," Calhoun said.

Sister Worth called from inside the bus. Wayne went to check on her. "Take me off the bus," she said. "...I want to feel free air and sun."

"There doesn't feel like there's any air out there," Wayne said. "And the sun feels just like it always does. Hot."

"Please."

He picked her up and carried her outside and found a ridge of sand and laid her down so her head was propped against it.

"I...I need batteries," she said.

"Say what?" Wayne said.

She lay looking straight into the sun. "Brother Lazarus's greatest work...a dead folk that can think...has memory of the past...Was a scientist too..." Her hand came up in stages, finally got hold of her head gear and pushed it off.

Gleaming from the center of her tangled blond hair was a silver knob.

"He...was not a good man... I am a good woman. I want to feel alive...like before...batteries going...brought others."

Her hand fumbled at a snap pocket on her habit. Wayne opened it for her and got out what was inside. Four batteries.

"Uses two...simple."

Calhoun was standing over them now. "That explains some things," he said.

"Don't look at me like that..." Sister Worth said, and Wayne realized he had never told her his name and she had never asked. "Unscrew...put the batteries in... Without them I'll be an eater... Can't wait too long."

"All right," Wayne said. He went behind her and propped her up on the sand drift and unscrewed the metal shaft from her skull. He thought about when she had fucked him on the wheel and how desperate she had been to feel something, and how she had been cold as flint and lustless. He remembered how she had looked in the mirror hoping to see something that wasn't there.

He dropped the batteries in the sand and took out one of the revolvers and put it close to the back of her head and pulled the trigger. Her body jerked slightly and fell over, her face turning toward him.

The bullet had come out where the bird had been on her cheek and had taken it completely away, leaving a bloodless hole.

"Best thing," Calhoun said. "There's enough live pussy in the world without you pulling this broken-legged dead thing around after you on a board."

"Shut up," Wayne said.

"When a man gets sentimental over women and kids, he can count himself out."

Wayne stood up.

"Well boy," Calhoun said. "I reckon it's time."

"Reckon so," Wayne said.

"How about we do this with some class? Give me one of your pistols and we'll get back-to-back and I'll count to ten, and when I get there, we'll turn and shoot."

Wayne gave Calhoun one of the pistols. Calhoun checked the chambers, said, "I've got four loads."

Wayne took two out of his pistol and tossed them on the ground. "Even Steven," he said.

They got back-to-back and held the guns by their legs.

"Guess if you kill me you'll take me in," Calhoun said. "So that means you'll put a bullet through my head if I need it. I don't want to come back as one of the dead folks. Got your word on that?"

"Yep."

"I'll do the same for you. Give my word. You know that's worth something."

"We gonna shoot or talk?"

"You know, boy, under different circumstances, I could have liked you. We might have been friends."

"Not likely."

Calhoun started counting, and they started stepping. When he got to ten, they turned.

Calhoun's pistol barked first, and Wayne felt the bullet punch him low in the right side of his chest, spinning him slightly. He lifted his revolver and took his time and shot just as Calhoun fired again.

Calhoun's second bullet whizzed by Wayne's head. Wayne's shot hit Calhoun in the stomach.

Calhoun went to his knees and had trouble drawing a breath. He tried to lift his revolver but couldn't; it was as if it had turned into an anvil.

Wayne shot him again. Hitting him in the middle of the chest this time and knocking him back so that his legs were curled beneath him.

Wayne walked over to Calhoun, dropped to one knee and took the revolver from him.

"Shit," Calhoun said. "I wouldn't have thought that for nothing. You hit?"

"Scratched."

"Shit."

Wayne put the revolver to Calhoun's forehead and Calhoun closed his eyes and Wayne pulled the trigger.

13

The wound wasn't a scratch. Wayne knew he should leave Sister Worth where she was and load Calhoun on the bus and haul him in for bounty. But he didn't care about the bounty anymore.

He used the ragged piece of bumper to dig them a shallow side-by-side grave. When he finished, he stuck the fender fragment up between them and used the sight of one of the revolvers to scratch into it: HERE LIES SISTER WORTH AND CALHOUN WHO KEPT HIS WORD.

You couldn't really read it good and he knew the first real wind would keel it over, but it made him feel better about something, even if he couldn't put his finger on it.

His wound had opened up and the sun was very hot now, and since he had lost his hat he could feel his brain cooking in his skull like meat boiling in a pot.

He got on the bus, started it and drove through the day and the night and it was near morning when he came to the Cadillacs and turned down between them and drove until he came to the '57.

When he stopped and tried to get off the bus, he found he could hardly move. The revolvers in his belt were stuck to his shirt and stomach because of the blood from his wound.

He pulled himself up with the steering wheel, got one of the shotguns and used it for a crutch. He got the food and water and went out to inspect the '57.

It was for shit. It had not only lost its windshield, the front end was mashed way back and one of the big sand tires was twisted at such an angle he knew the axle was shot.

He leaned against the Chevy and tried to think. The bus was okay and there was still some gas in it, and he could get the hose out of the trunk of the '57 and siphon gas out of its tanks and put it in the bus. That would give him a few miles.

Miles.

He didn't feel as if he could walk twenty feet, let alone concentrate on driving.

He let go of the shotgun, the food and water. He scooted onto the hood of the Chevy and managed himself to the roof. He lay there on his back and looked at the sky.

It was a clear night and the stars were sharp with no fuzz around them. He felt cold. In a couple of hours the stars would fade and the sun would come up and the cool would give way to heat.

He turned his head and looked at one of the Cadillacs and a skeleton face pressed to its windshield, forever looking down at the sand.

That was no way to end, looking down.

He crossed his legs and stretched out his arms and studied the sky. It didn't feel so cold now, and the pain had almost stopped. He was more numb than anything else.

He pulled one of the revolvers and cocked it and put it to his temple and continued to look at the stars. Then he closed his eyes and found that he could still see them. He was once again hanging in the void between the stars wearing only his hat and cowboy boots, and floating about him were the junk cars and the '57, undamaged.

The cars were moving toward him this time, not away. The '57 was in the lead, and as it grew closer he saw Pop behind the wheel and beside him was a Mexican puta, and in the back, two more. They were all smiling and Pop honked the horn and waved.

The '57 came alongside him and the back door opened.

Sitting between the whores was Sister Worth. She had not been there a moment ago, but now she was. And he had never noticed how big the back seat of the '57 was.

Sister Worth smiled at him and the bird on her cheek lifted higher. Her hair was combed out long and straight and she looked pink-skinned and happy. On the floorboard at her feet was a chest of iced-beer. Lone Star, by God.

Pop was leaning over the front seat, holding out his hand and Sister Worth and the whores were beckoning him inside.

Wayne worked his hands and feet, found this time that he could move. He swam through the open door, touched Pop's hand, and Pop said, "It's good to see you, son," and at the moment Wayne pulled the trigger, Pop pulled him inside.

The Bible Repairman
Tim Powers

> "It'll do to kiss the book on still, won't it?" growled Dick, who was
> evidently uneasy at the curse he had brought on himself.
>
> "A Bible with a bit cut out!" returned Silver derisively. "Not it. It
> don't bind no more'n a ballad-book."
>
> "Don't it, though?" cried Dick, with a sort of joy. "Well I reckon
> that's worth having, too."
>
> —*Treasure Island*, by Robert Louis Stevenson

Across the highway was old Humberto, a dark spot against the tan field between the railroad tracks and the freeway fence, pushing a stripped-down shopping cart along the cracked sidewalk. His shadow still stretched halfway to the center-divider line in the early morning sunlight, but he was apparently already very drunk, and he was using the shopping cart as a walker, bracing his weight on it as he shuffled along. Probably he never slept at all, not that he was ever really awake either.

Humberto had done a lot of work in his time, and the people he talked and gestured to were, at best, long gone and probably existed now only in his cannibalized memory—but this morning as Torrez watched him the old man clearly looked across the street straight at Torrez and waved. He was just a silhouette against the bright eastern daylight—his camouflage pants, white beard and Daniel Boone coonskin cap were all one raggedly backlit outline—but he might have been smiling too.

After a moment's hesitation Torrez waved and nodded. Torrez was not drunk in the morning, nor unable to walk without leaning on something, nor surrounded by imaginary acquaintances, and he meant to sustain those differences between them—but he supposed that he and Humberto were brothers in the trades, and he should show some respect to a player who simply had not known when to retire.

Torrez pocketed his Camels and his change and turned his back on the old man, and trudged across the parking lot toward the path that led across a weedy field to home.

He was retired, at least from the big-stakes dives. Nowadays he just waded a little ways out—he worked on cars and Bibles and second-hand eyeglasses and clothes people bought at thrift stores, and half of that work was just convincing the customers that work had been done. He always had to use holy water—*real* holy water, from gallon jugs he filled from the silver urn at St. Anne's—but though it impressed the customers, all he could see that it actually did was get stuff wet. Still, it was better to err on the side of thoroughness.

His garage door was open, and several goats stood up with their hoofs on the fence rail of the lot next door. Torrez paused to pull up some of the tall, furry, sage-like weeds that sprang up in every stretch of unattended dirt in the county, and he held them out and let the goats chew them up. Sometimes when customers arrived at times like this, Torrez would whisper to the goats and then pause and nod.

Torrez's Toyota stood at the curb because a white Dodge Dart was parked in the driveway. Torrez had already installed a "pain button" on the Dodge's dashboard, so that when the car wouldn't start, the owner could give the car a couple of jabs—*Oh yeah? How do you like this, eh?* On the other side of the firewall the button was connected to a wire that was screwed to the carburetor housing; nonsense, but the stuff had to look convincing.

Torrez had also used a can of Staples compressed air and a couple of magnets to try to draw a babbling ghost out of the car's stereo system, and this had not been nonsense—if he had properly opposed the magnets to the magnets in the speakers, and got the Bernoulli effect with the compressed air sprayed over the speaker diaphragm, then at speeds over forty there would no longer be a droning imbecile monologue faintly going on behind whatever music was playing. Torrez would take the Dodge out onto the freeway today, assuming the old car would get up to freeway speeds, and try it out driving north, east, south and west. Two hundred dollars if the voice was gone, and a hundred in any case for the pain button.

And he had a couple of Bibles in need of customized repair, and those were an easy fifty dollars apiece—just brace the page against a piece of plywood in a frame and scorch out the verses the customers found intolerable, with a wood-burning stylus; a plain old razor wouldn't have the authority that hot iron did. And then of course drench the defaced book in holy water to validate the edited text. Matthew 19:5-6 and Mark 10:7-12 were bits he was often asked to burn out, since they condemned re-marriage after divorce, but he also got a lot of requests to lose Matthew 25:41 through 46, with Jesus's promise of Hell to stingy people. And he offered a special deal to eradicate all thirty or so mentions of adultery. Some of these customized Bibles ended up after a few years with hardly any weight besides the binding.

He pushed open the front door of the house—he never locked it—and made his way to the kitchen to get a beer out of the cold spot in the sink. The light was blinking on the telephone answering machine, and when he had popped the can of Budweiser he pushed the play button.

"Give Mr. Torrez this message," said a recorded voice. "Write down the number I give you! It is important, make sure he gets it!" The voice recited a number then, and Torrez wrote it down. His answering machine had come with a pre-recorded message on it in a woman's voice—*No one is available to take your call right now*—and many callers assumed the voice was that of a woman he was living with. Apparently she sounded unreliable, for they often insisted several times that she convey their messages to him.

He punched in the number, and a few moments later a man at the other end of the line was saying to him, "Mr. Torrez? We need your help, like you helped out the Fotas four years ago. Our daughter was stolen, and now we've got a ransom note—she was in a coffee pot with roses tied around it—"

"I don't do that work anymore," Torrez interrupted, "I'm sorry. Mr. Seaweed in Corona still does—he's younger—I could give you his number."

"I called him already a week ago, but then I heard you were back in business. You're better than Seaweed—"

Poor old Humberto had kept on doing deep dives. Torrez had done them longer than he should have, and nowadays couldn't understand a lot of the books he had loved when he'd been younger.

"I'm not back in that business," he said. "I'm very sorry." He hung up the phone.

He had not even done the ransom negotiations when it had been his own daughter that had been stolen, three years ago—and his wife had left him over

THE BIBLE REPAIRMAN

it, not understanding that she would probably have had to be changing her mentally retarded husband's diapers forever afterward if he had done it.

Torrez's daughter Amelia had died at the age of eight, of a fever. Her grave was in the dirt lot behind the Catholic cemetery, and on most Sundays Torrez and his wife had visited the grave and made sure there were lots of little stuffed animals and silver foil pinwheels arranged on the dirt, and for a marker they had set into the ground a black plastic box with a clear top, with her death-certificate displayed in it to show that she had died in a hospital. And her soul had surely gone to Heaven, but they had caught her ghost to keep it from wandering in the noisy, cold half-world, and Torrez had bound it into one of Amelia's cloth dolls. Every Sunday night they had put candy and cigarettes and a shot-glass of rum in front of the doll—hardly appropriate fare for a little girl, but ghosts were somehow all the same age. Torrez had always lit the cigarettes and stubbed them out before laying them in front of the doll, and bitten the candies: ghosts needed somebody to have *started* such things for them.

And then one day the house had been broken into, and the little shrine and the doll were gone, replaced with a ransom note: *If you want your daughter's ghost back, Mr. Torrez, give me some of your blood.* And there had been a phone number.

Usually these ransom notes asked the recipient to get a specific tattoo that corresponded to a tattoo on the kidnapper's body—and afterward whichever family member complied would have lost a lot of memories, and be unable to feel affection, and never again dream at night. The kidnapper would have taken those things. But a kidnapper would always settle instead for the blood of a person whose soul was broken in the way that Torrez's was, and so the robbed families would often come to Torrez and offer him a lot of money to step in and give up some of his blood, and save them the fearful obligation of the vampiric tattoo.

Sometimes the kidnapper was the divorced father or mother of the ghost—courts never considered custody of a dead child—or a suitor who had been rejected long before, and in these cases there would be no ransom demand; but then it had sometimes been possible for Torrez to trace the thief and steal the ghost back, in whatever pot or box or liquor bottle it had been confined in.

But in most cases he had had to go through with the deal, meet the kidnapper somewhere and give up a cupful or so of blood to retrieve the stolen ghost; and each time, along with the blood, he had lost a piece of his soul.

The phone began ringing again as Torrez tipped up the can for the last sip of beer; he ignored it.

Ten years ago it had been an abstract consideration—when he had thought about it at all, he had supposed that he could lose a lot of his soul without missing it, and he'd told himself that his soul was bound for Hell anyway, since he had deliberately broken it when he was eighteen, and so dispersing it had just seemed like hiding money from the IRS. But by the time he was thirty-five his hair had gone white and he had lost most of the sight in his left eye because of ruptured blood-vessels behind the retina, and he could no longer understand the plots of long novels he tried to read. Apparently some sort of physical and mental integrity was lost too, along with the blood and the bits of his hypothetical soul.

But what the kidnappers wanted from Torrez's blood was not vicarious integrity—it was nearly the opposite. Torrez thought of it as spiritual botox.

The men and women who stole ghosts for ransom were generally mediums, fortune-tellers, psychics—always clairvoyant. And even more than the escape that could be got from extorted dreams and memories and the ability to feel affection, they needed to be able to selectively blunt the psychic noise of humans living and dead.

Torrez imagined it as a hundred radios going at once all the time, and half the announcers moronically drunk—crying, giggling, trying to start fights.

He would never know. He had broken all the antennae in his own soul when he was eighteen, by killing a man who attacked him in a parking lot with a knife one midnight. Torrez had wrestled the knife away from the drunken assailant and had knocked the man unconscious by slamming his head into the bumper of a car—but then Torrez had picked up the man's knife and, just because he could, had driven it into the unconscious man's chest. The District Attorney had eventually called it self-defense, a justifiable homicide, and no charges were brought against Torrez, but his soul was broken.

The answering machine clicked on, but only the dial tone followed the recorded message. Torrez dropped the Budweiser can into the trash basket and walked into the living room, which over the years had become his workshop.

Murder seemed to be the crime that broke souls most effectively, and Torrez had done his first ghost-ransom job for free that same year, in 1983, just to see if his soul was now a source of the temporary disconnection-from-humanity that the psychics valued so highly. And he had tested out fine.

He had been doing Bible repair for twenty years, but his reputation in that cottage industry had been made only a couple of years ago, by accident. Three Jehovah's Witnesses had come to his door one summer day, wearing suits and ties, and he had stepped outside to debate scripture with them. "Let me see your Bible," he had said, "and I'll show you right in there why you're wrong," and when they handed him the book he had flipped to the first chapter of John's gospel and started reading. This was after his vision had begun to go bad, though, and he'd had to read it with a magnifying glass, and it had been a sunny day—and he had inadvertently set their Bible on fire. They had left hurriedly, and apparently told everyone in the neighborhood that Torrez could burn a Bible just by touching it.

He was bracing a tattered old Bible in the frame on the marble-topped table, ready to scorch out St. Paul's adverse remarks about homosexuality for a customer, when he heard three knocks at his front door, the first one loud and the next two just glancing scuffs, and he realized he had not closed the door and the knocks had pushed it open. He made sure his woodburning stylus was lying in the ashtray, then hurried to the entry hall.

Framed in the bright doorway was a short stocky man with a moustache, holding a shoebox and shifting from one foot to the other.

"Mr. Torrez," the man said. He smiled, and a moment later looked as if he'd never smile again. He waved the shoebox toward Torrez and said, "A man has stolen my daughter."

Perhaps the shoebox was the shrine he had kept his daughter's ghost in, in some jelly jar or perfume bottle. Probably there were ribbons and candy hearts around the empty space where the daughter's ghost-container had lain. Still, a shoebox was a pretty nondescript shrine; but maybe it was just for travelling, like a cat-carrier box.

"I just called," the man said, "and got your woman. I hoped she was wrong, and you were here."

"I don't do that work anymore," said Torrez patiently, "ransoming ghosts. You want to call Seaweed in Corona."

"I don't want you to ransom a ghost," the man said, holding the box toward

Torrez. "I already had old Humberto do that, yesterday. This is for you."

"If Humberto ransomed your daughter," Torrez said carefully, nodding toward the box but not taking it, "then why are you here?"

"*My* daughter is *not* a ghost. My daughter is twelve years old, and this man took her when she was walking home from school. I can pay you fifteen hundred dollars to get her back—this is extra, a gift for you, from me, with the help of Humberto."

Torrez had stepped back. "Your daughter was kidnapped? Alive? Good God, man, call the police right now! The FBI! You don't come to *me* with—"

"The police would not take the ransom note seriously," the man said, shaking his head. "They would think he wants money really, they would not think of his terms being sincerely meant, as he wrote them!" He took a deep breath and let it out. "Here," he said, extending the box again.

Torrez took the box—it was light—and cautiously lifted the lid.

Inside, in a nest of rosemary sprigs and Catholic holy cards, lay a little cloth doll that Torrez recognized.

"Amelia," he said softly.

He lifted it out of the box, and he could feel the quiver of his own daughter's long-lost ghost in it.

"Humberto bought this back for you?" Torrez asked. Three years after her kidnapping, he thought. No wonder Humberto waved to me this morning! I hope he didn't have to spend much of his soul on her; he's got no more than a mouse's worth left.

"For you," the man said. "She is a gift. Save my daughter."

Torrez didn't want to invite the man into the house. "What did the ransom note for your daughter say?"

"It said, Juan-Manuel Ortega—that's me—I have Elizabeth, and I will kill her and take all her blood unless you *induce* Terry Torrez to come to me and him give me the ransom blood instead."

"Call the police," Torrez said. "That's a bluff, about taking her blood. Why would he want a little girl's blood? When did this happen? Every minute—"

Juan-Manuel Ortega opened his mouth very wide, as if to pronounce some big syllable, then closed it. "My Elizabeth," he said, "she—killed her sister last year. My rifle was in the closet—she didn't know, she's a child, she didn't know it was loaded—"

Torrez could feel that his eyebrows were raised. Yes she did, he thought; she killed her sister deliberately, and broke her own soul doing it, and the kidnapper knows it even if you truly don't.

Your daughter's a murderer. She's like me.

Still, her blood—her broken, blunting soul—wouldn't be accessible to the kidnapper, the way Torrez's would be, unless...

"Has your daughter—" He had spoken too harshly, and tried again. "Has she ever used magic?" Or is her soul still virginal, he thought.

Ortega bared his teeth and shrugged. "Maybe! She said she caught her sister's ghost in my electric shaver. I—I think she did. I don't use it anymore, but think I hear it in the nights."

Then her blood will do for the kidnapper what mine would, Torrez thought. Not quite as well, since my soul is surely more opaque—older and more stained by the use of magic—but hers will do if he can't get mine.

"Here is my phone number," said Ortega, now shoving a business card at Torrez and talking too rapidly to interrupt, "and the kidnapper has your number. He wants only you. I am leaving it in your hands. Save my daughter, please."

Then he turned around and ran down the walkway to a van parked behind Torrez's Toyota. Torrez started after him, but the sun-glare in his bad left eye made him uncertain of his footing, and he stopped when he heard the van shift into gear and start away. The man's wife must have been waiting behind the wheel.

I should call the police myself, Torrez thought as he lost sight of the van in the brightness. But he's right, the police would take the kidnapping seriously, but not the ransom. The kidnapper doesn't want money—he wants my blood, me.

A living girl! he thought. I don't save living people, I save ghosts. And I don't even do that anymore.

She's like me.

He shuffled back into the house, and set the cloth doll on the kitchen counter, sitting up against the toaster. Almost without thinking about it, he took the pack of Camels out of his shirt pocket and lit one with his Bic lighter, then stubbed it out on the stovetop and laid it on the tile beside the doll.

The tip of the cigarette glowed again, and the telephone rang. He just kept staring at the doll and the smoldering cigarette and let the phone ring.

The answering machine clicked in, and he heard the woman's recorded voice say, "No one is available to take your call, he had me on his TV, Daddy, so I could change channels for him. 'Two, four, eleven,' and I'd change them."

Torrez became aware that he had sat down on the linoleum floor. Her ghost had never found a way to speak when he and his ex-wife had had possession of it. "I'm sorry, Amelia," he said hoarsely. "It would have killed me to buy you back. They don't want money, they—"

"What?" said the voice of the caller. "Is Mr. Torrez there?"

"Rum he gave me, at least," said Amelia's voice. "It wouldn't have killed you, not really."

Torrez got to his feet, feeling much older than his actual forty years. He opened the high cupboard and saw her bottle of 151-proof rum still standing up there beside the stacked china dishes he never used. He hoisted the bottle down and wiped dust off it.

"I'm going to tell him how rude you are," said the voice on the phone, "this isn't very funny." The line clicked.

"No," Torrez said as he poured a couple of ounces of rum into a coffee cup. "It wouldn't have killed me. But it would have made a mindless...it would have made an idiot of me. I wouldn't have been able to...work, talk, think." Even now I can hardly make sense of the comics in the newspaper, he thought.

"He had me on his TV, Daddy," said Amelia's voice from the answering machine. "I was his channel-changer."

Torrez set the coffee cup near the doll, and felt it vibrate faintly just as he let go of the handle. The sharp alcohol smell became stronger, as if some of the rum had been vaporized.

"And he gave me candy."

"I'm sorry," said Torrez absently, "I don't have any candy."

"Sugar Babies are better than Reese's Pieces." Torrez had always given her Reese's Pieces, but before now she had not been able to tell him what she preferred.

"How can you talk?"

"The people that nobody paid for, he would put all of us, all our jars and boxes and dolls on the TV and make us change what the TV people said. We made them say bad prayers."

The phone rang again, and Amelia's voice out of the answering machine speaker said, "Sheesh" and broke right in. "What, what?"

"I've got a message for Terry Torrez," said a woman's voice, "make sure he gets it, write this number down!" The woman recited a number, which Torrez automatically memorized. "My husband is in an alarm clock, but he's fading; I don't hardly dream about him even with the clock under the pillow anymore, and the mint patties, it's like a year he takes to even get halfway through one! He needs a booster shot, tell Terry Torrez that, and I'll pay a thousand dollars for it."

I'll want more than a thousand, Torrez thought, and she'll pay more, too. Booster shot! The only way to boost a fading ghost—and they all faded sooner or later—was to add to the container a second ghost, the ghost of a newly deceased infant, which would have vitality but no personality to interfere with the original ghost.

Torrez had done that a few times, and—though these were only ghosts, not souls, not actual people!—it had always felt like putting feeder mice into an aquarium with an old, blind snake.

"That'll buy a lot of Sugar Babies," remarked Amelia's ghost.

"What? Just make sure he gets the message!"

The phone clicked off, and Amelia said, "I remember the number."

"So do I."

Midwives sold newborn ghosts. The thought of looking one of them up nauseated him.

"Mom's dead," said Amelia.

Torrez opened his mouth, then just exhaled. He took a sip of Amelia's rum and said, "She is?"

"Sure. We all know, when someone is. I guess they figured you wouldn't bleed for her, if you wouldn't bleed for me. Sugar Babies are better than Reese's Pieces."

"Right, you said."

"Can I have her rings? They'd fit on my head like crowns."

"I don't know what became of her," he said. It's true, he realized, I don't. I don't even know what there was of her.

He looked at the doll and wondered why anyone kept such things.

His own Bible, on the mantel in the living room workshop, was relatively intact, though of course it was warped from having been soaked in holy water. He had burned out half a dozen verses from the Old Testament that had to do with witchcraft and wizards; and he had thought about excising "thou shalt not kill" from Exodus, but decided that if the commandment was gone, his career might be too.

After he had refused to ransom Amelia's ghost, he had cut out Ezekiel 44:25—"And they shall come at no dead person to defile themselves: but for father, or for mother, or for son, or for daughter, for brother, or for sister that hath had no husband, they may defile themselves."

He had refused to defile himself—defile himself any further, at least—for his own dead daughter. And so she had wound up helping to voice "bad prayers" out of a TV set somewhere.

The phone rang again, and this time he snatched up the receiver before the answering machine could come on. "Yes?"

"Mr. Torrez," said a man's voice. "I have a beaker of silence here, she's twelve years old and she's not in any jar or bottle."

"Her father has been here," Torrez said.

"I'd rather have the beaker that's you. For all her virtues, her soul's a bit thin still, and noises would get through."

Torrez remembered stories he'd heard about clairvoyants driven to insanity by the constant din of thoughts.

"My daddy doesn't play that anymore," said Amelia. "He has me back now."

Torrez remembered Humberto's wave this morning. Torrez had waved back.

Torrez looked into the living room, at the current Bible in the burning rack, and at the books he still kept on a shelf over the cold fireplace—paperbacks, hardcovers with gold-stamped titles, books in battered dust-jackets. He had found—what?—a connection with other people's lives, in them, which since the age of eighteen he had not been able to have in any other way. But these days their pages might as well all be blank. When he occasionally pulled one down and opened it, squinting through his magnifying glass to be able to see the print clearly, he could understand individual words but the sentences didn't cohere anymore.

She's like me.

I wonder if I could have found my way back, if I'd tried. I could tell her father to ask her to try.

"Bring the girl to where we meet," Torrez said. He leaned against the kitchen counter. In spite of his resolve, he was dizzy. "I'll have her parents with me to drive her away."

I'm dead already, he thought. Her father came to me, but the book says he may do that for a daughter. And for me, the dead person, this is the only way left to have a vital connection with other people's lives, even if they are strangers.

"And you'll come away with me," said the man's voice.

"No," said Amelia, "he won't. He brings me rum and candy."

The living girl who had been Amelia would have been at least somewhat concerned about the kidnapped girl. We each owe God our mind, Torrez thought, and he that gives it up today is paid off for tomorrow.

"Yes," said Torrez. He lifted the coffee cup; his hand was shaky, but he carefully poured the rum over the cloth head of the doll; the rum soaked into its fabric and puddled on the counter.

"How much is the ransom?" he asked.

"Only a reasonable amount," the voice assured him blandly.

Torrez was relieved; he was sure a reasonable amount was all that was left, and the kidnapper was likely to take it all anyway. He flicked his lighter over the doll, and then the doll was in a teardrop-shaped blue glare on the counter. Torrez stepped back, ready to wipe a wet towel over the cabinets if they should start to smolder. The doll turned black and began to come apart.

Amelia's voice didn't speak from the answering machine, though he thought he might have heard a long sigh—of release, he hoped.

"I want something," Torrez said. "A condition."

"What?"

"Do you have a Bible? Not a repaired one, a whole one?"

"I can get one."

"Yes, get one. And bring it for me."

"Okay. So we have a deal?"

The rum had burned out and the doll was a black pile, still glowing red here and there. He filled the cup with water from the tap and poured it over the ashes, and then there was no more red glow.

Torrez sighed, seeming to empty his lungs. "Yes. Where do we meet?"

Father Dear
Al Sarrantonio

He never beat me, but told me stories about what would happen to me if I did certain things.

"The crusts of bread," he told me, cutting the crusts off his own bread instructively and throwing them into the waste bin, "gather inside you. If you eat bread with the crusts still on, you will digest the bread but your body will not digest the crusts. They will build up inside you until..." Here he made an exploding gesture with his hands, close by my face. He smiled. I smiled. I was four years old, and cut the crusts off of my bread.

"The yellow pulpy material left after an orange is peeled," he told me another day, a bright sunny one as I remember, with thick slats of sunshine falling on the white kitchen table between us; I recall the sound of a cockatoo which flitted by outside, and the vague visual hint of green and the smell of spring that came in through the bottom of the window, which he had opened a crack (I believe now that he opened it that crack for effect, to accentuate the brightness of spring outside with the stuffy dreariness of our indoor habitation—he told me other things about dust and about the indoors), "will make your teeth yellow if you ingest it. With the eating of oranges, which, by the way, you must eat, Alfred, for your condition, any specks of this pulp will be caught in a receptacle just to the back of your throat, just out of sight, and will creep up like an army of ants at night to stain your teeth. In time, your teeth will become the deep shade of a ripe banana; perhaps, someday, that of a bright lemon just picked." How I remember the hours I spent whisking those orange fruits clean of pulp, examining my fingernails afterward to make sure no bits had adhered to them; O, how many other hours did I lay awake at night in my bedroom, hating him and at the same time believing him (no, that's not right; the hate came later, much later; there was only love then, and if not that at least a respect for his knowledge, for the things he was so gently trying to save me from—no, it was Love after all) and waiting, with a dry ticking at the back of my tongue where the saliva had dried as I lay fearfully waiting for those tiny insect bits of pulp to march up my mouth, dousing my gums and teeth with yellow spray from their bucket-like tails; O! How many hours did I spend in front of a mirror, trying to see, my mouth as wide as my jaw would allow it, that "receptacle" where those lemon-ants waited!

I hate him now; came to hate him slowly, inexorably, and, in time, I have come to love that hate, to relish and enjoy it since it is the only thing I have in this world that I am not afraid of.

He taught me nothing of value. He taught me to hate books, to hate what was in them and the men who wrote them; taught me to, above all, hate the world, everyone in it; everything it stood for. "It is a corrupt place, Alfred," he lectured endlessly, "filled with useless people possessed of artificial sensibilities, people who respect and cherish nothing. They live like animals, all of them, huddled into cities chockablock one on top of the other; they are of different colors, and speak different languages until all their words mix in one jumbled whirr and none of them understand what any of the others are saying. I know, I come from that world, Alfred. They don't know what life is. They don't know what's safe. But you know what's safe, don't you?"

I remember grinning eagerly up at him at times like this, like a puppy; he always bent down over me, his hands behind his straight tall back, and I remember at times reaching up to him with my tiny hands, begging him, "Pick me up, pick me up, swing me, please!"

"Swinging you will make your stomach move in your body," he answered, smiling wanly, "and once moved, at your delicate age, it will stay in that new spot, perhaps where your lungs or pancreas should be, and will make you sick for the rest of your life. It may even turn you into a hunchback, or make you slur your words if it moves, on the high arc of your swing, into your vocal cavity. You do understand, don't you?"

My arms lowered slowly, tentatively, to my sides.

I was not allowed to play on the swings on the grounds, either, but would stare at them for hours through my bedroom window.

The grounds, naturally, were beautiful, wooded and sprawling. No one, I heard it whispered among the servants, had grounds like this anymore; no one,

THE URBAN FANTASY ANTHOLOGY

I once heard a Chinese servant say, deserved to have such grounds. The world, he whispered to mute Mandy, my sometimes guardian (when He was away), was still far too crowded for this type of thing to crop up again; there were too many other problems to be solved without one man shutting himself up in such a way. I am sure that Mandy went straight to my father after this bit of sacrilege had been imparted, and the man, if I remember correctly, was gone the following day. Another servant, of course, was in place instantly.

The grounds, as I say, were sprawling, but I was not allowed to make use of that sprawl. There were too many opportunities to be "hurt." The swinging motion I have already described could, of course, be accomplished to dire effect by the swing set just beyond the Italian-tiled patio; there was also at that spot a set of monkey bars which "would upset the balance of your hormones if you were to use it, since hanging upside down by a boy of your delicate constitution would only lead your body to hormone imbalance. The features of your face would begin to move about by the action of the blood rushing to your head, and you would end up looking something like this." He made an extremely grotesque—and terribly funny—face then, and I laughed along with him until I abruptly began to cry. If my memory serves me correctly, I ran and threw my arms around him, thanking him for saving me and asking him to promise never to leave or send me away; and, yes, I remember pointedly and now as clearly as if the moment were again occurring that my teary eyes were staring at his hands, still behind his back, and I was willing them to move around toward me, to show me anything parental and physical. I believe that may be the moment when I thought something was not right between us; for a fleeting second I entertained the thought that maybe he didn't love me after all but then quickly dismissed it, knowing that it must have been me, that I may already have been in danger of contracting some vile disease, something transmitted by a touch of the hands to the head, something transmitted by a loving hold, and that he was merely, as lovingly as he could, trying to avoid exposing me to it. He was saving me from himself. I threw myself from him, aching with apology for what I had almost accomplished. I don't remember if he thanked me or just went away.

"If you gaze at the sky too long," he said, after catching me leaning out of an upper-story window at the moon overhead, "your head is very liable to fall off or stay locked in that position at least. Never look up in the daytime."

"Not even to watch a bird fly overhead?"

"Never. How old are you now?"

"Seven."

"Never look up again, Alfred. Until now you have been lucky, but with the age of reason comes a severity of life that you will only too soon realize."

I never looked up.

"If you sit in a chair for more than five minutes, your feet will begin to lose their circulation and may never get it back. If you stand for more than five minutes, too much blood will rush to the bottom of your body and your feet will become heavy, as if filled with lead." I crouched when I walked.

"Meat will cause you to turn red."

I did not eat meat.

"Vegetables will cause you to turn their own color—yellow, green, orange." I only ate vegetables when desperate.

"Chocolate will cause you to turn black. Wheat you may take, and potatoes, and you may drink water in moderation after boiling, cooling and then boiling again. Do not drink milk: it will make you white as paper."

He showed me a book with these things in it, or rather read to me from one. The book, I later discovered, was *Moby Dick*. Such a thick book, such thick lies.

And yet I followed his instructions and thanked him for it. I grew. I grew fat. Wheat and potatoes were my diet, and teenagehood found me stout and ugly. I wore glasses thick with mottled glass, because he told me a lucid pair would cause my eyes to change color and shape. My teeth hurt, and he scolded, saying that I had eaten something, possibly so long ago I could not remember, something that had gone against his wishes and was now catching up with me.

I will kill him when I find him.

He left abruptly; abandoned that massive estate in the dead of night when I was fifteen years old. There was only one hint that this would happen. Late in December of the winter he left, during the coldest part of a cold month, Mandy, the ghostly mute, took to her bed believing she would die. She was attended to by other of the staff, and even my father occasionally visited her. I was told never to go into her bedroom. I had once had a peek into that room— enormous and cluttered, with a high sculpted ceiling (there were paintings on

THE URBAN FANTASY ANTHOLOGY

it, clouds and blue sky which made me fearful lest my eyes and neck lock on it) and deep brown carved wooden walls. A huge bed, with high spikes at the four corners. A green-and-yellow coverlet. This was all I remembered. In the very last days of December, when it was made known with the usual whispering (whispers were what filled that manse, whispers and lies) that she would die before the night was gone, I went in to see her.

I knew she was alone. There were statues on that floor, as on every floor, behind which I had often hidden and which I had no neuroses about since my father did not know or had never caught me at it. There was one particular statue, a golden, tiny wood goddess with bow, set prominently high on a pedestal just to the left of the wide winding staircase (I used to occasionally slide down that staircase railing also, until He found me at it one day and told me that my genitals would be forced back into my body by the pressure of the railing if I continued), which gave an excellent view of Mandy's sickroom entrance. Shortly after supper I secreted myself there, watching the comings and goings of the servants, the dour doctor who came from somewhere and departed again to it, and, finally and surprisingly, my father, who came quietly out of the door somewhere just before midnight. He had no reason to check on my whereabouts, since he had made sure I was tucked solidly into my bedchamber just after dinner and had no reason to believe I would be anywhere else (he told me as a baby of the "things that were abroad after dark"), but this was one of the few of his lies that I had managed to outgrow, even though at times on my nightly sojourns I thought I spied one of his "beasties of the night"—more likely optical illusions of the night. It occurs to me that he was neglectful in this, but why quibble; I seem to recall he was getting a little old by this time and had forgotten to reinforce some of the foul walls he had built, brick by blood-red brick, around me for my fifteen years. Anyway, here I was when he hobbled off (he was getting old, and I remember him making use of a cane just before he left the next month) to his own voluptuous quarters somewhere to the other side of the building and one flight up (I had seen those quarters once, too, and they made Mandy's into a tent) and, probably, to one of his live-in paramours, servant-man or-woman or possibly someone from outside who was occasionally flown in, usually around the holiday season (which was not, naturally, celebrated, in this household).

I waited a full ten minutes, crouched in my hiding spot and beginning to balance the two fears—fear of discovery by leaving the shadow of that statue too soon and fear of my legs being lost to me since I could feel numbness setting into them—before slowly moving out toward the door in a rabbit's crouch.

The lock ticked open easily. The room was not as big as I had remembered, but the bed seemed even bigger. Grey moonlight suffused the room, throwing a pale line of light across the bottom half of the bed; there was also a low wattage bulb set into the wall over the bedstead, illuminating the upper half.

All I could see was a pile of pillows and that same green-and-yellow comforter, which looked as flat as if no one were under it. At first I thought that this might be the case; perhaps they had moved her without my seeing; perhaps she had died and they had lowered her from the window into the waiting arms of the dour doctor to be carted off for burial or burning; perhaps this had all been a setup to lure me to this spot so that my hiding place behind that wood goddess could be uncovered and I could be mind-tortured further. I whirled quickly around but saw no one at the doorway behind me and no one, seemingly, in the corners of the room ready to jump out.

By this time I had moved close enough to see that, yes, she was in bed after all. Barely there, what was left of her. There was a head above the line of the quilt that looked like the head of a monkey, shriveled and nut brown; and below that the coverlet stretched as flat as I had imagined it did, scarcely revealing the outline of an evaporated body.

I leaned down over her, wanting very badly to peel up her eyelids as I had seen once on television (before He had decided that this pleasure, too, should be denied me for my own good), when her eyes opened of their own and she stared straight into my face.

She tried to scream, but nothing came out. Her features contorted, her lips pulling back over her teeth, making her look even more like a monkey. It was now that I saw why she was mute: her tongue ended in a surgically sharp line at the back of her throat, giving her nothing to articulate with. Or so I thought.

After a moment she ceased trying to scream, and a curious calm descended on her. She looked at me for a few moments, apparently recognizing me now. Why had she tried to scream? Possibly she had thought I was someone else. But now, recognizing me as she did, her eyes brightened and she tried desperately to say something.

"What?" I asked, leaning down close with my ear to her mouth, wanting to draw back because of the disease she might impart to me but overcome with a violent compulsion, for the first time in my life, to explore a mystery on my own. "I can't hear you."

She was muttering something, so far under her breath and with such obvious effort that I hushed my own breathing, concentrating doubly hard to pick up her faint, insect's voice.

"Mo..." she was saying. "Mot..."

"What?" I rasped at her, impatient and now with one eye on the door lest someone hear the faint struggle going on in here.

"Mot..."

"Mot? What do you mean, mot?"

"Mot...Mother," she said, so far in the back of her throat that it was like listening to an echo off somewhere in a cave.

My body became ice. I nearly grabbed her by the mouth to make her repeat that word; but her eyes had filmed over and her lips were slack. For a moment I thought she had died there before me, but as I watched her eyes cleared again and once more she looked straight into me, through me.

I said nothing, and then I whispered, "You are my mother?" Her mouth said nothing, but it formed the word, yes.

"*Oh*," I said, my throat gagging. I threw myself from the bed, instinctively going for the window and then pushing myself away from it when I looked up to see the full moon staring down at me from above. I fell to the floor. My throat would not work; I lay gasping for air like a reefed fish. My head was on fire, too; I thought for a moment that one of the terrible things my father had warned me about for so many years had come true, that the moon, or my disobedience in being out of my room, or my visit to this chamber, or the sight of this woman or what she had said had triggered one of those ugly reactions which had for so long hung above me like a sword. I had eaten too many crusts when a baby, I thought desperately; possibly it was lemons; or bananas, or my brains had blown up to balloon size from hanging upside down, or not hanging upside down, or from bumping into a doorjamb, or not.

With a Herculean effort I staggered to my feet, to the door, into the hallway past the Hunter Goddess (her bow for a moment as I came out of the room pointed straight at my head) and into my own room, clawing my way into bed and so far under the covers that everything—the light, the evening, myself—

was extinguished and a sudden darkness dropped upon me...

Only to rise again into dim light later, much later, when the first tepid hints of spring were manifesting themselves, and when my father was long departed, my mother long dead. My father brought most of the staff (at least those he had comported with) with him, leaving only a skeleton klatch of indifferent menials to attend to me, supplemented by his own horrid ghost, hanging in the air, usually in dusty corners, wherever I went in that house, reminding me of what I was and what he had made me and, in his absence, daring me to be anything else.

For the next twenty years I listened to that ghost. Haunted, bloated by shame, starch and nightmares, I lurched from room to room (save one, of course) in that mansion, trying once again to be an infant by following my father's twisted directions on life. I was not rational; I was nothing but a bundle of neuroses held together by muscle and bone matter. I shouted much, screamed much, cried much except when I remembered what he had told me about crying: "If you weep, Alfred, the water reserves in your body will never be filled again. Recall that you are born with a certain amount of tear-water in you; that all other water which you take in is used for other purposes or expelled; and recall that once that tear-matter is depleted it can never be restored and you will never be able to cry again. Your body will try, throwing you into horrid convulsions, but nothing will come out of your eyes. Eventually your tear ducts will take the liquid they so crave from your eyeballs themselves, turning them into dry, paper-like orbs. Needless to say, you will go blind."

I tried to go blind. I cried incessantly, half-waiting for (and not caring about) the coming moment when there would be a crackling sound from deep within my eye sockets signaling the end of vision and the beginning of physical darkness. It never came, and after many months (years?—there is much about those twenty summers, winters, springs and falls that memory does not serve) I came slowly to realize that here was one of His major lessons that turned out not to be history but fiction. Might there be others? I began to explore. Carefully, of course. The litany of my fears was a long one, and there were some areas where I would not tread—those fears were so deep-rooted. But there were many—"You must always, Alfred, walk with a measured step, throwing one foot out in front of the other, pausing before letting it touch the ground, and then letting it down in two phases, heel and then toe, two separate stages, heel then toe, or the feet will become flat and useless and hurt you incessantly"—that I was able, with patient years of self-imposed physical and mental therapy, to be rid of. I never, when speaking, doubled the letter "a" when using it as an article anymore (He had assured me it would prevent further stuttering, an offering to the Stutter Gods, I suppose). I didn't knock my knees together when standing up anymore. I didn't blink consciously before looking at something close up (to adapt the eyes to closeness).

And so, at age thirty-five, I was ready to find and kill Him. It must have appeared quite comical, this fat (though by now not so bloated since I had learned that my diet could be expanded to include a healthier assortment of food; I had also discovered vitamins, something He had never spoken of), squinting (I had done away with the glasses, learning that they were not needed, were actually destroying my eyesight; I would squint with or without them now), white-haired (is it any wonder my hair had turned snow white—actually it was that way after I came to my senses after my mother's death) middle-aged man with enough tics, bad habits and eccentricities to fill two thick volumes, fumbling his way into the world beyond his little castle (I made it a point to pass by those monkey bars, even swinging once upon them, pulling myself upside down and screaming my father's name at the deepest of blue skies that was evident that day) and out onto the Road of Vengeance, a road I, this abnormal specimen of man, knew nothing about, cared to know nothing about, begging only that it lead him through the maze of the terrible big world to the front door of the man-monster who had caused him to hate not only it (the world) but also his father and himself. Curiously, I had come to love one thing: the image of my mother on her deathbed: a deep and mysterious totem she became for me since I really knew so little about her; any of the servants who were left after my father's abandonment knew nothing of her, and my own recollections were so dim—she took care of me, I seemed to recall, in those odd periods when my father was ill in bed or occupied with one of his paramours. Never saying anything, she was hardly noticed. She had become safe, become, in fact, much larger than life. She was my mother; she had nurtured me, brought me into the world, possibly even loved me secretly, had certainly done nothing to harm me directly; and so, she became Sacred. She became the image I could hold up to Him; and when I found him I fully intended to flay him alive—peeling the flesh from his now-ancient bones, as many strips for Her as for myself.

I found him easily.

Almost too easily; I admitted a little disappointment that the chase did not go on longer because the scent was so strong. The City was a strange place but not all so horrible; I had heard him speak about it to me for so long in revulsive tones ("You must never, Alfred, I repeat, never go into the outside world, the vile City waiting out there, for it would be your end"); I found it somewhat less than my imagination had made it out to be. It seemed merely too many people pressed into too small a space; but they were, after all, people, and did not frighten me or revolt me as I had expected they would.

I had fully expected the Hunt to go on for some time, and so found myself immensely surprised when the most discreet inquiries as to my father's whereabouts led to his discovery. He seemed to be someone of import; I had never had doubt as to his monetary worth since the very fact that we had resided on such a vast expanse of land, at a time (you'll remember the comments of the servants as to this) when no one seemed to live this way, but I was duly shocked to find him so readily known outside of our isolated manse.

I was careful in approaching him. He resided in the most well-to-do building in the most well-to-do part of the City (naturally), holding an entire floor in a dreamlike blue metal and glass monstrosity; it overlooked the river, which, in its flowing blueness, hurt the eyes with all that visual concentration at one far end of the spectrum (he had once told me the color blue would hurt me; would make me, he said, "see nothing but blue until you are driven mad and want to tear your eyes out"). I had also been told, by one overly cautious individual who had easily succumbed to bribery for information; he insisted that we meet in a series of brief encounters in a park, where he imparted, on a bench by an ice cream custard stand—once, even, in the bushes by a children's zoo—tiny snatches of information that, when added together, gave a picture of a man of immense power in the last throes of life. This hurt me terribly, because if He were already dying he would be that much less horrified by my appearance, never mind my actions, and would probably already be faced toward the last dark precipice which I would gleefully tumble him over. I didn't want him to die. I wanted to kill him.

I made my way to Him with the utmost caution. Ironically, and to my delight, there was in the entrance to his entire fourteenth floor a statue remarkably like that wood goddess in our manse, which I remembered with so much fondness and which, in a way, was the catalyst to my new life; with her arrow she had pointed me in the direction of Salvation and Revenge and had, in her smooth and godlike way, brought me to this delicious point.

I hid behind this statue, distinct from that other only in that this one was clothed, and I methodically, patiently mapped the comings and goings to His suite. I did this for days, managing to hide myself from the watchful (or half-watchful—he was not very attentive to his job) orbs of the guard who seemed always to be present. There were visitors, all during the day—men with briefcases, dull brown suits always buttoned, grim grey faces; but I noticed that in the evening there were never any visitors, and that somewhere around nine o'clock the bored guard usually slipped off for a cigarette no doubt shared with other bored guards on other floors of the building. He invariably stayed away a half-hour, and no one ever checked on him, so after a week of this surveillance I quietly slipped from my lair (knocking my knees together once as I rose—damn Him!) and stole my way into his metal manse.

If possible, this abode of his was even more regally attired than the other; the richness of the furnishings—velvet-covered furniture in blacks, reds and greens, tapestries, oiled wood walls and floors and antique ceramics—not to mention the other artworks, paintings and, yes, sculpture everywhere—that I began to gag in reaction to it. He had been a Pig before; but the realization that he was now an even greater one, a public one—this was all too much. I fingered the blade in my overcoat pocket—I had searched long and hard through the manse for just the right instrument, finally settling on one that, if the little blurbs often found in museums next to art treasures are to be believed, was once used for ritual sacrifice in Celtic Ireland. Oh, yes, I would use it again for just such a purpose, reviving a custom....

Room after room of nauseating ostentation passed before me, until the hairs on the back of my head ("Don't ever let the hairs on the back of your head rise in fright, Alfred: it will cause you, in time, to lose your hairs as they are pulled into the back of your skull by the action of forced straightening") (!!!) stood on end and I knew that the richly carved, heavy hinged door (hares and hunters on that door, how delightfully appropriate!) before which I stood was the last in the apartment and would lead to his bedroom. And indeed it did, for as I edged it open I heard a faint but unmistakable voice call out questioningly,

"Grace? Grace?"

I was going to answer that no, it was not Grace and that the state of grace was what I hoped he possessed for the journey he would soon take, but when I saw that the room was so completely black-dark that he would not see me until I stood just over his bed I decided to slip through that oily darkness and do just that. He called out again, very faintly, and then lapsed into a ragged, even breathing that told me he had slipped into sleep.

In a stealthy moment I was at his bedside, and leaning over him to turn on the Tiffany lamp by his bed.

At the instant I turned on that lamp he awoke.

"No!" was all he said, hoarsely. He tried to mouth my name, but I knew at that moment that he had suffered a stroke at this very instant of nirvana and would have trouble saying anything at all. I drew my blade out slowly, running it over my nails in front of his straining red face; he was gulping for air like a blowfish out of water.

"Alfred," I said slowly, quietly, completing for him what he was trying so hard to say. He shook his head from side to side, his eyes never leaving my face.

"Yes, Father, it is I. Are you surprised?"

He was puffing hard, and I lowered my ear (as I had done so long ago for my dear mute mother!) to hear him say, "Go...back."

I laughed. I pulled my head back and spat laughter, and then I put my face close to his.

"I don't think so, Father."

Again he was straining.

"Must," he said.

"Why? To keep me away from you? Don't you want me by your living side?" I lowered my wide eyes just inches from his, and brought the blade up close to his straining, yellow nostrils. "Would you rather I didn't speak? Would you rather I cut my own tongue out, make myself mute like my mother?" His eyes went very wide and he shook his head violently from side to side.

"What, Father? What is it you want to say?"

I pulled him up by the shoulders, a little frightened by how light and frail he was, and pressed his lips to my ear.

"No..." he said.

"Speak, damn you!"

THE URBAN FANTASY ANTHOLOGY

"Did it...herself..."

"Did what?"

"Cut her...own...tongue out..."

I pushed him back down into his pile of silken pillows.

"Liar!" I said, raising my fist to strike him.

"No!" he said, suddenly finding his voice from somewhere down deep before it cracked off into a whisper again. "True..."

Calming abruptly, or rather moving off beyond rage to a calmer, more clear, more vicious place, I once again lowered my ear to his lips.

"Why did you leave, Father?"

There was a gurgle in his throat, and then, "...her...house..."

"What do you mean, 'Her house'?"

"...kept me there. Gave me everything to keep me silent. Made me..."

"Made you what?" My voice was regaining its edge.

"Made me..." He was breathing very unevenly, and said with great effort, with what a fool could have taken to be pleading in his eyes, "You."

My voice was very calm now, and I made sure he could see me drawing the blade through my fingers, letting it glint off the weak light from the amber reading lamp.

"You're lying," I said. "You're lying like you always have to me. Your life is a lie from beginning to this, the end. You twisted my mind from as early as I can remember. It's a sewer now, Father. It always will be. I am scared to death just to be outside that mansion. Just coming here made me tremble and sweat. My life is a catalog of unnameable things, sick things, tics and neuroses that I can't escape. I fear everything. Except you." I brought the blade down slowly, delicately toward his old man's chicken neck.

"Did it for you, go back," he croaked, looking at my eyes, not at the blade. "Hybrid. She...hated you. Only way to keep you alive. Statue," he said, his face suddenly getting very red, blood pumping into it from the ruptured machine in his chest and making his eyes nearly pop out of his face. His voice became, for a moment, very loud and clear. "Alfred! She was from the woods, not like us! Go back, save your life!" He grabbed at me with his spindly arms, his twiglike fingers. He tried to pull himself up, tried to clasp his vile body to mine. "...back..."

His grasp loosened then, and he slipped, like a flat rock into a pool of water, down into death.

I sat up, panting, and looked down at him; the blade felt sharp in my hand and I entertained for a moment the notion of carving him up anyway, of taking the pound of flesh I had come for and at least giving to my mother the sacrifice I had vowed. But instead I lowered it into my coat and stood up. He was pitifully dead, and in death he appeared much less the object of hate; the soul had left, leaving only meat behind.

It was then, when I was leaving his bedroom and passing the massive, gilded mirror over the dresser by the doorway, that I saw something that made me stop.

My skin had turned red. I thought immediately of the meat I had eaten in the past months, of the bounteous meat I had eaten in the past days in the City. I shook my head to clear it, turned on the bright lamp on the dresser and once again my color was correct. I smiled knowingly at myself: for a chilly moment my teeth looked yellow and I thought of all the oranges I had eaten—the back of my throat became uncontrollably dry and it felt as though something tiny was ticking around back there—but then this passed too.

"Fool," I said, and left the apartment in haste, throwing a fleeting glance at the statue in the foyer before passing on.

Everything outside was blue.

Overhead, there was a fat full moon, and as I looked up at it, it turned indigo and my neck began to ache, giving me trouble in lowering it.

I sat down on a bus and then a train, and my feet went numb.

I now felt, inside me, the movement of my organs and the gathering of bread crusts as they pressed out through my ribs, hernia-like.

Somehow, I made it back to the grounds of the manse. I think a servant found me outside the front gates in the morning, curled up like a gnarled root, my face pointed at the killing sky. I don't know how he recognized me, since as they carried me in I passed a looking glass and saw that the features of my face had rearranged themselves, grotesquely mimicking that funny face my father had made at me so long ago.

They placed me in my father's old bedroom; the dour doctor came and went, and from the look on his dour face I knew that he would not return from the woods from which he was summoned.

I don't know what color I am now—red, black, blue, green, bone white. I do know that the pulp-ants are active this morning and that therefore my teeth must be a particular shade of yellow. Lemon yellow, perhaps. My genitals have retracted into my body. My head feels as though it will shortly fall off my shoulders.

I have had the statue of my mother moved into my new bedroom and placed in my line of sight. The arrow in her bow points directly at my forehead and I now see a look of lust and self-loathing on her features that I didn't see before. I want to look at that statue; I want to look at it hard and long.

I think often of my father.

I know that soon my tear ducts will rob the liquid they need so desperately from my eyeballs, turning them into crackly paper orbs, and that, naturally, I will go blind.